The Secret Life of

Kris Kringle

as told by his brother Olaf

ISBN 978-0-615-25323-7
Third Sun Media website address:
thirdsunmedia.com
FIRST EDITION
ILLUSTRATIONS © BY JHON KILGORE

To

G

and others

who wish to

believe...

Contents

The Secret Life of Kris Kringle

as told by his brother Olaf

by Jhon Kilgore

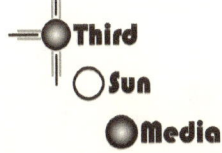
Third Sun Media

View from the coffee shop out over the Puget Sound

Prologue
Pike Place Market

The storm clouds rolled over the Olympic Mountains, heading for downtown Seattle, as I walked into the Pike Place Market. I was looking forward to visiting my favorite coffee shop. A little out of the way for me during the week, but it was Saturday, so I had the time. The café was at the back of the market, behind the famous three-foot tall brass pig.

The coffee house had large thick windows that looked out over the waterfront piers and the bay called, Puget Sound. The place really didn't have a name but the regulars liked it that way. The tourists hardly ever came

there and it looked small and rundown from the front, a further induce-
ment for people to go to the Starbucks at the top of the market.

I paid for my order and spotted the prized corner booth that had a
great view. I made it there before anyone else, bulldog edition of the Sunday paper in tow, and settled in for a long, lazy read.

The rain had just started to drizzle on the windowsill beside me, making the bustling coffeehouse seem even more cozy. As crowded as it was
though, the thick vinyl and oak booths dampened the murmured con-
versations as much as the dismal cloudy sky above Seattle. I was into my
paper and didn't see the old man who came up to my small booth in the
corner.

"May I sit with you?" he asked.

"Sure," I replied, hoping that he wasn't one of those people who mistake tolerance for hospitality.

He sat down quietly and I soon forgot he was even there. The Dow was
down again and my portfolio was taking a beating. Then, the thunder
rolled in, like twenty jumbo jets coming towards Seattle from across the
Puget Sound.

Now don't get me wrong, it really does rain in Seattle, 300 days year or
more, but a thunderstorm makes people stop and take notice. Everyone
turned towards the big bay windows that looked out over the waterfront,
across the Sound, over to West Seattle and Bainbridge Island. Waiting
for the first flash of forked lightening, the storm didn't disappoint us.
Three separate bolts lit up the darkening sky in an eerie green over the
gray choppy water. The crowd's hush was broken by oohs and ahhs then
drown out by the rolling thunder that shook the heavy glass panes in their
frames.

I felt the old man's eyes on me, so I glanced over at him and was locked into his stare.

"Kinda makes you feel small," he said.

I wasn't sure if he was talking about the storm or his gaze that was making me feel like a bug under a magnifying glass.

"Uh, yeah," I managed, as usual light drizzle turned into heavy sheets of rain that started to hit the windows. As he glanced out to the deluge, I studied his face. He had a well-trimmed white beard, shaved close to his ruddy skin. Thick white hair, in a short Steve McQueen no nonsense cut. The tiny crows' feet around his eyes were the only other sign of age.

He was wearing a knotted sweater that was stylish without looking G.Q. and his hands enfolding his mug of tea were large and muscular. I guessed he'd worked as a fisherman all his life.

He must have noticed me studying him because, his mesmerizing eyes slowly returned to me. He looked me up and down a few times then concentrated on his drink.

I found the silence uncomfortable so, I picked up the paper again to see that my idiot of an editor had mauled my exposé on the mayor. The story was on A 13, which reporters call the 'graveyard'. If your story is past A9, it's toast. I toss the paper down.

'Well crap,' I thought. I worked three weeks on that story. It had facts, photos, and figures on the mayor's reelection campaign. Now it was seven paragraphs short and as good as dead.

'I'm never going to get off the 'Ask Aunt Sally' column,' I continued my silent lament. Seattle's local public affairs, fix the pothole on my street / my view is being blocked by my neighbors trees what can I do about it, column. It was buried in the back of section D on page 10, four days a week. It paid the bills, but I didn't want to be stuck doing a rant column forever. I had a degree in journalism and felt that I was being wasted on a daily column that didn't even have my name on the byline.

I was startled out of my funk by the absence of the old guy. I panned the room and saw him over at the hot water dispenser putting more honey and adding another teabag to his mug. I watched him closely as he weaved back to my cherished booth.

He stealthily stepped around a couple who were trying to keep their spat quiet and then between two people who shoved their chairs back into his way, that made me rethink judging him as being so old. 'Maybe his hair just turned white early,' I thought to myself. He slid into his side of the booth with, and I'm being honest here, catlike grace.

"I thought that guy at the third table would have nailed you when he backed up his chair so quickly." I quipped.

I was feeling a little more sociable and the storm had moved over, so I was a little bored and looking for some conversation.

"Hmmm," was all I got back. Then the man smiled and asked, "Do you play chess or backgammon?"

"Either," I said noncommittally.

"Well there are some games over there near the sugars and straws." He offered.

"Ok, I'll bite," I said getting up, maybe this would be more interesting than grumbling about my 'big story' getting canned. Yeah, a rainy morning, a great espresso, and a good game would definitely hit the spot. I found the backgammon board and most of the pieces, 'oh well,' I thought, 'I'll just use some of the sugar packets for my chips.'

Heading back to the table I saw the clouds returning to their normal depressing gray and the rain had slackened to just being an annoying drizzle.

"I'm Jack," I said, offering the game board to him, my hands were still too full to offer my hand.

"Call me Olaf," the older gentleman replied, without any accent.

I settled into the over-stuffed cushion and was curious about his name.

"You don't speak with an accent," I realized that I was being a little politically incorrect.

He laughed and smiled a broad friendly smile, "Well, a man who speaks his mind, I thought I was the last. Do you mean am I from Ballard?" He asked, showing a broad, bright smile.

Ballard is the 'little' Norway of the Northwest. A small suburb of Seattle were people were notoriously polite and said "Uff da," instead of hello, how is your day?

"Aaaa yeah," I said blushing.

"No, I'm from village on the coast of Norway. I've just been away for a long time." He grinned.

"I didn't mean anything..." I started.

"Don't apologize, I was just starting to like you," he chided. Something in his voice echoed the thunderstorm that had passed. "Let's put the spotlight on you for a minute." Olaf said, raising an eyebrow. He'd finished setting up the game while I had been fumbling with my investigative reporter shtick. "You are upset about a story in the paper. You always sit in this booth if you can get it and my studying you... surprises you. I would have to ask you why, since you were studying me earlier..." The old man raised the other eyebrow at me, looking a little comical.

"Fair enough, I replied. I'm a reporter for the Daily and one of my stories got over-edited." I huffed. "I usually write the 'Ask Aunt Sally' column," I finished lamely.

"I won't hold it against you," Olaf said smiling again.

We finished two games without saying anything. He took the first and I just got by with a lucky double sixes at the end of the second game.

"So the story you were writing, was it the local scene or something political?" Olaf asked, trying to wheedle more conversation out of me.

"It was actually a story about the Mayor and some of the shady dealings that got him reelected, but now instead of proof, the story reads as though the facts are just unfounded allegations by some third party." I quipped back, not trying to conceal my disappointment.

"Well your still a pup, so give it fifty years or so and they'll give you the front page." He said, with a straight face.

"Look," I replied, not trying to humor him, "I'm really not into paying my dues every time some old geezer feels I need to earn his respect."

"Fair enough," Olaf seemed nonplussed, "but there are other stories, and far stranger than are dreamt of in your philosophies," he waxed on quoting the bard.

I put up my hand, "I get it and your sympathy is duly noted." I mumbled as I was getting up.

"You're not leaving yet," he stated it as though it were a fact, though it was sounding more like a command. "We still have a game to play."

"Uh, no just getting a refill." I replied uneasily to his paternal tone.

I went up to the counter to get my second Mocha. 'Hey it was just another Saturday,' I thought. 'I'll stomp this guy at backgammon and feel a lot better about the whole thing.'

By the time I got back to the table, Olaf had already set up the board with all the remaining pieces and sugars packets to complete the white set on my side of the backgammon board.

"Tell you what, I'll tell you a story and if you choose to write it, you can sell it as a novella or to a magazine if you like." He offered.

"What are there, wild dogs roaming the streets of Ballard or something," I smirked, regretting my words as soon as I had said them.

This old guy had tagged me earlier with the 'fifty years' crack but, I didn't need to try and one up him. The white haired man just brought out some kind of competitiveness in me, I still don't know why.

"No, it's a story that has love found and lost, of great success and failure, of sacrifice and redemption or so it may be. But more than that, it's a story about hope," Olaf piqued my interest with his sales pitch, but I wasn't going to make it easy for him.

"Sounds a little long to be told over just a couple of games of Backgammon." I told him honestly.

"You come here every Saturday, you have two of those coffee drinks and sit and read the entire paper, if you were to forgo the paper and play Chess or Backgammon with me for that time, I could tell you a chapter or so a week. I assume you have one of those mini tape recorders?" he asked.

"Yes, but is the story worth my time?" I wasn't going to pull any punches with this guy.

"That will be for you to decide. Give it two weeks and if your not satisfied I'll buy your drinks for you, for say... four weeks?"

"Deal," I do love free coffee, "but why is this story needing to be told? There are millions of tales, tall and ordinary, what is it about this one that people would want to read?"

"I'm a storyteller, and far too old to be a writer. Stories, all good stories, need to be passed on, but the life of this particular person needs the telling. Now that's all that you're getting this week, so roll your dice." Olaf replied to my challenge.

The rest of the game was played as fierce as two people can play without throwing coffee in the opponent's face. Olaf doubled me as soon as he thought he had the upper hand and I did likewise, finally he pulled out the win at the last roll of the dice and won by two chips.
"Well that's one game multiplied by 32," he said.

"Are we going to keep score for the duration of this story that 'needs a telling?'" I sparred at him.

"Why not." Olaf beemed with confidence. "I like a challenge. Be sure to bring your recorder and two tapes next Saturday." He chided.

"Yes sir," I shot back. With that being said, he got up from the table and left without looking back.
'Strange man,' I thought to myself. Well if nothing else I would get some free mochas out of the deal, so sure, at the very least it was a little something to look forward to next Saturday. I finished the paper without much thought of the drizzling rain outside or the weird bargain that I'd gotten myself into.

The next week went by without too many hassles and the 'Ask Aunt Sally' column was finished long before its deadline, so I decided to go out with some people from work to celebrate Friday and stayed out late. When I woke up Saturday, I almost forgot the tapes and some batteries and the recorder I'd told Olaf I'd be bringing.
'This had better be good' I thought to myself, as I headed out into the city of ever present rain. When I entered the cafe, Olaf was getting a refill in

his cup of tea and the look in his eyes told me, this is not a person you'd want to be angry with you. I got my drink and settled into my side of the table. Olaf was already waiting with the game board setup.

He sat there looking out the window at the drizzle as it increased to a downpour. The old man had a faraway stare, like a disappointed parent, who had grown weary of a child's mischief. I quietly set up the recorder and the tapes and made sure that they were in working order, as he slowly turned his attention back to me.

"Well, I'm guessing vodka," Olaf stated flatly.

"Just celebrating a good week," I replied. I didn't feel I owed the story-teller anything for not being there on time, so I acted like everything was cool.

"If you write this story you will make your money and get the fame that you seem to crave." He said, eyeing me.

I didn't like where this was going. I sure didn't want to be some old man's ghostwriter, doing his memoirs and listening to him prattle on, for weeks at a time.

"Look, this is a little more serious than I want to get with you," I replied defensibly. "You wanted to tell me a story and I agreed to listen and if it was worth writing about, hey I'll give it a shot, but I didn't promise you the New York Times best sellers list or anything. You got a story, so spill it."

Apparently, the hangover that was just kicking in, was making me a little more venomous than I wanted to be. The craving fame comment Olaf had made, had just hit a too close to home for my liking.

"Diogenes, would be happy to find an honest, if somewhat surly man, sitting across from me." my backgammon opponent said smilingly. "I don't want any fame or any money. I just want you to hear my tale with an open mind. An open mind is the corner stone of intellect. And I'm sure that it's a story that you'll find interesting." Olaf finished, in his paternal lecturing tone.

"So can you give me a hint what this story is about?" I queried him.

"Are you too old to believe in... Kris Kringle?" he asked, with a twinkle in his eye. "Now turn that thing on and roll your dice."

The story, I'll say, does take an open mind and more than a grain of salt, Okay, more like a pound of salt.

As for what follows, I transcribed the tapes as they were recorded with my interjections, where I thought that they were needed, to clarify a point. I also included my own reactions to this man, Olaf Peterson, and of how the story changed my, 'oh so jaded perspective,' as he called it.

Map of Haven

Chapter 1
The Past is Prologue

So let's start at the beginning.

There was a small fishing village called Haven, deep in a fjord on the southern coast of Norway at about the ninth century. Christianity hadn't reached Northern Europe, despite propaganda to the contrary.

There was a boat builder, Sven was his name, who had only one son. This young man was one of the few men of privilege in that time and he flaunted it. The girls all swooned when he paid them any attention. I guess the closest thing to him today would be one of those ungrateful children that are spoiled to the core. You must understand that this was quite a rarity in that day and age.

His name was Petr and he was to be married by an agreement between his father and another prosperous family further down the coast. Being the Alpha male of the town, he could have his pick of the girls. Apparently, he picked them all more than once. But, no girl who ran her fingers through his thick blonde hair could've loved him, more than he loved himself.

Being the original playboy was a burden he carried well. None could out swim, out fight or out drink him. His marriage to Anika, the daughter of a wealthy southern trader, was something he would have put off as long as possible.

Petrs' mother had died giving birth to him, so he'd run wild ever since his wet nurse had set him down. Women had their use, when he became of age, but the thought of being tied to just one made Petr all the wilder.

With only one month until his wedding, he lived his life like he was trying to enjoy fifty years all at once. Drinking and climbing the razor sharp fjord walls that surrounded the tiny hamlet, to the top on a bet and riding a horse to death on one of his famous hunts. And in those days horses weren't cheap either.

Some blamed his father for not remarrying. Some said there was just an untamed fire in the boy. Indeed, he was a boy in a man's body. I think that it's called the 'Peter Pan Syndrome.' Kinda funny it bears his name, at least indirectly.

"I thought you were going go tell me about Kris Kringle... you know Santa Claus," I said; though it sounded more like a whine.

"What is past is prologue and Kris' past determined much of his life. Now do you want to hear this or not?"

"Sure, go a head," I muttered.

"Alright then," Olaf chided me. Though something smoldered behind his eyes, again I was pretty sure that I didn't want to see him angry.

Anyway, Anika and her family showed up in a festively covered long boat the day before the summer solstice. The boat was laden down with her dowry of sheep and furniture. Huge wreathes of flowers covered the ships sides. All the people in the village came down to the small bay to see the sight. Sven had to drag Petr there, because the night before he'd tried to drink the meadhall dry. The groom was a sight to see, all red and blurry eyed in the bright morning sun, with his disheveled hair and ale stained clothes. The townsfolk agreed that his handsome face had a look of terror on it, like the beautiful boat was carrying death herself.

The ship glided into moor and the people all craned their necks to see the bride, but apart from the deckhands tying up the boat, there was only one other person on deck. A man, smallish, barrel-chested and bald, with a huge red beard and with a gaze from his eyes that pierced right through a man. He stood, straight as a post there on the raised stern of the ship looking down at Sven and his son.

"It looks like your son fought a barrel of mead and lost, Sven," He bellowed.

"Aye," replied Sven, "though it was more like a wagon of ale."

Everybody laughed except Petr, of course.

"Eric," Sven called back up to the red bearde man, "did you forget to bring a daughter with you? I see you've brought plenty of sons to hold mine down for the hand-fasting." Again everyone laughed and Petr turned three shades of red.

"Aye" the man bellowed back, "and don't cha' be worrying I'm hiding her so's not to scare away the groom." He shot back.

The ears of the girls in Petr's harem perked up at this. Every last girl in the village of marrying age had secretly hoped that the bride would be horse-faced, and round as a barrel so that Petr would run away with one of them instead.

The ship was tied off and Eric jumped down to be at the head of the gangplank that his five strapping sons were putting into place.

"Anika," He called over his shoulder, and a hush went over the crowd.

In fact, the only sound that was heard was the gently lapping of the waves on the beach. Even the constant cries of the sea gulls had stopped. The sound of a board creaked, then the entire town including the bride-groom held their breath.

Then Anika appeared, stepping up to her father and placing her foot on the top of the plank, like she was walking down from her throne.

No one said anything; the whole village just stared.

Eric finally broke the silence, "Well it seems you've made quite an impression," he said with a smile. As she slowly walked down the board to the small beach, people parted before her like a wave. No one had ever seen a girl so regal.

The bride had small white flowers woven into her flaming red hair. Her face was without a freckle and her skin was the color of buttermilk. Anika's lips were full but when she smiled, the sun was said to dim in comparison. A slight breeze fluttered the white dress she wore, that had leather wrapping that showed her figure to its best. The belts were adorned with silver oghrams, symbols of wealth and happiness, and they caught the glints from the sun when she moved. Truly the most remarkable thing about her, were her eyes. A deep green, with depth enough to swallow a man and as she reached Petr they did.

"I hope you're not looking your best," she said to the Groom, in a voice that sounded like music.

"Aaahhh," was all that he could say.

And as the people enjoyed this spectacle, Petr was enjoying it more. He was beyond smitten, he was enthralled and she with him, in spite of his disheveled state.

Sven called out for all to hear "To the hall!"

A cheer went up around the two lovebirds, but they were listening to a sweeter music and had to be moved along so that the dowry could be unloaded from the boat.

The meadhall was in the center of the village, situated on a small hill with the smithy and the drawing stream. The stream came from the glacier that had carved out the fjord millennia ago. The ice flow had melted two miles back up the canyon. Leaving a sharp and high cliff wall to the north that kept out the worst of the winter storms and a small hole in the southern wall that led to the thick forest, that Sven and his men harvested for boat building. The acreage behind the village was said to be one of the most fertile places that anyone had seen. The old people swore that you could drop a berry there at nightfall and come back to find twelve full bushes the next morning. The farming was shared by all the village folk for staples like onions and turnips, but it also grew lingham and elderberries for making strong wine. This brought the village a little fame and a lot of trade at the summer festival. The festival took place in Vigfjord, the town down the coast where Anika's family lived.

Most of the houses were in a semi-circle around the meadhall looking out to the fishing boats in the southern facing fjord. Next to the small bay, higher up the shore was the long house where Sven and his men made the fishing boats and the longer trading vessels.

Finally, the dowry had been brought up to the meadhall, that was already overflowing with the feast that had been laid out by the whole town.

The Hall was ready for the wedding party with fish and cheese, fresh spring fruit that overflowed from wooden platters. Large brass bowls held lingham berry wine and mead for everyone and a great wild boar was roasting in the fire pit at the far end of the hall. To this was added the wreaths from the ship that were hung from rafters. The mead hall had a dizzying amount of smells with all the food, people and flowers. The large doors at the front were left open and the roof panels were lifted for light and air. Petr and Anika had been escorted to the mead hall by their fathers and were the last to take their seats at the far end of the hall nearest the roasting boar.

As the party went on around them, they talked quietly to each other, holding hands and eating very little of what was heaped before them. Sven and Eric took turns toasting each other's health and joking about Petr. One of Eric sons, Eric the younger, began playing a pan flute, a villager brought in a drum and another a lyre and they began to get the village to dance out in front of the great oak doors of the meadhall. So as not to disturb the people eating inside.

The feasting had went on into the evening, when the oldest man in the village was asked to tell a story. The fragile-looking elder raised slowly up on his staff and walked to the chair that was placed beside the roasting pit.

The boar had long since disappeared and the pit now held a glowing pile of banked embers.

He was helped to his seat by one of his granddaughters, who then brought him his bearskin cloak. Even on a warm solstice eve, the temperature could give the elder a chill.

"Olaf tell us of Odin's Peril" called out one of the young girls "No, no, tell the tale of Thor's battle with the frost giants," shouted one of the young bucks from the back of the hall. Then, as others called for their favorite stories, Olafs' wrinkled face cracked a wide smile. Happy to still be of use and honored with all the attention.

"You're in for a treat," Petr told Anika, "he can really spin a tale." Anika looked at the old man seated by the hearth, the weight of the bearskin seemed as if it would pull him off his chair. Petr squeezed her hand and smiled a boyish smile, "He only tells stories at special times of the year now that he's older than a glacier," her groom chuckled to his bride.

"Enough," a loud voice boomed out. Anika was surprised to find it came out of old Olaf. "The spinner of tales has decided." All eyes looked up to him with anticipation. "The Tale of..." he drew a long breath, not so much that he needed it, as to make the tension last. "Odin and Frigga."

This seemed to please everyone. Fighting, frost-giants, love lost and love found and Olaf would play up the romance for the mood of the betrothed. As he began to tell the legend, he idly began to roll the end of his staff in a pool of boar tallow that had been left near the fire pit. When he got to the part when Odin fought the frost giant and killed him with a fiery bolt of lightning, Olaf stabbed at the fire with his staff and the fat caused a small fireball to shoot straight up from the banked embers, to the delight of everyone. Petr and Anika watched the old tale-spinner weave the legend through many twists and turns, capturing the whole audience in the experience. He ended with the two gods swearing eternal love for each other and Odin giving the Norse people fair weather and good growing seasons ever since.

"Here endth the tale... but it is not over as long as their love lasts and we have nights like this one." Olaf finished. The wedding couple thanked him for his telling and Anika told him it was the finest telling of her favorite story. Others offered their thanks as well. There were no TVs and movies or books in those days, you must remember. So anyone who could keep people entwined in a tale was revered.

The party started up again with the music outside and drinking inside the meadhall. The couple went out into the night, Petr showing her the village and the fields. They lay on a blanket under the stars and watched the moon rise, music playing off in the distance....

The next day was the day of hand fasting...

"Wait, wait and wait you're just going to skip ahead to the next day? Aren't you leaving out anything from the stars, blanket and music in the background?" I wanted to know.

"I'm telling you this story the way it was told to me" My storyteller said tersely.

"You weren't even there?" I said, regretting it. as soon as I said it. Of course he wasn't there it was the ninth century after all. Why was I getting so caught up in this story anyway? 'Jack just let him tell the story,' I thought to myself. He sat there waiting for my mind to play catch up, looking very nonplussed.

"So the next day, was the day of hand fasting," Olaf began again. Anika had refurbished her red hair with tiny white flowers and wore a deep emerald green dress that showed her figure again to its best. Once again she had donned her leather belting that wrapped her midriff and crossed her chest in an ex, with the silver runes of wealth and family glinting in the sun as she moved. Petr looked far more presentable than he did the day before. Wearing studded leather armbands and a sleeveless suede shirt that had made all the maidens swoon as the gentle breeze tossed his flaxen hair.

The wedding of lives and fortunes, as it was known then, was held in front of the meadhall so that all had a view and witnessed the two speaking their vows. As they began the ceremony the old wise woman, Helga, asked if there was any to oppose the union of the two. 'A good way to get any troubles out of the way or to at least know your enemies,' thought Helga.

Many of the maidens hoped that the marriage wouldn't take place but, seeing Petr looking at Anika had dashed their hopes. All the maidens looked forlorn except Brenda, the blacksmith's daughter. She'd had it in her mind to have Petr for herself. The match would make perfect sense, the smithy and the ship builder's family worked very close together. Brenda knew in her heart that she should be the one with flowers in her hair. Petr had never made cow eyes at her the way he was with his bride. All her dreams were being taken from her and Brenda wasn't going to let him go without a fight.

"Aye" she yelled from the back of the crowd. "We all know she's a beauty," Brenda cooed, as she walked up to the front of the gathering.

"But why should we give up such a man, to this witch, when there are so many fine, well propertied-women," she said, placing her hand on her own chest, "in this village?" The question caused the crowd's mood to somber.

Anika waited for the woman to come up to her. Brenda kept on talking, not letting anyone get in a word edgewise until she was up on the wedding platform. "This is where I should be!" Brenda finished her speech, stomping her foot on the wooden stage. She spun on her heel and glared at Anika. Petr started to move between the two as Anika held him back with one hand to his chest.

"Betrothed, we are not yet joined," she said, with the same music to her voice that he'd come to love. "I'll deal with this." Though not taking her deep green eyes off of the interloper.

Over Brenda's shoulder, Anika could see the maidens all edging closer to the platform, to see the carnage.

'This has to be stopped once and for all' Anika thought to herself. 'I need to make an example out of this one or I'll be fighting these hens off forever.'

"How would you get rid of me?" Anika chimed to Brenda.

"A good beating and you'll be rowing a boat back to wherever you came from!" Brenda fumed.

"Then you'd best get to it, for I'm in the middle of my wedding." The bride goaded.

Brenda could stand this red-haired-dream-wrecker no longer. She balled up her fist and swung as hard as she could. The blonde pigtailed girl closed her eyes as she pulled back her fist and let it fly straight at Anika's face.

Brenda's ears was greeted with an obliging thud. She opened her eyes and was surprised to see Anika still standing and even more surprised that Anika held her own balled up fist in her hand.

The bride twisted the fist around quickly, pulling up Brenda's arm with it, so that Brenda was spun around with her arm up her back, facing the crowd. Anika then forced the interloper's arm up higher, making Brenda bend over the edge of the platform.

"Now then, what were you going to do after that?" Anika's voice still had an unerring lilt.

Brenda's face turned red as she was forced to look at the smiling and laughing villagers. Maidens in the rear were glad they hadn't decided to voice their own disapproval of Anika. Brenda wasn't given much time to think, as she went flying off the platform, Anika had let go of the interloper's arm and kicked her in the rear. The crowd moved out of Brenda's way as she tumbled on the ground, her blonde pigtails flying about her head.

Brenda had underestimated the witch but she was broader and stouter than the redhead and was going to use this to her advantage. When Brenda got her legs under her, she kept low and rushed for the stage, half expecting for Anika to show her true colors and either run for her daddy's boat or hide behind her bridegroom. Anika did neither. The red head-stood her ground as Brenda ran up the three steps of the platform to grind her into meal. The bride took a short half step forward and threw out her open palm, level with Brenda's neck. The blow flattened the wench as she covered her throat with both hands, trying to breathe.

"That red hair doesn't lie," Eric said, to break the tension. As the crowd laughed, in a lower tone he said to Petr, "She's Druid trained, in staff, knife and hand combat. If you hurt her heart, I'll be the least of your worries."

Anika bent down, much to the shock of the villagers, they thought that she was going to finish the poor girl off. But the bride helped the pig-tailed interloper to her feet and did a very fast motion with her hands over Brenda's neck and the blonde-haired girl started to breathe again.

"I wouldn't try to speak for a few days if I were you." Anika said, letting the double meaning sink in, "but you'll be fine." Then to a person in the crowd, "Some wine for my wedding guest."

Brenda's father, Joar, came forward and helped his daughter to sit on one of the benches, giving her a goblet of strong mead. He was grateful to Anika for showing as much compassion as she did. He knew at a hand-fasting, words could easily become swords and the challenge had ended in the best possible way. Though Brenda was still in shock at what had just happened, thankfully she sat on the bench speechless and dazed, holding her goblet of mead through the rest of the ceremony.

"Now then." Helga began again. "Is there anybody else who oppose this joining?" She said as loud as she could.

The maidens in the back kept their silence and seemed to shrink when Anika shot them a glance. Helga let Anika have her moment to clear the air, and then they both smiled as Anika faced toward Petr and offered her right arm for the ceremony. Helga held it by the wrist intoning the song of the Goddess. Placing a fertility rune made of stone into Anika's hand as she sang the ancient melody.

Helga finished the first part of the ritual by folding the bride's fingers up into a fist around the stone. She then motioned Petr to put out his right hand. Then the old wise woman placed Anika's balled up fist into Petr's open palm saying,

"You Anika, daughter of Eric are now the carrier of life," then Helga turned to Petr. "You Petr, son of Sven, are now the protector of life." She then wrapped the couple's hands with the binding that Anika had woven for this day. It had fine embroidery of Olgams and symbols of marriage, happiness, health and protection in silver thread on a fine green cloth.

As the old woman finished tying the knot, she called out in a commanding voice, "What the Goddess has joined no one dare put asunder!" Then in a much lower voice, the old woman said to Anika, "Wife kiss your husband... if this is the man you truly want," The wise woman finished with a smile.

Of all the marriages the wise woman had done, this one seemed to be the most blessed, for these two surely loved one another.

Anika looked deep into Petr's eyes and raised her eyebrow.

"Well... okay," she said, with a mischievous smile. Then she pulled him close and they wrapped their free arms around each other with their bound arms between them, over their hearts, as a sign to all that they meant their commitment to each other.

A cheer went up by most of the villagers, some of the maidens of the village were already busy fawning over Eric's five sons. After all, they were all eligible and not bad looking. Much feasting went on that day and into the night.

"But that's not really important," Olaf said, looking up from the game board. "Next week, I'll tell you about what happened years later."

I just sat there as he got up, putting his mug on the shelf near the kitchen, and walked out without looking back.

'What did I get myself into?' I thought. 'This isn't what I expected at all.' I put my tapes in a plastic bag to keep them from getting ruined by the rain. Then I slowly packed up my backpack and headed home. Looking out over the Puget Sound I saw the gray clouds getting darker.

Drombeg

Chapter 2
Brenda's Revenge

I quickly wove my way through the crowds at the market, as I didn't want to be late, after last week's scolding by Olaf.

On Saturday, the local farmers and craftspeople seem to have their best to show the public. I walked passed the fish throwing guys and the big brass pig down a little used corridor to the espresso shop.

Olaf was already there in the corner, mug of tea in his hand staring out the window. The game was set to go. I looked at my watch to see if this was going to be a repeat of last week, but I was on time. So I got the double shot low foam with a touch of hazelnut syrup and headed over to the table, ready for more of his story. I had to admit to myself that Olaf was a good storyteller. If the rest of it was as good, at least it would be entertaining. As I slid into the naugahyde bench, Olaf looked a lot older than he had last week. The storyteller caught me looking at him.

"Bad memory," was all he said. Then his disposition brightened. I set up the tape recorder and made sure I had the extra tapes handy.

"So okay what happened years later?" I asked, hitting the record button. I had finish transcribing the last week's tapes just the night before, so the story was still fresh in my memory.

"Well…" Olaf began…

The village had come to embrace the red-haired girl that the Druids had trained. Her ways were strange, most had thought at first. At odd times of the night, Anika would go out into the great forest that lay on the other side of the southern fjord wall, through a break in the massive rock. Then, she would return a little after sunrise with her basket full of herbs and mushrooms. Anika never asked any of the villagers to go with her on these foraging jaunts. And truly, no one needed to go to watch over her. With her staff and a small dirk for cutting the herbs, Anika could better protect herself than any in the village. Once, in the late fall, she came in early with a wild boar that had crossed her out in the forest. Anika had killed it with the pointed end of her staff, then cleaned it with the sharp knife she'd had for cutting the herbs.

As Helga, the old wise woman, was getting along in years, someone needed to take her place. Anika, as well as being taught Druid combat techniques, had also learned the herbal arts as a part of her education. So she was exactly what the village could use. This knowledge wasn't lost on any of the people there.

Well, any except the Blacksmith's daughter, Brenda. The broken-hearted blonde couldn't reconcile the fact that she wasn't Petr's wife. It wasn't that Anika wasn't gracious and forgiving. In fact, that just made Brenda all the more upset. Though she'd hid her spite and loathing from even her father, Joar, it boiled up in her more over the years. Brenda made excuses to avoid Anika and Petr whenever possible. The way they fawned over each other after seven years, it just wasn't natural. Petr was just as handsome as he ever was. His thick blonde hair was longer and his muscles were bigger from honest work. And the witch, Brenda didn't even want to say her name. She actually had gotten more beautiful. She hadn't seemed to age, even after three children. Her belly always went flat within a moon of every birth. 'Very unnatural,' the pigtailed blonde brooded.

Brenda had had other suitors, but she couldn't let go of the image of Petr in her head. Before the suitor would open his mouth, Brenda was already comparing him to her perfect Petr. She knew that her father worried about her since she was his only child. That year, he was going to take her to the midsummer fair to get her a husband once and for all.

Well, she could learn to love another. Maybe, and that would be revenge enough, or would have to be. Brenda watched the townsfolk that weren't going down the coast to the fair, bring their wares and things to be traded and sold down to the large trading vessel. It would be the last time she ever wanted to see these people. All of her friends had eventually deserted her and became the witch's friends.

"You really should find something else to complain about," the women would say. Then, after a few years of hearing her complain, they just tried to avoid her. If they had to interact with Brenda at all, they would talk about the weather or the crops or something equally safe. No, she would not miss any of those girls. Most had gone on to wed within a couple of years after Petr was taken. Taken from her.

Joar, her father, would always love her, but he would chastise her to look for a better man than Petr. And as she sat near the mast amidst all the barrels of elderberry wine and fresh smoked goat cheese, she vowed to herself to do much better, elsewhere.

The ship was loaded by midmorning, a fine treasure to sell at the fair down in Vigfjord. Joar was pleased that his daughter had willingly got on the boat this year. He'd secretly gotten a love potion from the old wise woman, Helga, to use on his daughter at the maypole dance. There were many men who would want her, though she had waited a little too long. People had thought she didn't want a husband, she had certainly turned down enough offers. The concerned father had decided to take matters into his own hands. After the first dance, he would give her a mug of watered down wine, as was the custom. Only he would stir in the love potion of herbs that would dissolve in the drink. And by the end of the day she would have forgotten all about Petr.

Joar knew that Petr was the reason that his daughter had refused to take any suitors, and the blacksmith had watched Anika over the years. Her three children were a joy and the training that the Druids had taught her allowed Anika to work right up to the birth. Then she'd be back to work the next day. If his daughter were hoping for the red-haired 'witch' to die in childbirth, she would be waiting a long time.

Joar had tried not to like Anika, for his daughter's sake. Though over the years, he couldn't find anything to hold over the Druid. Helga didn't feel threatened by the younger earthwise-woman. Anika had actually taught the older woman some new herbal remedies. She'd even came up with some warming salves to help with the stiffness that the older villagers had in their joints. Anika was also very helpful with the burns and cuts that Joar got from working the metal in his forge, giving him creams out of that large chest that came with her dowry.

It looked like a sea chest that had washed up on the shore that had been cast back after the mermaids had tired of it. Queer it was, encrusted with shells, the likes of which he'd never seen before. Strange symbols were carved around the shells that looked like seaweed at the corners. They curled and flipped back on themselves in a way that looked like letters of some forgotten language that changed slowly in the shadows of firelight, if you looked at them long enough. In the chest, Anika kept the salves she made and other herbal concoctions that she'd gather at the odd hours in the great forest. Joar had offered to make her a short sword that she could carry to protect herself.

She declined with her musical voice saying,

"I've protection enough," showing him her quarter staff made of ash and the small knife, that looked like it was made of pewter, but was sharper and stronger than anything that he'd ever seen, she kept the small knife in a sheaf at her hip. Anika's staff was carved with oghrams of the Druids and was sharpened at one end. Though a little taller than her and seeming to be ungainly, she could wield it like it was a part of her. Joar had seen her practice with it early one morning. The staff buzzed through the air like the wings of a humming bird. Joar could just barely make it out. Between the staff and the way she moved around, in what looked like fighting stances, the Blacksmith wondered if it was some kind of dance that the red-haired woman had learned. Joar had stopped worrying about their new earth-wise woman when she came back from foraging with the boar across her shoulders. That settled any question of her value to the village. With that, even her protective husband had learned to trust her skills.

Standing at the bow of the ship, the blacksmith checked his own stock of wares that he'd trade for more copper and tin. Small items that made life a little easier, kitchen utensils, hooks, and some silverwork that he was known for making. Studs that he'd trade with the southern leatherworker, Alvis. It would be nice to visit with a friend of his childhood and Alvis was always honest in his dealings, even with those Viking slavers from the far North coast.

The slavers were men that would only trade with villages that they couldn't raid. If a village showed any sign of weakness, they would turn on the townsfolk, even if they were blood-kin.

Fortunately, the way the glacier had carved out the valley, gave the people of Haven little to worry about. The walls went straight up for several hundred feet and the south wall only had one narrow passage that was easily defendable. The approach from the sea was but a small inlet and since it was the only one for miles, ship's crews kept on good terms with the small hamlet. Many times during the fall and winter, a ship would harbor in Haven, away from the maelstroms that could dash a vessel on the rocks of the jagged coast. So even though it was prosperous, it wouldn't be easy prey. The villagers of Haven felt safer from the slavers than most port towns.

That year had been very prosperous for the village and all that they couldn't use was loaded for trade on the long boat. Casks of wine, barrels of goat cheese and other crafts that filled the ship had almost grounded it in the shallow end of the cove nearest the village. The boat hardly had room for the provisions and crew. With Sven and Joar trading Haven's goods, the ship was sure to be just as loaded down on its way back. With the midday-tide coming in, the two men rallied their crew to push off and start rowing out to sea.

Anika watched the ship that was filled more with the hamlets hopes and dreams than with goods. Many of the girls asked to trade their shares in for exotic threads and fabric, of what little would make it this far north at anytime of the year. They would be happy with some dyed cotton or a bit of ribbon, but they weren't likely to see the fine cloth that could be had much farther south.

During her training with the Druids, Anika had seen the great southern city of Constantinople. A city of many delights and deviations but it was made very clear to her, that the church of Rome held sway over the people and her kind were hung and burned, if they were lucky. Far worst things were done to any that were deemed heretics by the church of Rome. So the group of Druids she traveled with, that were called Pagans by the people of the Byzantine Empire, traveled as Christian pilgrims to avoid being detected.

Those were strange times in her life. At seven, Anika's mother had given her over to a Grey robed wanderer without any protest from her father, Eric.

"It's the ways of your mother," was all her papa had said.

None of her brothers had to go, but they had failed the test the old man given all of Eric's children. The grey bearded man, would take the children, one at a time to a nearby stream. Then he'd ask them to hum a note, then look into the water and tell him what they saw. All the boys said; water, rocks, a trout. None of the answers pleased him. The old man would bring them back in a huff and take the next one down to the stream. Finally, he took Anika to the little creek.

"Now lass," he tried to remain calm, this had been an exasperating trip and this was the last child to be tested. "Breathe deeply and match my tone." His voice was steady and deep. Anika swallowed as much air as she could.

"No girl, you're not a frog," he chided her, making a face that bloated out his cheeks and crossed his eyes. That made Anika giggle and relax at his silliness. He then took a slow deep breath, which she then mimicked and as he began to sing a pure perfect note, Anika almost lost her breath.

'How could this old man sing such a high note,' she thought to herself. Before she lost her breath, she concentrated on the note and started to match him. After a moment, Anika got it right then she saw little bits of light flitting around in front of her eyes. The old Druid watched her, knowing the small girl was seeing something, maybe this was the one he was looking for after so long. He let his tone die out long before he got tired, to match her smaller lung capacity.

"Now child," he said softly, as to not disturb her state of mind. "Look deeply into the pool, here near the edge of the stream." The gray bearded man pointed to the nearest deep spot he could find. Anika leaned over holding onto a small ash sapling that grew out over the steam, because she felt dizzy. Anika stared and stared in the clear water. Her eyes went out of focus then into a focus she'd never experienced before that day.

The sunlight that played on the water, made images of places Anika had never seen in her young life. A great city and scenes of a war between metal clad warriors and a red-haired army of men, women and children that were fighting fiercely with wooden weapons against overwhelming odds. Images blurred and came together. She saw herself, though much older, looking back at her younger self lovingly, then a sudden darkness came across her vision, that had an animal's shape but blurred. The little red-haired girl felt the animal blackness peering through her... into her soul.

"Yes, she'll do," it said, with a voice that rang in her mind. This scared her out of scrying the pool. The sun was much higher in the sky when Anika got her wits about her and turned around. She was surprised to see her father and mother standing with the old man, watching her. At once, sad and happy expressions played on her parents' faces. It was her mother that explained that she had a gift and her grandfather, the old man she'd never met before today, was to teach her how to best use that gift. Anika wouldn't be gone for very long, her parents promised her. When she returned to the village Anika would be a great help to all her family and friends. Anika was a little more than scared to leave all she'd known but somethings she'd seen in the pool, a blur of a man that she'd marry, a thing, very important that only a few could do, and the intelligent darkness that shimmered, felt too important to her not to persue.

The little red-haired girl knew the rightness of going away. So Anika agreed to leave the village and learn to use the natural gift she had, not knowing the twisted path it on which her choice would take her.

Anika left with the strange old man that same day, having little time to say goodbye to anyone. They traveled in a roughly made cart that held enough hay for the donkey and a few wooden boxes of her strange tutor's goods. The grandfather's name was Elwyn but Anika soon learned that everybody called him by his title, 'Merlyn.' Within a day's travel, the little girl and her grandfather met up with the rest of his people. There were two couples and a woman that the little girl happily found out was her grandmother. Once the troupe broke camp they headed inland, far from the girl's known world. Rowena, Anika's grandmother, sat in the back of the cart comforting her granddaughter about her loss by showing Anika a way to see her family anytime she wanted. It took singing and breathing a certain way, then Anika had to be still as the dead. After a lot of practice the granddaugther was accomplished at doing this new skill and wanted to learn more. As the days passed, she was told stories of how the Druids came into being and the mandate that they needed to fulfill.

"Long ago, a few humans were taught by the elves to know and work with the magicks of this world." Ysbail, one of the other old women told her.

"The knowing allows us to use our natural gifts to their fullest." Brigit, the last woman in the trio finished. "And we've been given an importatn task to complete."

"That is our journey," Rowena said with a smile, "farther than any of us have traveled." The grandmother finished with her eyes wide, showing Anika that she was also excited in the adventure, catching the small girl up in her emotion of the great quest.

Onward they went slowly over the land, many days through the wilds, on more of a cow path than a road. The women would teach the young girl more complex tasks, ways of reading the land and its creatures moods.

Upon reaching the coast, they all found passage on one of the long-boats that traders used on the long trade routes. Elwyn donned the garb of a wandering priest and cautioned the group, mainly for Anika's sake, that they were on a pilgrimage to Miklagard, the name the Vikings used to describe Constantinople. It means, 'the great city,' they told Anika. They were to go to the city anyway and being pilgrims on the way to see Hagia Sofia, the Church of Holy Wisdom, was the perfect cover. Anika hadn't really believed tales of such a city, that the women had described. A city of several hundred thousand, the Hippodrome with room for 100,000 spectators, it was more people than the little red haired girl could imagine.

The old women continued to teach Anika, mostly in her dreams on the long voyage.

At first, it seemed strange, but after waking up and knowing how to read and write, all from one night's teaching, Anika could hardly wait to go to sleep again. Many weeks went by and the little waif absorbed all that she was shown. When the women had taught her all that they knew, the men took over to show her different magicks, Bryce and Glynn, the two other men in the party, taught her the martial arts.

Bryce had traveled far in his long life and taught the young girl the pike in a way that only a few outside of the forbidden kingdom of the East would know. Glynn showed Anika military tactics of all the armies that he'd known, then he taught her, the assassin's art of the knife. This took up most of the voyage. Once the party left the great sea through the Norvasund, later called the Straits of Gibraltar, Anika thought that her head would burst. Memories of her tutors' lives mixed with what little she had experienced. Elwyn came to her as she leaned over the side of the last boat that they had taken passage on, to reach the great city.

Anika was throwing up from the migraines she'd kept having, not from the seasickness that the crew had thought. The Merlyn felt her troubled mind trying to make sense of all the knowledge, yes, it was more than a little girl should have to bear, but there was no one else. Anika would need the knowledge and experience to find her way to the elves safely. So it came to him to ease her pain. He'd been too long playing the part of a priest instead of watching over the care of his ward. Anika finished emptying her stomach and turned to find the gentle stare of her grandfather. "Come child, I have a remedy for your head." He said kindly.

The Merlyn took her aft and gave her a mixture of herbs and wine that calmed her as he sang a low song of making over the small child. It would cause Anika to forget most that she had learned until she was older and would be able to use the knowledge wisely. The grandfather kept up the herbal treatments until a few days before the ship reached Miklagard, then he started to teach her his own knowledge. 'Just in case something happens to me,' the Merlyn thought to himself.

The day came when Elwyn would meet with his contact in Miklagard. The sun came up over the peninsula called the Golden Horn. Even the sailors who'd seen it before, stopped their tacking of the sail to watch the sun break through the clouded horizon to light the great city in its splendor. The city jutted out from the coast, as if in defiance of the Mediterranean Sea. The wall around the city was 7000 yards long, the inside wall was 12 yards high. There were 100 high towers along the length of the wall to defend the great city. Where the penisula joined the coast, there were defensive moats. In the cities main harbor, a heavy iron chain was in place to block raiding ships.

And above all of it's fortifications, was Constantinople — The Golden Horn.

Anika was slack-jawed at the sheer size of it. The huge city walls facing the sea dwarfed the 'pilgrims' when they sailed into the harbor of the Golden Horn.

As soon as the group found lodgings, Elwyn, their leader, the Merlyn, had gotten his land legs under him. By noon, Elwyn had met their contact in the Bazaar and had arranged to take the package that his group had traveled so far to get. His long journey wouldn't be at an end though. The others that had came with him to help with his latest student would stay here among the Christians in the city. Their teaching Anika all their knowledge at an accelerated rate was their last task for his fellow Druids. Elwyn and his wife Rowena would finish Anika's education and take her to the calling place called, Drombeg, in the land of Erin.

Drombeg was a stand of stones at one of the sacred places in the world where the Druids could interact with their patrons from the other realm. If all went according to plan, there Anika would be directed to finish the work that had taken so long to complete. When the Merlyn came back from the bazaar, he found that Bryce had given Anika his fighting staff, since the man was too old to wield it any longer. In the small courtyard of the house that had been prepared for them, the little girl danced with the staff swinging deadly blows at imaginary opponents and giggling. As was agreed, Glynn would surrender his fighting dirk to her as well.

"I might as well give it to her, she knows how to use it and with her youth, she will be more than ready for any task that she's set upon." He told Elwyn honestly.

"What concerns me is that I blocked the skill out of her wakefulness," the Merlyn said, "I'll talk to her later about it. She's happily cracking skulls now," He finished, watching her spin the staff around her in a blur.

But that week, the whole city was plundered by rogue Vikings. The year would come to be known as 860 ad. The Viking raiders cut down everything that stood in their way, set fire to churches and houses. The emperor was forced to offer the marauders a large amount of gold so that the citizens would be left in peace. Two weeks went by, before Elwyn could find anyone who knew the man he was to meet in the great church of Hagia Sofia. The news wasn't good, whatever the Merlyn was to take back to the Isle of Erin was lost. The Druids contact, an Eastern man had been killed on the first day of the fighting. Elwyn wouldn't have known what to look for anyway. It had been kept secret, even from him. All he knew was that Anika was to take it on the journey with her to the elves. The old man was crushed; he was the last of his order, Merlyn, high priest of the Druids. All that had come before him had added to the knowledge of his people. Now at the culmination of their work, he'd failed. One last task lost from him. It could have been anything. A power wand, a sacred plant, he just didn't know and he was far from any of the sacred places of power to contact the elves as to what was to be done. He was inconsolable for the next few days, alone in his chamber. He told the others that he was meditating on the problem, but all knew why he stayed in solitude.

Meanwhile, Anika played with her new toys. The staff could shatter rock if she sang power into it. With the dreamtime teaching and the practice of holding the notes in certain ways, power would be pulled up from the earth into the little girl. Then she could direct it into any object. 'All the nightly instruction was worth it after all,' Anika thought to herself.

She hummed the perfect note then one of slightly higher octave, making a vibrato of the two notes and felt the energy encase the staff. The wooden pole wouldn't even have a scratch or nick after hours of shattering rocks as big as a man's head.

The pewter-gray colored dirk, that Glynn had given Anika, that was a wonder. It was double edged, with a blood-groove down the middle and light as a feather. The knife was perfectly balanced for throwing and with all the skills that the old assassin had given her, she wasted no time in practicing with it. Using the other half of the day that wasn't spent with the staff. "Strength will come in time child," the assassin, Glynn told her. "Just you mind to do the drills."

Anika did all the stances that not only kept her lightning fast, but they also would keep her flexible even after a long day of training.

"Mother... mother are you far-gazing?" her oldest son, Olaf asked. He'd watched her slowly stop working in the communal field, then she stood motionless barely breathing for some time.

"No just wool gathering, an old memory, maybe if you're good I'll tell you it tonight." Anika said, tempting him. Of course she would leave out a lot of details and she couldn't tell Olaf half of a story without him falling to sleep. A blessing really, he eldest son took after his father in that respect. She looked up from the basket of turnips and took the six-year old with her back to the village.

She just caught sight of the trade ship leaving the fjord, as it headed for her home village three days south. Anika dearly loved her birth mother and father and all her brothers, well pretty much, but the village of Haven felt more like where she was needed and accepted than anywhere else she been. Yes, they thought her ways strange, but she was an asset to the community and many had said as much. Not just for taming Petr either. The healing arts and herb craft was sorely needed and with Helga's eyesight starting to wane, the older wise woman was unable to pick the herbs at night when they were the most potent.

'Well, enough of that,' Anika thought to herself, the healer turned her attention to the story that she should tell tonight.

Maybe she would tell the children of the end of the adventure. When Elwyn took her to Drombeg, the circle called the 'Druid's Altar,' where she finally understood why she was taken from her home in the first place. 'Perhaps it would be better to tell the story as something she had made up, rather than as what actually took place. Yes, that seemed to be for the best.' The Druid mused.

Anika saw that Petr was just coming up from the inlet and the loading of the ship for trade, smiling at her, as she beamed at him. He'd never pried into her past, indeed Petr was just happy that she was here. After seven years and three children, Anika would see how much truth her husband would glean from the story.

After the dinner was cleared and the children were getting to bed, Petr hadn't been too surprised that their eldest son Olaf, was telling his younger brother Kris that their mysterious mother was revealing one of her Druid stories.

"This is more tale than story," she started. "It was a long voyage from Miklagard, to the land of Erin. After many weeks at sea, we came to the beautiful emerald isle. There, your Great grandfather took me to meet the elves, beings of tremendous power, who had taught the Druids all of the knowledge to be earthwise. When we landed, the people who weren't preparing for the ritual had come down to see us.

So many that I was lost in the mob, which cheered and congratulated my grandfather for fulfilling the quest that was laid upon him. Though

I wasn't lost for long, the Merlyn had sent his spirit on ahead the night before and had arranged everything. As the people in the crowd clamored around their leader, a small girl about my age of ten, came to my side.

"I'm Mara," said the blonde wisp of a girl with a smile, "I'm to be your guide here."

I followed her up the stone steps of the hillside to a winding path and up to the altar area, about three leagues from the sea. There was a small rocky terrace with a fine view of all directions. The locals called it Drombeg, which in their tongue meant, 'the small ridge.' The sacred place had 17 pillars of smooth-sided sandstone arranged in a circle about fifteen paces across. Like many of the stone circles that the Druids used, it was also used to mark the winter solstice. This one was setup to the alignment of the winter solstice sunset. Mara took me over to one of the old stone huts to acquaint me with what I was to do for the ritual.

Later, as twilight drew the day to a close, several men began blowing very large horns, while other men beat a slow steady rhythm on large drums, around the circle of stones. Women began to chant low in the ancient tongue; words that rose with power as the rhythm grew. I stayed at the stone hut, one of the two that were side by side, joined with a common doorway. To one side there was a stone flagged pool, that looked like an ordinary cooking trough that was filled with water. Red-hot stones were dropped into the water-trough and the pit could boil for almost three hours, cooking even the largest elk. That night it was to be used for a different purpose. I'd learned from Mara that the horns and chanting over at the circle were used as a 'calling,' a knocking at the door so to speak, the pit was where all the action was to take place."

Olaf and Kris, who had been almost dozing at this point, became very bright-eyed at the sound of something juicy. Mary, Anika's joy, had already drifted off to sleep at the sound of her mother's voice and Petr sat there by the fire not wanting to interrupt.

"Well now," Anika chimed as she finished surveying her audience. "The pit had been filled to the brim with fresh water and the red hot stones were put in when the horns had started at the stone circle. The water began to steam then after a little while, the pit started the long boil that would last three hours. Grandfather appeared in all his splendor with a clean white robe and his ash staff that for this occasion had an animal's horn strapped to the top. He came over to me and together we circled the boiling water. He chanted the same words that the women at the stone circle were chanting; I tossed herbs that Mara had given me, in the boiling water. As we continued to go around the pit I felt the energy build. It started as a small feeling in my feet and grew until I felt it moving through me, like standing in the tide, being pushed and pulled by the unstoppable force of the waves.

Then, grandfather came to a halt at one end of the pool facing away from the stone circle and looking out at the darkening sea. Steam rose and swirled in many shapes, not all pleasant. The vapors came together over the pool; not a hand's breadth above the boiling water and started to form a kind of dark doorway. The fires that were used to heat the stones for the pit still gave off as much light as before, but the doorway seemed to draw the light, all light into it. Even the horns and chanting that weren't eighty paces away, faded away to nothing. Grandfather, high priest of all the Druids, rightful Merlyn, leader of the people who learned and followed the Earth-wise ancient knowledge of the elves, raised his staff to summon.

"Aaaaaaaaaa, I'm here," the voice was in our minds, not spoken aloud.

"Could you please not wave that thing around, you could put someone's eye out." The voice had a rye sense of humor to it.

"I have failed you in retrieving the, the".... Grandfather never had learned what he was to bring back from the city of Miklagard. It had caused him much grief, that one of the few things that the elves had asked in all of the time that helped his people; the Merlyn had let the elves down.

"Yes, the package. That is unfortunate, but do not trouble yourself, Merlyn. You could not have seen the unexpected war that fell upon Miklagard." The voice was softening, comforting and reassuring to grandfather. "It only tells us that the 'article' was genuine, besides," the voice brightened, "you have found a perfect candidate to help us finish some other work." The voice implied me.

I felt soft, kind eyes looking into the depths of my soul seeing all that I was and could be, that which I'd been taught and my progress.

"Your granddaughter does you credit," the voice from the black door chuckled. "Send her back to her family for now, it may be a time before you are called upon, Anika." I felt its full gaze upon me. "Others must be informed about the 'package' then we will call for you. Great, is the burden that you must bear child, but you are more than up to the challenge." Grandfather thought that voice had finished at that time so he backed away from the steaming pit and faded from my view. I remained frozen in place.

The being turned its full attention towards me.

"One other thing for you missy..." the voice chuckled again.

"Well that's another story," Anika said, to her two boys that had been wide-awake for the juicy part.

"Oh please tell us more!" they begged.

"Maybe another night, If you're good I'll tell you more about Mara and the adventure that we had just getting off of the Isle of Erin."

The children knew better than to press their mother about anything. So they bedded down and soon they were dreaming of far away places and having adventures of their own.

Petr, still sitting by the fire next to his beloved finally asked, "Just how much of that was true?" He pressed her as gently as he knew how.

"All and more," she replied sweetly, batting her eyelashes at him. Petr wasn't sure about any of his wife's past, before they'd met. After her tale, he didn't know what to believe.

"Do you trust me?" Anika asked pointedly, looking at the troubled face before her. She hadn't told the story to torment him. Now she was glad to have left out a few of the details. She searched his stormy countenance for a sign, seeing his boyish grin return told her all she needed to know.

Months passed without any more stories from Anika. She felt that enough had been said for a while and she'd revealed enough to get Olaf and Kris to faithfully do the breathing and singing exercises that she had started to teach them.

The trade ship had came back full of goods and much needed supplies that the village couldn't make. Joar was happy to report that his daughter Brenda had found a big strapping lad, though he was one of the slavers, and would live in his village that was very far north, up the coast. So with the great harvest that had been put up for the cold season to come and the abundant amount of fish that had been caught and smoked, the village was ready for even the worst of winters.

The fall harvest festival had long since past, though down in Erin it was called Sowen, the Night of the Dead. Anika had checked in with her good friend Mara on the dream paths then. The blue-eyed weather witch had two children of her own. She was one of the few Druids that had survived the massacre at Craggenmore, and had escaped to live far to the north in the middle of Ulster, deep in one of the many glens that the slaver Vikings hadn't reached. Anika thought about Mara, it had been a long time since they had talked on the dream paths. The healer decided she would find her friend and visit that night, if she wasn't too tired. With all the salves and ointments needed to be brewed that night, the last full moon before the solstice, Anika was in for a long night's work.

Her sons had stocked up the wood outside for the fire she would need for her elixirs and ointments. Since some of the roots and mushrooms gave off such an awful smell, the healer made all of her salves outside.

Anika made a quick dinner for her family. A hearty meal of seaweed and fish soup and flat bread, it was filling and she could make enough in her large cooking kettle to even feed her growing boys. As the large kettle simmered, the Druid checked all the supplies that she would need for the long night ahead. Anika went to the old sea chest that the Selke had given her and pulled out her ingredients to take out to the makeshift altar / worktable.

'Wolfsbane, Yarrow, Shadow moss,' she thought to herself, checking all of the roots, herbs and mushrooms that she'd collected for the medicines that she'd make to see her village though the winter. Anika gingerly handled the fragile ingredients, thankful that the chest had preserved the stores as if they had just been picked.

That was the one wonder of the chest. It could preserve anything that fit in it, even meat, without going bad. The Selke, magic folk that changed from human to seal and back again when they chose, had many things from the 'old times' as they called them. They rarely gifted anyone with such a wonder. It was when she and Mara had been asked to take a Selke's baby daughter from a place near the 'giants causeway' over the sea to the Isle of Mann. The baby's mother had been killed by a barbarian when she was in the form of a seal. The baby couldn't be taken by the father, for he was hunting the barbarian down, as was the Selke custom, so it fell to the Druid healer, Anika and the weather witch, Mara. It was one of the many adventures that she and Mara had had on the way back to Anika's village. Safe to say, it ended well and the father Selke was so grateful that he brought the chest to her for a dowry gift as thanks for taking care of his only child.

Anika stocked a makeshift shelf, that Petr had set up behind the longhouse, with the contents of the chest and started what would be the blending fire as the sun went down behind the western sea. The stars were already filling up the sky, as she lined up the pots that would hold the old people's bone warming salve. A honey and arnica mixture that the village folk used to keep cuts from getting infected and heal bruises over night, there were many other ointments but those were needed the most. Anika pulled on her cloak that her stepfather had brought out to her. She thanked the father of her beloved Petr.

Sven liked her right from the start and had come to think of her as his own daughter.

Anika smiled and shooed him back inside so that she could work. Then she pinned the heavy woolen cloak at her shoulder with a brooch that Joar had made her. That little silver gift had surprised her greatly. The black-smith had waited until his return from the festival when he'd finally found a husband for his daughter. While Sven and the others told the story of the journey, Joar found Anika outside the meadhall and had presented it as a gift to her for all the burn salve that she's given him over the years without asking anything of him in return. Anika suspected it was also for putting up with his daughter, Brenda, but the Druid healer didn't press the blacksmith for conformation of her thoughts.

The sound of the crackling fire brought her back to her task at hand. It would be an hour before the moon would crest the southern shield wall. The Druid felt it in her bones, so she stoked the fire and pulled the cloak, that had been warmed in the hearth, tightly around her and watched the constellations move slowly across the sky.

As the moon came up over the south shield wall of the fjord Anika came out of her meditation. She'd left her body and had looked in on her dear friend, Mara to find that she was dealing with two sick children. 'I'll recommend something for that fever in the baby, and some houndsmort for the toddlers cough, then they all can get a proper night's rest,' she though to herself. Anika put the warm woolen cloak aside so that she could work. With the breathing exercises that her grandfather had taught her, Anika could be out in the coldest weather without getting a chill, but she didn't want the townsfolk thinking that she was any stranger than they already thought. So the Druid healer waited until they had all bedded down and she could work in peace.

Some herbs had to be blanched, some fire roasted and mixed quickly so she went to work, deftly going through the rituals that were far less magickal than they looked. A lot of the roots had to be heated and cooled again and again to draw out the juice that gave them the most potency, so she would have to wave them in the cold night air, then reheat them in the fire to extract the oils. Anika was sure that her waving the roots around in the moonlight would look like some weird incantation to 'draw down the moon.' When actually, she was looking at the roots in the full moonlight because the oil of the root would glisten a certain color when the root was ready to be mixed with mushrooms. As she went about her work she felt a tugging at her consciousness. She thought it was her friend and would get back to Mara as soon as she finished the warming salve.

With the two major projects out of the way, before the moon had almost reached its zenith, Anika decided to take a break. The other potions and salves were for gout, scurvy and for sleep, which were easy to prepare so they could wait. Anika breathed in deeply, relaxing, sitting back into the woolen cloak that she had set aside earlier. Her body always cooled a bit when she left it, so she wrapped the heavy cloak around her completely. Anika felt her spirit leave its shell and she floated for a moment above her body.

"There you are." She 'heard' a distant voice. Anika sensed it draw near.

"I tried to find you earlier, there is something you need to see. NOW!" the familiar voice insisted.

The Druid healer knew that this was the same voice that she'd encountered at the stone circle at Drombeg. Anika felt being pulled up far above the land where her village was located. High up above the atmosphere she went at the speed of her guide's thought.

'The moon took up a lot more of the sky from this vantage point', the healer thought. Anika was turned around to see what was the matter. She looked down at the peninsula of her homeland. She saw a blue light where her village should be and three other dots of red light. One from the North out at sea, and two coming up from the South, one from the sea and one over land through the forest towards the gap in the southern shield wall of the village. Immediately, the information entered her mind. Slavers were going to attack the village. Vikings of her own country, against Viking law were going to raid the prosperous little hamlet. This and more rushed into her mind from the guide. She had little time to think of a way that the farmers and craftsmen could organize against professional warriors that were about to attack her village of Haven.

'Use Mara to create a storm,' the thought rang in her head. 'I will help her direct it.' before Anika could ask any questions her companion was gone. The Druid healer thought of the weather witch Mara in the land Erin....

Mara felt the sensation of the presence of her friend tugging at her beside the bed. She'd just gotten the two sick boys to sleep, more out of exhaustion than medicine. It was times like this that she missed her best friend more than any other. While Mara had been gifted with the ways of witching the weather and bending it to her will, Anika had all the knowledge of the healing arts that would break the fever of the baby and the coughing fits of her three-year-old. Mara started to lift out of her body; her spirit was then unceremoniously pulled free.

"Wha...," she started.

"Listen please," she felt Anika pleading. "You must begin a great storm surrounding my village." The healer then gave Mara all that had transpired before, with the unseen guide, in a thought 'bubble' that the women used to give each other when they relayed large ideas or information.

Mara felt her healer friend leave to organize the villagers of Haven. The weather witch entered her own body and marshaled her strength for the task ahead. To make a storm used energy. To make and direct a maelstrom so far away was more than Mara had ever tried. That and being up for two days with the children being sick, made Mara doubt that she could help her dear friend. She went outside barefoot, luckily she had gone to bed with all her clothes on, so she didn't have to dress, not that she would. Barefoot was the way she connected with the earth to work her magick. Mara looked up at the moon now approaching its zenith; she reached out with her senses, feeling the night air. There was more power infused in everything that night and not just because of the full moon. Mara walked down the path to her own circle where she worked her power. It was ringed in stones that she'd placed around it to draw in and concentrate power. 'Yes,' she noticed, more energy and more coming in... swirling around, the circle. Large waves of it were being drawn in from the countryside at an amazing rate. The elf or guide or whoever that said they would help her wasn't kidding. After all the time that had elapsed, Mara and Anika had thought that the elves had forgotten about them, it was good to know they were watching out for the Druid women. Mara entered the small circle feeling more awake and alive than she'd ever experienced. The ethers coalesced around her; energy enveloped her, passed through her and waited to do her bidding.

Anika came back into her own body with a start. She quickly came up with a short list of priorities. Not knowing if the slavers would try to kill them all and leave no survivors to tell of the breaking of the sacred law or enslavement of the women and children. Or had the slavers planned to kill any able fighter and sack the village, Anika didn't know. Either choice had to be taken into account as to just fend off the attack, or prepare these people to fight to the death. 'Better to err on the side of caution,' Anika thought to herself, if she was wrong, at least they'd all be alive. Then the plan of the slavers' attack came to mind. To surround the village, cutting off any escape must mean that it was to be a battle to the death. Anika felt emptiness in the pit of her stomach. Not that she hadn't fought and killed before, she had many more times than people would believe. But with her life in Haven she had much more to lose. Anika rushed in to tell Petr and Sven to get them to wake the village, and then she woke her children dressing them more warmly than they needed.

"Where you are going, you may need the extra cloak so take it." She told her young. Then Anika shoved a flint stone in each pair of the children's boots.

"Go and take the other children up the glacier, there are caves in the north wall about halfway up. You must hide and stay unseen no matter what you hear. When it is safe, I will come for you." She then gave Olaf a thin hemp rope to use as a guide for the other children in the dark. "Now go and do not light a torch, you must use the moonlight." With that done, she turned to get her staff and fighting dirk.

Most of the village had been gathered at the front of the meadhall when Anika arrived. They weren't happy about being pulled out of their beds and warm long houses in the middle of the cold night, but the talk of an attack quieted the anger enough for the Druid to talk without inter-ruption.

"Good people, three groups of slavers come even as I speak, two block-ing the sea from North and South and another from the great forest to the gap in the southern shield wall." Anika let it sink in for a moment. "Don't ask how I know. I've never given you cause to doubt me. I've sent my chil-dren to collect the rest and take them up the glacier to the caves."

"Then we should all go to the caves, let the slavers raid the village, I will trade a barrel of honey mead for my life any day." One of the fishermen's wives said loudly, from the back of the crowd.

"There is not room enough for the children as it is," said her husband. Quiet fell on the crowd. Petr came up behind his wife on the dais where they had married seven years and five moons ago.

"We fight or we die." Petr said loud enough for all to hear. Off in the distance thunder rolled over the ocean.

Less than a candle mark later, the first ship entered the dark, sleepy cove. All the villagers of Haven had taken their positions. The wind had picked up and storm clouds covered the sky that had been perfectly clear. Anika knew that her sister Druid was amassing a great maelstrom from the sounds of the thunder and flashes of lightning that eerily flickered off of the shield walls of the fjord. The storm would be too late for keeping the slavers out of the cove but it could unnerve them into thinking that the thunder god, Thor, was telling them his wrath would fall upon them for breaking of the sacred law. That no Viking should ever raid upon his own people. Maybe this would give the villagers the edge they needed to fend the slavers off, some thought.

The second boat followed silently behind the first, pulling into the safe haven away from the storm that was about to break on top of them. As a lightning flash struck the rocks outside the little port, the villagers steeled themselves the fight for their lives.

Joar, the blacksmith, had a few swords and a great battle axe that he thought he could barter to the next trader boat that would come though in the spring. These he handed out to whoever could wield them. Most of the men had bows made of yew or ash, about a meter in length and in the small cove, deadly to anyone who didn't have on full armor. Though the men weren't used to warring, their familiar hunting weapons gave them confidence in the coming battle.

Thought was given to the fighting strategy. Only a few of the men had seen combat and the notion of grouping together into a shield wall battle tactic and facing the enemy would be suicide. With all the targets grouped together the slavers would massacre them quickly. The villagers chose to put the bowmen back a little, to pick off any of the slavers that fought with one of the village's swordsmen. As the boats softly beached, Petr lit a small torch and threw it onto the pitch that he'd hastily poured near the water's edge before the ships had entered the harbor. The hope was to give the bowmen of the village light as well as catch the slaver ships on fire. Anika had assured her bond-mate that he would need to use the pitch, which burned even in the rain, for a great storm would fall upon the village. Petr knew better than to question her about such things and made an arch of the flammable muck around where the ships would most likely land. The pitch flamed to life bringing cries of surprise from the slaver ships.

"It's that witch!" shrieked a familiar voice from the longboats.

The slavers leapt to the ground trying to put out the flames that threatened their ships.

"Now!" Sven's shout rang out through the valley, echoing off the fjord walls. Arrows flew in from all directions at the slavers fire-illuminated boats. With the fire in front of them, the Viking slavers couldn't see to aim at the villagers. Great shields soon covered the sides of the ships nearest the village. The few slavers that were on the beach trying to save the boats were left to fend for themselves.

Great drops of rain started to fall, lightning flashed; and thunder echoed off of the walls of the fjord. The fighters managed to get one of the boats free of the beach. It slowly drifted a few feet off shore where in came to a stop. The second boat was starting to catch flame in spite of the rain, which was now pelting the ground and the pitch fire. The villagers didn't press their attack in the hopes that the slavers would see that they had been out flanked and leave without bloodshed.

"Give us the witch and you will be allowed to live!" a female voice cried out from the boat that was slightly off the beach, out of the fires reach.

'All this for me,' Anika thought. 'They would risk this?' Then the shrieking familiar voice locked into Anika's memory. It was Brenda! Anika grabbed Petr and told him her theory.

"Brenda has been telling tales about me to her slaver village friends." Anika shouted into Petr's ear to be heard above the rolling thunder. She could tell by the look on his face that he'd guessed the rest. Brenda would have her revenge on the witch by making her a slave. The Druid dreaded the thought of being taken away from all that she loved and held dear, forced to use her healing magicks for the Viking slavers. She looked over at her husband. Petr's face was filled with rage. He dipped three arrows into a barrel of pitch trying to get as much of the thick oily stuff onto the arrows while still keeping them able to fly true. As he turned to kiss her, the Druid whispered in his ear,

"I'll watch the pass dear." She said, with a smile. In that one moment Petr sensed the power that his Druid wife could wield. He kissed her quickly and felt a charge of energy transfer from her lips to his, like a little jolt of lightning.

"Death to those who cross your path my love," he whispered back in her ear before another boom of thunder drown out his sentiment.

Anika watched him go to the far side of the meadhall then Petr disappeared in the sheets of rain that were coming down. The other villagers had had the same idea. As she saw someone's silhouette in a lightning flash readying more pitch arrows near the smithy.

"Your time is up, hand her over!" came a loud male voice from one of the boats.

The reply came quickly, as volley after volley of flaming arrows hit the invader's ships.

Cursing could be heard, followed by the blowing of a horn, three sharp blasts sounded, but no one left the boats. Anika knew it was the signal for the warriors that had traveled over land, who where waiting on the other side of the gap in the southern wall. The villagers had sent bowmen there, not enough to throw back a full on assault but enough to make the slavers think that they had greatly misjudged the village's defenses. Soon she could hear fighting in front of her. The gap was in danger of being taken or had already fallen. She just couldn't be sure with all the noise of the storm raging overhead. Two sharp horn blasts came behind Anika's position. Back on the long boats, the shields came down and men started poring out of the boats to form up as a 'boars snout.'

The Druid healer had seen this battlefield tactic before. The sheer weight and momentum of the wedge shaped charge could drive through an opposing shield wall of troops, turning the battle and spreading panic through the enemy. But the villagers had chosen not to group up in a shield wall of force against the raiders. So the tactic merely helped the villagers target the slavers more easily. The rain was giving way to a thunderous hailstorm. Anika couldn't imagine the amount of energy that her friend, Mara was expending, but Anika was thankful for all the help. The pitch fire had died down and with all the cloud cover that the Viking raiders hadn't counted on; visibility was limited to the flashes of lightning that lit up the sky in an eerie green.

"Find the witch, find her first!" the raider's commander yelled. The group tried to stay together but the darkness and the ice that was forming from the hailstorm were making it very difficult for the slavers to do anything but hold their ground.

Anika turned her attention to the raiders that had made it through the pass. Staff in hand, she laid aside her fur cloak and woolen tunic and took off her woolen skirt. She had always been in the habit of wearing leather breeches in cold weather or when she went alone into the forest. They never caught on brambles or branches like linen skirts did and though it wasn't the fashion up here, all the Druid warrior women fought in breeches.

Anika altered her breathing to enable her vision to change so that she could see in the dark like a cat. Off to one side she could make out a line of raiders that stretched from one side of the fjord to the other, spaced at about five paces apart. They were obviously going to herd anyone who was out hiding in the fields back into the fray and keep anyone from escaping. Anika couldn't see much further passed the line, she hoped that the children were safe. Humming softly the song of making, feeding power into her staff she went off to make war on the raiders from the North.

Petr had joined up with Sven to keep the slavers pinned down at their boats.

"They must have brought people from a neighboring slaver village,"

Sven said in Petrs ear. "Never have I seen so many pour out of a ship. They must have been shoulder to shoulder all the way here. I hope the pass holds." The father said to his son.

"Don't worry, Anika is taking care of that." Petr said laughing.

Sven wondered if his daughter in-law had turned into a dragon. He always knew that she could take care of herself, but there had to be at least fifty men back there. Sven started to turn around and head for the pass, but Petr held his father's arm to keep him from leaving.

"Come let's finish this!" Petr yelled to his fellow villagers over of booming thunderclaps.

The raiders broke into three different groups; one headed in the direction of the smithy, one headed towards Petr's group near the meadhall and the third moved to take the end of the crescent shaped village nearest the boat. The lightning still flashed over head; hail gave way to a pounding rain, which would make the ground a mud bog if it didn't end soon.

The villagers ran from the groups of raiders that came near them. The raiders had the upper hand, using tactics that the farmers and fishermen couldn't combat. Each of the small groups had large square shields in front and the second rank of men put their shields on top of themselves and covered the first rank so none of the arrows were penetrating the shield wall tactic that the raiders used.

Sven and Petr looked at each other, worry in their eyes.

"Time to use a sword," Sven said, setting his bow down and picking up a four foot broad sword.

"Aye, but I'll just use Joar's new axe. Petr hefted the huge battleaxe. Then the fight was in full swing. The raiders broke ranks to take on the charging villagers to mop up any resistance. But the farmers, fishermen and boat builders were fighting for their lives, their homes and their children. What the townsfolk lacked in experience, they made up for in adrenaline.

Anika slipped easily between the raiders and starting at the north end of the offense of invaders and proceeded to break one leg of every raider down the line. Cries could be heard from the advancing line of slavers;

"We've been ambushed!" Came from one.

"My leg!" Screamed another. With the night vision of a cat, Anika saw the warriors ranks ahead of her breaking up. Men in twos and threes were placing themselves back to back and swinging their spears and covering up as much as possible with their shields.

'That will slow them down a bit,' the Druid thought to herself. She leaped past blind spear jabs to one of the large boulders near the edge of the fields.

'Well if they want a witch, I'll give them a witch,' the Druid healer thought to herself. Anika increased her breathing and pulled as much earth energy into her staff as she ever had, then shouted out in a voice that shook the men in their sodden boots.

"Leave now or die!" her staff crackled with visible power illuminating her position. It was a gamble, but one she had to take.

"Take her," the raiders' captain yelled, but only ten of the men left standing rushed her. They ran at her screaming a war cry, more for their courage than to scare the 'witch.' Anika threw her staff at the one nearest her. It pierced his shield, armor and chest. Even with his forward momentum, it knocked him back into his comrades. They moved aside to let their captain fall to the ground. The dead man hit the mud with a thud,

Anika's staff sticking straight out of his chest, up in the air. The staff's glowing light faded after a moment, but it was plenty of time for the raiders to see what had happened to their captain. Some of the men on the ground counted themselves lucky to only have a broken leg.

Anika grabbed her dirk that was at her belt. Holding it over her head she sang out a note as pure as it was terrible, the men stopped in their tracks and held their ears. The small blade grew in her hands into a sword like none of the men had ever seen. It glowed as it grew, sheaved in a brilliant blue light. It grew to a little over three feet in length and curved nearer the tip. Anika felt the hair on the back of her neck straighten. She wasn't worried about the sword attracting lightning, its metal was Elven and didn't conduct heat or lightning. Maybe Mara was centering in on her use of power. The Druid checked her position, safe on the boulder with the raiders now charging again through the mud. A lightning bolt hit a few feet in front of the raiders killing them all instantly. The rest of the slavers watched with amazement at the witch who could call down lightning. Anika stood there, her braided red hair whipping about her head, glowing sword held high, she scanned over their ranks as if she could see each and every one of them in the dark.

The Druid jumped down and grabbed her staff, pulling the deadly weapon out of the slaver captain's chest. Anika spun the ash pole around and fastened it to her back, then bounded back to the village like a dear, sword in hand.

"Odin help us," was heard from some of the survivors. The men furthest from the Southern shield wall slowly, painfully, crawled back from where they'd come and tried to form a circle to protect themselves and their broken legs.

Brenda was livid; none of this was suppose to happen. Even if they got the witch, Brenda's position in her new village, would be lowered by her husband. They were to slip in and take the village when the full moon had reached its peak in the sky. The witch and her weirding sea chest would go with the slavers along with all the barrels of mead and all the winter stores that their longboats could carry. Brenda could then stay behind as a kind of ransom to Petr, that the slavers would bring the witch back in a year or two after they had conquered lands to the South. Of course, they wouldn't bring the witch back and she would be in Petr's longhouse. He would be lonely, and Brenda would have to be taken care of, in order to be traded back in the same condition. She had brought a few love potions from the wise woman in the slaver village. While the old crone's power wasn't close to Anika's, she made potent love potions. In fact, it took five of them to get her husband to raid her home village, long after the warring season. Well, that and all the stories, most true, about the amazing powers of the fine boned red-haired witch.

This however was a disaster. The village wasn't suppose to fight back, Brenda worried that her father might get hurt. The raiders were treating this like a siege when it could be handled with much more finesse. Even though Brenda had been told repeatedly not to leave the longboat, she knew she could end the battle quickly.

With all the men fighting, no one paid any attention to her which only helped her cause. She stayed low and went towards the meadhall. The fighting had mostly moved off to concentrate on the smithy. Brenda could hear the shouting and occasional clash of metal. Cries of the injured could be also be heard between the thunderclaps.

'Where were the children hiding?' Brenda wondered. 'If they sent them out in the fields to hide, the southern flank of invaders would have scared them back into the village. Just how much time did the village have to prepare?' Brenda wondered to herself. All of the arrows had started flying at once. Somehow, the witch must have known and rallied the townsfolk to protect herself.

'Well I'll put the kink in her little plan,' the spurned woman thought vengefully. Brenda hurried around some of the dying raiders and into the meadhall. There her husband Bjorn was fighting her beloved Petr at the back of the hall.

"No! Stop, we need him!" she cried out, as if that would stop the fighting on her command. Her husband backed up a step, but still kept up his sword.

"Why?" was all that Brenda's husband could get out between great gulps of air. Petr had been holding his own against the seasoned warrior with his battleaxe. Blood was spattered on both men, none of it their own.

"Trade his life for the witch." Brenda said, matter-of-factly. Her husband Bjorn, seemed as stupid as he was strong.

"That's her mate, dolt!" Did she have to explain everything to her husband?

Bjorn became enraged. "So, this is your beloved Petr!?" He yelled.

Brenda wasn't sure if it was all the love potions she'd given her husband that was causing his anger, or her constantly talking about Petr to him. Her husband's sword flashed at Petr cutting his arm in the dim hall.

"So he's not a god after all. See he bleeds and he will die." Bjorn taunted his foe and his wife with the words. Quickly, the raider's commander thrust out several more blows but these were easily defected by the double-headed axe. Petr used one every day that he'd worked with his father, even though this one was slightly heavier, he handled it like it was a part of him.

The few torches in the middle of the hall backlit any movement of his opponent. Though the light was in his eyes, Petr concentrated on the silhouette, easily countering the weakening thrusts of Brenda's slaver husband. Both men were tired but Petr had more to lose, so he gathered up his strength to kill this man. With their leader dead, the rest of the raiders could be forced to give up. And Brenda, that treacherous woman at the far end of the hall, Petr would give her over to Anika and some well deserved Druid justice.

Bjorn stood his ground but didn't move to strike or to flee. He just stood there gulping breaths, looking for an opening.

Petr heard a movement behind him, a small rustling sound. He froze, the back of the hall didn't have an entrance. Petr knew it sounded like a child squirming around in the dark, either trying to hide or trying to get a better look. The slaver hadn't heard the noise, so Petr fained a thrust and spun around fully hoping to get a glimpse of who was behind him, then finished the axe swing out at Bjorn and brought it up for the expected parry. The change in lighting from the dim of the torch lights half way down the large one room hall to the black of the corner behind the fire pit caused Petr's vision to blur slightly. The slaver saw his chance and swung, his sword passed down instead of thrusting again. Bjorn knew he would leave himself open if the swing missed its mark, but this seige was taking more time than he'd hoped it would.

The axe just missed blocking the blow that went into Petr's leg cutting a wide gash. Brenda screamed even from her vantage point she could see that Petr could die from that wound. This whole plan had unraveled in front of her eyes, now she would be stuck with the lout that her father had love-potioned her into marrying and her beloved Petr would die. Brenda had to stop the fight before her beloved lost too much blood, surely Anika would do whatever it took to heal him. Brenda rushed forward gathering up and ripping the bottom of her linen skirt for a tourniquet for the bleeding leg.

Petr knew he would surely die, his head had started to buzz like he'd had too much wine. And he couldn't try to stop the bleeding, the raider would finish him off as soon as he tired. Petr had seen his darling daughter behind him hiding in the darkness against the back wall of the meadhall. He knew he couldn't protect her and still fend off this slaver. The thought of his daughter, Mary, being the slave of this bastard was too much, rage came up in him even as his strength left his arms. Petr knew that his opponent would give no mercy even to such a worthy foe. Surveying the meadhall before his mind became too clouded, Petr saw Brenda rushing up to him and Bjorn, her blonde pigtails bouncing around her head. This was the defender's chance, Petr waited until she was almost upon them then he swung out with all the strength he had left, but the slaver wasn't distracted by his wife. Bjorn knocked the axe back at Petr then thrust his sword through Brenda's beloved's chest, driving the man back against the wall and pinning him to it.

Brenda heard a small girl scream the word "papa!" from behind her dying Petr. Mary had been trapped by her father's body against the wall and from where she was, Bjorn's downward sword thrust, had just missed the little girl's head. The woman hissed a curse at the victor of the death match and pulled the screaming girl out from behind her dead father.

"All this could have been settled without bloodshed, you dolt!" Brenda was overstepping her place in the slaver society, but none of this would've happened if Bjorn had listened to her.

"We ransom the child. See, easy." She said, getting a better hold on the girls' arm. "I'll do it! Since you wouldn't know subtlety if it hit you on the head!" Brenda marched Anika's daughter to the front of the hall out to the dais that was to one side of the doorway, not looking back at her husband who was about to turn his wrath on her if her little ploy didn't work.

Anika had just made it back to the village proper, looking where she could do the most damage to the invaders, when she heard Brenda's shout over the din.

"The witch for her child! The witch for her child! Come out now and I'll spare your hell-spawn offspring!" Brenda yelled it over and over taunting her rival that had stolen Petr's love.
"Just so you know, my husband killed yours." Brenda yelled out, even though her heart was breaking over it, she would take out her pain on the witch.

Anika came around the edge of a longhouse to get a better view of the front of the meadhall where the interloper was bellowing. From Anika's place in the darkness she could see Brenda up on the raised platform with a dagger at her daughter's throat. Mary's shirt was covered in blood, though it didn't look like she'd been hurt herself. The little girl just stood there shivering with tears running down her cheeks. Petr was nowhere to be seen and most of the fighting had ceased at this new spectacle. Anika felt the ethers for the presence of her mate. In the heat of battle she'd hadn't checked on him while she was out in the fields. There was emptiness where she had always felt him for the last seven years.

Anika checked herself, the last thing she could do was get emotional, that would give the invaders the upper hand. Anika would gamble with her own life, but not with her daughter's life at stake. The Druid summoned her will, channeling the emotion into something that she could use. Power... raw hatred that sucked energy from mother earth. Her anger stretched out like a balloon filling with a torrent of force. Quietly, Anika walked out from behind the longhouse. Not making a sound, she walked straight towards the platform where she had bonded herself to her now late husband. A slaver solider came up to within reach of her. Anika beheaded the man without looking in his direction; her focus was on holding the anger back until it would be useful.

Brenda spotted her prey coming towards her, sword in one hand and that damned staff slung across her back. As the witch approached the torchlight, Brenda glared at her long time rival. Her red hair braided back in a ponytail. That would be the first thing to go. Brenda would cut that pretty hair off her foe's head just for a start. The blonde-haired woman would make Anika pay for all the pains, real and imagined that the she had suffered. One of the captains in full armor came towards Anika to take her weirding sword away. The sword sliced through his shield, chainmail and neck in one clean motion. Anika could have been swatting a fly with all the effort she had put into it. The witch came closer, walking as if she was taking a leisurely stroll but her gaze never left Brenda.

"Another step and your daughter starts to bleed." Brenda yelled, with more courage than she felt. Anika was twelve paces from the meadhall and was enough in the torch light that Brenda could see any hand waving or witchery. Some of the raiders had gathered around the front of the meadhall between the witch and their commander's wife.

"Now put down the sword and that staff." Brenda tried to use the sweet musical voice that Anika had used on her at the wedding.

Anika spun the sword between her fingers slowly then stuck it in the ground in front of her. Then just as slowly, she pulled the leather cording that held the Druid staff from her back and dropped it in the mud. Anika was aware of villagers waiting to see a sign, something, to tell them to begin fighting, but their healer just stood there in the slackening rain. As Brenda started to tell Anika how it was going to be, Anika bled off some of the energy she was holding back.

The Druid used the mud and earth beneath her feet as a channel for the power she'd been concentrating. In second sight it looked like tentacles of a giant squid creeping under the ground to where the raiders and the blonde pigtailed horrible woman held a knife to her daughter's throat.

Anika let her nemesis prattle on about how she would be made a slave and all the bad things that would happen to her, blah, blah, blah. No one had moved since the Druid warrior woman had cut the head off of one of the raider's captains. And no one seemed to be in a hurry to subdue her.

Brenda laughed at the thought of her subtlety, bringing this whole raid to an end with so little blood shed. Maybe the slavers would start to listen to her and seek her counsel.

"You there, go and take the witch's weirding weapons, she's nothing without them." Brenda said, taunting Anika again.

But the Druid wasn't listening; she was springing a trap of her own. This night she'd suffered more than any other before and the pain opened new and deeper channels in her psyche than even she'd realized. Two of the men started to move towards Anika and found that their boots were stuck in the mud. In fact they couldn't move at all. Brenda wanted to cry out to her husband to take the witch down. She tried to draw the blade across the catatonic child's neck, but Brenda too, was as stiff as stone. The witch didn't pick up her weapons as she moved forward weaving in between the frozen raiders as if she were walking through a stand of trees.

Slowly, the Druid came up the three stairs to the platform were Brenda held her child. Anika looked deep in the frightened woman's eyes as she pried her fingers away from her daughter. Anika then looked into her child's face. A blank stare was all that greeted her. It would be many years of healing to undo what was done to this child. Anika gathered Mary up into her arms and left the dais. She walked over to the edge of the mead-hall where Sven came over to her. In this surreal happening no words were spoken, just a look from him, part sympathy for his daughter-in-law, part malice as he glanced at the raiders in front of the meadhall. Sven took the girl up in his strong arms and hurried off to some place safe. Other raiders stayed back not wanting to be a part of what was to happen next.

The Druid healer-warrior now turned her full attention to Brenda's men. Some had chosen to come to raid the village of Haven for the conquest and spoils, some because they had to for their families' sake. But all of them had chosen... poorly. In her assassin training that Anika had gotten in the dreams on the long voyage to Miklagard, she had learned how to kill a man three times before he hit the ground. But she had also learned to strike a man's nerve points in such a way that would give him a much longer and more painful death. Starting with the one farthest from Brenda she used all fourteen of the different blows of 'the slow death,' one to each of frozen raiders. After the man received the hit Anika released him from the paralysis cocoon that she held him in, to let him writhe in pain. The effect this had on Brenda was evident in her eyes, which continued to widen as the Druid witch came closer, leaving her troops flopping around in the mud and screaming in agony. Anika finally reached the platform again and this time Brenda didn't have a child to ransom. The pig-tailed blonde felt a rush of wind all around her… it seemed to pass through her.

'More witch magic, maybe she'll just kill me quickly,' the Brenda thought. Then pain started, the blonde woman wanted to clutch her arm that felt like it had been hit with a club, then her leg throbbed in agony. Brenda thought that her leg was somehow broken, but she couldn't move to protect herself. This continued and moved through her growing more intense and faster like being in a great howling wind of hammers beating at her. Time seemed to slow then stop for her, seconds had been drawn out into months she had long since wished she was dead, and the pain increased as the witch reached out a hand to Brenda's face.

Everyone who looked at the righteous revenge, saw Anika approach Brenda, then the blonde woman's feet seemed to catch fire, not her boots but her feet. Soon her legs burst into flame. Brenda didn't cry out, but looked like she wanted to very badly. Pain spasmed across her face that soon began to smoke and char. Anika turned away as the flames engulfed her nemesis forming into a fiery pillar of flame that burned despite the rain.

As Anika walked down from the platform and headed out among the dying raiders Bjorn, Brenda's husband leapt out from the darkened mead-hall and struck the Druid as hard as he could with the flat of his blade. After channeling so much power Anika had been temporarily weakened and hadn't the strength to kill all the rest of the raiding party. She crumpled down like a broken doll in the mud among the slavers.

"Thanks for killing my wife." The commander laughed. "She talked too much anyway." He finished by kicking Anika in head then yelled to his men to rally to him.

The villagers saw the scene from their dark hiding places. Some fled into the great forest rather than face what was left of the slavers, taking whatever they could pack on their backs in the darkness. By morning the raiders had gathered their wounded and killed the ones that couldn't be mended or splinted. The commander was amazed at all the broken legs that occurred to the raiders out in the fields. After a little coercion from two of them, he heard the story that the witch had did it all and killed their captain with her staff and ten men with a thunderbolt.
'Maybe she'll be worth the trouble of keeping her after all,' Bjorn thought.

By mid-morning the troop ship that had dropped off the men that had tried to take the southern pass, came into the harbor with its skeleton crew of five.

Bjorn figured that he'd lose a few men and the extra space would be filled up with precious cargo. That morning, the leader of the slavers had a boat for just the wounded and two boats that could be filled with the wealth of the village. The few people that stayed behind or were caught, ended up stocking the ship with all the winter stores that the township had. The people of Haven would come in one of the newly acquired long-boats as slaves for the raider's village. The witch's children had been found and were being as closely guarded as was the witch. Bjorn hadn't meant to hurt Anika as bad as he did, but he didn't know what he had been up against. The limp body of the red-haired healer was tied to the mast of his ship, tightly, and he had three man watch on her on the long voyage home.

The damnable rain had stopped, but the clouds told of the another storm that was just waiting to break. By evening tide the slavers were ready to leave the conquered village behind. Bjorn knew that he'd broken the Vikings most sacred law, not to make war on another Viking, but with the witch, Bjorn could conquer a better place for his people far to the south, so it still might be worth all the trouble his late wife had put him through. The raiders burned the village to the ground so that if anybody had escaped them, there wouldn't be any chance of surviving the winter. No witnesses, or survivors, just slaves, was Bjorn's policy.

The slavers had lost a lot of men in the pitched battle, better to show his new slaves how hard their new life could be, then offer them a chance to earn a place with the his men. As the leader of the raiders boarded his longboat to head North, Bjorn stood on top of the furs that were piled behind the mast. The carnage, that used to be a village, smoked behind him, as the ship headed out into the great Western Sea.

Two days passed, the storm had broke over the procession of boats as soon as the raider ships had left the safety of Haven's cove. The witch hadn't woken up and her children hadn't bothered Bjorn or any of the crew in the lead vessel, the entire time.

The children had been lashed down to their mother's sea chest before the raiders had left the little harbor. Actually, that had probably saved them from being tossed overboard many times since the maelstrom had started. The little girl seemed almost too still, but maybe it was a gift that kept her from screaming and crying.

The sail had been full since the raiders had left the safe harbor of

Haven, pushing them faster up the coast than they had ever traveled. The problem was, that they had passed their own homeport a day ago. The wind wouldn't let up enough for them to get the sails down. It was as if the ships were in a riptide that was pulling them along the coast racing in the storm.

Bjorn hadn't wanted to make this raid after the warring season anyway. He felt that if the storm didn't stop, his men would soon turn on him. They had already lost the boatload of wounded men and the slaves somewhere back in the night. No one had seen the ships go down. The other ship that was loaded down supplies, was spotted approaching some of the huge rocks that lined the coast, just before the light had left the sky on the previous day. Apparently, that longboat's rudder had snapped in the strong current.

The sky was a dark metal gray; there was no way to get any bearings. All that anyone could tell was, they were headed North.
Tor, Bjorn's second in command, climbed aft to the commander's position over the booty that had been lashed to the deck with thick hemp rope.

"It must be the witch!" he yelled, as loud as he could in his commander's ear. "We must cut her loose or we all will die!"

Bjorn heard the plea to him over the thunder that had boomed constantly for the last two days. The raider commander knew he had to do something and if she'd called down lightning then, she could be causing the storm. They still had the weirding children so maybe his crew could survive this after all.

"Odin, if I live through this, I'll never listen to a woman again!" Bjorn yelled at the sky.

Lightning flashed repeatedly and the raider commander took it as a sign.

"Cut her loose!" Bjorn agreed with his old friend. Tor grabbed the hemp tie downs and started for the mast where Anika was tied.

Olaf, Kris and their sister Mary were tied to their mother's sea chest. All of their mother's things were brought on board. The raiders didn't know where the witch's magic came from, so they took everything from her longhouse.

Kris sat huddled next to his siblings for warm. He and Olaf had gathered all the children and taken them to the caves, but lost Mary in the commotion. When they went to find her, the raiders were attacking the village and the two boys couldn't have imagined that Mary wanted to be safe and went to be with her father. Luckily, their mother had made them dress so warmly in heavy wool. The storm had soaked them to the bone, but wool could warm a person even if it is wet. The two boys huddled close to their catatonic sister, hoping to get her to respond, but she was as numb on the inside as their exposed skin.

Kris shifted with the heaving of the boat, causing his foot to slip on the wet deck. Something poked his numb foot sharply enough for him to remember the flint stone that his mother had given him. Kris dug it out after a little struggle between his numb hands and the wet hemp rope the raiders had used to truss him up. As quickly as he could, the small boy began to work on the ropes above an important knot that had been too hastily fastened. If he could cut through the rope, the slavers would lose half their cargo and his mother's precious sea chest. It would be a small victory, but it would be worth the beating, Olaf agreed as he got out his own piece of flint.

Aside from giving them some dried meat to eat and some fresh water, their captures had left them alone. So Kris and Olaf took turns keeping Mary warm and working the rope. They were nearing a rocky, dangerous looking part of the coast and the ship was being directed by the current at the huge monolithic boulders that would surely smash the ship to splinters. Kris cut the final bit of rope as he saw one of the slavers cutting his mother down from the mast. Quickly, he got out of the ropes that were around his wrists and feet and climbed on top of the chest to see what they were doing with his mother. The crewman tossed her off of the back of the ship into the raging water.

"No!" Kris screamed at the slavers and went to jump across the netting against the wind. The next wave that hit the ship caused the five year old boy to lose his balance and the ship went up over a huge swell that told of an approaching reef.

Off in the distance, Kris could see his mother's body floating out to sea. He lost sight of her as the ship started down the other side of the giant swell. The boy felt weightless, as the ship seemed to drop out from under him. Then the ship went into the underside of the swell, Kris' weight almost doubled, slamming him into the sea chest causing it to loosen.

"Get him!" Kris heard faintly over the storm and the crashing waves, the ship was getting dangerously close to the huge boulders that lined the northern coast. Kris looked over his shoulder to see which of the slavers were trying to get him. He allowed himself a quick smile when he saw his mother's sea chest and barrels of mead and salted fish falling into the churning sea. The small boy had nowhere to run to and was quickly caught by Tor who gave a glance to the commander to see what was to be done with the little trouble maker; Kris was unceremoniously thrown overboard.

I heard my tape recorder click, signaling the end of the story for that week.

"That's as good a place as any to stop." Olaf said.

I just sat there as he got up, went to put his mug away in the cupboard on its hook and walked out into the busy market.

The Portal to the Nine Realms, later called the Witch's Teeth

Chapter 3
The Witch's Teeth

The next week, I was waiting for Olaf at the table with the board set up and recorder at the ready. A lot of questions leapt to mind, but I really wanted to hear what happened next to the young Kris Kringle. The cliffhanger from last week got my attention and I was starting to enjoy these Saturday mornings anyway. It was the rainy season, September through June, in Seattle, and coffee can only do so much to lift a person's spirit.

Olaf came in a few minutes later and put his over coat on a peg near the front door of the cafe, he then got in line and ordered. After putting in a squeeze of honey in his tea, the old storyteller slowly turned and walked at an even slower pace, over to the table. Then Olaf slid in the booth with his usual cat like grace.

"Just building up the suspense," he said with a smile.

"I'm just making up for that week I was late," I smiled back.

My storyteller tested his tea with a small sip, "Okay, then," he seemed to be thinking about where he had left off last week.

The sea crashed around Kris, lifting him up and slamming him back down again and again. His small body was numb to the bone before the slaver had thrown him in the water, then the coldness of the sea took his breath away. There was yelling and screaming on the boat behind him, but it seemed like it was miles away. Kris vaguely remembered the sight of land that he had seen between the sheets of rain. Luckily, the Viking slaver had thrown him off the ship on the side closest to the shore. As Kris started to swim he saw the boat being pushed further away from him, closer to the jagged rocks that arched out from the coastline. Kris' arms and lungs ached as he worked them a little, feebly trying to stay above the waves. Then, the warmth started. Kris had heard enough stories to know that it was a sure sign that death was about to overtake him. Quickly, a warm-calm feeling dulled his senses. The brave young boy tried to fight it, thinking of what the raiders had done to his village, his family, and then he was to drown there in the middle of nowhere, a senseless death, for nothing. Kris pulled up all the rage left in him to spur his body on, to make it to the surf.

'If I could just make it there,' he thought, as sea continued to pound at his small body. Kris forced his arms to move, kicked hard with his legs and tried to avoid thinking about not making it to the shore.

'Let's see,' Kris thought to himself as he struggled in his wet woolen clothes, 'I'll kill any Vikings, help the survivors, then we'll need to get some driftwood for a fire.' The little boy let his mind keep busy so that fear wouldn't overcome him. Up ahead, the pounding of the surf grew a little louder. Kris lost sight of the ship, the swells blocked his vision and the saltwater burned his eyes. The little boy gave it all that he could, but the water was pulling him down, dragging him down. Kris felt his anger was failing him as well, slipping away from him as his mind dulled, thinking of how nice it would be to just sleep. The warmth was embracing him and Kris didn't try to fight it and just let himself start to float.

A loud sound disturbed his light slumber, but he couldn't quite place it. It sounded like the cracking of timber. Kris moved his head a little to see a keg that had fallen overboard, being smashed on the rocks in front of him. The next swell from the storm carried him straight at the huge monolith. Kris was just too tired to try to swim around stone and his leg hit it hard enough to pull him back from his stupor. The pain that shot up his thigh caused Kris to feel again, if only for a short time. As the waves came, he fought to get a hold on the jagged stone to pull himself up into a small gap in the boulders so that he could make the shore.

The sea picked the small boy up again, straight into the huge stones, but this time, Kris was positioned to go between two of them in the small space that separated them. With strength that came out of his very depths, Kris managed to get between two great, black, jagged boulders and fell into the little cove that was on the other side. Even with the maelstrom blowing at full force, the giant rocks sheltered the little safe haven, giving it an eerie calm. Kris used his remaining strength to paddle to the shore.

He lay there in the sand, trying to clear his mind of the fog that threatened to overwhelm it. Lifting himself up on one elbow, Kris surveyed his surroundings. Huge stones flanked the cove that was full of fish. 'The storms must blow them in,' Kris thought to himself, as he continued the explore from where he laid. The small beach had plenty of driftwood and there was a cave behind some of the bigger logs that lined the sandy shore.

The huge black stones blocked out the view of the sea so Kris didn't know if the ship had gone down or not. The only sound that he could hear, was of the constant tide hitting the rocks and of the storm which had lost most of its fury. Kris' clothes were torn and soaked and he had an awful pain in his thigh, but the numbness in his limbs and the need for warmth were his first concerns.

Fire was his first priority. Luckily, Kris still had his flint that had been in his boot. Using his elbows, because he didn't know how bad his leg was, Kris crawled over the wood into the cave. The driftwood in the cave hadn't been touched by the storm, so the fire was soon blazing. He collapsed by the small bit of warmth, too exhausted to worry.

When Kris woke up, thoughts of his mother and siblings fates were strangely forgotten. So he started a new fire, made from a stack of dry kindling that was laying on the beach and checked his leg. There was a huge black and blue mark that ran down the length of his thigh that hurt to the touch and he noticed that there were black, swollen places on all his toes and fingers, Kris wasn't sure if they were from frostbite or bruises. He didn't trust his leg enough to stand on it though, so Kris crawled out of the cave again on his elbows to catch something to eat.

The lagoon was full of fish, so Kris speared enough to fill himself with a piece of driftwood that he had sharpened with his flint, then headed back to the cave before the clouds overhead could start to pour down on him. He did the same routine for about a week never wondering about his siblings or mother.

Finding a small trickle of water near the back of the cave was the only other thing of note that happened.

Kris took stock of his situation and found that the frostbite had stopped in the tips of his fingers and toes, his mind still felt strange, and his leg hadn't gotten any better. The bruise on his thigh was still black and deep.

Kris finally tried to use his leg, putting his full weight on it the third day but it was too painful. The next few days, Kris would crawl out of his little shelter and spear a couple of fish that were trapped in the little lagoon from his tiny bit of sandy beach and cook them over his driftwood fire. This took up most of his energy. His only thought was on his survival. On the sixth day, the haziness of the pain and trauma he had endured started to subside and Kris remembered that he had to get out of there and get help for his sister and brother.

'I must have hit my head hard to have forgotten about them just when they needed me most,' he thought, feeling a little guilty for their plight. 'I should at least find out if the boat has wrecked.' The small boy decided. Kris fashioned a splint from the wood that was in front of the cave, securing the driftwood with leather lacing from one of his boots and he made a small crutch from a small forked branch of driftwood. The seventh day, he spent getting ready to leave the cove. From the scant growth of weeds at the edge of the cliff, he fashioned a small line of rope, then Kris ate and rested, as much as he could.

The sky was clear the next morning as he crawled out to survey the cliff side. From the little beach, he saw a chimney of rock. That's a crack in the rock face, about the size of the inside of a chimney, it looked passable for a small boy.

It was slow going, even with all the rest and food he'd had. His right thigh was still as bruised as ever and the splint made the climb seem twice as long as it should have taken. About half way up the cliff face, there were no hand holds for five feet straight up on either side of the rock chimney.

Kris knew he couldn't use his legs to inch his way onward, so he wedged himself in and rested, thinking of his options. He looked out over the ocean for any sign of a wrecked ship while he gathered his thoughts. The day was sunny and clear, allowing him to easily scan the shore for survivors or boat wreckage. Finding none, Kris surveyed the tiny cove that was ringed by the huge rocks. The fish still teemed in it, far below. If he would fall from this height, hurt leg or not, he'd surely die. Up above him about six feet away Kris saw a tiny spire of rock that looked stable enough to hold his weight. So he took out his small grass rope that he'd braided from the tough beach grass. It was too short for Kris to throw and make the outcropping without throwing himself with along with it. He threw the length of rope to see just how far he would have to jump on his one good leg. Since he really didn't have a choice, going back down and living in the cave might get him through the winter but no one fished this far north at any time of the year. Kris wouldn't be able to know if anybody was out there anyway, with the monoliths blocking the cove. Besides, he had to help Mary and Olaf, if they were still alive. The only choice he had was to go up.

Kris got as crouched down as he could get and jumped with all his strength. If Kris didn't make this jump, the rest of the climb wouldn't have mattered. He got the thin rope around the spire with an inch to spare. With each hand on one end of the rope, he slammed into the rock face knocking the wind out of him. Slowly, the little boy pulled himself up to the outcropping of rock, then by midday he reached a ledge where he could rest. Having climbed the walls of the valley of his village had taught Kris much.

He was more than three quarters of the way up the chimney. Considering he was short a healthy leg, he was happy with his progress. As Kris looked out over the sea while resting, he saw a thin line of clouds out on the horizon. The next time he stopped to rest, Kris saw that the clouds had become much more dark and foreboding, with flashes of lightning, quickly becoming great rolling masses of purple and black thunderheads. Kris knew that he had to race the storm to find shelter before it hit the coast. The little boy took greater chances to reach handholds that were further than he would have dared earlier. Kris knew from the look of the storm that it could blow him off the cliff face as if he were a leaf. Nearing the top, he looked back at the maelstrom brewing off the coast. It looked alive; churning and rolling in on itself like a bunch of giant purple and black snakes, fighting. He could hear the thunder booming in from the storm, growing louder.

Kris looked up, the top of the cliff was finally in sight, feeling the thunder vibrate through him. Faster, he pushed himself, faster still. Kris reached the cliff top, quickly scanning the horizon before him for somewhere to hide from the fury of the storm. There was a small group of boulders not far away on a huge open plain that ended three leagues off with a strange mountain. The mountain had ten peaks that looked more like a giant black crown than a rock formation. There was a band on snow around the middle of the strange mountain, with the bottom and the top, both bare black rock. Beyond that, lay a forest that went off to the horizon.

Kris pulled the crutch, that he had fashioned from the driftwood in the cove, off this back and started for the boulders, as he felt the first fat drops of rain pelt him. The rain soon turned into hail then got bigger by the time he reached the boulders. The massive stones gave him shelter from the brunt of the storm's fury, but didn't have an obliging cave as the cove had had. Kris tried to make himself as small as possible as the wind howled around him. With his back wedged between two of the boulders and his bad leg sticking out in front of him, he had a good view of the strange mountain that he knew had to be his next shelter. On the ground, he saw paw prints of a very large northern wolf, the kind that could take down a reindeer by itself.

The hail and the snow that was falling in great wet flakes soon covered the tracks so that he couldn't tell how many wolves that had been there, maybe it was only one or maybe a whole pack. As the maelstrom battered the coast, the storm changed from an ocean gale to a thunder-snow blizzard. Lightning flashed and the snow fell in great waves that blocked Kris' vision down to less than yard. His only hope was to make it to the distant mountain where he could find better shelter from the wolves. It was doubtful that they would be out in this storm, but if Kris waited until it was safe to travel for him, the wolf or wolf pack would be on him before he was halfway to his next shelter. The small boy marshaled his strength and set off in the surreal storm, adjusting his weight on the crutch as he went.

The storm wouldn't let him get a clear sighting of the mountain, with sheets of blowing snow and the lightning that flashed an eerie green-blue overhead. Thunder boomed right on top of the small injured boy, knocking him down several times and the numbness in his arms and legs started again. Kris had no idea how far he'd gone or if he was even headed in the right direction. He got up again feeling the pain in his leg shoot up for the hundredth time since he'd started. The crutch was harder to maneuver in the deepening snow. In between the sheets of freezing rain, Kris caught glimpses of the dark stand of rock off in the distance, he changed his direction slightly each time he got a glimpse of it, to keep on course.

The progress was slow and exhausting, the wind whipped the ripped shreds of Kris' clothes, now encrusted with ice; beating his arms and legs causing new bruises.

The thought of Mary and Olaf trapped in the hands of the Viking slavers drove the small boy onward. As Kris started to feel the numbness turn into warmth, he raced for the black mountain knowing that he would have to beat the warmth of freezing to death and the wolves to find a shelter.

Soon the fury of the storm lessened slightly; Kris heard the thunder rolling off in the distance, not the deafening thunderclaps that had knocked him down earlier. He sensed more than saw that the twilight was deepening, everything was growing darker and had a reddish quality to it. The snow slowed its descent and the wind had gone from a howling to a fierce blow. A large black object appeared through the falling snow.

Kris changed his bearing slightly and took a little hope in that he was much closer than he would have thought. As the little boy neared the strange looking mountain, he searched the terrain for a path up its base to a higher shelter, but the snowdrifts had covered any sure-footed way to the top. When he reached the base of the of the black mountain, Kris heard the howl of the Northern wolves.

Olaf, the old storyteller, had told tales of such beasts, on the long winter nights. Tales of beasts much larger than the wolves that village hunters had killed and brought back from the wilderness. These northern wolves were three times that size, with great teeth and one could bring down a reindeer by itself. Kris stopped and listened, the wolves howling was far off in the forest... he guessed. The warmth was now growing in his limbs making them heavy and sluggish. Kris took stock of his body quickly. His hands were growing a blue-black; they were blistered and swollen. He assumed that his feet were just as bad because he couldn't feel them at all. His right thigh was purple and bloated in spite of the cold.

The mountain towered over him, seeming to challenge him to climb it. The crutch would only get in his way, so Kris strapped it to his back, and crawled through the snow until he felt the rock underneath. The rock was warm to touch, which really worried him. Either his mind was going into madness as the cold tightened its grip on him, or the damage to his hands was so great that they would never have proper feeling again. The small boy pushed on; the hatred for the Vikings that had destroyed his life still burned within him.

The Northern wolves howled closer now, but with his mind starting to fog, the small boy could only guess that they had his scent. As the coldness drained his will, Kris crawled upward, around one boulder, then another. He felt the slopes steepen as he crawled, higher he went, driven on, not knowing where the strength was coming from. Was it the fear of the pack that was now hunting for him? Was it the burning hatred that he had for the slavers? But burning passion could only last so long, and that fiery hatred that had gotten him so far, had died down to an ember. Still he went on, up ravines and passed outcroppings of rock that stuck out of the mountain like giant black thorns. The wolves' howling was beneath him at the base of the mountain. Kris couldn't see the Alpha male loping up the slope with the other great beasts following right behind. With his last bit of strength, Kris heaved his battered body to the top of the mountain into the lowest gap that was between two of the points in the 'crown' of the mountain.

His small body, limp from exhaustion, slid down the inside of the crater that was at the top. Kris looked around waiting for the wolves to come over the gap in search of the easy meal. He thought that it might be easier to end his pain, taking his own life to cheat the wolf pack of their sport. Kris felt around in his boot feeling for the piece of sharpened flint that he could cut his wrist with and end his life.

Down the slope the Alpha stopped in his tracks sensing his prey, the fear and stink of death were on this one. It would be an easy meal for some of the pack. The wolf started towards the gap in the top of the mountain, then hit a wall of pain and jumped back in surprise. The other wolves that dared, ran passed him, only to be thrown back after having the same experience. The pack circled around growling in confusion. Circling the top of the mountain they tried every path, but the intense pain stopped them at every try. Finally, with hunger gnawing at their bellies they gave one final group howl and headed off to find easier prey.

Some time later, Kris awoke to the burning in his limbs trying to remember the last thing that had happened to him. The warmth had given way to the numbness that had given way to the blood finally running back into his arms and legs; the pain was excruciating for the boy. He'd remembered sliding down from the space between the spires of rock that crowned the mountain, then he must have passed out.

Quickly, Kris checked to see how badly the storm had punished his body. His clothes were tattered but at least they were dry, his hands were a dangerous black from frostbite, swollen and blistered. As for the place on his right thigh, the bruise had spread from his knee up to his waist on the right side of his body and was bloated, making the skin tight and painful to touch. Kris looked around to see why he was still alive, 'either the cold or the wolves should have finished him by then,' he thought to himself.

Could the wolves have lost his scent and went onto some easier prey? It just didn't make sense. What could be easier prey than a frostbitten-boy alone in the wilderness? Still, if they were going to kill him, they would have done it already. Kris surveyed at his surroundings.

The top of the mountain had been carved out like a great bowl, with the thorny parts of the crown sticking out at the edge of the basin. Kris found it odd that even though he could see that the snow was gently falling high above, none of it was in the crater in which he was lying.

The whole area had a strange light that came from nowhere, everything was visible like when the moon is full, but there was nothing there to give such a light. Then as his eyes cleared a little more, Kris saw that the snow fell on something like a bubble that was high above the crater. The snow seemed to melt when it touched and ran down the outside of the bubble to the edge of the basin where it joined other drops of water to make little streams that all ran down the gentle slope to the center of the crater. Kris was so amazed with this, he forgot to feel the pain of the frostbite and his throbbing leg. He just watched the little streams collect and run over the black bowl shaped crater into a small pool that never got larger than the size of a small boat. 'Odd,' he thought to himself, 'with all that water flowing in the whole place should be full by now.'

As he started for the pool on his elbows, already bloody from the trek up the mountain, Kris noticed that the ground was as warm as it was black. He felt it through the remainder of his clothes too. This comforted him somehow; Kris should have worried about the soundness of his mind. Warm ground in winter, the thought went right out of his mind. As he inched down the slope, Kris saw a shape like that of a horse that faded in and out of his vision like the heat waves that came from a very hot embers in a fire pit that played tricks on the eye.

Olaf the old storyteller, for which his brother had been named, had once told Kris that the shadows on the back of the mead hall's walls, played to the shape of a man's desire and didn't tell the future like some people thought. Kris finally understood what the old man was trying to say to him.

A horse was what he needed most to get him to a healing woman or at least to some people who could help him. Kris dismissed the mirage as wishful thinking and concentrated on getting to the pool.

He crawled on, 'maybe the water would at least be clean and warm,' the boy thought. And he could dress his injuries better if he could see them. Kris had forgotten how long it had been since the last time he'd had a proper bath, the sea notwithstanding.

The shimmering shape flickered one more time in the strange half light, as Kris approached the pool of warm water, then it disappeared. He stripped the splint that had held his right leg still for so long, then instantly regretted it. Pain like Kris had never felt before, shot through his mind.

He thought that it would drive him mad. As he lay there trying to catch his breath, the pain throbbed all the way up his back to his brain.

Kris couldn't have imagined what a spiral fracture in his thigh would be, at that moment, he was experiencing all the pain of it at once, Kris wished the wolves had found him. The little boy laughed hysterically, tears coming to his eyes at the thought of dying here alone in the middle of nowhere in this crater; he laughed even as he rolled over onto his bad leg and into the pool. Kris started to scream from the pain underwater, but calmness overtook him as he started to fight for air. The waters warm embrace held him up to float on the surface. Kris breathed deeper than he had for a long time. All pain was instantly gone. He pulled his hand out of the pool to look at the frostbite. His fingers were covered with something that looked like sea foam after a storm. Kris looked closer, his small finger and thumb that had been blackened and swollen with frostbite were restored to a healthy color and feeling. Quickly, he put his hand back in the water. Gently, he kicked with his good leg to reach the edge of the pool, where he stood up on his good leg. Kris watched his hands under the water, great patches of foam came from around them and they tingled. After about a minute, the foaming and tingling stopped. So he checked them again. The hands were fully restored as if the frostbite had never happened.

Kris looked again to see that the pool still frothed around him. His feet and thigh tingled; he let his right leg float straight out in front of him, as not to interfere with the magick of the pool. Kris' foot was returning to its natural color and the great bruise on his thigh was much smaller and didn't hurt at all. Kris put it back down into the pool and hung onto the side ledge enjoying himself for a while. He hadn't remembered feeling so good.

As the warm water fizzled, Kris watched the snow far above grow heavier and heard the winds howl but they sounded very far away. Soon the water that was coming from the melted snow was trickling faster into the pool but the water level didn't get any deeper. 'Strange,' Kris thought to himself, he'd have to see why that was later on if his leg had healed. Kris had heard of such healing springs from Olaf. But he thought that the old storyteller was just trying to keep him busy with tall tales while his mother was off doing chores or had to talk to his father.

The water finally stopped fizzing and Kris checked his thigh. First by sight, then when it looked as good as new, he gingerly put a little weight on it, as he pulled himself out of the pool. Kris then took a step, then another; delighted that the pool had worked its healing magick on him. His clothes didn't smell either and clean clothes had less of his scent on them, he would be harder for the wolves to track. Kris lay on his back to rest and to dry his clothes on the warm, smooth, black rock that lined the crater.

While they dried, he took stock of his situation. He was whole again with clean, but ragged clothes, he had his flint for fire but didn't need it at present. His mind was clear and surprisingly he didn't feel hungry or cold at all.

He wished his brother and sister were with him, what an amazing adventure they would've had. Kris was sure that they wouldn't believe him unless he brought them here. Wherever here was, he'd have to get his bearings from the stars then travel as fast as he could to get passed the wolves and back to civilization. Kris looked around to see what other wonders this place held. From his view at the pool, he saw most of the blackened crater. To one side, there was a slight rise that blocked his line of sight. So Kris went to investigate. The little boy loped up the incline happy to have the use of his right leg again. Tattered furs of his pants followed along like streamers behind him.

The rise had a roughly circular indentation that had a much smaller pool, which was shallower than the magick pool that had fixed his leg. It was only a hands width deep and had the same ink black stone lining it's bottom as the rest of the mountain top had. Further on, across from the small pool, the crater wall had a mottled appearance. As Kris neared the one part of the whole basin that wasn't smooth black rock, he saw something that looked like metal. But like no metal that he'd ever seen. There were blue-black and dark red streaks of it lining the wall. They were shaped like pieces of armor. A part of a shin guard here, part of a great shield sticking out there. All jumbled up and with such intricate patterns that it took Kris a while just to figure out what the pieces were. He found the armor very warm as he ran his hand over it and the metal felt smoother than the finest cloth he'd ever touched. Kris looked for anything like a sword or axe, but there was no sign of any weapons, so he looked for any other wonders this place held. Nothing caught his eye in the luminescence of the crater, so he went back to the smaller of the two pools to rest. As soon as he lay his head down, Kris felt how tired he'd become. All the wonders of the black-spired place had been too much for him. Maybe the magick of the pool needed him to sleep for it to finish its work. Whatever the reason, Kris went fast to sleep.

He dreamed of the places that the storyteller Olaf had told him tales of; Bifrost, the rainbow bridge. That led to Asgard, home of the Norse Gods, of the Yggdrasil tree, the root tree of the nine worlds, where Odin, King of the gods had hung for nine days to have a vision. The dreams continued, Kris also saw Alfheim, The abode of the Light Elves and their ruler,

Frey on a balcony of his palace overlooking the Elven realm and its many wonders. After so many dreams, the boy awoke more tired than when he'd fallen asleep.

Looking up, Kris saw a shimmering light in the shape of a small horse standing over the little pool next to him. The outline was hovering barely above the water. The shape turned to look at him, and lowered its head. Kris felt that it spoke to him, but he hadn't heard anything but the distant howl of the North wind. The animal shaped shadow said into the boy's mind,

"It is a pleasure to finally meet you."

Kris thought that he was still dreaming. The shape whinnied and replied again into his mind,

"No, you are very much awake."

Kris didn't understand and said as much. The shape began to flicker then the outline began to glow. Kris backed away from the thing and looked around for the nearest escape route.

"Wait," said the voice in his head, "You weren't brought here to be healed and then just leave."

Kris turned back to the glowing shape but a small black horse with a single horn was in the spot where the shimmering had been. Its eyes were as blue as the ocean on a bright day, and it's strange horn was mostly white with a tiny amount of black at its tip. The pony's eyes seemed intelligent but not cruel, more like the eyes of one of the old people in Kris' village, of one who had lived a very long time and its horn looked like it could easily go right through a man. Kris wasn't afraid of a horse, but the horn and the fact that it seemed to be talking to him, was what worried the boy. Either this was a dream or he'd stumbled into some strange magick.

"I'm Emsaph," the Unicorn bobbed his head to the boy. "And you are?"

"Confused," the boy replied. "I'm sorry if I've trespassed, I meant no disrespect." Kris said.

He knew enough from the stories he'd heard that the elves and fairies didn't like to be put upon. Kris felt that he'd obviously stumbled into one of the places that he had heard of from the old story teller. Kris had thought that Olaf was just trying to scare and delight children or make the story more interesting by putting in imaginary creatures in it. The horned horse just snorted at him and shook its head.

Kris felt a strange sensation take hold of his mind, he saw his life in images flash by in visions that filled his head. The feeling was gone in an instant, leaving Kris with the beginnings of a migraine.

Emsaph turned his head slightly to the left.

"Ah, here come the answers to all the questions that are flying around in that mind of yours." The Unicorn mindspoke to the small boy.

Kris followed the direction of the pointing horn of the strange horse over to the edge of the basin wall. It began to shimmer, then three glowing outlines of human shapes came towards Kris. This time, the boy watched the brightening of the outlines, then as if stepping out from behind a sun-lit sheet, three girls appeared and became solid. They all looked like sisters except they had different colored hair. One was red-haired, like Kris, the second blonde and the third girl had hair as black as a raven's wing. The three all had on the same style of dress. A beautiful wine colored gown with threading and gems sewn into the bodice, the color of the jewels were that of fine honey. They also looked to be about fourteen years of age.

"Greetings," said the one with the red hair that reminded Kris of his mother.

"Truly you are your mother's son, but we didn't know if you would make it here," said the blonde girl.

"But come, we have much for you to see and learn," said the third girl, the one with black hair.

In unison, they all reached out to Kris in a gentle loving way. Seeing no threat and knowing there was nothing he could do about it if there were, Kris walked towards the trio. As he was to step in what should have been the pool, he didn't feel his feet get wet. Looking down Kris saw that the whole group was just barely standing over the water and the pool didn't even have a ripple on it. A mist came up around him, like in a sauna. Though it smelled of sulfur and oil.

"That's to confuse the nosy," he heard in his head. Kris braced himself for whatever was to come next, though he still could see the girls, he couldn't see anything else. Then the boy felt a shift, like when you misjudge a step that was farther than you thought and catch yourself. The Unicorn whinnied again off to his right and Kris heard in his head,

"Don't fret little one, I still can't get use to the feeling."

Kris then felt his hands being squeezed in a reassuring way by two of the girls and after being alone for so long, he welcomed the warm touch.

The mist blew around him, growing thicker. Kris tried, but couldn't see what was beyond the cloud, though he felt like they were moving very fast. Things swirled in the mist, forms fought to take shape; Kris tried to use the skills his mother had begun to teach him to sense the things trying to peer in, to see what was in the center of the protective cloud.

"We move fast to avoid any unpleasantness," one of the sisters said.

Kris couldn't tell which one, as they all sounded alike. The motion quickly slowed then stopped. There was a sensation that the mist cleared and brightened a little to Kris' eyes.

"Home," Emsaph thought loudly.

"No, not just yet," the Trio replied. The mist brightened and darkened with colors flashing from all sides for some time, but before Kris could get bored the cloudy-mist felt like it had stopped again.

"Hold on," the girls intoned. Kris felt uneven ground under his feet, as the mist fell away from them all, like a falling leaf.

The boy looked around to his amazement; Kris was in the realm of the gods. There, not far off was the Yggdrasil tree. Though it was not as big as Olaf the storyteller had said that it was. Off in the distance, a great mountain covered half the horizon, topped with the most beautiful buildings he had ever seen.

"That would be Odin's palace," Emsaph quipped like he was referring to an outhouse. Kris just stood there in silence, and tried to take in the awesome sight.

"Am I dead?" he asked solemnly.

"By the Norns, he is a cutie," said the blonde girl. The boy's ears perked up at this. The Norns held the fates of all men in their hands. Kris tried to remember their names so as show them the proper respect.

The trio led him to the pond at the base of the huge tree that was the root of the nine worlds. Talking of the sights, they told him that the tree actually spanned the nine worlds so it really was a lot bigger than it looked. They found seats on the great gnarled roots that came out of the base of the giant worlds-spanning tree. Kris' mind raced with many questions, so they let him ask about the places here in this world where his people's religion had started.

Then the sisters began again, after they'd let him ask all the tourist questions.

"Yes that's really Odin's palace. Yes, the plain that was further off in the distance was were many of the battles were fought many years ago. No, you're not dead or dreaming." The sisters reassured him.

Kris lost track of who was speaking to him; the sisters kept finishing each other's sentences. They also told him that it was his mother who was to be the one to come here, but her training was interrupted by war. The trio went onto explain that Kris' mother had been chosen when she was just a child to be trained among the Druids. So that Anika could come heal the breach between the worlds, but she left the Druids without something that the Elves had sought for a very long time and before the plan could be enacted. Emsaph had to travel back to get the sisters and since time moves differently between the realms it had been twenty years before they were ready.

Then, the sisters had watched and waited for a time when she could be contacted, but the village had been raided and Anika was lost at sea. Luckily, she had started to teach her children the Druid ways. The toning and meditating that his mother had taught him, that to Kris seemed like a waste of time, had actually tuned his mind so that the sisters could track him. The Norns had helped the weather witch Mara cause the maelstrom sending the ship so far north and had helped Kris survive the icy water, pulling him along to their place of power where they could reach him. They then dimmed his memory of his brother and sister so he could re-gain his strength in the cave at the small, sheltered cove.

Kris didn't understand most of it, but kept silent while they were telling the story. Kris didn't want his hosts to think him a braggart so he explained that he had just happened to be there by chance.

"We are chance," they told him.

That jogged his memory, Kris knew who they were and their 'jobs.' Their names were Urd, which meant fate, Skuld and who was necessity, and Verdandi, the nature of being. Kris waited for someone to use a proper name so that he wouldn't seem the fool for using the wrong name for the wrong sister.

"I don't want to seem improper, but should I be here in Asgard." The small boy said, trying to be as meek as he could.

"Your reverence does you credit," said the dark-haired sister. "But don't worry about Odin or Thor," the Norns smiled. They then told him of the final battle of the gods had happened in Asgard. The final battle, Ragnarok, when all gods would die and it would be the end of everything. Kris protested saying that happened only at the end of the world. The sisters then explained that time moved at different speeds, as a night and day moved differently at different times of the year, so time moved faster in some of the realms than in others.

They went on to tell him of the battle and at its end, in desperation Odin did the unthinkable.

"You were taught of the rune stones?" a sister asked.

"Yes ma'am, they are used to tell the future. There is an old wise woman in the village..." Kris tried to say.

"No, no the real Rune Stones, the ones of Odin's making." The red-haired one cut him off.

The sisters went on to explain the about the Rune Stones and that they had amazing power to do many things. One would gift you with the ability to see into the future of others, to see the outcome of their actions, another Rune Stone allowed you to move at the speed of thought and all of the stones gave the owner a very long life.

"Odin, in an effort to kill as many of the enemy as he could, broke one of the runes stones, the one called Hail, the stone of destruction, releasing its power killing everyone in this Realm. And Hail also ripped a hole through time and space all the way to Midgard, what you know as your world. That's where you met our Unicorn , at the hole that Emsaph was guarding, he's a little more fearsome than he looks," one of the sisters teased, pulling at the Unicorn 's tail.

"Hey," Emsaph shot back.

Kris interrupted the two before he lost his train of thought.
"So you're saying," he started slowly. "That the battle at the end of the world was for this world, not where I live." He reasoned, catching on.

The sisters replied that Ragnarok; the battle at the end of the world, was in fact only a prophecy about Asgard, the home of the Norse gods, not all of the realms. The rest was all exaggeration; that it would end everything. Storytellers always say a little more than they hear, the black-haired girl told the small boy.

"Okay, so then you wanted my mother to come here to fix this hole, which is where?" Kris continued.
"Here it can barely be seen, even by one of us. It has been eons since the battle in this place, if you look over at the great plain and breathe as your mother taught you..." The redheaded sister instructed.

Kris breathed in slowly, then held the air in his lungs to the count of eight focusing out on the grassy plain.

"Do you see a shimmer above the ground like heat off a fire?" One of the sisters asked. Kris concentrated past the end of the elfin girl's finger and let the 'second sight' take over his vision.

"Yes, but it is very faint." Kris said, shading eyes to get a better sighting. "And this goes through all the realms ending in...?" He didn't want to sound like a dullard, but it was a lot to understand for a small boy from a backwater world.

"You were there, at the mountain, the battle raged over into your realm and ended there. Did you not see the black crater or the armor in the walls?" asked the blonde one.

"So what did you need my mother or me to do?" Kris needed to know.

"We are Norns, you know that much, yes." said the sisters in unison. Apparently, they needed to start from the beginning.

"Your names are Urd, Skuld and Verdandi. That's why I thought I was dead." Kris countered. The Unicorn came forward beside the three girls.

"Actually, there are more than one set of Norns," Emsaph chimed in. "These are the Sisters of the Crossing." The Unicorn mindspoke, with as much grandeur as he could. He bowed to them showing the respect that was due to them, then finished the introduction.

"They are Titania," the red-haired one curtsied, "Elphaba," the blonde did the same, "and Nula," the dark-haired didn't curtsey, but just smiled at Kris in a way that made him feel a little uneasy. "They watch over the doorways between the realms to make sure that what happened here, never happens again. With a little help, that is." The Unicorn finished with self-assured smuggness.

"We need a human to heal the rip from your side of the tear." Said Titania.

"Using one of the remaining stones, we hope to reverse the process."

Elphaba seconded. "The stones are at the black mountain, in the pool that healed you." Nula finished the explanation.

"You remember when you came out of the water you also didn't feel hungry and the pool even cleaned those 'clothes' of yours." The Unicorn whinnied. Kris looked down a little self-consciously at his clothes.

"We can not possess the stones, the dwarves or frost giants would know, and war would soon follow. Only the humans of Midgard could wield them without anyone knowing. It is very far from the other realms, as you would understand. Emsaph show him," Nula said.

Pictures of what they were trying to convey flashed into the boy's mind. The great battle, Odin with his belt of stones and a mighty axe, Thor beside his father, with lightning coming from his thunder hammer. Frost giants were surrounding the two them from all sides and Loki, Odin's half-son, was behind the giants, goading them on against his father. The host of Asgard, the largest army ever created, laid to waste around the battlefield. The king of the gods of Asgard swung out the double-bladed axe that threw bolts of power that killed all that it touched. Thor, with his mighty hammer battled at his father's back, both gods fought with such poetry and ferocity that Kris wished Olaf the storyteller could have seen it to tell everyone of such bravery.

Finally, Thor took a fatal wound. Odin dropped the great axe and grabbed his son with one hand. He pulled the magickal Rune Stone, Hail, from his belt and sang out in fury and grief, a battle cry that shook all of Asgard. The giants with Loki behind them rushed in for the killing blow. A mist rose up around the entire army from the ground freezing their feet into place. Odin's one eye burned with hatred for all that they had taken from him. Slowly he squeezed the Rune Stone of destruction in his mighty hand and pulled his dying son close. A light that hurt to look at came from the stone and grew more and more intense. The world fell away and the vision ended.

"So it falls to you. The stones need to be drained of their power and we must charge you with finding another stone as well." The Norns explained further.

"It was the stone that started the war in the first place. Loki's stone. It was said that it contained all the evil the nine realms had, and more. Bright and shining, beautiful without equal. it was clear as the blue summer sky. If it was held out in the sunlight, it gave off a strange orange light long after the sun went down." The trio said.

"Emsaph put the picture of it in Kris' head." One of the sisters said.

The boy saw the Loki stone in the vision that the Unicorn placed in his mind. It was made of the hardest of stones and bigger than the boy's fists put together.

"You must find this stone and call to us. But do not hold it any longer than you have to... for it corrupts all that it touches. It must be found and destroyed. We will send help to you to destroy the stone in Midgard." The sisters finished.

"Won't someone or something be looking for the stones?" Kris asked.

"No one will come looking for them, our father, we sisters and this nag," they said, pushing on the Unicorn 's side, "and now you are the only ones who know for sure that Odin's Rune Stones and the Loki crystal weren't destroyed in the battle." The girls revealed to Kris.

They went on talking about which stone would be the best to use for the healing of the tear between the realms. Only one of the stones was needed to heal the breach. Kris asked if they could come and talk to him after the tear was healed, to counsel him on the best use of the stones that were left or at least give him someone to talk with occasionally. The sisters explained that there were natural holes between all of the realms, which were their duty to protect and that they would come to see him as their duties allowed.

The Rune Stones were of Asgard and had only a certain amount of power in them, not to be recharged, so he was counseled to use them wisely. The elfin girls then asked him if he had other questions.

"I know enough to know that the power of those things would give me all the revenge that I could want on the slavers who killed my mother, but the stones won't bring her back, will they?" The small boy asked.

"No. What is gone from the world does not come back, no one should have that kind of power," the Unicorn spoke into Kris' mind.

The Norns finally agreed that since it would take several hundred years to finally heal the tear through the nine realms, they decided that the stone with one long line down the length of it, called Ice, was the best choice. When used, it would change the climate nearest to the hole causing bad winters for many years to come, eventually the whole continent's climate would be effected. The fierce cold would hopefully keep the gateway safe from trespassers. And since the hole would take centuries to finish in all the nine connected worlds, it was one the Norns thought should be used.

Many outland creatures could have found the tear and the humans wouldn't be prepared to handle what would come through the portal at the black mountain. Though Emsaph had kept watch on the tear for many centuries, some creatures had made it to Midgard.

Like the Northern wolves, some halflings and some things that couldn't be identified by the Norns. All the information was a bit much for anyone to handle and certainly more than most five-year-olds, so Emsaph lay down next to Kris and the sisters departed to tell their father Frey, leader of the light elves, the news. Kris sat down next to the Unicorn and then leaned up against the little horned guardian. The boy started to relax and take in all that had been shown to him.

"Rest little one. Think of your questions and I will answer what I can as you sleep." Emsaph used the mind link to cause the boy to slumber.

Kris fell into a deep sleep that had many dreams with the sisters showing him the stones that were left and their many uses. How to use them without killing himself or others. And how to learn very fast, to speak, write and read different languages by holding the stones and intoning them in certain ways. Kris also learned that he could use the Rune Stones for a 'glamour,' to look different, be taller, shorter, a woman if need be, all the while being himself that no one could see, unless he deemed it necessary. Finally, Kris dreamed of his brother and sister far away in the winter camp of the Viking slavers. He awoke with a start, Emsaph at his side.

"I must go, how long have I been asleep." Kris asked urgently.

"Do not worry," the Unicorn nodded to him, "you can stay here a year and not be gone a week in your realm, that is the nature of things. It has taken a while though, to teach you all that you needed to learn." The Unicorn whinnied.

Kris actually understood what the beast was saying and knew that he couldn't leave without the sisters that had brought him there anyway.

"Come I will show you the wonders of this place." Emsaph said, as he pulled himself to his feet. The memories of Kris' brother and sister faded from the young boy's mind.

"Climb up on my back, I'll show you the great battlefield and give you a 'royal tour' of this now ungodly place, pardon the pun, before the girls get back." Emsaph showed Kris many incredible things there.

Asgard had many orchards with fruits that Kris had never tasted, there were giant statues of heroes long gone, that could tell the adventures of Odin and Frigga, Thor and the evil Loki. When Kris and his guide had finally passed the inner walls of Odin's palace, massive buildings that floated were there, bobbing up and down to their own rhythms. The Unicorn told Kris that the reason the buildings floated was that Odin was just showing off his power and the style had just caught on.

Many days had past before the sisters had returned. Kris and the Unicorn became great friends, playing and having adventures, as males will do. The pair awoke one afternoon in the one of the great halls of Odin's castle to find the trio of sisters standing over them.

"Well, if you're quite rested," Titania said with a huff.

"It is time to close the tear." Elphaba clapped her hands, as if that would hurry them up.

The sisters gathered close to the Unicorn and Kris. The mist arose around as it had before. Kris felt the group move through the walls of the castle and back to the place that they had taken him from so long ago. The journey didn't seem to last but a moment this time. As the mist fell away, Kris saw that the black crater looked as if they had just left. The same strange half-light filled the top of the black mountain. Snow was falling high above, he watched the frozen flakes of water hit the protective bubble and melt into droplets that ran down the outside. The water trickled into the pool at the bottom of the crater, same as when he'd left. Kris noticed that his clothes were a lot tighter. Though he had been provided clothes that fit him in Asgard, now they were too small. When he looked down he saw that he was taller and older.

"Remember years elsewhere can be, but a few weeks here," Emsaph spoke into the boy's mind, then he showed Kris what he looked like to the others. The young man had just aged ten years since leaving Asgard.

"But my sister won't recognize me, I'll be older than Olaf is," Kris said with bewilderment. The Unicorn projected the need for him to be gone so long in Asgard. Kris watched in his mind's eye, all of the learning had received as he dreamed when he slept next to Emsaph. More things rushed into his mind, triggered by the Unicorn .

The Northern wolves were actually from the outlands of the frost-giants realm that had found their way through the tear in the worlds. Other large creatures that now slept in deep caves in the forest, twice as large as a man with matted hair and beastly faces. Creatures, that storytellers couldn't have imagined. All had come through this hole that Odin had made. Titania motioned to Emsaph to instruct Kris on the job ahead. The images changed from what had come through the hole to the mechanics of how to seal the tear. Kris followed along with the scenes in his head asking silently any questions he had to Emsaph, then nodded to the Unicorn . As the young man started down the slope to fetch the Rune Stones from the pool that had healed him, Elphaba stopped Kris.

"We must leave you now Kris, thank you for trusting us."

"Take this," Nula said, handing the young man a sack that looked like it was made of fine red linen with the opening trimmed in a white fur.

"You will need something to carry those things around in," Titania finished smiling.

Kris thanked them and went off to retrieve the stones. When he was out of earshot the sisters turned to the Unicorn .

"You must finish his instruction. We will come to check on him when we can." Nula said.

"Once the power starts to flow, many creatures will be drawn to it and we'll have our hands full in the gateways of other realms." Titania cautioned Emsaph.

"So we leave this end up to you, old friend," Elphaba said, waving a perfectly manicured finger in the Unicorn 's face.

"Help him with his hatred of the Vikings that raided his village, there is too much power in the stones for one so young." The trio coached the Unicorn that had been their own instructor once.

"He won't be a problem. I see great good in this one. The pain, well leave it to me, I've something planned that I didn't even teach you children." the Unicorn thought to the trio, as he turned to watch the young boy.

Kris looked into the healing pool to see his reflection. He hardly recognized himself. The small boy he'd been was gone, now he was an ungainly youth. His red hair had grown wild since he'd been here. All the knowledge that his friend had put in his head amazed him. He knew and understood math and reading. He could hardly wait to tell Mary and Olaf. Though they wouldn't believe any of it. Kris saw in his mind what was to happen with the healing of the tear between the realms. The weather in this part of his world would become much colder in winter and the growing season much shorter, that would be the side effect of the destroying the Rune Stone called Ice. That would trap the creatures that had made it through, but they would die in no more than a few hundred years. Future generations would hear tales of great wolves and huge hairy monsters and not believe a word of it.

Kris dove into the pool to find the remaining Rune Stones. He remembered what they looked like from the great battle of Ragnarok, in Asgard. The teenager found the first one easily enough, the blue gray stone was bigger than he could hold in his two hands, oblong in shape, with a symbol cut into one side. The carving of the rune was smooth, like the stone had been made of wax. It had no rough edges, just the rounded corners. Kris brought it up out of the water and noticed how heavy it was. He barely managed to get it into the bag. If there were nine of them, he'd have to hitch up Emsaph like a plow horse to drag them out of here.

The next one that Kris found had the same marking as the runes his mother had worn on special occasions. The rune was called Wunjo, which meant joy. After getting nine of the stones into the bag, he left the tenth stone, Ice, out to seal the breach.

Emsaph came down to his ward and walked with the young man up to the smaller pool where they'd first met. The Unicorn told Kris not to worry about the stones; the bag that Nula had given him made everything in it very light. It would be as if he had thrown his cloak over his shoulder, instead of lugging the nine stones around on his back. Kris saw the outline of the three sisters glowing just above the pool.

"They need to work the power that we give them from their side," the Unicorn reminded his newest student.

Though Kris had already seen how it all would happen in his head. Emsaph had shown him in the vision. Kris would hold up the stone and Emsaph would stand behind him telling him what notes to intone and how to tune them into a vibrato. The stone would burst into dust and the power would flow out to the trio of Norns who would seal the tear from their side and Emsaph would do the rest from this side.

"That picture in your mind is just a theory you know. We don't know how it will work, for sure." The Unicorn whinnied.

One of the girl's outlines raised her hand to signal that they were ready to begin.

"Okay, now this won't hurt me a bit," the Emsaph thought into Kris' head. The boy didn't like the sound of that, but before he could say anything the stone rose in his hands to over his head and Kris saw in his mind the first thing he was to do. As he started to make a low hum, the stone began to glow. The light increased between his hands, an eerie bluish hue that grew more intense by the second. The light shone at the space where the girls would be standing, if they were here on Earth that is. Kris began to sing the note that he heard in his mind. The power between his hands grew, he felt like the stone was holding him up not the other way around. Images flashed in his mind of the stone being carved by a huge hand. Robed figures surrounded the Rune Stone at night in a place that had three moons, sang songs of power into the stone.

Then images of his mother rushed into his mind; the stone was now looking into him. He felt the pains that he'd hidden from himself... of her floating out to sea; the memories that he would never be able to share with her. Kris felt all of these pains and more, things he didn't even know he'd suffered. Images rushed and blurred past, this and more poured into his mind, the power continued to grow. The stone was singing through him. The blue light was blinding, Kris shut his eyes, but the light shone brighter still. Deep within him, Kris felt the pain building, rushing up his spine, he tried to cry out, but the song was too strong; it was now singing him. He had no control over his body, Kris saw himself outside of himself.

He was floating outside of his body watching the tear being healed.

Emsaph was behind his body, muscles straining as though he was holding a great weight. Sweat poured off the Unicorn as he struggled to finish the healing. Kris looked at his own body, arms out in front of him with the stone between his hands. The body was slack like he'd fallen asleep, except that his mouth was open singing a single note for much longer than he would have had breath to do. The stone burned a brilliant blue light at the tear, which was much smaller now. Kris couldn't see the tear when he was in his body, he just though it was the size of the cloud that they had come from Asgard. It was actually the size of the crater, he could tell that much. The rip was closing, but Kris could still see the seams that had been mended. They glowed a nasty red like a fresh scab on a wound and throbbed like they were alive, threatening to break back open at any moment. Still the Unicorn strained, and the body that Kris saw remained slack. He sensed more than saw the energy pouring into the gap between the realms, hoping that the girls were coping with the amount of power being directed at them. The seams where coming together, nearer to the base of the crater. The outer tendrils of the tear throbbed less and less and the Rune Stone looked transparent. Kris felt like he was being pulled back into his body. A slight tugging at first, then as he drew closer the feeling yanked him back inward.

Kris dropped to the ground gasping for air; the stone had disintegrated between his hands. Then Kris heard Emsaph thud onto the black ground behind him. Looking out of his bleary eyes, he saw the outline of the three sisters, one of them had fallen, the other two were attending her. Kris still felt the second sight that allowed him to see the tear. He focused in on using the power to see the unseen. The rip had been sealed, though the scar was immense. Emsaph had shown him earlier that the tear would eventually heal and would need to be tended to until it did. Kris collapsed from the amount of energy that had been channeled through him. He slept in peaceful dreamless sleep. The dark, calming and warm void embraced him.

When he awoke Emsaph was lying next to him, patiently waiting for him to awake.

"Did we do it?" the young man asked.

Instead of a reply, he saw pictures of what had happened, he held the stone, intoning of the sound, but all he was shown was from the Unicorn 's point of view. Next, the rip that had gone through the nine realms seemed to scream in his mind, the power that it took to mend the hole was beyond Kris' mind to comprehend, even with all that the Unicorn had taught him. Kris saw his body from behind, from Emsaph's point of view, being used as the fulcrum for the power rushing through him. Then, he understood why the pains he'd experienced had flashed acrossed his mind.

His parents deaths, the loss of his siblings and village. The sisters had seen into him, and saw his pain. Kris had carried the same pain in him that had caused the tear in the first place. Though not as intense as Odin's, Emsaph had used it like a trigger to funnel the energy into the hole. Lastly, Kris saw the result of the healing. On the other side of the tear the three sisters were repairing the damage to the other eight realms. Elphaba had been injured by some of the creatures that were trying to leave the realm of the frost giants and make it through the tear before it closed. Emsaph didn't know how badly she had been hurt, as soon as her sisters had finished directing the power into the breaches they had taken her to their father, Frey, ruler of the Realm of Light Elves, who was also a healer. The Unicorn then told Kris he would check on her as soon as he crossed though five realms to get to the Norns.

Since the hole had been closed, he would have to travel far to get to a natural throughway to see her.

"Now to see you on your way, there are some other things you must know. All that you have had placed in your mind, the knowledge of using the stones, the reading and writing of Druid ways and the rest. Other things were placed in your head that you won't know until you get a little older. Also, the Loki Stone is more insidious than the girls realize. If the stone fell into a stream, the people who drank the water would begin to change. Slowly at first, then over time they would be hateful, greedy and warring on everyone. Maybe you should check to see if that's where the slavers got their nasty disposition. Make no mistake, A gem that evil will find its way to power. Once there, it will be hard for the person to part with it. So, be careful with whom you reveal how much you know. Knowledge is power. Think on how much more powerful you are now compared to when we first met." The Unicorn lectured.

Kris had to agree, he had vast knowledge of his world and how big it was and the young man knew how to work with the natural energies using the Rune Stones to direct Midgard's untapped powers.

"Now that the realms are healing, our power here will diminish." Emsaph told his pupil.

"We can visit you at what are known as 'sacred places' but we can no longer wield our magicks here as strongly as we once did. The beasts that came through the tear will live out their natural life span here; we guardians are too few to be chasing after those things. While they're not all mindless, they aren't sensitive enough to feel the power of the stones. There maybe people here who can feel the unique power that the Rune Stones give off, but they will only feel it when you are working with the power directly. So if you use them, be far from harm, very far, or keep them in the bag that Nula gave you. But I've told you more than your head can hold, we must go our separate ways for now, but we will meet again in time."

With that the Unicorn got up from where he'd been laying next to Kris and without looking back, trotted towards the rim.

"But where will I go?" Kris called out, as Emsaph was at the rim.

"Go with what is in your heart, young one," the voice rang in his head, "And get some new clothes." The Unicorn finished.

Kris saw the way he looked to Emsaph, he did look frightful. The nice clothes he had been given in Asgard were rags now, what he wore barely fit him and his hair had grown long and wild looking.

'Well, I guess I'd better get started,' Kris thought to himself. 'I need to go save Olaf and Mary from the Viking raiders.'

Kris found that he didn't have any bloodlust for the slavers at all. He didn't know if it was the closing of the holes between the realms or maybe that Emsaph had worked a spell on him to take his hatred away. Anyway, he got the bag of stones, which hardly weighed anything, the bag that Nula had given him made everything that was in it, very light. Reaching in the bag, he touched one of the stones and hummed slightly, thinking of the nearest village.

It didn't have a name that he knew of, but it was an outpost of humanity and Kris looked forward to getting there. The sisters had taught him to use the stones to travel great distances very quickly, but cautioned him not to use the Rune Stones, except to get his bearing so close to the healing tear. They didn't want to take a chance on damaging the work.

'Luckily, I don't have to worry about the cold either,' Kris thought to himself, just being near the stones and thinking of being warm caused them to generate heat throughout his body. The Rune Stones also would create the same kind of bubble that had protected the crater for so long. Humming to himself, the young man with wild red hair, shifted his vision to 'second sight' to see the energies of the hole between worlds and the bubble in the crater from the rim where he stood. The tear throbbed slightly though it was much smaller than he'd seen it before. The Norns had said that it would take many years to heal and the shield that had only allowed him in, would gradually fade over time as the tear mended. Kris looked out over the great northern forest that ran from the horizon to the sea. He somehow could sense the wolf pack. Then, Kris knew why they were so big, coming from the out lands of the frost-giants. Many stories would be told of killing those huge beasts. He was glad that the only way that they could sense him was with their noses. Far off, near the sea, many miles south nearer to the settlement that he was headed to, Kris felt other creatures that had gotten through the hole before the trio of sisters and Emsaph had blocked the way. Great hairy monsters slept in a cave, that a man would have dive into the deep water of the marshy lake to find. There were only two of them, mother and child who were hibernating. As Kris passively scanned the horizon he felt another otherworldly creature, it was Emsaph who had traveled many miles to the East though the forest by the time that Kris had scanned in his direction.

"Get marching," the young man heard in his head, then a whinny. Kris smiled, looked out at the half twilight of the northern winter, then started south.

Kris headed back towards civilization with the stones in a sack that the Elven sisters had given him. The wolves that had hunted Kris in his younger
days were in the area, but wouldn't come near him. He'd set up his own
little bubble of protection just after he had left the crater. The huge wolves
stayed away, baying at a distance until he finally thought one night,
'Why don't you wolves go away from me or just be quiet.' The wolf pack
didn't leave, but they went instantly quiet and followed him for many days
until he reached a village.

Kris looked down on the small hamlet, the roofs sagged with snow and
the drifts reached up the 'A' frame roof of the meadhall, threatening to
engulf it in their icy maul. Not knowing how long he'd been with Emsaph and the three sisters, Kris thought that it must have been the dead of
winter. He saw the townsfolk going about their business with weariness to
them, as if the cold and snow had made them numb to their very souls.

The red-haired youth didn't know that winter was holding over,
delaying the spring. The people of the hamlet had been wondering if
the mythical wolf, Fenir, had swallowed the sun. The gray overcast skies
should have already gone and Spring should have started, they reasoned.

Sensing something was amiss, Kris buried the bag of Rune Stones in a
snowdrift near the edge of the forest. Kris then extended his own protection onto the village, this he did without thinking of it consciously. Intoning protection, had been taught to him in his sleep by the Unicorn back
in Asgard, and now it had become second nature.
'Besides,' Kris thought, after catching himself directing the protective
energies to the outskirts of the township, 'bringing the wolves with me to

attack the village would not be looked on as being a good guest.'

His red hair and wild look was noticed as soon as he came in plain sight and entered the village. The children ran to tell the men cutting firewood at the far end of the clearing. Kris strolled up to and entered the mead hall, it was a tavern, meeting hall and church all rolled into one.

In groups of five and seven, the people came in to hear any news of the outside world or at least get a look at Kris.

The young man's clothes had been tattered by his sudden growth spurt, the villagers would want some answers as to the stranger's appearance and would also want to know how Kris could be coming to their village out of the northern woods. Kris quickly thought up a story of the ordeal of reaching this little hamlet after he'd left the crater that Odin had made.

Later Kris named the mountain where he met the Norns, the 'witch's teeth', a bit mellow dramatic I thought, but it kept worker elves away.

"Santa really had worker elves?" I asked incredulously.

"That's a story for another weekend. "Now where was I ?" Olaf thought out loud. "Yes", he said as he took a sip of tea for dramatic pause.

'The village that would become known as Harborg, the most Northern of the villages at the time.

Don't bother looking that one up to challenge me with it next week", Olaf said seriously, "It's still under a mountain of ice."

"Could you clarify that point please", I chimed in.

"I'm getting to it." He replied dryly.

The town's leader came in with the last of the men. His name was Hrothgar, a giant of a man and as Kris said, not really friendly.

"Who are you to have come in from the North untouched by the wolves?" The leader thundered at the youth, fists at the ready. Kris knowing that the people were upset about something and they seemed to be looking for a reason to see any omens in him, good or bad, so he carefully chose his words.

"I was on a ship that had been caught in a great storm and I was cast overboard. Being near enough to shore I made it there and used what little I had," Kris showed the nub of flint that he'd had in his fur boot, "to reach here."

"How did you manage to find our village?" Hrothgar pressed.

"I used the stars at night, if the weather was clear." Kris replied truthfully.

"What village are you from, whelp?" An old woman spoke in a rasping whisper between the murmuring of the crowd. Hrothgar grew quiet. Shooting a glance over his shoulder to the fire pit where the hamlet's hedge-witch sat warming her bones. Then back to the teenager.

"Well," he said it more like a command than a question.

"Haven," the youth replied, regretting it, as soon as he spoke. The villager's faces drew up in disgust.

"Our wise-woman had seen the village destroyed by the slavers, in a vision she had, are you one of them!?" Hrothgar roared as he pointed to the old woman who was sitting next to the fire.

"No, I'm the son of Petr the boat builder, my grandfather is Sven Longbow you must have heard of him!" Kris pleaded.

"Aye child," husked the old wise woman, "you must have the look of your mother's people."

Hrothgar had had enough of the interruption. His place was out guarding the woodsmen from the large hungry wolves. Since the delaying of Spring, the wolves had grown bolder, attacking the villagers night or day, who were foolish enough to go out alone.

"You can stay the night, but after that, you will have to leave this village," the leader insisted, Hrothgar was tired of wasting time on the interloper. With that, he turned with his scowl to the newcomer and hurried the rest of the men out to finish their chores before the twilight set. Kris moved closer to the hearth, near the old woman and took stock of what he'd heard and where to go the next day.

The seer leaned closer to get a look at him with her good eye in the flickering light of the fire.

"I knew your grand sire, you wouldn't know it to look at me, but I could have been your grandmother if I'd have left my family here. I just couldn't leave though, so he chose another lass." She took a long draw on a pipe and studied the young man from head to toe.

"You might want to have a story for being able to survive the cold with so few clothes to cover your skin." She pointed with the mouth end of her pipe to the tattered remains of his garments. He looked at them with surprise. No wonder the townsfolk had gawked at him. His pants were more ribbons than cloth.

"Ailsa," the woman called out to the darkness in the back of the mead-hall. "Ailsa?"

"Yes grandmother," a young girl's voice called back, as Ailsa appeared into the flickering half-light.

"Dear, where are the breeches and shirts that your father had?" The senior asked.

The young girl stared at her grandmother in horror. Wolves had killed Ailsa's father a fortnight ago and now the girl was being asked to give up her dead father's clothes to a boy not much older than her.

"Grandmother no..." she started but was cut short by the seer.

"Those clothes are doing your father no good now and they weren't his best clothes anyhow. Just bring the lad your father's work shirt and breeches."

The girl left in a huff and returned much later with the clothing, laying them at Kris' feet, more out of reverence for the memory of her father than deference to Kris.

After changing, Kris made it a point of thanking Ailsa for the clothes, "You have honored me with these garments, I will bring them no shame." He said, trying to appease the upset girl.

When he returned to the fire, it was dying down to embers, which the old woman, Halga, was banking to keep it alive until the men, came in with the night's wood.

"It's just like this place," she said waving her hand aimlessly around in the air talking to no one.

Then she turned to stare at Kris.

"I've felt something early this winter... something, a drawing, pulling at the edge of my dreams. Terrible things are coming here, but the people will not leave. They will stay and die or be driven out of their homes in fright. Winters longer, colder... still my people will not leave. Now you come, in from the North.... Dark forest, black crags. I feel you young, alive, but more." She was looking around Kris like she couldn't keep him in focus. "You know what I say is true? Don't you! Why the cold comes and the dark things that have rested in the land are coming here? Don't you? Don't you?!" the seer pleaded. Grabbing Kris' shirt desperate to hear her fears confirmed.

"Yes," was all Kris could say in a whisper. He watched as her eyes glazed over and she sat there swaying to music that only she heard, nodding her head until the men came in with the wood for the night's blaze. Behind them, the others villagers came in to help cook or get the bedding ready for the night. Ailsa attended to her grandmother, Halga, getting the old woman out of the way, so that the fire could be stoked and the meal prepared. The young woman gently pulled the fisted hands away from Kris' shirt and helped the old woman over to a bench nearby. Then she came back to get Kris.

"I'm sorry about earlier," she said, gesturing to the clothes that Kris had been given, "You must have lost all of your family when the slavers raided your village. I've heard that they kill all the men and take the women and children as their slaves. Is that true?"

"Yes," Kris replied stoically. "It's all true and worse. Be thankful that you don't live too near the sea," he finished.

She smiled at him. 'How brave and fearless he must have been to make it all the way here on his wits,' she thought, smiling absently.

Ailsa returned to her duties, helping prepare the meat for dinner. She knew that grandmother would give her no trouble tonight. When the seer had a vision-spell, she would just sit there for hours. Ailsa would feed the old woman and put her to bed and grandmother would be her old self again in the morning. That would give Ailsa a little time to talk to Kris and hear of the world beyond her tiny village. She'd gathered mushrooms and herbs in the woods with her grandmother, but that was as far as she'd ever gone away from the place of her birth. At night, Ailsa would look at the only road out of town. The South road, the townsfolk called it. She guessed everybody else in the world called it the North road or maybe the road to the end of the Earth.

'Maybe I could go with him South,' she thought. Out of this cold. Kris and her could go to places that she had only heard about. Morgan-plorgg, a city of eight hundred people. More people than she'd even seen in her life. Kris seemed nice enough and he managed to find his way here through the wilderness, so he could obviously take care of himself. Except for his shredded clothes he'd shown up in, he looked little worse for wear. Maybe she would go with him in the morning if Hrothgar was in the far fields watching over the woodcutters, then the village leader wouldn't come after her and by nightfall she and Kris would be too far out of reach for the mighty warrior. Ailsa knew that she would become Hrothgar's wife in a season or two, definitely by the fall festival, at the harvest. Then, she'd be trapped here for the rest of her life. It was more than she could bear. There was just too much to see and she was going, 'Hrothgar could just find a new bride at the Midsummer's fair to drag up here,' the adventurous girl decided.

Ailsa finished the serving and helped clean up, humming a little tune to herself. Then she edged in near the fire to hear the rest of Kris' story of his village, the slavers that had raided it and his 'escape.' Kris had edited out all that had happened at the Witch's Teeth and instead put in an abandoned bears cave that was near a lake where he ice fished until he recovered his strength enough to make to journey here. He really thought it was better than the truth. The villagers reveled in the novelty of having a new story and one man that had been up in the north woods in the summer time chimed in about the fictitious lake saying,

"Yes, that sounds very familiar. Good fishing there. You were lucky to have found that cave with no bears in it." This seemed to clinch it for the villagers who felt a little uneasy that Halga had forced Ailsa to give the stranger her father's old clothes, but now that they'd heard Kris' tale, they felt that it was just to give them to the young man.

Even with the scant meal, the townsfolk happily bedded down with a good story filling the emptiness in them. Kris felt the tension in the group relax with a tale of courage, even though he couldn't tell them the whole truth. He imagined that was what Olaf, the old storyteller of his village felt like after spinning a good tale. After a little more talking, the people all bedded down in the meadhall for warmth and safety it gave them from the large wolves that hunted them.

After a long time away from people with just a Unicorn for company, Kris didn't just fall asleep, he felt claustrophobic with all the townsfolk around him. Finally, out of exhaustion he drifted off. In his dreams, he saw the wolf pack was drawing closer to the village each night. The deeper he dreamed the farther out he went, past the tear in the world with its magic shielding. Circling the North Pole, he looked down on the earth from a great distance. Then thinking of his sister, he found himself floating over the winter camp of the Viking slavers.

It was up a river, close to the sea. Barrels of salted fish and mead were left on the boats either because of the weather or possibly for trading with other villages. Without knowing how, Kris understood that the Vikings would trade with villages that they couldn't take by force. He heard laughter and shouting coming from the Meadhall. The band of raiders were still celebrating their year of prosperity, at other's expense. Thoughts of his sister pulled him nearer to a small building at the edge of the small village. He sensed many small children were housed in the poorly built stone hut that was surrounded by a fenced area that had been shoddily roofed. Kris' spirit floated down to the roof hearing some of the children crying inside. Coming closer to the front door, he heard his brother Olaf consoling their sister Mary. Suddenly, he felt the urge to be with them.

Kris was pulled back into his body and awoke with a shot. The fire was a little lower than it was when he fell asleep, but everything else was the same. Kris got up slowly and made as if to go out into the night to relieve himself. As he made his way out of the village, Kris felt more than saw where he'd buried the bag of Rune Stones. The chill he'd felt left him as soon as he touched the red linen sack.

Kris was concentrating so hard on digging up the stones and leaving the village quietly, that he didn't notice the shadowy figure who watched him from the house closest to the southern road. Bag in tow, he felt the Northern wolf pack prowling the woods near the far end of the village.

Ailsa watched Kris dig up a red bag out of a snow bank. He turned and headed right for her.

'What a fine specimen of manhood he was.' The girl mused. Ailsa had sneaked a peak at his bared torso yesterday when he had changed into the clothes she had given him. Well muscled and handsome as a young man should be. A thousand other thoughts raced in her head as he came closer. It seemed for a second that he'd seen her shadow at the edge of the out building next to the road. She slowly circled around the building so that by the time he'd passed she could sneak after him. She watched him from her new vantage point, around the other side of the shack. The wolves howled off in the distance, Ailsa jumped and headed off after Kris for protection. She saw that he hadn't even turned around in the direction of the noise, 'he must be very brave', she thought to herself. Though she tried to be quiet, he turned toward her as soon as she left the shelter of the small shack.

Kris heard the wolves' familiar howls of frustration; he'd set up a field of protection around the village while he was there. Now that he was leaving, the wolves thought that they could attack the village, but they didn't understand that it would take several more days for the energy that Kris had charged into the hamlet to dissipate. A buzzing not unlike a hive of bees entered his inner hearing. Kris quickly turned towards the disturbance that marred the silent predawn. Ailsa was running up to him as graceful as she could. The young man tried not to laugh, spooked as she was by the wolves and carrying all her most precious possessions in her own sack, she lumbered towards him in the knee deep snow. He let her approach without telling her to go back to the village.

'This little pond of a village was too small for such a big fish.' Kris thought as a smile came to his face.
Ailsa smiled her most winning smile at her rescuer as she reached out to him. The young girl had already prepared to tell him of her great plans.

Kris stopped Ailsa before she got too far along about the beautiful children that they could have.

"We must travel quietly through this country, for the wolves may hear us," Kris told her, in a hushed whisper.

She was suddenly somber and nodded, pursing her lips. Ailsa walked behind him in his footsteps to avoid the snow that would soon soak through her boots. Kris plodded on through the knee-high drift that had filled the roadway. Even though it was wide enough for a large ox cart, the trees loomed over as if to claim the road back within a season of growth.

The pair traveled silently for a long time after the predawn of the northern day had broke over the southeastern horizon. With only a few hours of 'daylight,' Kris wanted to make good time. After many bends in the road, Ailsa felt like she was far enough from Hrothgar to take a break.

"Can we rest for a little while?" she asked, seeing a few boulders sticking out of the snowdrift at the edge of the road. Kris thought for a moment then smiled at her.

"Sure," was all he said. They reached the rocks and Kris helped her up to a flat space near the top of the boulder. Ailsa looked off in the distance hoping for a sign of civilization. Some smoke or sounds that meant that she wouldn't have to be out in the wilderness for the night. But nothing answered her thoughts but the lone cry of a distant hawk. Her traveling companion just sat there with his eyes closed, apparently listening for the cry of wolves. The few clothes that Granny had made Ailsa give her future husband, hung on Kris' young frame. She was amazed that Kris wasn't even shivering from the cold; come to think of it, she'd been so excited about getting to see the real world, Ailsa hadn't thought about the cold at all. She looked down to find that her boots that hadn't been treated with the seal oil, that made shoes waterproof, were still completely dry. The young woman didn't know what to think of the high strangeness. Was this young man an elf? She didn't see any pointy ears on him. Maybe he was one of the magick folk. But he didn't look or act like one of the Earthwise. They were usually old and strange in their ways. He seemed every bit as amiable as she would want in a suitor. Whether he knew it, or not.

Kris had gotten Ailsa to sit and then tuned into his inner sight that Emsaph had taught him. Those lessons seemed like ages ago, back when he'd been spelled by the Unicorn to forget about his brother and sister and all his troubles, while he was a small boy in Asgard. Emsaph had done it to make room in the small boy's head for other things besides hate and grief. The Unicorn taught Kris to use the natural talents that all humans had, but had long been forgotten. He breathed slowly, calming his mind reaching out to the stones to amplify his sensitivity to the tear so many miles to the north. Kris felt the power there; the magick that was slowly healing the tear was still throbbing like a freshly bandaged wound. He was almost far enough away from the black mountain to start using the Rune Stones to get to his siblings.

'First, I have a little problem to fix,' he thought. Kris knew that they were still three days walk from Morganplorgg. So he scanned the road ahead in his mind, yes near, but not too near the village. Kris opened his eyes and turned to Ailsa.

"I think we can be there by night fall," Kris said to her honestly.

"No, I've heard it said that it's a long way off. It could take days." She replied knowingly.

This was farther than she'd ever traveled from home. The wilderness seemed to close in on the wayward girl as the thought sank in like the cold, chilling her.

"Well, we should get started then," Kris finished.

They trudged on through the snow hearing only the cry of a lone hawk that circled far above, looking for a snow hair. The two travelers stopped again in the afternoon; Ailsa gave Kris some of her dried venison and part of the cheese that she'd packed. Afterward he sat there with his eyes closed again. Ailsa felt that she should get him to talk about his plans once they reached the big township. 'Over eight hundred people,' she thought, 'more than I've ever seen.'

"So what are you listening to?" she started.

"Close your eyes and listen to the world," Kris said in a whisper. Ailsa did and said she didn't hear much of anything.

"Just close your eyes, I'll guide you." The young man countered.

"Fine," she said, trying to keep the edge out of her voice. She was getting exasperated, why didn't he just tell her what he was listening for? Kris watched her close her eyes; he made sure that they were really closed by waving his hand in front of her eyes.

He summoned some power of the bag of stones slightly.

"Now listen for the water, it's very far off." He started to weave the tendrils of power from the Rune Stones simultaneously around the rocks that they were sitting on and a similar bend in the road very near the village of Morganplorgg.

"Now, there, if you really concentrate, you'll hear the sounds of children playing." Kris continued, feeding the energy to cause the teleportation, directing, focusing on both places at once. Ailsa was getting tired of this game, then she heard the water faintly at first then slightly louder. Then her betrothed, whether he knew it or not, told her to listen for children. What would children be doing out in this lonely country? She strained to hear anything. Her brow furrowed, as she heard something. Yes, it was the sound of children! But how? She opened her eyes, the road seemed different somehow. Though all the mountains in the distance looked pretty much the same, something was a little off to her. Ailsa felt dizzy, probably from the excitement, she assured herself. Kris sat there smiling at her.

"See you can do it." He said, encouraging her. Far off she heard the low murmur of civilization.

"I think we're a lot closer than you thought, Kris said honestly.

'Maybe the people in her village didn't know how far it really was to Morganplorgg,' Ailsa thought to herself. The twilight was heading into winter darkness when they rounded the final snowy bend and into the township. 'What a great Meadhall,' both teenagers thought.

"That's the biggest building I've ever seen," the girl exclaimed. Any tiredness Ailsa felt left her and she led the pace into the village.

"I've seen bigger," Kris bragged truthfully, thinking of Odin's hall in Asgard. Though the girl wasn't listening, she had wanted to see the great township more than anything since she was first told about the place. Everything was bigger, more, and brighter than even she had imagined.

Kris decided to stay with her a little longer to erase all memory of him from her mind. Emsaph had told him the importance of keeping a very low profile, at least until he got some experience using the Rune Stones. A couple of hundred years, the Unicorn had told him with a whinny. So Kris let her lead as he focused on her mind. Olaf the storyteller had once told him, that any good story has at least a bit of truth in it. Kris left her part of the journey in her mind, gently, he pushed thoughts of himself to the back of her mind, so he could put in the fiction of the tale.

Ailsa didn't realize the clumsy attempt to rewrite her recent memory; she was far too busy looking at all the new people and their clothes. They had clothes that actually fit them well, she marvelled.
Kris finished giving her a story that would delight the crowd at the mead-hall with all the danger of the wolf pack, a daring escape and her tenacity to persevere. That would certainly give her a place in the village and hope-fully a couple of suitors that were more attractive to her than Hrothgar

had been.

The town didn't look as weary as Ailsa's, but the effects of the extra long winter did seem to be creeping up on the outer buildings. Drifts were up to the edge of the roofs and one of the shacks had collapsed under the weight of the extra long winter's snowfall. Kris carefully stayed in Ailsa's footsteps, 'easier for her story to be believed,' he thought. The girl was enchanted with her new adventure. She'd made it all the way here safe and ... Ailsa stopped in her tracks, she tried to wrap her head around the memories that were being rewritten as she watched the mental images of her journey change. Ailsa stood there and tried to think of how she had gotten to Morganplorgg. Brand, the blacksmith's apprentice, saw a strange girl standing outside the smithy.

"Are you alright?" The strapping youth asked.

"Now I am," the winsome girl replied, with her best smile. "I've just arrived from the North Country after a long and dangerous journey." She said, after reviewing her recent memory.

"All by yourself?" The strapping young man looked behind her only to see one set of footsteps that lead back to the northern road. Something flickered at the edge of town, 'just a shadow of the twilight,' Brand thought to himself.

"Well, we are hard pressed for good tales, this far north. Would you come with me to the hall to tell the good people of Morganplorgg your story." He bowed as cordial as he knew how.

Ailsa hoped that she could find a man so fine down here, but this one was nice as well.

"Thank you," was all she could stammer out.

The young man took her bag with the few positions that she had in it and walked her towards the hall.

Kris watched them go inside from the edge of the village. It was best to make sure that she would be okay before he left her. Besides the darkness would now hide him, as he readied to go get his brother and sister. Kris lifted the enchantment of invisibility. He needed all his concentration for his mind to locate a place near the slaver camp and to open the portal to it. Kris felt the area around the slaver's camp, looking with his mind to be close, but not too near the great hounds that the slavers used for watchdogs. He found a spot, out of the wind, on a ridge above the winter camp, but it wasn't easy. The Vikings had obviously thought about the approaches to their settlement. The central building was part armory and part barracks. The great long boats had been positioned to block any ships that could make it that far up the shallow river from the sea. Kris had wondered how the huge longboats could travel in less than water knee deep. His curiosity caused his mind to go to the closest one. 'Ah, these ships had even a shallower draft than any that Sven had built,' Kris thought to himself. 'Enough sightseeing' he chided himself. Kris refocused his attention and directed his mind to a place across the river and up a steep bank, 'perfect' he thought.

Kris reached out with his mind pulling his body into the space between space and towards his hiding place above the raiders' camp.

"Well Jack, is it going to be worth your time to sit here and record the story or do you want to get four weeks of free coffee instead?" Olaf looked at me quizzically as he set down his empty mug.

"You win," I gave in to his amazing ability to spin a tale. I'd forgotten all about the bet. "You tell a mean story," I confessed. "I thought that this was going to be some fluff about... well never mind. I'll concede, but it doesn't mean I'll let you win at backgammon." I finished, trying to retain some of my dignity.

Olaf laughed and went to go put his mug back on the shelf that the regulars used to keep their personal coffee cups and tea mugs. I watched him as he left the coffee shop then, I packed my tapes and recorder as two young couples waited impatiently for me to exit the booth.

The Rune Stone called Hail

Chapter 4
The Raiders

The next Saturday was much like the last, with the ritual of me getting my coffee, Olaf getting his tea and the setting of the game board without much talking. I watched the gray skies out the window, ferryboats coming and going from the waterfront, carrying cars over to the Olympic peninsula, while Olaf got his drink just right. Once all the preliminaries were out of the way, I had to challenge my storyteller, Olaf, on at least one small point.

"So I have to ask," I started.

He looked at me like I was a bothersome child.

"Just one?" My storyteller asked nonplussed.

"Well, I checked on a few little details that were in your story," I said offhandedly. Olaf's eye lids went to half closed, sort of that John Wayne movie squint, the one that the Duke would get, right before he shot someone.

"Well, how is it that Kris and Mary had Christian names?" Hey, I thought it sounded reasonable.

"You know, I never thought to ask my mother. I would assume she heard them in Constantinople. Now, as usual you're getting ahead of the story." Olaf chided. "I'm sure even more questions will come up and I will answer them in due time and if I don't, then we can always go for a question and answer session, though I'm loath to do it." His reply sounded like a teacher that had taught the same subject for far too long.

"Okay, that seems fair, I just wouldn't want anything to go unanswered. You know, for the sake of the story." I added.

Olaf looked out the window for a minute, with a far off gaze at the Olympic Mountains that spanned the western horizon.

"Yes, for the story," he looked back at me, "Roll your dice," the old man said, starting the backgammon game.

"Okay, but just one more question?" I asked quite nicely. He nodded as a reply.

"So what did Anika's children do for a thousand years?" I asked quizzically.

"We all had a part to play, I took care of the reindeer at times, Kris was a saint twice, well sort of, we should cover that topic. Of course, you know about Saint Nick, but he was also another Saint. But I'm getting way ahead of myself here."

"So he was Saint Nicholas and some other semi-famous people that didn't have their pictures taken." I asked suspiciously.

"Well no, besides we generally stayed out of the public life, instead we had our own little community, so to speak." Olaf looked reminiscent.

"Yeah, at the North Pole," I interrupted. "These trips to the outside world, did all three of you go together or one at a time? Was Mary anyone famous?" I was very curious.

"Look up Babouschka, and Lady Belfana, in Russian and Italian myths respectively." He replied.

"What about you? Were you anyone I'd have heard of, or did you do anything of historical note?" I wanted to know.

"I traveled the seas and went to remote areas, city life is a taste I've only recently acquired in the last five hundred and fifty years." He said bristling.

"So what, did you just shovel reindeer crap for a five hundred years or did you know anyone famous?" Now I was goading him, waiting for him to slip up.

"Charles Dickens, he was a good man, way overburdened with his family responsibilities, so I helped him a little with *Scrooge*. It's not like he was a hack, but I had to encourage him to do revisions of over half the chapters in the book. Then, when he toured, giving recitations of the book, I coached him on doing the different voices for each part, it was my way of helping send Kris' message.

"What message?" I asked. Then, I threw his own words back at him. "It's later in the story. Okay, but Dickens?" I asked pointedly.

"You can easily tell with, that 'best of times, worst of times' fluff he did later. You're a writer, can't you tell the writing styles are different?" Olaf questioned me, in a lecturing tone.

"Well of course they're different," I replied, "but Dickens wanted a dark story and used an Oliver Twist touch on it." I countered

"That sounds like your college professor's lecture, not what you think," Olaf argued back.

"Fine, I'll read all three of Dickens' classics in the next two weeks and give you my opinion." That settled that, I thought, then something else came to mind. "I suppose that you wrote the famous, Yes Virginia, There is a Santa Claus editorial?" I was still looking for Olaf to crack under all the questions I was lobbing at him.

"Heavens no," he replied, "I ran the New York Sun at the time and it did come up at dinner. Frank Church and I talked about how it should be handled and when it should be published. The letter came in September and I thought it would be a treat if it were published in the December 24th edition. He didn't really want to put his name on it at first." Olaf finished sincerely.

I just kept quite waiting for him to start laughing and to tell me it was all a joke, well, he didn't.

Olaf continued, "At the time, it didn't seem as important as it turned out to be, but Frank realized that this could hurt the paper if it wasn't put into the proper frame of mind and I just steered him in a more... esoteric direction."

"Any other things you helped with in history?" I was almost afraid to ask. "Putting men on the moon, the gas-powered engine, new Coke? Wait did you have anything to do with the Coke ads in the thirties?" I quizzed.

"The artist was acquaintance of mine, that's all I need to say." Olaf smiled, finishing his tea; he got up to get the refill. I just sat there. It was all too neat of a package. I needed proof of something. I just didn't know what to ask him. The old storyteller returned and just sat there studying me.

"Hard pill to swallow?" Olaf asked knowingly.

"It's a lot to take on faith," I answered honestly.

"It's just a story Jack... isn't it?" He asked with a grin.

I sat there, he wasn't going to offer anymore information. The noise in the café rose and fell as I shifted position on the padded bench. After about a minute Olaf said, "Well, you've turned one question into about twenty, read Dickens if you must, but for now, roll your dice."

Kris had sighted the slavers' winter quarters in his mind's eye and opened up the way 'in between' to make the long journey to the raiders camp in an instant. Emsaph had shown him the techniques but hadn't apparently told him everything. As the space between Morganplorgg and the slavers' winter camp started to fold and warp, Kris saw that he wasn't the only one who traveled through the 'in between.'

The young man was fast approaching, a very hairy something, in this space that he'd come to think of as his own. The beast seemed as startled of him as he was of it. It didn't look like the creatures that Kris had been warned about that were near Ailsa's village, though it was at least twice as big as a man. No, this creature had the look of intelligence and kindness about its face and motioned for him to stop in the 'in-between' to talk or communicate in some way with the startled young man.

Kris lost his focus on his destination and tried to stop in the space 'between' space and time, but his Unicorn teacher hadn't taught him that maneuver. The young man phased out of the 'in between' without the clear picture in his head of the exact spot where he would land.

Kris 'landed' four feet in the air and slightly further up the steep embankment than he'd intended. Instead of the stealthy quiet approach Kris was hoping for, he fell out of the air on the icy snow which avalanched as he hit the ground. Kris tried to fall backwards flailing his arms, trying to slow his descent towards the river, but that just caused more snow to dislodge from the hillside. As he slid towards the icy stream, the sack of Rune Stones swung around and crowned him, knocking him out. His body continued on downward towards the riverbank, breaking small branches and snapping twigs as it went. The bag had enough force after hitting Kris in the head to complete its arch and ended up at his feet, getting lost in the snow of the small avalanche, as it stopped short of the river behind a large fallen tree.

All the noise that Kris had made, alerted the huge guard dogs over in the winter camp across the river and started them barking and growling. They left their nighttime resting place, out of the wind, but near the slave pen and gathered directly across from where all the noise had come.

The Viking slavers locked up their watchdogs during the day so that the slaves could work. Then, when all the labor was done, they would throw blood or cooking fat on the slaves before locking them up for the night. So if a slave managed to break out of the pen, the half-starved dogs would have a little extra to eat. It was a very effective way to control their captives and remind them at all times of their place in the slavers' society.

The mongrels had all gathered at a spot directly across from the fallen tree where Kris' unconscious body had finally stopped. The Viking raiders came out of the their meadhall armed for battle, though they were already half drunk. Nobody had ever attacked the camp and the slavers never came out of the warm hall in the cold winter night air if they could help it. If they heard a slave scream, it was beneath their concern. But, the fierce barking was something new and the slavers didn't like surprises.

Bjorn, the leader, signaled to his second Tor, to follow him as he kicked his way through the pack of starving mongrels, leaving the more inebriated Vikings on the shore with the dogs. The two slavers cautiously waded across the frigid knee-deep water, Bjorn with his sword drawn and Tor with an arrow notched in his longbow. They scanned the opposite bank of the river looking for any sign of movement, but all was quiet. Tor could see the avalanche that Kris had started, it cleared a swath from the top of the embankment to a fallen log near the rivers' edge. The path was easily visible in the waxing moonlight. Tor motioned to his commander who nodded and gave the closing circle sign meaning that they would separate and come up the bank from opposite ends of the fallen tree to hopefully surprise anyone who would be hiding there. It didn't look like much cover to Bjorn. Maybe a yearling stag had lost its footing up on the ridge and had killed itself on the way down. The two friends were more than a little shocked to find a thinly dressed red-haired teenager asleep on the other side of the log. Bjorn jerked him up grabbing the young man's neck. But, instead of intimidating him to get some answers, The slaver captain saw that Kris was unconscious. Tor rescanned the top of the ridge. Nobody would be out at night in only a shirt and some breeches. The stranger's shirt didn't look that warm either, which meant that there was a camp near by, an enemy camp.

The two men nodded at each other and signed the same suspicions to each other. Bjorn sheaved his sword and carried the unconscious lad back across the river with his second covering their retreat, bow at the ready.

The dogs were pushed back and herded towards the slave pen. The drunken slavers that had waited on the shore, followed quietly behind their leader to the meadhall.

The hall wasn't built as well as the great mead hall that they had raided in Kris' village. It was smaller and had been shoddily made; a dirt floor with the one large table took up the center length of the room. Furs and animal skins covered the benches that ran along the walls in the long house. The slaver women were gathered around the large fire at the far end when their mates returned. The women were tending to the dinner of several large pieces of mutton and some turnip soup that bubbled in a large cauldron off to one side of the fire. Others were melting snow in a large kettle to soak grain for porridge for the next morning's meal.

The old wise woman had told the other women of the village that if the slavers raided the village with the red-haired witch, that only evil would come from the river. So they took the extra time and effort to melt the snow instead of drawing the water from the wide stream. The men didn't care as long as the food appeared at the right times.

Bjorn called out to his latest wife to bring him some ale, then he had the more sober of his men get ready to stand watch out in the bitter night air of the extra long winter.

Kris awoke to find himself with the large boot on his chest, which was attached to the man who had led the raid on his village. The commander stared down at this strange young man that somehow looked familiar.

"How many men in your camp, boy?" the half-drunk slaver spit at him.

Another man came in the long house with a very large hound.

"This will make him talk," the besotted Viking slurred, bringing the hungry beast closer to its next possible meal.

While Kris was still under the boot of his captor, one of the women poured some mutton juice from the dinner kettle on his new clothes. The half-starved mongrel pulled on the lead around its neck eager to eat the gravy-covered boy. The leader lifted his foot off of Kris' chest. At last the young man could breathe again. He rolled away from Bjorn, nearer to the banked embers of the cook fire. The man holding back the dog produced an evil grin of half missing teeth and released the hound. Kris saw the dog racing at him in slow motion, when he was back at his own village so many years ago, he'd heard the storyteller say that your life flashes before your eyes at moments like this, but something about this fight seemed familiar to Kris. Like he had seen it in a dream. The animal leaped at the boy's throat ready to get a decent amount of food for once in its life.

Kris couldn't believe his eyes, he saw his arms actually reaching out to grab at the front legs of his would-be devourer. The Vikings only saw a blur of the lightly dressed boy grabbing the legs of their meanest hound and somehow twisting and flipping at the same time, threw the hungry mutt into the banked embers of the fire.

Two large cries rang through the hall. One from the slavers and one from the dog who thought he was being given an easy meal, only to find another cruel punishment at the hands of a human. The mongrel wasn't going to allow his gravy soaked meal to get away that easily though. The dog jumped forward, keeping low this time until he could get within striking range. Kris saw his own leg shoot out, connecting with the side of the dogs' head, disorienting it. The young man then fell upon the animal like a wrestler grabbing its neck to control the dog's fangs. The hound was beside himself, so hungry, with one of the slaves covered in tasty drippings and he couldn't move any closer to have a bite. The boy had expertly locked the hound's muscles, not allowing even a nibble. The dog howled in frustration, then really howled as his body was thrown back in the fire. Defeated, the animal moved off snarling. He'd bide his time, the humans had to sleep sometime, then he'd feast on the boy if he got the chance.

"Well, if we knew you'd be worth gambling over..." the slaver commander started. "Put him in with the rest of the slaves." Bjorn commanded, looking closely at Kris' clothes for the first time.
"Only a fool would try to attack our camp!" The leader said with bravado. "This whelp probably ran away from a little hard work."

This was good enough of an answer for most of the warriors who were more interested in finishing off the keg of mead, than fighting out in the cold of the extra late winter night.

"You'll soon know your place here, boy." Bjorn snarled at Kris.

Tor, the captain's second grabbed the red-haired young man roughly and lead him out of the warm hall and into the cold.

Kris let his eyes adjust to the moon lit night. The slaver was half dragging him to a poorly made pen filled with ill-fed slaves huddled together to keep warm. This was the same pen he had seen in his dream on his first night back in civilization. Tor shoved the young man into the crowded pen and headed back to the warmth of the meadhall.

The people of Kris' village didn't recognize him. He had only been gone for a couple of months in their time, but he'd been away for years thanks to the Norns. The group looked at the newcomer with suspicion. Lightly dressed as he was, in good shape and he didn't have the under fed, gaunt look of a slave. Something was suspicious. One of the older women, Thyra was her name, as Kris recalled, came forward to size up this new potential threat.

"Who be you to come among us!" The tone of her voice told Kris much of her suffering. In the short time he'd been gone, the people of his village had been turned from the peace loving kindred he'd known into a feral mob. He'd have to go slowly with this or he'd be dead by morning.

"Calm yourself woman, Kris said gently. "If I were here and be a slaver, would I be covered in the grease and blood, a meal for the dogs." He firmly replied.

He'd show no weakness, 'just calmly reply from a position of strength,' thought Kris. But Thyra wasn't finished with him.

"You come here lightly dressed, upsetting our masters' dinner?" She asked slyly, if this was a test she was sure to pass it, calling the vile slaver's her masters. Bile rose in her throat to say it, but better that, than be fed to the dogs.

"Indeed as you see, woman." Kris replied truthfully. He then sat down on the cold ground and leaned up against the wall.

"You wouldn't want to be doing that stranger," a man said. "The dogs will snap at you between the boards and you'll bleed to death before you know what's happened." The familiar voice finished.
It was Joar, the blacksmith of Haven; a very tired and beaten down Joar, but the deep base voice held a note of kindness.

"Thank you..." Kris caught himself, he didn't want to start calling everybody by their names, it would frighten them and that wouldn't help anybody. "Friend," he finished.
Thyra wasn't going to trust this newcomer until she could see what he was to the slavers. Maybe he was being punished, having to sleep out here with the slaves. Too many unanswered questions ran through her mind. Let

that old fool Joar offer advice. It was his daughter that had brought down this ill fortune on the rest of the village. Right then, she could be back in her long house with her children helping her make the evening meal of mutton stew; waiting for her husband to return with more firewood.

Her husband, the word gnawed at her mind. Durin was a good man and they'd loved each other deeply. Yet, to be so happy and to watch him die at the hands of the slavers still haunted. Killed because he was one of the last fighters to surrender after Anika had been taken. So long ago... now she was reduced to this, fighting for each scrap of food that was raided from her village.

'Dear Odin... why have you punished us so,' she constantly thought to herself during her waking hours. Thyra moved back into the group to keep warm, but kept a watchful eye on Kris. No one else came forward to question him and since he didn't try to come any closer to his former friends and kinfolk, they left him to his own thoughts.

'Well, wouldn't the Unicorn be laughing at my current state of woe,' Kris chuckled to himself. 'How did I lose the bag again?' He questioned himself. The last half-hour had gone by in a blur. 'I must have dropped it somehow. Wait, what was that beast that was in the in-between?' Kris had started to piece things together.

He slowed his breathing and deepened it to fully clear his mind then, thought of the Rune Stones. Emsaph had imparted many gifts to Kris, when he was a young boy back in Asgard. A link to the stones was one of those gifts. Kris reached out with his mind casting for a feeling of their power. There... across the river, behind a fallen tree.

'Well, at least the slavers hadn't gotten their hands on them, not that they would be able to use them.' He mused to himself.

Before Kris and the Unicorn had parted company, Emsaph had told him that the stones were only 'keyed' to Kris and his bloodline. So they would be of no use to the Viking slavers. But Kris was glad he wouldn't have to go through his captors to get the sack of Rune Stones back.

When he came out of his revelry, he noticed that Joar was still standing slightly apart from the group. This was either to guard them from Kris or the dogs that prowled around the enclosure that Joar and the other men had been forced to build to keep themselves in at night, away from the hungry mongrels. Joar stepped forward and motioned to the young man to move towards the far wall away from the rest. Kris got up to stretch and slowly headed in the direction that the old blacksmith had been motioning Kris closer. After a short while, Joar started checking the enclosure's walls to see if they would keep out the dogs. No one paid any attention to his actions; it was something he did every night. When Joar got close to Kris, he pointed out to one of the nearest of the dogs that could be seen in the low light, commenting on how vicious it was. Kris nodded in agreement saying that was the very hound that the slavers had used on him.

"Do tell," Joar asked, openly curious. Kris relayed an abbreviated version of waking up in the hall and the rough questioning of him by Bjorn, the leader of the slavers. Joar didn't press the strangely dressed young man about showing up on the other side of the river. While Kris' clothes were a little big for him, he wasn't wearing a sleeved jerkin of thick wool that even the slaves were allowed to keep in this long, cold winter. Maybe they're punishing the boy, Joar thought to himself.

In a lower tone, the blacksmith queried. "I notice you sit on the cold ground and breathe in a way that... well, I've only seen one other not bothered by the bitter night air. She was a woman from our village, she had hair as red as yours." Joar finished, his comments trailing off to a mumble. He still kept pointing off in the darkness, as if pointing out another mongrel to watch out for. Kris felt a lump in his throat. The Norns or maybe it was that Unicorn that had blocked out the memory of his mother, when he had been with them. All those memories came flooding back in an instant. The last one still vivid in his mind of his mother tied to the mast of Bjorn's ship and he and his siblings tied in the bottom of the boat. All he could do was nod his head. Kris hoped that Joar couldn't see the tears running down his cheeks in the low light. If the blacksmith could see him shedding tears over his mother, the man didn't say anything about it.

"Are you of her kin? Did she really escape? Many of us didn't believe what the slavers told us. We knew she didn't die the way they had said she did." Hope rose in the blacksmith's voice.

Kris just smiled, thinking of one of teachings that Emsaph had imparted to him, 'hope springs eternal, little one, sometimes it is all we have.'

The blacksmith took this for a sign that confirmed all he'd been wishing for, an escape. Joar was so happy, he almost lost control of his whisper. The young man was staying very quiet and Joar knew better than to push for information out of this stranger. Joar had never raise his voice to Anika, not that he'd ever needed to, but you didn't trifle with a witch, they were subtle and quick to anger. He'd seen what she was capable of during the raid on his village. If her children had been older and had the 'weirding way' of the Druids, they probably would have won the battle all by themselves. Finally, the young man spoke.

"All that can be done... will be done." Kris managed to keep his emotions in check. "Can you tell me of her children," Kris asked haltingly.

Happiness welled up in the old smith's heart; 'This must be one of her kin sent to free us' he thought to himself.

"Two of her children remain," the blacksmith started, looking for any sign that this information pleased the stranger. "They dare not hurt the little girl for they think that they can use her, if she grows up to have her mother's power. As for the remaining boy, he is pig-headed and has been beaten for any reason that the commander can think up." Joar explained further.

Kris smiled, 'That sounds like my brother,' he thought.

"Would you like to meet them?" Joar asked. The children were put in the little stone hut that the slavers had let them build to keep their children a little safer from the hounds. The blacksmith tried to appease the newcomer with the knowledge that at least some of his kin were safe.

"No, let them be, awaking them won't change a thing tonight." Kris replied offhandedly. Of course he wanted to see them, but it would do no good to raise their hopes just yet.

"Very well, my friend, we will see our plight on the morrow," Kris reassured Joar. "Don't worry about the dogs tonight." He finished the conversation and turned to connect to the Rune Stones to pull what little power he could, as tired and bruised as he was. The stones ethereal power warmed him to his bones then Kris set about playing with the dogs' minds, that there were fat lazy rabbits just beyond their sight. 'That will keep the mongrel dogs away from the pen tonight, so that people could get some sleep without hearing a low hungry growls from the watch dogs in their dreams,' Kris reasoned.

Joar had gone over to his kin and friends and told them, the walls would keep out the hounds for another night. The rest of the remaining villagers knew that Joar was as good as his word and settled in for the night on the tattered animal skins that the slavers had discarded. The former residents of the village of Haven, huddled close to one another for warmth, leaving the newcomer to sit by himself next to the wall.

The next day, the slaves were awoken as usual, by the yelling of their captors, calling the dogs back to the camp. The hungry mongrels came back only reluctantly, to the little scraps of food that they'd get, their training was just enough to call them back. It took a lot longer because of the big fat rabbits that were so close the hounds could smell them, but their prey was clever enough to keep eluding the dogs and had kept them hunting all night.

Tor collected Kris from the pen before the people of Kris' village lined up to do the chores for their masters. Firewood detail had been assigned to the stronger of the men. Women went to clean and the children were made to collect fresh snow in buckets, instead of getting the water from the river that was only yards away. Probably to keep them out of trouble the older survivors thought. Not knowing of the slavers wise-woman's prophecy of the evil that would come from the river if the commander went on that last raid against the people of the red-haired witch's village.

The dogs were rounded up and put in the pen that the slaves had used for the night.

'No sense wasting time to build a separate pen for the animals,' Bjorn had reasoned. 'It helped break the moral of the captives to let them know that they were thought of as animals,' the leader thought. The sooner the slaves spirits were broken, the easier it would be for everybody. As for the newest addition to the slaves, Bjorn would have to break him personally. It wouldn't do to have any thoughts of rebellion with Spring finally on the way. The leader thought he could get more answers out of the young stranger since Kris had seen how the other slaves were treated.

Bjorn had visited the old wise woman in her bed three days ago, just before she'd died. She said to watch for 'the spirits of the slaves to rise as did the Spring.'

'Why did the 'wise' have to talk like that?' Bjorn had thought to himself. 'Why can't they just say this or that will happen in a fortnight?'

It would have been easier on him, if she had just talked without all her vaguely poetical nonsense. And that's what he was trying for, the easiest possible way for him to lead his people. Now he still had the mystery of the young red-haired boy who seemed to appear out of nowhere. Bjorn hated mysteries. They always meant trouble for him. The last mystery the slaver commander had encountered had gone badly. The Druid witch he'd meant to take from Haven, the red-haired woman, his dead wife had hated so much. It had made his head hurt. Bjorn put the mistake out of his mind by counting his blessings.

Brenda, his wife who had obviously used a love potion on him to get him to raid a village in the dead of winter, was killed by the red-haired witch so that was a blessing really. And having his former father-in-law as his new blacksmith was a bonus. With all his years of experience in boat making and repairing, Joar was a highly valuable slave to have with the warring season coming up.

Bjorn had suffered great loses of men and boats at the hands of the witch and her village. The best things to happen from that raid was an expert smithy and the witch's daughter, hopefully she had her mother's powers. It was clear that the witch's son didn't. He was just a stubborn lad who liked to have his back whipped. His second in command, Tor, had said he'd had been better to have thrown Olaf overboard, like they did the other son.

The door to the hall opened and Tor came in with the new slave. The young man seemed to be no worse for wear, after having slept out in the slave pen. He seemed even more confident than after he'd thrown the mongrel into the fire last night. The leader's temples began to throb. Tor pushed the young man down opposite his captain at the table. The two just sat and stared at each other for a minute.

"Leave us," Bjorn finally said, after taking the measure of this new slave. Tor didn't know what his captain was going to do with the red-headed boy. Usually, Tor would hold the slaves' arms while Bjorn would beat them senseless. Maybe he had something else in mind for new slave.

"Leave us!" Bjorn bellowed to all in the hall. The women completed breakfast and the snow was melting for the turnip soup for dinner, so they didn't need to be there except to keep warm. The women left without a word. Tor was the last to leave. Then, he stood guard outside the door so that no one would disturb the interrogation. For what seemed like hours, the two men, Tor and Kris, just sat across from each other. Bjorn thinking he was beating the truth out of the young boy but in reality he just sat there while Kris put false memories into the leader's mind.

With the raider's commander in a trance, Kris pulled even more of the power from the Rune Stones to look into this murder's mind. Viewing all that Bjorn could show him of; Brenda's need to capture his mother; Brenda showing the power hungry slaver commander how it would benefit him to raid the village even if it were against people of the same clan. How and why he had killed Petr, Kris' father and the loss Bjorn felt as he saw the witch and that damn magic herb chest float away in the maelstrom. All this and more, until he could understand the man who had killed his father, destroyed his family, and enslaved his village.

Killing Bjorn wouldn't bring back his parents, Kris could hear Emsaph in his head with all the reasons that this man, this killer, was not to be killed. Memories of what happened at Asgard with Odin and his son Thor, flashed through the young man's mind.

'Did that make killing the host of frost giants and the hated Loki worth it?' Kris knew that evil begets evil, he'd heard over and over, looking into the mind of yet another brutal man with a might makes right mentality. It just made the young man sick to his stomach to see the world as such a rotten place. If he killed all such men, Kris knew that others would step up to take their place. What could he do? Nothing at that moment, he couldn't undo the past. Kris had to somehow free his people and fast, the man guarding the door was listening and not hearing much, Tor would soon look in, even against his better judgment, to see what was going on. Kris saw a glimmer of an idea in a memory of his capture.

The door to the meadhall was roughly pushed aside and Tor had to jump out of the way as Bjorn tossed the young slave to the ground. The commander had a look of self-satisfaction on his ugly mug.

"Well if you're worthy of joining our village and will fight for me unto death, obey me or my second," he nodded to Tor, "then we can use you during the next war season, but first a small test." The leader grinned with malice.

Tor knew that the tests the leader would give a slave, who wanted to fight for the village were very harsh indeed. What better way to recruit then within your own ranks and with some training the young man could come in handy in close fighting. The leader half lifted half pushed the young man towards the river's edge. In winter, the test usually started with having the slave cross the river. When he was good and soaked to the bone, they would make him work very hard for the rest of the day. Then, stay up for the full watch of the night still in the wet clothes. It would definitely show if the candidate was serious about the position.

"Tor, notch your bow." The Bjorn ordered.

Tor already knew the drill, he would shoot a couple of arrows into the far shore and the slave would have to remember where they fell and find them quickly.

'It was a good test for eyesight as well,' Tor thought.

He fired three arrows, at length into the under brush of the far shore. Bjorn threw the young red-haired boy headfirst into the cold water. Kris struggled and choked in the cold clear water as he surfaced and got his feet under him. It was more for show than anything else. Since he'd linked up with the Rune Stones, he would be warm enough. But Kris was new to controlling the stones of power, he needed to be able to touch one to get his plan in motion. Kris only had control of the leaders mind and that was using up what power he could pull from the Rune Stones at a distance. Tor still had a very deadly bow and a quiver of arrows, so Kris played his part in the game.

The other raiders stopped what they were doing and came to see if the newcomer was going to drown in the cold water before the test even really got started. They watched the young man splash around and trip a couple of times getting out of the water on the far bank. The snow had drifted deep where Tor had shot his arrows so that Kris was digging with both hands, just to stay upright on the steep bank. This made the raiders gleeful while most were born in the village, all had to go through this ritual or one just as hard, to show the leader they had what it took to be a warrior.

An arrow swished by Kris' left ear.

"Be sure to get that one as well, boy!" Tor yelled across the river.

Laughter arose at Kris flailing about trying to get to cover in case there were more archers shooting at him with less accuracy than Tor. Finally, Kris was reaching the last arrow, the one that was just in front of a fallen log that had collected a huge snowdrift behind it. Kris then had his chance. If he was going to do anything to help the slaves he'd better do it quick.

Kris made a production out of pulling out the last arrow by making it seem harder than it was. As it came out, he fell backwards out of sight of the raiders and more importantly out of sight of Tor's aim. Quickly, he dug for the stones. He needed to touch one to jump to the in-between.

Yelling came up from the far side of the river. First, it was laughter, then it was anger. Bjorn didn't remember why he was out here next to the deep stream. The last thing he remembered was sitting in the longhouse across from the young slave he'd meant to break.

"What the..." was all he got out before his second ran into the cold river bow drawn and commanding the rest of the men to arm themselves. It seemed that no one was following Bjorn's orders anymore. Men scrambled to get their longbows and axes. Within a minute, most had returned, the rest encircled the slaves and waited for their next order. Bjorn bellowed at Tor.

"By Odin's left eye, what is happening here!" the leader bellowed.

Tor ignored his captain, something wasn't right there. Had they all been bewitched? Why send a new slave to the very place where he could be out of their reach? Bjorn would have to wait for an explanation for a breach of his authority. For all Tor knew, his commander could still be under the spell of that red-haired whelp. As Tor finished making it to the other side of the river, the other bowmen pulled back on their own bowstrings ready for combat. Tor searched the snow bank where the boy had fallen but there were no tracks to be found, no hole to be discovered.

'Bjorn was going to have a big headache over this mystery,' Tor thought to himself. He checked to make sure the bowmen were covering him and the hillside, then headed back as fast and quiet as he could.

Bjorn stood there bewildered by what had just happened. Tor had never tried to usurp his authority and how did he get out here without remembering it. Did he have a brain fever? Oh, he could feel a headache coming on right then. With Tor again on slaver side of the river, the men formed their defensive battle position by overlapping the edges of their broad, thick wooden shields. Both Tor and Bjorn were glad that the training of the men was so effective that they did it without having to be told. Tor looked to his leader then for commands.

"Back to the hall." Bjorn, then in command of his senses, fell into his lead roll again. He called for the women to take cover and the rest of his men to guard the slaves and release the hounds.

'Let their keen senses alert his men.' Bjorn thought to himself. 'I've lost enough men, good and bad in the past two seasons.'

Kris had expected the slavers to withdraw in their battle formation.

'They were afraid but really what were they afraid of, he reasoned?' A young boy who disappeared out of their reach? No, they were afraid of what they couldn't control. That's what would defeat them, not some superior force of imaginary men who would do to their village what they had done to Haven. Kris watched the men retreat back into the longhouse leaving a semicircle of guards to watch the far shore. The slavers would regroup soon enough. Bjorn would see to that, once he had his wits about him and Kris couldn't influence him anymore without Tor becoming suspicious. So, Kris decided to stir up a little chaos from the 'in-between.'

In the realm between time and space, the 'real world' had a haze that formed around people and objects. Due to Emsaph's dream teaching, the young man understood that around people, different colors meant different emotions and temperaments. The color around the guards was a sickly red, meaning fear. Kris would have to use that fear to free his people.

He moved at the speed of thought over to the slave pen. The dogs had been released so it was easier to herd the slaves back in the pen to free up the men to come to the meadhall and help to defend the village. The men at the river wouldn't have used battle tactics if there hadn't been a great danger, the raiders who had been watching the strangeness unfold from over near the slave pen agreed.

Joar and the others were all looking in the direction of the river where the boats were beached and tied off.

"If there is an attack, the boats are what I'd go after," Joar said, matter-of-factly. Kris stepped out of the in-between at the back of the group. He would need Joar to pull off this plan to get everyone away. He'd already found a place that was far away from the slavers, in fact it was far away from just about everything. Kris just had to think of a way to keep the raiders camp busy and get his people away without frightening them anymore than they already were. The 'in-between' was tricky if you weren't ready for it and fifty screaming people would make it impossible for Kris to get them all anywhere safely. From the back of the group, he called to Joar, "Are you ready to leave this place?"

It was a clear voice that cut through the murmuring of the other people in the pen. All turned to look at him. Joar was happy to see this young man alive. The blacksmith assumed that he'd been killed by one of Tor's arrows.

Kris' brother Olaf, saw his younger brother for the first time in months but because Kris had aged ten years Olaf didn't recognize him. As over-worked and underfed as the rest were, none but Joar thought that this stranger was related to them in any way. Joar was the only one who had guessed correctly. He was better fed and had his wits about him more than the others, because the slavers valued Joar's blacksmith skills and he'd never given up hope that somehow they could escape one day.

Back at the meadhall, Bjorn was finalizing his battle plan. If the young stranger had bewitched him and was just here to size up the village's defenses, he would have sadly underestimated the amount of arms that Bjorn had stored away in the benches that lined the wall of the meadhall.

There had been some debate over the amount spent on the weapons at last midsummer's trading festival but all that talk had stopped with the provisions acquired from the village of his newest slaves.

Fearful yelling came from the direction of the front door of the mead hall as Bjorn recognized the voices of the guards he'd posted. Cries of the darkening sky and of a sudden night that was falling on the camp. Bjorn grabbed his own warlord sword and headed out to see this new magic.

Tor had pushed the door wide and Bjorn could see the daylight wane, though it was it was still a bright cloudless day.

"What in the seven hells are you talking about...!" the commander started then his own eyes fell dim as though twilight was happening all at once. Then the leader saw only blackness... only there were no stars, no moon and no light coming from the meadhall's fire when Bjorn turned around. It was as though the whole village had gone blind at once. The leader found it hard to quiet his people, frightened as they were; he had to steady his own voice to be understood by his men.

"Is anyone hurt? Has anyone been attacked?" He called out in the most steady voice he could muster.

Odin! He hated mysteries. No one could say that they were injured, so he called for those who could hear him to find the outer walls of the meadhall and follow the sound of his voice back into its shelter. People hurried to follow orders that seemed reasonable. At least, their leader hadn't lost his head.

The slaves had left the pen as soon as the yelling had started and following Joar, they made for one of the long boats as fast as they could, not worrying about their captors anymore. Only two slaves stayed behind. Kris was keeping all of the slavers and their dogs busy with what can best be thought of as, 'a hood of blindness.' As for his brother Olaf, he was giving a beating to the slaver who had liked to punish him the most. Kris pulled his little, older brother off of the screaming man and pushed him towards the boat.

"One more hit, just let me hit him one more time, real good." Olaf said, murder dripping from his voice.

Kris could not deny his brother anything so Kris handed the stick back to his brother and said lowly,

"Hit him once for Anika and once for Petr as well." The older boy said to Olaf. This stunned the boy. But questions could wait; he had some whacking to do. The man started screaming again, more from the not knowing where the beating was coming from due to his sudden blindness, than from the pain inflicted by the small boy with a thin tree branch.

Finally, Kris herded his brother to come with him, past the meadhall where the blinded guards were now swinging at any noise they heard and yelling battle cries to frighten whoever or whatever was out there.

Joar separated his fellow villagers in two groups; one group to each of the most well-provisioned boats. He had gotten the gist of Kris' plan. And as long as Kris,the young witch, could keep the slavers off their backs, Joar knew that there was a chance for his people to be free once again. That would put renewed vigor in their veins. Sure enough, the two groups had readied the boats in record time. Nothing like freedom to lighten the heart and load, off of the backs of the soon to be ex-slaves. Joar saw the last two of his people come over from near the meadhall. The older redhead standing next to Olaf the younger, of course when seen next to each other, Joar saw the family resemblance. This must be a cousin from a distance clan of the Druids sent there to save what was left of Anika's family. Joar laughed at the strangeness of it all. It was a long and happy laugh, the kind a free man makes. Joar waved to Kris to signal that all was ready, but the longboats were almost totally beached. A high tide was needed to push off the boats, the witch boy had promised Joar that it would come early today.

One of the other men grabbed Olaf's arm and raised him up onto the ship. Kris waved back to Joar signaling him to make a little speech that Kris had had the blacksmith, and appointed leader, make if they made it this far.

"Everyone is to get as low as you can and cover your heads once we are underway. The arrows of our enemies will be close behind us," he announced.

The men in the other boat helped cover their own charges with skins and the extra thick sails the Vikings used, to help keep them out of harm's way. The river seemed to dam up just around the boats. Within a minute, the ships began to float. The men pushed with oars to get the large crafts into the deeper part of the river. All this had been prearranged by Kris and Joar a head of time. As soon as they reached the deepest part of the river, they positioned the boats to head down stream and out to sea, which was about three leagues away. Men from both boats threw lines to bind the two boats together. It was nothing that they had ever seen done before, but the witch boy had gotten them that far.

Kris waited for the boats to get around the bend before he picked up the sack that was in a small skiff, beached with the remaining boats. He turned to the village where the slavers had heard the noise of the slaves taking their boats and couldn't do a thing to stop it. Kris heard them yell in anger at their workforce being taken from them, and fear of being permanently blinded. Cursed for the raid on members of their own clan. Kris listened a while longer until he could see, using his second sight in the in-between, that the ships were close to the coast and the sun was waning in the western sky. Twilight would soon be come. Kris walked along the beach, down the line of boats, large and small, touching each one, which burst into flames as he passed.

One more deception and he could be free from these slavers for good. Kris touched one of the Rune stones in the bag, then thought of the in-between and it folded around him like a warm blanket.

In the meadhall the slavers eyesight returned to them all at once. Cries of joy arose, then cries of anger when the men poured out to see two of their long boats missing and the rest burning down to the last board.

"They couldn't have gotten far," Bjorn shouted as he ran for the last remaining boat, a little skiff that remained unburned. No one followed him. He turned to look at his men. Tor called to his leader.

"Let them go, old friend. They have the weirding way about them and I like being able to see." Tor said wearily. Grunts of approval followed by other men who would never have spoken this way to Bjorn.

The leader cursed at the rotten luck that had befallen him. Not realizing the suffering that Kris could have brought down on his village.

Back on the boats that were slowly escaping, Joar was having difficulty convincing the other men to keep the boats tied together.

"We must go North while you go South." The men of the other boat argued. "If the witch boy didn't burn their longboats that means we should each go a different direction, maybe half of us will be able to escape." The man with the knife in his hand said, as he started to cut the ropes.

"All will be safe if you do as I say!" Kris' voice came from the back of the boat. Joar just looked dumbfound at the young witch boy in the stern of his boat. They had left him on the shore back at the village.

"The slavers are close behind now, you must get under the skins and sails," Kris commanded them. "I will put a spell on the boats and as they sail West we shall sail Eastward. The men didn't understand the logic of the witch boy. They were just now sailing out into the West fall sea, There was no way to sail East, the Coast ran only North and South for hundreds of leagues and to sail back up the river was madness. Kris saw that these sailors needed a little incentive so he put the images of an unburned longboat full of angry slavers in the men's heads to scare them under the sail and out of his hair. As the sun finished setting on the West fall sea, Kris made sure that his people were all covered and touched the stone to open the portal to a land very far away.

"Well, that's enough for this week, take care." Olaf said, as he started to shuffle out of his side of the booth.

I stopped him before he got up to go.

"So you were that little boy beating that man with a stick?" I hadn't wanted to interrupt him, Olaf had a way of rendering the story that made me not want to break in during the good part.

"Yes, but I didn't want to confuse you by breaking from third person to first person, now did I?" He finished smiling.

I sat there having been beaten again by only one game chip, Olaf had gotten a lucky roll of the dice at the end of the last play of the game of our little backgammon tournament.

I watched him stride out of the coffee shop. My tape recorder clicked off as I gathered my things to go. 'Just a story,' I thought as I put my things into my backpack. 'I still have to read those Dickens novels,' I thought idly to myself as I headed home.

Kris Kringle's Workshop

Chapter 5
Kris Kringle & The North Pole

'd finished speed-reading the Dickens novels by the next Friday night. Though I didn't want to, I had to admit, the books could have been written by two different authors.

A quick biography check of Dickens revealed, that indeed he was greatly burdened by his family, just as Olaf had said. I tried to find the editor of the New York Daily Sun during the time of the famous, 'Yes, Virginia, There Is a Santa Claus' letter but it went out of business in the late forties. I couldn't find any pictures in the archives, so I still had nothing that could either prove or disprove anything that I had heard.

Then, sometime early Saturday morning, I finally caught myself obsessing, 'It's just a story, Jack,' I told myself. I knew it couldn't be true. I chalked it up to my journalistic need to find out the truth, that had gone just a little too far. Maybe, it was the left over frustration I'd had, when my story about the mayor's campaign scandal had gotten trashed. I slept a little, but still got up in time to make it to the Pike Place Market, tapes and recorder in my backpack, looking forward to seeing the old storyteller.

When I walked into the out of the way café, Olaf was at the sidebar where all the sugar, cream and coffee condiments were kept. He'd just finished pouring honey in his mug when he spotted me in line. He smiled at me and grabbed some extra sugar packets for us to use as the missing white chips on the backgammon board. I paid for my espresso and grabbed the game board and worked my way through the crowded little café to our usual table.

"You look like you stayed up all night," Olaf said flatly, as I got situated.

"Well I had to read those books and did some fact checking... it's a hobby." I replied tiredly.

"And... what did you find out on your reading and fact checking mission?" the storyteller asked with a bored expression on his face.

"That I should just shut up and quit trying to look for holes in your story," I said sheepishly.

I resigned to the fact that Olaf, whether he was a thousand years old or sixty, he could spin a yarn better than anyone I'd heard. The storyteller sat there looking smug, like I thought he would be, Olaf just looked at me waiting for my next question.

"Did you ever think of just going to Hollywood and dictate story plots for TV shows?" I asked. It blinked into my head, if I had a talent like that, I'd be on the first plane to L.A. to start my new career in a flash. "Okay, strike that, I don't even want to know." I came back to my senses quickly.

Hell, I could just hear him start in on how he helped Desi Arnez with the idea of camera placement and recording the I Love Lucy Show, starting a whole new era of television. I probably just couldn't stand to hear about it. I didn't want to go looking for facts and pictures all of the next week at the newspaper on things that he'd tell me, that I probably couldn't corroborate.

Olaf smiled and said, "You don't want to know what happened in Hollywood in the twenties, thirties or fifties?" He was trying to see if I'd really stopped being a reporter for one day a week and just be a listener.

"No, no, let's just concentrate on Kris Kringle this week. I'm sure you'll tell me why he has a different last name than you and I can only assume that he was headed for the North Pole which was far away from the Viking slavers' camp." I finished, and then I pushed down the record button on my tape recorder and took a sip of coffee.

"Actually that's a myth, Kris never did have a workshop at the North Pole, it was in Siberia." Olaf corrected me. "How Kris got his 'Kringle' last name... well, we'll probably be there in a couple of weeks, but it depends on how much we get through until then." He said, scratching his beard.

I arranged the pieces on the game board as he watched a car ferry come in to dock from the peninsula. I stopped to see what he was looking at, but all I saw was the perennial dark gray sky and water that make up the view of the Puget Sound from Seattle.

Olaf turned his attention back to the game, "As I recall, you're behind by only two games?" he asked nicely.

The Siberian forest was thick indeed; the upper canopy was so dense in fact that it didn't allow the snow to get through to the ground. Most of the villagers from Haven sat near the base of one of the massive tree trunks while Kris went off to talk to the person who had been there waiting for him on the other side of the encampment.

'This red-cloaked local was apparently the leader or holy man for his own tribe.' Kris thought, as he approached the shaman carefully.

When the two ships full of villagers had 'popped' out of the in-between into the small lake near his settlement, Batu was waiting for them. The Shaman had known of the travelers that came from the Far West before the party had reached the small lake and sheltering trees of the great forest. The dream paths held a large disturbance that could only be, many unprepared minds being taken where they were not ready to go. The spokesman that approached him had flaming red hair of a demon man though he also had a kind youthful face.

'Well, this would make a good fire-story for the tribe when he returned home,' Batu thought to himself.

The shaman raised his arms in a sign of greeting to the stranger. Kris did the same arm movement and sat on the ground in much the same way that the Shaman did.

'Good, he must be their holy man as well, though he looks a little young to have all of his tribe's trust,' Batu thought to himself.

Kris made a motion of flapping his outstretched arms while he stayed seated, the local shaman nodded as a reply. After a few moments, the two had left their bodies and were floating on the dream paths. Pictures appeared before Kris showing the fear that Batu's village would have with the strange people that had appeared in their small lake. The strange boats each had a dragon's head carved into the keel of the ship, Batu didn't know what to make of them. Kris knew that his people couldn't stay there long, they would want to go back to their own village, destroyed or not, but the winters would get much worse and Kris didn't want to see them wiped out by disease or starvation. This mental picture he showed to his Siberian host.

The two reentered their bodies and Kris leaned forward to touch the shaman. Batu didn't pull back as Kris had shown him what he had wanted to try before they had reentered their bodies. The red-haired stranger touched the shaman's forehead and reached into his bag of magick rocks.

When Kris pulled away after a minute or so, he could speak the local language very well. He didn't want to scare the man who had actually been there to welcome them, but it would be easier to speak to him in his own language rather than gesture or go on the dream paths to communicate with his host.

The shaman listened to the story that Kris told him about saving the people of his village and picking a place as far away as possible to make good their escape. Batu had seen distant lands in his shamanic travels on the dream paths and had some information about the strange hairy beast that Kris had seen on his way to rescue his brother and sister.

"They are the Almas." The shaman told Kris, after letting him finish his story. "They live mostly in the dream paths, that they call the 'Astra.' But sometimes they take a shortcut and appear here where we live. Usually, they don't stay long, they prefer being with their own kind. Humans hold little interest for them. But if one tried to stop you to talk to you...well, that is a good sign."

Batu was impressed with this stranger. Kris had brought two boatloads of people safely from a distant land through the in-between realm, not in spirit... but physically. The shaman was amazed that anyone but the Almas could move through the dream paths and take their bodies with them.

The red-haired young man had done that and brought his people with him. All this and Kris had managed to peak the interest of the guardians of the dream paths as well.

'Very interesting' thought the shaman. Batu had had a few dealings with the Almas. Being the shaman of this region, it was his job to know all that might concern his people. The creatures used many of the forest paths in this area to go around dangerous places in their own realm.

Kris watched his kind host play catch up with all the implications that his tale held. The shaman was a quick study and brought the one question that hadn't been asked.

"So what happens now?" Batu assumed the stranger had a plan for the next step in this bizarre exodus.

"Well, I was kind of hoping that we could talk about that, this is your land to watch over and we didn't mean to trespass. I only chose this spot because this is near a gateway to the outlands that my teacher had shown me."

The Unicorn had given Kris a mental map of the natural portals to the other Realms of Asgard. This region of Siberia was the farthest portal away from the slaver's winter camp,that Kris could reach safely.

"How long are you to be here?" Batu was thinking of the logistics of the extra populous on the tribes reindeer herd as well as local mushrooms and what little crops they had managed to squirrel away in their stone lined root cellars.

"We will not be tresspassing on your land for long, Kris saw what the shaman was thinking and quickly tried to put his new host at ease, "We have brought our own food with us and if you will let us," Kris made a sweeping gesture towards the boats, "We would like you to share our drink." Kris pointed to the barrels of strong spirits on the back of one of the ships.

"I think that will smooth over any problems with my leader or my people." The shaman replied smiling.

They then worked out the details, since the shaman was the only one of his tribe to see the strangers and knew that they were no threat to his people, he would go back with a small barrel of mead to make introductions. Kris would move his people further away from the Siberian Tungus tribe and set up a temporary shelter deeper in the great forest.

By the next day, Joar had calmed everyone's fears about the weird magic that they were experiencing. Kris had yet to tell them who he was and it wouldn't make things better if he did. So he played the part of one of his mother's distance relatives that wanted to help the people of her village. While the refugees had slept in a shelter made of the sails, roped to the tree trunks with bedding of old furs, Kris searched a little deeper in the thick forest and looked for a place to build a great meadhall, like the one back in Morganplorgg. He wanted to give the people from his village something that would be a comfort to them.

"Nobody wants to be a refugee.' Kris thought, as he searched for a perfect spot to build a place for them. He summoned up the picture of the town that he'd left Ailsa in to make her fortune and found a grouping of trees that were massive in girth and very close together. Kris decided not to use the power of the Rune Stones to make the large long house, instead Kris decided he would call up the Earth energy stored in the forest. The Unicorn had taught him to use the Rune stones to focus local energies to be formed by thought. That isolated area of the world would be a good testing ground for all those lessons that his teacher had put into his head back in Asgard.

Kris touched one of the Rune Stones, the one of hearth and home, then started humming softly the song of making that Emsaph had put in his mind. It was more complex that the singing lessons that his mother had made him practice, but having started his Druid training made holding the notes a lot easier.

Earth Power became visible in his eyes. He saw the currents that flowed in this ancient forest. Deep in the Earth the power had grown, now it slept and only Batu, the shaman of the Tungus tribe disturbed its dreams.

Kris reached down with his mind to call the power to wakefulness.

Slowly it came... thick and sweet in his senses, like cold honey that warmed to his bidding. The power that had lain silently in the great forest for so long, started to expand to his will, growing bigger and harder to control. With such a huge amount of energy to direct, Kris lost focus on the mead hall, the Power that was at his disposal was more than enough to build ten such halls. His mind drifted back to a time much happier that had bigger buildings. The great trees started to twist and groan as their natural growth was changed. Kris did not want to kill them. They had lives of their own, but he needed them to grow in a way that could house his people. The trees continued to twist and turn in and around each other. Doorways and windows appeared in the wood... the bark on the lower sections fell away revealing the beautiful grains of wood that molded to the thoughts of their shaper. Kris had thought that the structure might scare his kin because of its size and the fact that it was one great big tree.

Sizing up his handy-work Kris walked through the front door. Low benches lined the walls and storage space for boots and coats was off to one side. It was much like he'd imagined it, similar to one of his favorite mansions in Asgard where he and the Unicorn had played and explored.

Except it had strange scrollwork everywhere, running through the walls, tables and stairs. All the furniture looked as if it had sprung out of the floor, for it was part of the growing tree. Kris marveled at his handi-work, with the delicate scroll work that looked so familiar to him, it was all over the sweeping arches of the halls and rooms.

In the kitchen there was a rather odd looking table that stood in one corner. It was oblong, a little lower than could be easily used, with a hole in the center. This was to be the hearth of the house. The fully wooden house would need no fireplace if it had the proper heat source.

Kris went through his bag of Rune stones to find the one called Hearth. He placed the stone in the oblong hole in the low table and hummed a note until the wood closed over the Rune Stone completing the transfer of power into the structure of the house.

The 'tree house' would be heated without needing fire, using the power of the stone. The magick of the Rune stone wove its way through the veins of the wood, out to the shuttered windows and all the way to the stable at the far end of the great house.

'This should be more welcome than the tent that Joar and the men made out of sail yesterday,' Kris thought to himself.

But he was wrong... very wrong. The people saw the scrollwork that was like that on Anika's sea chest and took it for a bad omen. None but Joar would even come into the great house. Even though the blacksmith was impressed with the hot running water and indoor plumbing, he told Kris that his people had just been through too much and couldn't take much more. The young man was beside himself. Kris went back with the blacksmith to refugees roughly made camp and asked them what they wanted.

"To go home." was the cry from most.

"That place is gone to ash and the next winter will be hard, then after that unbearable. Until the whole fiord is full of ice and not even a snow hare could forage within leagues of the place." Kris tried to reason with them.

"We can't stay in this place, all seems unnatural here, we thank you for saving us... but we must live near the sea, it is our way." Joar said plainly.

Kris understood finally. "This is just a way stop for you all," he told them emphatically.

"The house is just for the next fortnight until you get your bearings. A holiday... if you will." This seemed to ease their spirits quite a bit. They'd thought that they had traded one master for another and they'd rather die than go through slavery again.

"Did I mention the great house has hot running water and indoor priv-ies." Joar said, trying to get even the holdouts to agree.

After that statement, most of the camp emptied out to get a look at this wonder where they could stay.

Joar lagged behind because Kris had motioned to him as the others were beating a path to their new spa.

"Where can we go if our township will be buried in snow with little to catch in our fishing nets?" the blacksmith wanted to know.

Kris had an idea, "Tonight, you and I shall go there and see that what I've told you is true, then we can consult as to what is best to be done from there, agreed?"

"Agreed," Joar said, spitting in his hand and shook Kris' as a sign that it was a deal that wouldn't be broken. "Now, I would really like one of those hot baths…" the blacksmith headed down the path after the rest of his kin.

After a time, Batu showed up with several of the warriors of the tribe to see these interlopers who had such strong beer. Kris explained that most had left camp to go bathe deeper in the woods. The hunters were more interested in the mead than anything else. The strangers didn't have any weapons and had women and children with them so the Tungus men didn't see any threat. Besides, Batu had been their shaman for twenty years and had never been wrong about the strange goings on in the deep forest East of their village. So with a few barrels of mead, the men headed back to give their report on the yellow and red-haired strangers.

The shaman stayed behind to talk to Kris.

"There was much movement in the power of the forest, last night." Batu said flatly. 'Best to not push this conversation into unfriendly terms' he thought. Kris knew that nothing would go on around here that Batu didn't know about.

"Ah yeah, I needed to build a more suitable camp for the short time that we will be staying here," Kris explained waving his hand around the camp made of sails and old animal skins.

"Show me this new camp…please. I would very much like to see it," the shaman said. Batu was interested in what could have disturbed the power that lay sleeping beneath their feet. Surely, anything would be better than the camp he was now seeing.

Kris led him to a small cleared space a little further east in the forest. At first Batu couldn't understand what he was seeing. He saw people through the windows and doors of the structure, it was as though the trees had swallowed them and the trees were stripped of bark had woven into a... words failed him, he'd never seen a home that had more than one story to it. He and Kris walked around the entire great house without saying a word. Kris watched the shaman take it all in; the sky bridges that connected the house to the steam sauna high up near the tree top, the huge stables at the far end of the house and the scrollwork that ran all over the outside. It was a bit much, but the energy that was called up had to be used or it would have been unsettled.

That could be bad for everybody. Wasted energy that pooled was like stagnant water. It would draw creatures and evil shamans to feed on the leftover power that Kris had called up from deep in the earth.

"Wondrous doesn't seem to cover it." The shaman finally spoke.

"It is a bit big, but it was my first house." Kris said, as an excuse for the excess. He still hadn't realized the amount of energy that the Rune Stones had channeled out of the Earth. Even with the training he'd had in his dreams in Asgard, it would still take practice using the stones to get the hang of them.

"We could teach each other much, my friend," Kris held out his hand. Batu knew better than to turn down such a valuable friendship though he didn't think he'd have as much to teach as to learn from this red-haired young man.

That night while Joar was sleeping, Kris escorted him on the dream paths back to the village they used to know. Cold winds blew into the fiord from the South, 'that had never happened' Joar thought to himself, as the two floated over the small valley that had been their home. Snow had started to cover over ash heaps that used to be houses, a smithy and a meadhall. Not a scorched stone of their fine village was left standing.

'Where do we go from here, my young friend?' Joar thought to his guide.

'I will show you a place that is far to the South with excellent fishing, good earth for crops and friendly people that will not try to enslave you.' Kris replied.

The two backed away from the planet so that Kris could show Joar where he was talking about exactly. Far down the coast even passed the kingdom of the Danes down into what is now known as France. In a small cleared area near the sea with large rocks to keep out any boats larger than a skiff. It had all the resources that a village could want but was remote enough not to be preyed upon by Viking raiders.

With that settled, the rest of the two weeks that the villagers stayed with Kris, were some of the happiest of their lives. Fresh hot bathes, in-door toilets and the Tungus tribe had given them all the reindeer that they could eat. More than a fair trade for the casks of mead and berry brandy that the Tungus had never tasted before in their lives.

As the people feasted, Kris got to know his brother and sister again. His brother watched intently as Kris performed magic tricks for the children. Olaf wanted to know everything about the place and how the hot water worked. Mary, on the other hand, was shy at the best of times, so Kris visited her in her sleep. The girl's dreams were all nightmares about seeing her father die. Over and over these scenes played out in Mary's mind. Olaf's dreams tended to be more of the time where they were all trapped on the ship. Sometimes they ended with Anika, their mother, going over-board. But most times, the dream ended before that happened.

Kris started to change his siblings dreams by stopping them before they became violent or giving them a happy ending. Adding to this, a spell of forgetfulness so that the pain that scarred their young minds, lessened each day. By the end of the two weeks, his siblings were much happier and played with the other children.

Finally, the time limit that the villagers had agreed upon had come. They were to be taken to this new home near the sea with all the details that Joar had promised them. There was fresh water, good land, eas-ily defendable, with good neighbors. They didn't want to go through an ambush again. Though they dearly loved the 'fairy spa,' as they had come to call it, they didn't feel at home there. It was too much strangeness for them, the stars weren't in the right place in the sky, and if they couldn't smell the salt air and hear the waves loll them to sleep, then they couldn't be at rest.

Kris had stepped up his presence around his siblings, the last two days that they were to be in Siberia, so that Mary and Olaf could get even more used to him. He would have to tell them his secret or they would go away with the rest of the villagers. Before the red-haired teenager could work up the courage to get them to one side, he felt a tugging at his consciousness, it was faint at first then a little stronger, after a time. His old teacher was coming with news of the Norns. Emsaph mindspoke from a long way off, like from the bottom of a deep cavern.

"Don't tell your brother and sister anything until I get there." That was the complete message. 'Didn't the Unicorn trust him to say the right thing?' Kris thought.

The camp was getting ready to be shifted back through the 'dream paths,' whatever those were. So people were reloading the boats with all they had used to set up the camp, sails and furs, cooking pots and wash tubs. When all was loaded, Kris was nowhere to be found. Joar sent runners to the great house and to the Tungus tribe to bring him to work his magick.

Kris had gone to the portal that wasn't very far from the tree house. He was waiting for his mentor to appear. The portal was just a small spring that came out of the ground and was slightly covered a large flat rock. The spring water ran down the hill towards the great house. Kris could hear the runners that had been sent, call for him to come back, but he wanted to be there when Emsaph came through.

The young man had so much to tell his mentor and looked forward to seeing the Unicorn that felt more like an uncle to him, than a dimension-skipping mythical creature. The runners from the refugee camp had searched the house by the time a shimmer of a small horse appeared not a hands breadth above the little spring at the portal between worlds.

The Unicorn solidified all at once over the spring water, then stepped gingerly down onto the dry earth as if stepping off an unseen pedestal.

Kris knew that his mentor was actually straddling two dimensions as he'd been standing in mid-air and then when he was on solid ground, Emsaph was actually there on Earth.

"You really have got to be a little more careful with those Rune Stones, Kris." The Unicorn mindspoke firmly into the young man's mind. "That little stunt of bringing all of your people half way across the world almost opened up the tear that we tried to fix."

Images flashed into Kris' mind of the hole that Odin had ripped back at the black mountain where he'd first gotten the Rune Stones. The mountain had been just a hill with an outcropping of granite near the sea. But when the god of Asgard had crushed the stone called Hail, Rune of destruction, the upheaval it caused pulled the rock out of the Earth then destroying the top of the mountain with its power. Kris watched it all unfold, ending with a smoking crater that was ringed with spires of scorched stone.

His mentor then showed Kris the damage that was caused by bringing the people of Haven to this far away land. Even though he'd been hundreds of leagues away from the Witch's Teeth, the power used to bring two boatloads of villagers, was enough to pull at the ethers that coursed over and through the planet, almost causing a rupture at the black mountain. Emsaph showed him of the seams of the tear that throbbed violently and looked as if they would break at anytime.

Kris knew that a 'sorry' wouldn't suffice. The healing of the breach between the worlds had never been done before, so there was no telling what would happen if the tear broke open, maybe it would not be reparable next time it happened.

'So that's why Emsaph had come to see me so fast,' Kris thought to himself. With all that had happened to him, it had seemed like a long time since he'd been with his mentor but it had only been a few weeks.

"Elphaba is fine, by the way," the Unicorn mentioned offhandedly. More images flooded the young man's mind. Creatures had attacked her as she stood between the Realms of three worlds, channeling the power to seal the holes that were much smaller than the one at the witch's teeth. She'd been hit with bolts of power that the Frost Giants of the frozen lands could wield, using their combined efforts to try to keep the doorway open.

"Elphaba will make a full recovery," his mentor explained further, "but she learned a valuable lesson about playing around with something she thought she could handle. Emsaph was going to turn the Norn's mistake into another of his lectures.

Voices called from not far off in the distance.

"Mage, the people are wanting to leave. You promised us that you would honor your word!" It was one of the villagers that had been sent to find their mysterious benefactor.

"Well, we mustn't keep them waiting, Oh, powerful shaman." Emsaph had taken the liberty of reading his young charge's mind to see what mess the young man had made of things. To his surprise, Kris had done quite well, the overuse of energy of the Rune stones notwithstanding.

Kris climbed onto his teacher's back as he was instructed, not knowing what the Unicorn had in mind. Emsaph asked if he could shepherd Kris in his use of the Rune Stones for the exodus of the people back to the other side of the world. The young man agreed, he didn't want to have the tear at the 'witch's teeth' burst open. The Unicorn was far more adept at directing and shaping such powerful energy than he was, maybe Kris could get a lesson in the practical application of using the stones, not just more of the theory of how to use Odin's powerful Runes.

The villagers were relieved to see Kris return to the lakeshore campsite with one of their runners who had been sent to go look for him. The young magick man was riding bare back on a small black horse; Emsaph had thought it best for Kris to disguise the Unicorn's horn with a glamour. 'No sense giving the people of your old village more to be disturbed about,' Emsaph had mindspoke to his passenger.

"The sun is setting, shouldn't we be off?" Joar asked the question that was on everybody's mind. "We thank you for letting us use your house, and for saving us, but we are anxious to go to our new home." The blacksmith was trying to voice the gratitude and concerns of his people without upsetting the redheaded magick wielder.

"Yes of course, I was summoning the power to send you to your new home. Not to worry, all is well." Kris relayed what Emsaph had told him to say. "It is easier to work this magic at sunset." Kris reminded them of the first trip through the in-between that was at sunset near the slavers' winter camp. It wasn't true, but the little lie would comfort them even more, hopefully.

Then, Kris instructed the refugees to get in the boats as before with the sails and furs over them as cover from the magick's of the in-between. This was a white lie as well, Kris knew, but it would be easier for Emsaph to put them all to sleep once they were under the sails. Normally, the Unicorn didn't have the power to effect much in this Realm of Asgard. But Emsaph could channel power through his young pupil who had been bonded to the Rune Stones. So as Kris raised his arms at the two Viking longboats that floated just off shore in the small Siberian Lake, the people under the sails and furs became very sleepy all of a sudden. Their eyelids became heavy and their thoughts turned to a warm, tired feeling of a welcomed nap.

"Well, that will keep the distractions to a minimum." Emsaph showed his student the eddies of the ether realm that they were about to breach. The in-between had been swirling around the area rather quickly, now it was calming down to an even flow, like a stream that has passed a rapids then flowed into a deep channel. The Unicorn waited until the ethers were almost still before he advised moving the sleeping villagers. Kris understood what he was seeing. Even though he'd had the refugees cover their heads on the journey to Siberia their mental state was so turbulent that it was a small miracle that they had made it safely. 'Thoughts and feelings shape the in-between... as much as tools and fire shape your world. Didn't I tell you that.' Emsaph mind spoke to his pupil.

Batu, the local shaman, had come down to the lakeshore from his village to see the strangers leave. Kris had told him that the house was too much trouble to destroy, so it was going to be left standing in the forest to the east of the Tungus village. The shaman had spoken to his own people of the powerful young shaman and they all had met Kris. So when Batu mentioned that it would be nice to have Kris be honored as a Tungus shaman, the village was amendable to the suggestion. The honey mead and berry brandy had certainly helped the idea along. Besides, if the tribe's trusted shaman could make such a powerful ally that could make the forest bend to his will, it would be good to make him one of the Tungus tribe. With that, Kris was given the red cloak and hat of the office of shaman.

From his vantage point on the far side of the lake, Batu calmed his breathing so that he could see into the dream paths, to see how this magic was to be accomplished. Curiously, everything seemed calm in the area around the two ships. The only evidence of anything strange was the blue glow that surrounded Kris and the horse he rode. Still, in second sight Batu could see that it was more than a horse that his new friend was riding, it was a spirit animal. One of the guardians that Batu's own teacher had told him of, that was on the highest Realms of the Dream Paths though no shaman had seen one in the flesh let alone been invited to ride one. 'Good that we made friends with these outlanders,' Batu thought to himself. The blue aura around Kris and the Unicorn began to increase and move towards the boats. Slowly, the field of power enfolded the ships, stem to stern. Power quickened and the two boats and the 'horse' and rider vanished from all sight. Batu looked for a disturbance in the energies that such a huge amount of power should cause, but the space where the ships had just been didn't seem to even be bothered by the young man's magical feat. Very impressive, Batu would have to ask his new friend about that kind of making.

Kris had told the Tungus shaman that he would be gone for a while and the great house was sealed to keep out wild animals. Batu knew that there was more to that line of reason then could be told, but all of his village were already afraid of the large, hairy Almas that walked in woods to the east of the village, so the if the new shaman wanted to live there, the tribe wouldn't mind. All of the good land was to the South of the village anyway. Batu was glad to have everything work out so well, he'd longed for someone to talk to about the dream paths. He had his own spirit animal, a golden hawk, but it didn't have a human perspective. Kris would be a good ally and maybe Batu could find out from his new friend where to get some of those magick rocks.

On the coast of Gaul, what would become France, the two ships appeared beached on the shore at high tide. It was a little after noon and the Spring sun was warm on Kris' face as he got down off of his teacher's back. It would make the villagers feel a little better to introduce them to their new home in a fashion that was as if they had traveled over the sea to get here. Emsaph had guided the energy the whole way, using Kris as the fulcrum of the power as he had done back at the witch's teeth, when they had closed the hole between the worlds. Kris was amazed at the control his teacher had had over the tremendous force that was contained in the Rune Stone that they were using.

"That's the way you're going to be doing it... soon." The Unicorn thought to Kris. The young man didn't understand the implication but knew better than to ask.

"Should we wake your blacksmith friend first?" The Unicorn had released his hold over Kris and the stones, so now he was back in his advisory mode.

Kris touched the one of the stones in his bag and thought of Joar being awake.

"Gently now, show a little finesse," his teacher wanted him to tone down the amount of power that was needed to bring the blacksmith out of the deep sleep without mentally slapping the man awake.

"Good... now a tiny bit more." Emsaph instructed. Kris felt like he'd been in this position before, back in Asgard when the Unicorn had instructed him during one of the many teaching sessions that had happened as Kris had slept.

With Joar awake, the red-haired young man introduced him to his new home. Up the beach that was guarded by large sharp rocks out in the surf, Kris led him to the place that Joar had seen in his dreams during the last two weeks. Miles of open fields with good earth to grow crops, the area was the highest for as far as the eye could see. No invader could sneak up on the villagers. And natural springs for fresh water, enough to supply the village's needs, ran from a source in a small wooded glen near the shore.

It was too much for the old man, after all the bad luck that had befallen on them to come to such a wonderful place, tears ran down his face.

"More wood and supplies will be here tomorrow." Kris told the black-smith. Emsaph had already thought ahead of what was to be needed as far as farm animals and wood for building, enough to get started was there in a sheltered glen where the villagers could start a new life. The rest would be delivered while they slept that night.

"There is one little request I would make of you." The red-haired stranger said to the blacksmith with great emotion.

"I don't think there is anything that I could deny you, even if I wanted to, Mage." Joar said honestly. "Though I thought there would be a price for all this good fortune." He finished.

"Anika's children," Kris started "They have family that would raise them...back in Vigfjord."

"If they have family, who are we to say that they can't go?" Joar was a sensible man and clearly this youth had the weirding way about him, none would dare question that he was Anika's kin.

Emsaph was waiting on the beach next to the boats when the two came back.

'Nice touch bringing all that wood and pigs along, you even brought Joar an anvil and tools...' Kris was cut short. 'Don't thank me,' the Uni-corn whinnied. 'Thank the slavers.' Emsaph showed the misfortune that had happened to the slavers' stores and supplies in the short time it took the villagers of Haven to cross from Siberia to Gaul in the in-between. Emsaph had not only managed to get the people here safely but had raided the camp of the Vikings that had enslaved them. Putting the sup-plies in the small glen even as Kris had walked Joar up the beach.

Emsaph had his student remount and let Kris say his goodbye to Joar while the Unicorn was relinking to the Rune Stones through his rider.

Joar watched the two fade out of his vision as he heard people in the beached ships come out of the deep sleep spell that had been put on them.

Olaf and his sister, Mary, awoke to see their maternal grandparents over them as they sat up in bed in the village of Vigfjord.

"Questions can wait," their Grandmother said, looking at their puzzled faces. "What you need now is a big bowl of stew." She got up from where she had kept her watch on the two orphans, little darlings of her only daughter, Anika. Olaf looked like he'd grow up to look like his father and little Mary was so much like Anika was at that age, that it made the old woman tear up just to look at her. The grandmother, Inga, went to the far side of the longhouse to get the children a large bowl of her mutton stew that was in her kettle at the fire. The children's Grandfather, Eric, was sitting near the ample blaze with a mug in one hand and a pipe in the other, just watching the shadows that the fire cast on the back of the stone hearth of their longhouse.

"I don't know what to make of the tale, Inga." He said out loud, as he sensed her presence. The strangely familiar young man on the small black horse had told them of the raid on the village that had happened back near the beginning of the winter. Few boats traveled up and down the coast in the winter season, so news of Haven would have to wait to be shared until the Spring when trading and planting season commenced. The people of Vigfjord had heard nothing of the destruction of the neighboring village to the North. The tale of the rescue and the trip to Siberia Kris had left out, let his brother Olaf and Mary have their say in the tale if they wanted. Emsaph thought it best to keep the story from becoming an epic adventure. It was easier to let the grandparents know that most of their Northern kin were all right and safe in a new home far to the South, with supplies and enough food to see them prosper.

As for Olaf and Mary, they had been through a terrible ordeal and hadn't had the luxury of ten years of Asgard and a Unicorn to keep them from dealing with their grief. So while Kris was showing Joar the new village site back on the coast of France, Emsaph had looked in on the children's Grandparents to see an older couple that had few grandchildren from their sons and wanted in their hearts to see their daughter's children. So when Kris and Emsaph faded away from Joar's sight, they took Olaf and Mary with them.

"You've done right by your brother and sister, lessening their pain and helping them have good dreams," the Unicorn mentor mindspoke to his pupil, "in that you've used all those lessons that I taught you about helping recreate memories very well. Now then, if you could learn the subtleties of moving through the mental space of the in-between." Kris could hear the hint of a whinny in the Unicorn's mind speech.

"You didn't tell me about those 'Almas' creatures that live in these dream paths, " Kris thought to his mentor, using the term he'd learned from Batu. "I saw one on the way to rescue Olaf and Mary and that's how I lost my balance when I popped out near the slavers' camp. It'd wanted me to stop and talk I guess and I don't remember that being covered in any dream-lesson I had." Kris tried to get his own jibe back at his friend.

"It's a mental plane of the Earth," the teacher started his lesson. Pictures appeared in Kris' mind of the Earth having several layers above its surface, much like clouds but in different colors. "When you saw the Almas, you lost focus on your goal, your mental focus." The Unicorn wasn't trying to make his student out to be a simpleton, indeed, he hadn't taught his young charge everything he'd ever have to know. It was brought up in the dream-lessons but not fully explored. 'How much knowledge can be crammed into a human's mind?' Emsaph had worried over giving his young pupil too much and thought it better to err on the side of caution. But there was no way to know that Kris would try to rescue everyone at once. True, it showed the boy's kind-heartedness to save all the people of Haven. But the lack of foresight of what channeling so much power would do to the freshly patched hole back at the black mountain meant that he was going to be a danger to himself and his world without some more proper training. And that training that was better handled by humans of this Realm of Asgard. But first, Emsaph needed to tend to Anika's children.

The conversation happened in an instant in the in-between as the Unicorn and the three children winked into the home of the Eric and Inga, father and mother to Anika and maternal grandparents to the children. With the story told and assurances that Olaf and Mary would be well-taken care of, the magical rider and the black horse shimmered into a twinkling of stars and blackness.

"I thought you would leave me with my grandparents,' Kris mindspoke to his teacher, 'not that I mind going with you, I guess. So where to... back to the Great house near the portal?" Kris asked expectantly.

'Ah... no.' Emsaph had made sure that Mary and Olaf had been properly linked to the Rune Stones and through that link they could visit with Kris when they slept. In time, they would come to know their brother again and be able to share in his memories of all the things he'd learned and seen. But at that moment, Kris needed to work on his focusing the power of the stones he carried.

The young rider and the Unicorn stepped out of the in-between on a steep mountain pass. Emsaph waited for Kris' eyes to adjust to the intense sunlight.

"Where are we?" Kris said out loud.

"The roof of the world, the place that blinds you with its snowy peaks and simple wisdom. Long had I wanted to come back and visit this kingdom, my own personal vacation spot in this Realm." Emsaph waxed on. "This is where you will find the path to the temple of the Black Hat Sect. It is a twisted and dangerous road." He finished, pointing with his horn down the mountain. Kris tried to find a recognizable trail on the face of the Himalayan mountainside. Something of a path that only a mountain goat could use, was all he could find.

"This way," the Unicorn walked up a few more switchbacks before showing his ward the path that led down into a hidden valley.

Kris wouldn't keep silent about the conversation, that as far as he was concerned, wasn't finished. "Can't I just stay in Vigfjord with my brother and sister?" He'd just started to get to know them again. Emsaph relayed that Kris could spend time with them as he slept and that he wasn't being left here. Emsaph chuckled to himself. Though his charge had been through and seen much more, than most in this world, he still didn't like going to his first day of "school."

"You need to be here for only a few years and you can go back to Vigfjord for Summers if you wish. But I must ask you to learn all you can from these people," the Unicorn's teacher voice rung in Kris' head like a bell. "They can help you master the Rune Stones by mastering your mind, young one." The tone was soft but firm. The path widened and the two visitors headed towards the far side of the valley at a slow walk.

"So where is this school?" Kris couldn't make out much except the lush vegetation on the valley floor, the white stone walls with the fool's gold running through it and the deep blue sky above them.

"Your eyes will adjust in a minute or two," the Unicorn chided. "Maybe you can learn a little patience while you're here as well." Emsaph finished.

As they passed the outer marker the late afternoon, sun poured into the valley of Khembalung, the hidden kingdom. Kris' eyes adjusted to the sky that shone an azure blue, deeper than any Kris had seen before. The fool's gold veins that ran through the stone of the mountain valley that lined its walls glinted the sunlight into the young students' eyes

"It's a long walk to the other side of the valley, Kris said, excepting this schooling, at least in theory. "Can't we just 'pop' to the other side of the valley or just into the school?" Kris wanted to get started as soon as possible.

"You will find that your stones aren't useful here." That's why we had to go to the entrance to the valley. The Unicorn instructed. "The monks here know secrets of the ancient times of this world. So that the knowledge won't fall into the wrong hands, they shelter this valley using mental techniques that shield their monastery from the outside world." The Unicorn then hushed his pupil.

One of the younger disciples of the order came down from his perch at the foot of the high stair to greet them. He saw their presence long before Kris could sense his. The youth that greeted them wore a white robe that had golden threading that ran through his garment randomly, much like the stones of the temple.

'If he'd covered his arms and head with the robe, he'd blend into the stonework.' Kris thought as they came closer.

The disciple had tanned skin and slanted eyelids much like the people of the Tungus tribe. But, where the Siberians were stocky and short, this boy was tall and graceful.

"I am to take you to the 'Master of the East.'" he mind spoke to Kris.

"It's an honorary title, don't get too worked up over it." Emsaph chimed into the conversation.

The two boys walked up the steep white stone steps while the Unicorn went to feed on the fresh mountain timothy and wild oats that the valley grew in abundance.

At length, Kris and his guide enter the Temple. It was hard to tell where the outside of the building stopped and the rock wall of the valley began. The inside of the Temple was a wonder to Kris even though he had been to the halls of Asgard. Columns thicker than a great oak supported a roof that was so far up it could only be glimpsed by the lamplights that ringed the columns at twice the height of a man.

As corridors went off at regular intervals, Kris followed his guide through the maze of great expanses filled with monks sitting on floors of polished stone meditating, down low passageways that were so low that even the boys had to stoop very low. They passed walls that looked to Kris as if they were maps of the night sky with every star represented by a jewel or a pearl of great price.

The redhaired young man was beginning to wonder just how big the monastery was, when his guide took a sharp left and went up a narrow staircase that had many switchbacks. The two climbed on in silence, their path lit by the torches that lined the rough hewed walls. The stairs were obviously carved out of the mountain like the rest of the Temple but the passage was the only one that looked unpolished and unadorned.

Up they went, a hundred stairs or so, then another switchback to a new set of stairs. The guide pulled one of the torches out of its holder and said,

"Not much further now."

Kris was glad to hear it; he was in good shape for a boy his age but the high thin air of the mountains made it hard to keep up with the apprentice monk. They reached the top of the stairs and entered a small room that didn't seem to be finished. The floor had a few tools laying about on the unfinished rock. The young boy handed Kris the torch and looked through the tools to find a thin rod of some metal that was about the length of one of the boy's forearms. He held the strange looking tool and walked towards the far wall humming a low tone from deep in his throat. Kris watched as the boy walked through the solid rock.

'They must use sounds the same way that my mother's people do,' Kris thought to himself.

"Okay, maybe this is a test, I'll need one of those rods." Kris spoke out loud, in case he was being watched from secret hole in the wall. Kris hunted through the pile of chisels and crudely made hammers to find a rod like the one his guide had used. It had the color of his mother's dagger, a pewter gray and was so light it might as well been a feather. Putting the torch aside he cleared his mind and thought of the tone that the other boy had used. He concentrated on the voice exercises his mother had made him do all those years ago, then Kris tried to mimic the low sound he'd heard. As he came closer to matching it, Kris thought he saw the wall becoming transparent. It flickered back and forth, from a solid wall to a doorway where his guide stood waiting for him. Kris refocused on the tone and sucked in enough air to keep the tone going long enough for him to make it through the wall.

Kris passed through the solid rock to the doorway on the other side. It had ornate gilding of mystical beasts around and large multi-colored circle that was filled with geometric shapes that blended in a way that was at once confusing and comforting. His guide knocked on the thick mahogany doors with one of the animal shaped knockers. Presently, one of the doors opened slightly. Kris' guide motioned for the rod that he was still holding. Taking the metal rod from Kris, the guide hummed a different tone than the one that they used to get through the wall and turned to his left and disappeared through a different wall than the one that they had come through.

"Well come in, let us have a look at you." The voice came from behind the ornate doors. The Unicorn teacher had never misled Kris before, but the young man still felt that he was being abandoned somehow. The monastery's newest student approached the doors cautiously.

The great doors swung back with ease to reveal a very large room that was richly furnished with heavy woolen rugs and low hanging oil lamps that flickered with the slight cold breeze that came from the windows that looked out over the hidden valley.

The sun had set and a waxing moon had risen over the horizon, illuminating the valley in a silvery half-light. Kris walked further into the room and over to the window to see if he could spot Emsaph grazing on the wild oats that covered the floor of the valley.

Kris smelled the amber resin that permeated the chairs and couches and wafted through the air from dozens of brass incense burners that lined the inner wall.

'You're looking in the wrong place,' the voice at once playful and familiar entered the young man's mind. Kris felt he should look over towards the back of the room. Oddly, the room seemed to curve with the outside of the mountain. 'How big is this place,' he thought to himself.

The room had such a gradual curve to it that it didn't need walls for privacy, you'd only have to go a little further along the room to find a secluded spot.

"Warmer, warmer still, come on young one." It was definitely Emsaph; 'young one' was his pet name for all the 'two legs' he cared about, whether it was Kris or the Norns, they were all children as far as the Unicorn was concerned. As Kris continued to walk the length of the room, he noticed that windows became less uniform and less frequent, lamps were on low tables in this part of the room, unlike the torches that were between the windows that over looked the valley near the entrance.

The smoke of the incense burners still filled the student's nostrils as he came around the graceful arc of the room to see his mentor standing next to a bald man who had similar features as the boy that had brought him here. Though this man was old, he had age spots and little wrinkles around his eyes, Kris couldn't see any other signs that the ravages of time visit on us all.

"Welcome, we have much to teach each other," the old man said in a language that Kris could understand. He hadn't noticed it before, with all the mindspeech that he and Emsaph did. This man was speaking a language that Kris shouldn't have been able to understand.

"That was my doing," the Unicorn chimed in. "As we were walking the valley I put the language in your head. To make it easier on you." Emsaph lowered his head slightly and turned it slightly towards Kris' new teacher.

"I am Lobsang." The new instructor said, "You've many questions, I'm sure, but all will be answered in time."

Emsaph chimed in; "Master Lobsang was impressed to hear that you've had dealings with the Almas." Was that pride in the Unicorn's mind speech that Kris heard?

"Yes, but here they are called the 'Yeti' or 'Yeren,' Lobsang added. "Rarely, do we attract their attention, no doubt they were interested in your ability to travel in their realm as they do," the old monk finished.

Kris had thought that he would have to talk to the Almas eventually, being that he'd created the great house near their territory in Siberia and Batu had told him that the creatures used the forest to side step something in their own realm. Kind of like a shortcut.

In his two weeks at the great house in Russia, the people of Kris' village didn't report seeing anything strange in the forest. So he didn't get the chance to talk to the creatures that lived on the dreampaths. This had worked out to Kris' advantage, because he didn't know how much or what to tell them. As though reading his mind, Lobsang said,

"Would you like to meet one now?"

What better time to talk to the creatures than when having a world-spanning Unicorn at his side, not to mention a bag of magical stones that could protect him. This reassured the young man.

"Ok, when do we leave?" Kris said, he was a little tired and hungry in spite of the rest and food he'd had at his Grandparents house.

"Not to worry little one, this will be a short trip," Emsaph told him.

With that, the old monk got up from the low, heavily embroidered cushion that he'd been sitting on and led the other two to a wall hanging at the end of the room. The black robed monk pulled at one side of the tapestry and it moved aside as if it were a sliding door. Kris was amazed by the view.

The windows that got progressively rougher as he went further into the arcing room now made sense. Far below and to the horizon all that could be seen were mountaintops. The monks had made the windows that faced their valley beautifully. But the ones that could be spotted by someone in the outside world, were made to look as though they were just crevasses in the mountainside, a trick of the light reflecting off the snow to fool the eye. The three walked out to a low balcony that looked out on the rest of the Himalayas. Emsaph moved to stand next to Kris as Lobsang took out of his robe sleeve what looked like two flat pieces of metal that had the look of brass, held together by a leather cord. The monk tossed the object in the air where it floated in front of the trio. The leather cord was drawn up slightly by an unseen force and the two metal symbols clanged together softly. The sound was wonderfully rich and pure to Kris. After a minute, the sound echoed off the mountains in the distance. The symbols continued to chime, as the echo of one died away it was replaced with the pure resonance of another.

The moon hadn't moved very much, when Kris smelled an animal scent. Not unpleasant, but it definitely had a musky odor to it.

"Monk, why do you summon me?" Kris heard the sound in his head and he noticed that Emsaph had changed his stance slightly. It looked as though he was just shifting his weight but Kris felt that the Unicorn was a little tense all of a sudden.

"Will you not join us" Lobsang said pleasantly. "We mean you no harm."

"Men do not see what they are not ready to see... Many things exist in this world but pass unnoticed by man, and with good reason." The Almas said out loud this time.

"One of your kind tried to talk to our young friend as he traveled in your realm," The monk pointed to Kris who now wished he could just go back inside. There was something in the air that sent a chill up his spine.

The shape of the Almas shimmered near the edge of the balcony. "So, you're the one I've been hearing about." The voice rang with laughter; "You're not as big as you were reported to be. We thought that the barbarian humans had found a way to enter our world and were trying to hunt us."

Much explaining from both sides then took place. The Almas 'felt' the two boat loads of scared humans traveling to and from Siberia through the mental plane of the Earth that the Alamas had thought of as their own. Now the whole thing had made sense. That's why they had left the area where Kris had created the great house near the Tungus tribe. When the story of the Rune Stones had been related to the Almas and that only Kris and a few others, including Emsaph would ever be crossing into their realm... the tension relaxed. With that said, the shimmering shape of the Almas gave way to the large, hairy body that stood at the edge of the balcony. "Well then, if you're going to be using our realm as we use yours, a proper introduction is in order," the Almas said in the tongue that the monks used.

"We do not have names as you do but you can call me 'Uten,' it is our word for friend." The creature with the apelike face and kind, intelligent eyes, put it's arms across its chest, flattened them together and extended them towards Kris, so that the palm of one hand touched the palm of the other. Kris thought it must be a way of saying hello or showing respect so he imitated the gesture back to 'Uten.'

"I must leave to tell my tribe to stop hiding in the far continent," Uten said. "Will you be here long? Others of my tribe would like to know you as well."

"He will be here for the foreseeable future, Emsaph chimed into the conversation. "Though the place that he created in Siberia will be his home. If your tribe doesn't object to that arrangement." The Unicorn finished in a diplomatic tone.

"That should not be a problem, if you don't mind, my tribe using the forest to go around a large void that lies in our realm." The Almas was also good at bargaining.

"I think we have an accord." Emsaph seemed pleased about whatever deal he and the Almas had struck, it was over Kris' head. The teenager just wanted to get something to eat. Sure, he could touch the Rune Stone and think of his favorite meal. But it wasn't the same as tearing into a large loaf of bread and tasting the seaweed soup that his mom had made. Full of shellfish and large chunks of cod and turnips. His mouth was watering just thinking about it. Kris was so caught up in savoring his next meal, he almost missed the Almas finishing his goodbye, as the creature turned and disappeared off of the balcony into the brisk mountain air.

"I must be going as well," Emsaph mind spoke both to Kris and the monk. "You have a lot to learn about focusing that brain of yours," the Unicorn chided Kris gently. "There is more in this world to worry about than an empty stomach."

Kris watched his mentor stick his nose in the bag and sensed Emsaph draw up a tiny amount of power from the stones. "I just need a little to get back to your house," he explained.

"I go to bring a container for that cursed stone."

An image of a strange basin filled the young man's mind, that looked as though it was made of the same type of crystal that the Loki Stone was made of, in a shade of ethereal blue.

"The sisters will bring it to that "house" you made. If that isn't a sign of misuse of power I don't know what is." The Unicorn whinnied a little. He was just joking.

Kris blushed, it had been his first real use of drawing energy from the Earth and trying to form it by using the Rune Stones.

"Also, I'll see if I can get the Elves to make you a belt for those rocks. Like the one that Odin had." An image of a belt that would go around Kris' waist with leather loops to carry some of the Rune Stones, popped into the yong man's head.

Emsaph pointed to the sack that had the stones that Kris had been carrying around.

"Your power to use those stones here," the Unicorn lifted his head back towards the monastery, "is severely limited. Maybe you will learn to rely on your mind a little more. Then, all that information that is sleeping in that brain can awaken." Emsaph turned and trotted towards the edge of the rough-hewn balcony.

"Take care of my ward, Lobsang." A shimmering blue light started from the tip of the Unicorn's horn and flowed down his neck and back. As it reached the end of his tail and base of his hooves he mindspoke, "Don't worry Kris, I'll be back in a few months." It was meant to sound reassuring but Kris only thought of it as a very long time not to see this being that he'd come to think of as a family member and a friend.

His mentor started to step forward into the abyss and disappeared.

Months passed and Kris found that the lessons he needed to learn, weren't very different than what his mother had started to teach him. A lot had to do with sound and breathing a certain way so that the low hum that the monks used could be held for incredibly long time. Lobsang also showed him some of the secrets of this hidden Temple. It had relics from distance ages, long passed. There were machines that flew that were made of gold and had large jewels inset on the arm of one the crafts' seats that let a person control it in the air. That wasn't the only treasure from the distance past that the monks were guarding in the catacombs that they called the "Hall of Records." There were spheres of glass that floated in the air that would light to the touch, all you need do was think of how bright you wanted them and they would go to their proper setting. Even the monks didn't know how the glass balls worked. No fuel could be added to them since they were perfectly smooth with no spout to be seen. But they had never needed fuel and according to the legends, they never would.

Many other things were shown to Kris as well. At times, he had one on one instruction with Lobsang in the room that he had met the 'Master of the East'.

That class was about man, freewill and fate, after the lesson the young man asked,

"How do I know that this is the right path that my life should take?" It seemed like a fair question.

Lobsang smiled. He seemed that he'd been waiting for this question. The monk turned to a low shelf that was to the below the windows that over looked the hidden valley in the great arcing room where Kris had learned most of his lessons. On the shelf were assorted incense burners, chunks of half-burnt amber resin and books but also two things that had been covered by ornately embroidered silk. Kris had seen them many times during his study with Lobsang but never thought enough about them to ask what was under the richly covered cloth. He just assumed that it was some other dusty relics that the monk didn't want to be exposed to the light. Pulling on one edge of the cloth slowly the monk sighed.

"Long have we heard that question from our own minds and from our students mouths but you will have an answer that we do not." The silk slid off revealing a mask that looked strangely familiar. It was a bronze likeness of the god Loki.

"I think you know who this is?" the monk asked, handing the mask to Kris. Having seen the battle of Ragnorok with all of the destruction that it had caused, in his mind back in Asgard, Kris didn't reach for the pointy-faced-evil-grinning usurper's mask.

"Go ahead, take it," Lobsang urged. Putting it squarely into his young pupils' hands. Kris looked at it. Whoever had made the bronze mask had a good idea what evil was all about. The angles of the cheekbones and set of the mouth spoke of pure malice that had filled the soul of the wicked Norse god.

"How does this prove anything?" Kris said, glad to be handing it back to his teacher and not to be touching it anymore.

The monk put it back on the shelf and made sure to cover it completely. He then reached for the second piece of ornate cloth. The old man cradled it so that the silk that covered the second mask stayed on as he handed over to Kris. Lobsang motioned his free hand as if mimicking to Kris to pull off the cloth.

A sense of dread came over the young man. Kris had asked the question, why did he not want to look at what the second piece of cloth was covering? The two sat there in silence for a long pause. Kris finally pulled the silk off to reveal the image of the second mask. The image that he saw had many of the same features that he did. The face was a little broader and it had a bushy mustache. Kind of like his Grandfather Eric had.

He looked up to his teacher for an explanation.

"These masks were made long ago in the ancient times, even before the founding of this Temple, the legend that went with them was that one would cause great harm and the other would come to fix the damage the other had caused. From what I've heard, you've fixed the tear between the Realms.... Lobsang left the rest of it unsaid. Better that Kris figure it out for himself.

'The second mask could be me,' when I'm much older, the young man thought. It kind of looked like him. The broad forehead and high round cheeks were like the men of his father's family and the full lips and oval face were like that of his mother's family. Maybe, the eyes were a little too closely set, but how could they know that he would be the one to come here? It should have been his mother. Or if the Druid's high priest, Merlyn, had gotten the Loki Stone back in Milkigard then his mom would have closed the tear and probably came back to the village and continued with her life. Maybe, telling the tale like one of her other stories, so it would sound more like something made up than a real adventure. All the 'what ifs' and 'if onlys' filled his head. Of all the choices and things that would have to happen to bring him there... at that moment in time, to ask that question... to be shown these masks, one that was definitely Loki and the one that would be him when he was a man. He handed the mask back to the monk.

"So what do I need to learn next?" he asked.

The tape recorder clicked off as Olaf stopped the story.

"Before you ask, the masks are real. Kris took them with him and eventually they ended up in a museum of ancient Tibetan artifacts. Look it up on the Internet if you want." Olaf finished his tea and waited for me to ask any questions that I had.

I just sat there sipping my second espresso. We both got up and he cleaned up the table and put away the backgammon board. I stuffed the tapes into a Ziploc bag and then into my nap-sack, three people were waiting for me to exit the booth.

I hadn't thought of that before. Why hadn't someone tried to sit with us before? The café had a, sit where you can policy, so that no one could hog up a whole booth for themselves. Our booth could have easily sat six people, but when Olaf was telling his story, no one sat with us. The thoughts got lost in the laundry list of things I'd have to do for the rest of the day. My mind forgot about the little mystery as I headed out to get some groceries at one of the many produce stalls.

The Rajah's Treasure Vault

Chapter 6
The Casket of Gems

By the sixth week, we'd fallen into a routine. One of us would have the table ready, which in and of itself was strange. Before Olaf and I started playing our backgammon games, while he told the hidden history of his brother, it was almost impossible for me to get the corner booth in the little café.

I thought of this while I was getting my drink. I watched over my shoulder to see why no one sat in the coveted corner booth. No one seemed to know that it was even there, though the locals crowded the coffeehouse, the booth stayed empty. And, when I got there before the storyteller, no one asked to sit across from me. Since the booths were pretty much communal, people sat across from you without needing to ask for permission usually. I thought someone would try to sit with me, but nobody even looked my way.

Olaf came in, as I was finishing getting my tapes ready and checking my batteries in the recorder. I watched the people in the busy coffee shop, the old storyteller tooled around them like a ghost on his way to the table. They didn't register that he had even passed by them.

Olaf placed his mug down on the table and locked eyes with me.

"Well, I see you finally noticed." He said, in a voice that sounded like a teacher chiding a daydreaming student.

"What kind of spell, are on these people?" I asked suspiciously.

"It's not a spell as you would think of it," he explained, sitting down. Olaf took a long slow sip of tea and savored the taste. "It is merely a 'glamour' on this end booth... that it appears to be fully occupied until we're ready to leave." He continued, "If you'd like I'll include you in the 'spell' sometime, so you can see it for yourself. More importantly, I'm going to tell you about..." he drew out the thought. I already suspected he knew what tale he was going to tell, Olaf just liked to see if his audience was listening.

In the land of the Rajahs, a stranger appeared one day. Literally, out of thin air, to offer a service to the prince in the inner court of the ruler. He offered the Rajah travel, fast travel, to any part of his kingdom. The prince's eunuchs pointed their spears at Kris' chest, waiting for a nod from their ruler to dispatch this strange looking demon with his flaming red hair.

"I'm not one to go running around my lands," the prince said lazily. "Nothing happens that I do not know of, and quickly. I have a seer and the fastest runners in the world to deliver my decrees and bring back news even from my farthest province. Besides, bad news can always wait and good news is meant to be savored." The Rajah said dismissively to the new arrival.

"Then, what if I showed you your future?" The young man asked politely, eyeing the spears that were pointed at him.

The spears edged closer...

"Wait!" the Rajah lifted his hand a little, and then sprang his trap. "And if you show me something I don't like?" He asked, liking this new diversion to an otherwise boring day.

The prince guessed that if the stranger showed him, revered throughout the world for his wisdom and good judgement, then red haired interloper would be lying. The Rajah was a learned man and knew that rulers come and go and usually not soon enough for the ones who endured their sovereignty. If on the other hand, if the ruler was shown a ruined palace in decay filled with vermin and monkeys, he could just have the interloper killed for upsetting him. As if reading the Rajah's thoughts Kris said,

"I'll only show you the truth," he let his disheveled red hair droop forward as he bowed to the ruler. "If you want, I can also show you what you could achieve... if you chose to actually do something with you time here on earth," the stranger finished.

That breach of etiquette caused the high-pitched eunuchs to gasp at his audacity. A few drew back their spears to get more power behind their fatal thrushes at the imp from one of the seven hells.

"Well, this will be an eventful afternoon," The prince said, as he was silently thanking the gods for answering his prayers for some challenge to his intellect.

"What will this cost me," the prince of the 'Land of Delightful Pleasure' asked. "This superlative good fortune sounds like it will cost me dearly."

The ruler smiled showing his gleaming white teeth.

"The prince is very wise," the strangely dressed red-haired imp replied. Kris bowed slightly again to the royal. "I ask for only one jewel from your vast treasury," the stranger had raised a single finger. "A single gem from the thousands that you possess." Kris then raised the rest of the fingers on his right hand and carelessly tossed his hand to the side as if to say, 'a pittance', with the gesture.

The Rajah lowered his own hand, causing the eunuchs to lower their weapons and stand at attention.

"Who are you to judge the ways of a Rajah?" the ruler asked, testing him.

"Let me say, that there exists a slight gap between what could be and the path that you are choosing now." said the red-haired man carefully. His slight red beard moved very little when he spoke, the prince noted.

The ruler looked at the stranger closely, as if for the first time. The intuder was a little smaller than an average man of his own kingdom, with flaming red hair and the most outlandish clothes. The stranger wore a heavy cloak had all the colors of a peacock's tail feather. Though his shirt and pants was as dowdy as a peahen's. The prince also noticed the stranger's skin. It was white as a Saba melon but he had red cheeks, much like the exotic girls from far to the West. Slave traders brought exotic women to sell twice a year, but they had sunflower-colored hair and spoke a barbarian tongue. Maybe, the demon couldn't change his hair color, showing his true nature to the wise. 'Shiva be praised,' the young prince thought.

"Leave us!" The Rajah commanded his guards and servants. Slowly, they plodded out of the many doorways that led out to the more public parts of the palace. Finally, only his viseer was left.

"Go Nandi, I do not fear this man." The prince said 'man' as though it rhymed with scum.

"As you wish... my prince." The Rajah's advisor oozed. He turned to give the stranger one last burning glance. The viseer had worked too hard to be the true power behind the prince. While the fool of a prince had sat idly on the throne, his senses numbed with too much wine and women, the court high counselor was free to do as he wished. Then, this demon from hell was sent to ruin his nice arrangement. Nandi could not bear it; this would not be! He reached for his poisoned dagger and threw it with a practiced ease.

That took the Rajah by surprise. Before the ruler could recover from the shock of his counselor and trusted friend's new talent, Kris said,

"Well Rajah of the 'Realm of Delightful Pleasure,' maybe you would like to start with me showing you... the secret talents of your subjects." Kris opened his hand and raised his palm up slightly; to receive the poisoned blade. It had been stopped just short of his right eye, then floated down like a feather, slowly into his outstretched hand.

The viseer, Nandi, turned back to look at his puppet, who had the look of someone who had just discovered a nest of cobras in his house. The high counselor tried to cover up his deadly skill.

"Sire, I only thought of your safety." The sickly sweet tone oozed from his mouth. "I thought you were under his spell." Nandi said, in the most sincere voice he could muster.

The Rajah recovered from his shock as best he could, and replied.

"Of course you were." The prince mimicked back. "I must say, that I'm glad to have such a close friend with such a useful and hidden talent." He finished.

The viseer seemed genuinely pleased with the Rajah's response. He backed away out of the room, as had all the others who served the prince.

"Take a turn with me in my garden?" the dark-skinned royal got up from his gold and jewel encrusted throne. He stepped down from his dais; robes of patterned silk flowing behind him, with a grace that only royalty seemed to possess.

Kris studied the noble lord of the 'Land of Delightful Pleasure.' The young prince had long blue-black hair, bright intelligent eyes and the honey brown skin that people south of the Himalayas were famous for having. As the prince smiled at him and waved at one of the painted silk screens that kept out the heat of the day, Kris saw into the ruler's mind and heart. There before him was a man who had the lives of almost a million people in his hand. Nothing that the ruler had done however suggested that there was influence by the Loki Stone. Kris turned his mind briefly to the court high counselor, Nandi. Though the royal advisor was naturally a power-grubbing social climber, this was due to the lowly birth in his caste, which he'd managed to keep consealed from everyone. The court advisor was mostly harmless to the people that he was trying to rule through the prince. Unless, he felt that his power was threatened.

The screen parted before the Ruler and his guest as if by it's own accord. The Rajah watched the stranger to see if he was amazed by this little piece of engineering magic. But Kris showed no sign that he was impressed by the trick that the prince had installed for just such an effect on his guests.

The visitor had already seen the trick of hydraulics; the Turk emperor had doors that would open in a similar fashion. The whole palace of the Grand Turk was also lit with gas lamps, 'wouldn't that be a wonder to this Rajah,' thought Kris.

The royal garden was truly a paradise of scent and color, and it was known far and wide for its rare flowers. Huge pots edged to the sides of the path that were filled with plants, with all the colors of the rainbow. Delicate flowers from far off lands, with exotic perfumes, hung over the pair as they walked deeper into the princes private garden.

The two walked for some time, the prince pointing out interesting flowers along the way. All the while, studying his guest for any sign of peculiar regard for any of the garden's flora. But Kris just smiled and nodded at the right moments of the tour. He obliged his host by smelling the flowers that held scents, of which the prince was particularly fond.

Twice the Rajah managed to get the stranger in direct sunlight, to see if the red-haired stranger, would be burned by the light of the sun's rays. But Kris didn't even seemed to be bothered by the sunlight that streamed through the dense foliage.

'So this person was a man, not a demon,' like the prince had first suspected. No flames came from the stranger, not even a smoldering of his red hair. The Rajah was impressed that the outlander was more of a challenge to his royal intellect.

'Maybe the stranger was a fakir, one of the holy men that became hermits in the high mountains, far to the north,' the Prince surmised. The fakirs were said to have discovered the secrets of the mind and this gave them special powers, like being able to levitate, or lay on a bed of nails... but stopping a dagger in midair, that was a feat of the mind that even the learned prince hadn't read of, or heard stories about.

At length, the path wound around to a dais in the middle of the garden. The platform was lower than the planters that surrounded it, giving the Rajah and his guest more privacy.

"This is the most secluded sanctuary that I have," the prince gestured for Kris to sit across from him on a bench that wasn't as richly adored or as high as the chair the prince had chosen.

"Show me what you will... be you a man or demon come to destroy my kingdom, I do not fear you." The Rajah smirked.

Kris knew that the prince was expecting some waving of his hands or chanting like the charlatans that had visited him in the past had done. However, the red-haired stranger just sat there, hands resting on his lap.

The divine ruler of the kingdom started to get impatient and it was starting to show. Anyone spying on the pair would think that the prince was about to threaten his guest. The royal advisor, Nandi, had seen to that detail. He wasn't about to let the prince out of his sight, much less out of his grasp. So from behind a particularly thick fern, that was close to the pair, the high counselor watched and waited.

Knowledge was power, and since the oddly dressed stranger had stopped his dagger in mid-air, showing the prince a different kind of magic, Nandi wanted all the knowledge he could gather of this red-haired imp.

In the prince's mind, the ruler felt that his spirit was being lifted out of his body. It was a most peculiar feeling. Like pulling a hand out of a bucket of honey. The royal had the sensation of a buzzing in his ears, a fluttering around his eyes, which blurred his vision. After a moment the Rajah's sight cleared. He looked around to see his body.

'Yes, there it was below him,' he thought, he could see his body just sitting there in his private garden across from the imp who had tricked him out of his physical form.

"Calm yourself, my prince," came the stranger's voice from far away. "All will be as you wished to see."

This didn't calm the ruler very much, he was used to being in control, the Rajah wasn't used to brooking disappointment. Before he could work up a sense of princely indignation, the scene changed from his beloved garden to a landscape of deep jungle with little outcroppings of stone. The prince and his guide landed softly on top of the tallest set of stones. "This is your kingdom, one hundred years after your death. We stand on the remains of the tallest tower of your palace." Kris said honestly to the prince.

"Oddly enough, this doesn't please me." The ruler said with a sardonic tone.

The two stood there observing their surroundings, the prince noted the mountains to the north. Indeed they were the same mountains that he could see from one of his bedrooms at night. A rustle in the foliage startled the Rajah out of his revelry. The sound grew nearer but the red-haired wild-man didn't seem to be bothered by it.

A small girl appeared who was foraging for food. Either by hunger or not paying attention she had gone too far afield. And at that moment, she was looking for a high place to see her way home. She didn't seem to notice the two overly dressed men standing there in the middle of the jungle on the outcropping of rock in the hot sun. The little girl had on a beautiful sari of yellow and green print that her mother had made for her. It was the only thing she had to call her own. Her feet were bare but she had a wonderful smile on her face as she climbed the stones that used to be the palace of the Rajah of the 'Realm of Delightful Pleasure.' The prince had never had to share anything in his life, let alone his personal space with an unwanted visitor.

"Be gone from me, child," he commanded.

She didn't seem to hear or care about the richly adored prince. She put her hand above her eyes to shield them from the intense sunlight and scanned the horizon for some sign of her house that lay on the edge of the jungle.

The prince looked to his guide on this very unsatisfactory journey to see a blue outline of the god Ganesha form around the red-haired stranger. The girl gasped as the God of Abundance appeared before her, she was so shocked that she lost her footing only to be caught by the blue trunk of the elephant-headed god.

"Well child, why are you so far from your home?" Kris, as the blue skinned young god with the head of an elephant, asked sweetly.

"I was looking for Saba melons, for my mother." The little girl replied sheepishly. "I'm sorry if I disturbed you, great lord."

"Not at all, not at all, Sonji." Kris had looked into the child's mind for her name. If he knew her name and where her home was, it would ease the girl's worrying. Kris sat her down with his 'trunk' on a near by stone. All the while, the prince was rethinking this visitor to his court. If this were the great God Ganesha, the royal was not endearing himself to the Lord of Abundance. The Rajah decided to keep his mouth closed for the present.

"Now Sonji, Kris started to lecture the little girl, "This is not a place to be getting lost." Kris had given this lecture to thousands of children over

the years, in the guise of many different gods and helpful creatures. Whatever would put the child's mind the most at ease.

"I know you want to help feed your family, but right now your mother
is worried about you, calling out your name, to call you to help with the
dinner." Kris just wanted the girl to think about her home a little more so
he could match up the picture in her mind with all the homes that were
close to the forest.

"Now, before I take you home here is a small gift for you, so that you
can get your melons at the market in the village and maybe your mother
will buy you those hair combs that you want so badly."

Kris knew that if he showed up as Ganesha and mentioned the combs
the mother would buy them for her daughter that day. The little Sonji
watched the Lord of Abundance lower his trunk down into the space between the boulders and dig around past a couple of skeleton arms to pick
out an anklet made out of six rubies, each the size of the girls fist. A large
cobra lashed out from an unseen hole at the trunk, holding the prize. The
little girl jumped at the sight of the large snake.
"Not to worry, little Sonji," the Ganesha reassured his new small ward.
"You see, that the cobra passed right through my trunk." Kris calmed the
girls' mind. "This is why you must avoid the jungle when you can. At least
until you are a little older, yes?" As Kris said the words he put it in her
mind to not be so reckless in her wandering.

"Yes, Ganesha." The little girl was awed that the Lord of Abundance
cared so much for her. Would her mother believe all that had happened to
her since being lost? The little girl was gathered up in the elephant god's
trunk and given the bauble from the Rajah's palace. Happy and smiling
she asked the god if this was a dream. He had saved her from a cobra,

given the poor girl a treasure that would feed her family very well for a long time to come and now he was taking her home.

"Ready Sonji?" Kris asked. He could think the three of them to her front door in an instant but he wanted her to enjoy that brief moment in time. The girl nodded, she was so happy she couldn't speak. They slowly lifted off the boulders and hovered above the trees. Sonji thought, 'this is how the birds see the world, what an amazing feeling.'

The wind whipped her braids around behind her head as they headed for her home. All too soon, they arrived at the edge of the forest near the little girl's house. The elephant-headed god set the little Sonji down lightly and gave her a hug saying, "I have to go help other little children who've wander too far from their mothers, so I must go now." Ganesha nudged Sonji with his trunk and waved goodbye, then he stepped back and started to fade as a cloud of glittering light appeared around his outline.

Sonji's mother came running to see the sparkles fade and her little girl home safe.

"Where have you been?" The mother started, with a rant that was as old as motherhood. "I've been so worried about you." The little girl's mother stopped short of finishing her tirade when Sonji showed her the bauble from the Rajah's palace.

"Where did you get such a treasure?" the mother asked looking around as if the owner would be there to claim the ruby anklet back from her daughter at any moment.

As the girl started to tell her story, the Rajah listened from a few feet away. He was standing right in front of the mother and daughter but he was on the other side of a shimmering vale with his guide.

"That was very generous of you to help that girl even if it was with a trinket from my palace." The Rajah emphasized the word 'my.'

"Well you aren't using it anymore, Kris said off handedly. "You are long forgotten, war destroyed this land and your palace had been ransacked and left to rot in the jungle."

The prince stood there trying to absorb the information as the girl and her mother turned to go back in the small house.

"I was promised..." the prince began and was cut off.

"How do you know that little girl isn't you in another life?" Kris wasn't about to reveal his mission and go through endless questioning from another pompous ruler, and what better way to stop this princely fit than to riddle him into silence. This gave the Rajah something to think about as they returned to the palace, the one that wasn't destroyed, where their bodies were much as they left them. The prince shivered, he wasn't sure if it was from the future he'd just seen or from the thought that it couldn't be altered.

Kris sat there watching the wheels turn in the Rajah's mind. Thinking, sifting through what he'd seen.

"I will give you as much gold... as much gold as the strongest man can carry, if you can help change that future." The Rajah pleaded with the stranger. "I don't want my kingdom laid to waste, even if I'm not remembered. What can I change to make the future better?" the prince looked to Kris for guidance.

"You are already on the path to saving your people and your legend, great Rajah of the 'Realm of Delightful Pleasure.' The strange guide smiled at the prince. 'Another convert to humanity' Emsaph would mind speak to Kris upon hearing this tale.

While Kris didn't like having to go through so much trouble to look for the Loki Stone, he did like to use the mind puzzles that the Black Hats had taught him on those who thought that the world was here to serve them. It would be easier to sneak into the treasury and look at his leisure but he couldn't detect the Loki Stone except by touching it with his hand. Better to use the treasurer and others to speed the work. Besides, Emsaph had told him to interact with the rich and powerful, 'knowing their minds and hearts will teach you much about yourself' the Unicorn had counseled him.

The Rajah got up to go back to his inner court. The sun had barely moved in the sky from when he had sat down. The red-haired stranger motioned at the prince and at once they were just inside the palace's treasure chamber, leaving Nandi to wonder what had happened, as he was spying on the pair, crouched behind the large fern.

The torches that lined the walls suddenly flamed to life, causing a riot of colors from chests of gems, gold and off of statues with inlays of mother of pearl. The prince always loved standing here among his forebears' holdings. So many of his line had added to this vault. At that moment he could only see it as a way to pay for an army to defend his kingdom from the barbarians that would soon fall upon his people.

Kris had seen many such vaults in his search for the Loki Stone. He knew that riches could bring out the worst in people, and the evil gem of the Norse god Loki would amplify the abuse of power but the Rajah while foolish and lazy wasn't particularly evil.

The 'Masters of the East,' as the Black Hat sect was so reverently called, said to check wherever wealth or power ruled a land. The Loki stone was sure to be as drawn to power as the powerful would be to it.

Once Kris explained the size and properties of the stone that he was looking for, the prince summoned the treasurers to help searching. No records of such a stone were found, but at length, a sliver of the strange stone was found at the bottom of one of the many trunks in the back of the vault.

It was brought to the stranger. Kris could feel its malevolence as soon as it touched his hand. Quickly, he dropped into a leather bag that he had on his belt and questioned the treasurer.

"This is part of the stone of which I seek, why is it not on the accounting of the vault?" He thought that it might have influenced the treasures of the past to not include it on the register.

"If the stone was as big as you say, the treasurer chose his words carefully, "And chipped so easily, a former treasurer or Rajah might have gotten rid of the stone." The clerk was guessing, but Kris read his mind and saw he was telling the truth.

The rest of the treasury was searched, then searched again, but nothing else turned up.

Lastly, the treasurers were all gathered together and Kris wiped the whole day from their minds with all the information that he had told them so that the evil of the jewel would be kept secret.

That night as Kris and the Rajah parted company on one of the high towers in one of the large bedrooms. The prince took out an anklet of six rubies and asked the stranger to give it to the little girl if she had need of it in the future. Kris took the gems from the prince and touching his own Rune Stone that he kept with him at the back of his belt unseen, he pushed the anklet into the stone wall to keep in a safe place if he'd needed to give to little Sonji in a hundred years.

"Good luck be with you, great Rajah." Kris said as a goodbye. "May I never have to retrieve those rubies, my prince."

The Rajah watched the stranger walk out to the parapet and stepped out onto the night air. The prince had stopped being amazed by the strange man, his guide of a possible future. Kris faded into the night, and the ruler turned his mind to training warriors and strategies of battle that his ancestors had used, not noticing that the tale of the Loki Stone was fading from his memory.

Back in the thick forests of Tunguska, Kris was happy to report to Emsaph that at least he'd found out some important news about Loki's evil gem. After contacting the Unicorn using the portal that was very close to the great house, that was made of fused trees, Kris had dumped out the little leather bag's contents into the crystal crucible that the Sisters of the Crossing had brought. Kris avoided even going into the room it was in, to stay as far away as possible from the otherworldly evil that looked so harmless in its crystal form. Within a week, Emsaph showed up to see his nemesis only to find a tiny shard of it in the crucible.

"Well, the Loki Stone seems a bit smaller and cloudier than when I last saw it." the Unicorn joked lamely.

He stared at it for a long while not saying anything. Emsaph's blue eyes glazed over a bit, then the shard lifted out of its container, that would keep its harm shielded from the world.

"Aah... yes, come see," Kris heard the Unicorn calling to him in his own mind. "See the outside of the stone, it's a milky white... and the stone I remember... it was clear and perfect, so hard that it couldn't be broken. Yet this is no harder than a common diamond." Emsaphs mind spoke to Kris with the tone of deductive reasoning, sounding clearly.

"When Odin tore a hole in the universe, it must have damaged Loki's gem quite a bit." The Unicorn finished his theory.

"Is this good or bad," Kris wanted to know? Maybe, it would just fall to dust and he'd be done with having to look for it. The shard floated back into its container, Then Emsaph turned towards his young student.

"Both," the beast said flatly. "It may be in twenty pieces but they will be easier to destroy. If this shard is a true sample then the stone has lost much of its power." The Unicorn explained.

Kris was shocked to hear it. Just by touching it slightly a week ago, still made him feel sick to his stomach.

"I see you've been busy looking." The Unicorn tossed his head to the side, meaning the chest of gems that Kris had collected on his travels.

"One gem for every; Royal Prince, Sultan, King, Rajah and Emperor that I can find." Kris said with a sigh. "It seems that all these lords on high do is amass more and more wealth." Kris said, running his hand through the box of baubles. "Oh, and you were right, all of them were more interested in how they would be remembered by future generations than any other thing that I could do for them." Kris said, dejectedly.

"You'd think that feeding their people and trying to improve their subjects lot in life would be enough to make a legend out of a sovereign, but don't feel down Kris," the Unicorn counseled the young man. "It's like that in most of the universe as far as I can tell." Emsaph mind spoke his sigh. "Luckily, it's not like that in the Realm of the Light Elves, and speaking of which your sister, Mary, will to be coming home very soon." He thought to his student, lightening the tone.

"Why did you want me to keep these gems anyway." Kris asked, still tossing the diamonds, emeralds and pearls around as if they were marbles in the chest instead of each being a small fortune.

"You may need to trade them some day or impress the wealthy with this collection, that's why. I had you take only one gem for one service rendered to these rulers. You could go and rob the treasures of all their wealth, but for what? You are not that kind of person and if you were, the Loki Stone would make you a tyrant in this world."

Emsaph had seen into the young man's heart and knew that Kris cared far more for his family than for all the gold and gems in the world. That goodness of heart made Kris the ideal candidate to collect the pieces of evil that were loose in this world. Truly, the Elves could leave this world to suffer under the evil that the stone; would eventually bring out in this backwater realm but they chose to help. In a limited fashion, for the laws that governed, this realm of Asgard were not the same as the rules that gave the Elves long life and powers of mind over matter in their own realm. So the Norns and the Unicorn that had roamed all of the outlands of Asgard were tasked to help the Druids. An Earth-wise friendly people, who in time came to understand the natural powers that could be used in this world and that had finally bore fruit, a tiny shard that lay in the crucible. 'Well it's a start,' the Unicorn had thought to himself.' Kris had lost interest in the gleaming stones that he'd collected and went to feed the reindeer that the Tungus tribe kept bringing every year. After the first one was killed for its meat, Mary couldn't stand the thought of killing any more animals and since his mentor was of the four legged variety, Kris kind of felt guilty eating meat as well. 'It was a good thing I like fish so much,' he thought to himself as he left the Unicorn in the warmth of the Rune Stone heated house, styled after a house that he'd stayed in while in Asgard and went to do his chores.

Emsaph reached out in the ethers to find Olaf, Kris' brother, on a boat in a sea far to the West. The ship was being tossed around by the huge waves in a violent storm. It was a merchant vessel heavily laden down with cargo from Genoa bound for Cairo to trade for fine Egyptian cotton and spices from the Far East. The Unicorn trotted out of the large house into the stables beyond. They were richly appointed with carvings and scroll-work much like Anika's seachest. Kris probably didn't even realize that he'd subconsciously formed the details of the great house from the memories of his childhood. Now at forty years of age, reckoned by this world, Kris was a well propertied man. A high alchemist and worldly in his travels, educated in languages and customs of a dozen cultures, Kris was still a child at heart. More than anything he wanted to be fishing with his father and helping his mother.

"Did you want me to prepare a stall for you," Kris asked hopeful, maybe his mentor would be staying for a while.

"Actually, I thought you should know that your brother is in trouble again." The Unicorn whinnied. Emsaph showed Kris a mind picture of a merchant ship on its way from Genoa to Cairo to trade wool.

"The ship was being tossed about roughly, in danger of being swamped." The Unicorn mind spoke a little more urgently in his tone.

"He can 'pop' back whenever he wants to," Kris replied flatly. Olaf could use the Runes Stones just like Kris and even though he couldn't draw as much power from the stones as Kris could, Olaf could still easily teleport back to the great house that Kris had formed out of the forest in Tunguska, Siberia.

Since Olaf had chosen to go a Viking, adventuring and exploring in the wide world, instead of helping Kris try to locate the Loki Stone or go with

Mary to see the Elves, Kris tried to act like he didn't care what his brother did.

"I'm sure he would have if he were awake." The Unicorn showed his charge that Olaf lay at the stern of the boat, dangerously close to falling overboard. The mast that had been broken by the fierce winds of the storm had hit him, knocking him out.

Kris ran back into the house to grab the sack of Rune Stones, and disappeared before his mentor could counsel him as to what was best to be done.

Kris appeared several feet above the boat and floated there for a minute to get his bearings.

His brother was still lying on a bale of wool at the back of the trade ship. Cries of woe turned to astonishment as the crew saw a red cloaked being floating above their sinking ship. Kris had been in such a hurry to get here that he'd forgotten about leaving his red cloak and breeches that the Tungus tribe had given him as their honorary shaman. Neither had he scanned ahead to see if there was a common figure that the crew thought could save them from their peril. Emsaph watched his pupil recover quite quickly and glamour himself as a bald, older man that had a halo of sorts around his head.

"St. Nicholas! Our prayers have been answered!" The men cheered. "Save us, please, I shall give all my profits to the church in your name if you would but help us." The Captain pleaded.

Kris had already scanned the captain's mind to find the legends of this St. Nicholas that he was about to impersonate.

"Calm yourselves, sailors of Genoa," Kris was slowly calming the waves and dissipating the storm for a league around the trade ship as he spoke.

Standing there mid-air, smiling at the sailors.

Emsaph mind spoke from Tunguska.

"I see that you've been practicing your lessons, well, I'll leave you to it then...." The Unicorn would monitor the situation in case he were needed.

"Peace be with you all," Kris continued to comfort the men. The boat lifted slightly out of the water so that it wouldn't sink on its own. With so much water in the hold and the wool soaked clear through, it was a wonder that it hadn't gone under by itself already. 'St. Nicholas' caused the water to be drawn out of the boat rapidly. It washed overboard back into the sea. Then the boat lowered down into the calm ocean. The tradesmen were beside themselves with joy. All of the wool was dry and the hold that had been full of seawater, threatening to swamp the boat was cleared.

"You will have safe passage to your destination." Kris assured them. "Next time, don't overload your boat." 'St. Nicholas' chided the merchant captain.

"Thank you, thank you," The captain shouted up to his rescuer. "I shall give the church all of the profits of this trip in your name." He said again.

"Better you feed your family first." Kris replied. "Charity begins at home. Now to your injured crewman." Kris floated down to the rear of the boat.

Emsaph had mindspoke to Kris as he was calming the storm that Olaf was okay but would have a rather large headache upon awaking.

'Serves him right for dragging me halfway across the world' Kris thought back. 'St. Nicholas' was seen touching the hand of the only injured crewmen and floating away with him. The rest of the traders didn't know if he was alive or dead when 'St. Nicholas' carried him skyward. Oh, the stories of this journey were ready to be told as soon as the Genoa traders reached Cairo.

The nearest landfall was to the south and Kris really had to focus his will to channel so much energy to save his brother and the trade ship. He left the ship and took his unconscious sibling and flew to the land of the ancient Pharaohs. It would have been too taxing for Kris to mentally shift back to their home in Tunguska. His Unicorn teacher hadn't been kidding when he'd told Kris that it would take a couple of hundred years to get the hang of using the stones all the time.

The storm was just now reaching the coast, so Kris stayed far above the thunderheads and landed further inland. Near exhaustion, Kris landed quite hard outside of Cairo, with the massive pyramids off in the distance.

Finally, Olaf awoke, rubbing his head at the pain of being struck with a glancing blow, of the mast from the trade ship.

"You are lucky to be alive Olaf, my oaf of a brother," Kris chided. "I wasn't paying you any attention and if Emsaph hadn't been looking out for you..." Kris let his brother finish the sentence in his own mind.

Olaf was in enough pain already and Kris didn't need to rub salt in an open wound.

"I guess this means I'll owe him a brushing of his flea bitten fur coat." Olaf said, jokingly. He loved the Unicorn almost as much as his brother, though he didn't like to owe favors to anyone.

"That and warmed oats with spring timothy grass, just the way he likes it." Kris added to the chore list. "And you might as well consider yourself his indentured servant for the next hundred years." Kris finished.

"Better you'd have let me drown little brother." Even though Olaf had been born before his younger brother, Kris' time in Asgard had aged him ten years older than Olaf.

"Now that you're both safe, sound and on the ground," Emsaph chimed into the conversation in both of the brothers minds, "I'm going now but will soon return with your sister." The Unicorn informed them. "You should rest for a while Kris," Emsaph suggested though it sounded more like a command. "The land you're in has many wonders to be sure." He finished mind speaking with the two. His presence faded from their minds and the Unicorn headed for the portal to retrieve their sister.

Olaf with his headache and Kris realizing how much energy he'd used, looked like a couple of hung-over sailors that had wanted to see one of the last remaining of the seven wonders of the world as they stumbled forward.

The people of Cairo were used to seeing strangely dressed foreigners wandering around. But there was a strange sight indeed; one who looked like most of the Italian traders and one who had a scarlet cloak and breeches that carried a linen-sack also of bright red.

After a time, Olaf's head stopped throbbing and Kris got his strength back in his legs and they made their way towards the Pyramids. Kris felt something tugging at his mind, thinking it was Emsaph he open his consciousness to the mind paths of communication.

"State your business here!" a voice rang in his head. Olaf had grabbed his own head again, 'so he'd heard it also,' Kris thought. Both of the brothers looked around for the source of loud challenge that had been directed at them.

"Who am I addressing?" Kris asked, neither returning the challenge, nor sounding timid.

"Call me Sphinx." A voice said.

Kris switched to second sight and looked towards the Great Pyramid. A shimmering image of the stone Sphinx that would be uncovered, hundreds of years later started to form. It solidified in the in-between of second sight. Though it looked much more feminine in appearance than the stone structure that is around today.

It was larger than a Viking long boat. Its fur was like that of a lioness, that Kris had seen in one of his travels in India, a pet in some ruler's personal zoo. The creature had a coat of a golden tan of fine nap but with slightly darker spots near her hind. The Sphinx's wings remained tucked in at her sides, but looked like they could unfold to an amazing width. The forepart of the Sphinx was a beautiful, if somewhat feline looking woman. Her nose was more animal than human and her eyes were slitted and iridescent, like a cat's. Kris tried to fix his gaze on the eyes of the Sphinx but they shifted slightly out of focus, much like trying to see the desert horizon through the heat of the day.

Kris and Olaf were taken off guard by this entity. Why hadn't Emsaph told them of this strange creature that was a part of their world. The Sphinx turned its body fully towards them, so that it could study them intently. Finally, the great Sphinx spoke to them.

"Long have I slumbered beneath these sands, after that pompous Pharaoh carved his likeness into the rock that holds open the doorway between my and your worlds. He destroyed my image in stone. That a grateful people had made of me, when I agreed to be their portal guardian," The lion-bodied woman explained. Nodding at Kris, she said,

"You come bearing the power stones of the gods of the far north." It was more a statement than a question. "I see through you," she continued, "They are all dead," she went on with a visible sigh. She sat down on her haunches and looked at the pair of men that had awoken her.

"It's the way of things, I suppose. That's the great mystery... the ultimate riddle. No matter what is done with your life, be you man or god... why does the end always come as a surprise? It was a rhetorical question, my young men. Though you may look for the answer for the rest of your lives if you choose." The eternal lion of the desert laughed lightly. She was enjoying the company that she had missed for so long. True, many men worked and lived close by, but few had the second sight and still fewer wanted to talk to her. So she slept at the portal between her world and that of Earth at the edge of the land of Africa.

"So... my travelers from distant lands, let us tell our stories." The Sphinx offered. "I'm guessing that's why your Unicorn friend sent you my way." She smiled. "He did promise to stop by once every five hundred years or so." Her voice had a sorrowful tone to it. "I can't go running about your world like he does all the time," now her voice was envious. "While I can see distant lands in this world, I am charged to guard this portal for a few more millennia. So I don't get the run of the place like that horned pony. Her eyes twinkled a little. Kris thought that meant she was joking. But he didn't want to press the issue.

"Did he ever fix that hole he was always going on about?" This question allowed Kris to begin to tell his and Olaf's story, which delighted the Sphinx to no end. A great tale with mind pictures supplied by Kris and partly by Olaf of their adventures. She was more than happy to return the favor, telling the brothers of the ancient days of Egypt and the wonders of Africa. She did stop them from traveling any further beyond her portal into the continent though.

"Many are the portals, as you call them, in the Earth... each land mast has its own 'Realm of Asgard,' so to speak." She explained. "As Odin, the dwarves and elves are connected to the land to the North so I am connected to this land here and behind me to the east is the land of the Jinns. Long-lived they are, like your elf friends but are not to be trifled with, especially with you carrying those power stones with you. You'd be asking for trouble to go there." She suspected that the Unicorn had sent them here to not only be taught but also that he could send her word that he was much engaged elsewhere. Still, she liked the new stories, so it wasn't that much of a bother to instruct these two on the places to watch out for danger.

"Far across the sea that lies to the West is yet another land with many doors to other worlds that have no contact with this side of the Earth." Now that they had gotten her started, she was a chatty thing.

Emsaph long ago had showed Kris, Earth, as a globe, but the man hadn't thought that there were any boundaries that he couldn't cross. The Sphinx had told him that walking around with the Rune Stones could be dangerous for him. Even if others couldn't use the power, they would still be attracted to it. Suddenly, Kris felt that his world was much smaller and more dangerous than an hour ago.

"Do not be troubled... little man," the Sphinx cooed. "You have eight other worlds to see that others of your realm don't even dream about."

She had enjoyed their time together and even though he was just a human and she an ageless being that spanned worlds, she was fond of Kris and his brother, Olaf. As they parted ways and Kris was fully rested and about to blink back to Tunguska, the Sphinx asked them to visit once in a while to tell stories or just to visit.

The two humans vanished and the Sphinx was settling down for a very long nap as the sun set yet again on the horizon of the Great Desert.

"Well that's a good place to end this week I guess." Olaf told me as he got up to leave.

I knew better than ask questions... though he seemed to always answer them with the next week's story. I hadn't thought of why there was no Santa Claus in Africa or South America. It just didn't occur to me. But to have it explained so simply was very disarming.

'Maybe, I should rethink my approach to this storyteller,' I thought to myself. I'd tried to push him into making a mistake by throwing questions at him to see if he'd trip up. I'd looked for a flaw in the story, maybe it was my journalistic need to look for the truth behind the tale, maybe I was just uneasy about being caught up in something that was pushing me out of my little comfort zone. Either way I wanted to know more about the man who was pushing my buttons.

I was right behind Olaf as we left the café, but a mob of tourists blocked my view and by the time they had moved through the narrow hall of the market, I'd lost sight of him again.

Augustus Krup's Wagon

Chapter 7
The Elves

The next weekend, Olaf was already sitting in the booth waiting for me. I remembered what the storyteller had said about the 'glamour' that he had put on the booth. I thought to myself, 'Jack, why are you disappointed that you didn't see any of the magick that Olaf claimed to possess?' As I saw him waving to me, I got my drink and headed over to sit across from him.

"So where's the 'glamour?'" He asked the question that was on my mind before I could ask it. "Well, Jack, I didn't think you believed in any of that mumbo jumbo so I didn't bother to include you in the little spell that I've worked up, sorry," He said, shrugging his shoulders.

"Okay, if that's what you want to say," I didn't try to hide my disbelief from the storyteller. "So what's the tale about today?" I asked, as I rearranged my backgammon chips lazily, not looking up to see his disapproving stare.

"Well now, we've covered quite a bit already," Olaf said stroking his closely trimmed beard. "Maybe it would be..." He continued to rub his facial hair. "This happened around the fourteenth century. It was definitely between the plagues, of that I'm certain," he seemed to be pondering. Then Olaf drank some of his tea as he collected his thoughts.

From Nicholmas, the festival of Saint Nicholas on December 5th, until Twelve-night, the last day of the Christmas holiday on January 5th, Kris traveled across Europe and upper Asia delivering gifts to children and food to the needy. He loved the feeling of giving a toy to a child, knowing that the little boy or girl would feel loved. Hopefully, when the child grew old enough to see the toy for what it was, a token from an unnamed benefactor. That thought enough of them, to give them a toy of their very own.

The child's parents would look dumbfounded as the child emptied out their shoes that had sat by the fire to dry overnight. The squeals of joy at receiving the little gifts, brightened up the small country cottages in the darkest days of winter. More often than not, a goose and a bag of oats were left on the table for a little Christmas feast. In some of the more remote places that Kris visited, he would leave the whole family presents, most were practical, a new axe, some kitchen utensils, and obviously food, but also he'd made sure the children got a toy or doll to cherish. The parents would stand over the delighted child and just stare at each other, both thinking that the other had somehow found some money for such an extravagance. Then a smile would start on either the mother's or father's face, when the memory of their own childhood Christmas present came mysteriously, during the longest nights of the year. And the looks on their own parents faces when their gifts came from that unknown source.

"Don't forget to look in your stockings." The mother would say, remembering the exotic fruit called an orange and nuts that had to be from some far off land that she had found in her own stockings when she was a child.

While Kris was playing Father Frost in the Western part of Europe, Mary, his sister, was gift giving in a similar fashion to the children in Russia and Italy. As a rule, she didn't like to leave the local vicinity of the greathouse in Siberia, unless it was to go visit the Elves. But something deep within her, the shadow of the memory of her own childhood and her father's death, made her want to help give a happy memory to children everywhere.

In Italy, Mary played the part of the local folk legend as the Lady Belfana. Belfana was an old woman who rode a broomstick through the air and gave Italian children presents at Christmas if they were good and coal if they were not. Mary didn't really fly around on a broomstick though. It would have been hard enough just to balance her full bag of toys and treats on a broom if it were just hovering in the air slightly off the ground, let alone with her on the broom as well, swishing across the countryside. So, she would put the image of a flying witch into the minds of the sleeping children she visited as she filled their shoes and stockings with small toys and treats.

In Russia, Mary became known as the Lady Kolyada. Wearing jewel-encrusted white elfin robes and with her strawberry-blonde hair, Mary looked very otherworldly in her reindeer driven sleigh. Giving toys and sugar candy out of a sack that was very similar to her brother Kris'. It was bright red, trimmed in white fur and had a Rune Stone at the very bottom. The stone had been magicked to keep the bag filled with toys and candy. Everytime, Mary pulled out a toy or stick of candy out of the bag, it was immediately replaced with an identical copy, using only a tiny-bit of power that was held in the Rune Stone. It was an inspired idea to use the Rune Stones in this way, to drain their terrible power in the most benign and beneficial way for the children.

One Christmas eve, Kris had finished his gift giving early in the eastern providence of the Gelderland. There weren't that many families in this remote part of the country, so the night's work had went quickly. He'd filled the children's shoes and stockings that were drying by the fire with nuts and toys in the small villages that he had visited. As he was carrying on the legend of Father Frost, the local gift giving old man of the Winter Solstice.

Kris stopped his white horse, named Rishka, at a crossroads, to see if there were any houses left to visit in the region that he had missed. The mare stomped her hooves in protest for having to stand in the cold wind while her rider just sat on her back.

Kris couldn't concentrate on mind casting to sense any human life with his horse so agitated. He patted her neck and read her thoughts to see what was disturbing her.

Rishka was remembering how much the cold was like life on the farm, before Kris had saved her.

She had been a plow horse once and had been forced to have a metal bit in her mouth as she pulled a plow for an owner that abused her and fed her only enough to keep her alive. Usually, the farmer left her out in the cold, in winter, not caring if she lived or died. Then one day, Kris was passing the farm and saw the farmer whip the poor horse for refusing to work. She fell over from exhaustion and lack of food as the farmer raised his whip to finish beating her to death. Kris called to the man to stop.

The farmer's arm seemed to be frozen in mid-air, the painful blows of the whip had ceased for the beaten animal but she was too tired to care. Kris had ridden over on his own horse, a black stallion, and bought Rishka her freedom from that horrible man right on the spot. The farmer laughed when Kris paid his asking price saying,

"All you've bought is meat for your table." As he counted his pieces of silver coin.

Kris didn't reply, instead he placed his hand to the injured horse and put a picture of green fields full of sweet grass and a shaded stream for her to drink into her mind. Rishka thought that man was death come to call her to a better place. But it was a kind man who had the strange magick of the fairies that Rishka had seen playing at the edge of the forest on midsummer nights.

They would pop in and out of space in the low brush from twilight until well after midnight. This is just what happened to Rishka. She found herself swept along in a swirling blackness to a stable lined with fresh straw and a feed bag, full of oats that tasted sweeter than anything that Rishka had ever been fed by the farmer.

Her new owner was more of a caretaker, seeing that she was well fed and groomed. Pictures of calm scenes filled her mind as she was being attended. Rishka came to trust her red haired savior and let him ride her bare back. Kris knew he had to be gentle with his new refugee. And, after a time, the mare's sweet temperament came back to her. But sometimes, she would have a flashback to the farm where Kris had found her, like that frigid night.

Kris soothed her wounded memory and mentally warmed the mare with power from the Rune Stone that was on his belt. After she settled down, he cast his mind out in this remote corner of Gelderland, feeling for any houses that he might have missed on his gift-giving mission.

As Kris reached out further with his mind, he 'heard' a cry of desperation that far off in the distance, near the border with Germany. Kris was taken aback by the despair in the man's mind. The man, Hans, had been in an accident when his single horse driven sleigh had caught a tree root that was just under the freshly fallen snow, causing the sleigh's rung to break off, just as it was rounding a narrow corner above a steep ravine.

Hans had tumbled out as the sleigh and all of his family's supplies had come down the steep slope behind him, starting a small avalanche that buried him at the bottom of the ravine. Kris sent his mind forward to view the damage.

The pin that held the horse's harness to the sleigh had snapped as it had started to tip over, so the horse was unhurt, if a little scared. It had trotted on ahead, knowing the way home. Using his second sight. Kris went to where the injured man lay. Hans had a broken arm and a lot of bruises from his fall but the snow that had covered him had also protected him from the weight of the sleigh that had rolled on top of him. The small avalanche also had trapped the man who thought that he'd die from the cold before his kin would be able to find him in the morning.

Kris touched the Rune Stone on his belt and folded the space around him and his horse, to go to the wounded traveler in the blink of an eye. Kris then quickly dismounted Rishka and put the huge sack of toys and goods down so that he could dig through the snow covering the injured man.

Hans was sure he was hallucinating things when he heard a horse snorting nearby. He remembered falling out of the sleigh at the top of the ravine and hitting the snow bank hard as the sleigh had rolled over him; breaking his arm. Even if his kin had gone looking for him on this cold wintry night, there was no way that they would be able to get down into the ravine without ropes. Hans was certain that there wasn't a trail that a horse could find down into the ravine. All of the absurdity of a possible rescue was going through his head as a hand thrust through the snow and grabbed his cloak near his throat. In one swift movement, he was dragged clear of snow that had entombed him. Hans sputtered and coughed as he lay on top of the snow looking up at his rescuer.

The man had flaming red hair and a kind face, with cheeks either redden by exertion or by the cold night air, stood over him. The stranger was of average height and obviously very strong. The rescuer reached down to feel Hans' arm. The injured man had thought he'd heard it snap on the way down the ravine and now was worried why it had stopped hurting.

The stranger stood up and Hans grabbed his arm where he thought he'd had broken it. The arm felt fine if a little cold but that was hardly surprising, considering that he'd been lying there since a little after sun down.

"A little brandy, I think," the red-haired stranger said, and turned get a flask out of his sack.

Hans struggled to get to his feet, his left arm may have been fine but the rest of him was badly bruised. He felt a hand under his right arm help him up to stand. The world swayed back and forth in front of Hans' vision. A flask was put into his left hand and he took a small sip. Hans felt his blood start to warm again. As his strength returned faster than Hans would have thought, he watched the stranger dig his family's winter supplies out of the snow bank, he accidentally created on the way down the ravine. Soon the red-haired man in a bright red cloak had all of the stores in a pile. Then, he grabbed the sleigh and flipped it as though it was a child's toy, throwing the snow that it was full of, into the air starting a small blizzard that obscured Hans' vision for a minute. When he could see again, Hans was amazed that all of his supplies were in the sleigh and the large white horse that he had heard while he was under the snow, was standing in front of his sleigh ready to be hitched up, waiting to depart.

After Kris had made sure that the man, Hans was his name, didn't have brain damage from such a bad fall. He slipped the injured man a flask of strong honey wine and found the packages while Hans tried to stand without falling over. Flour, beans, and oats enough to feed a family of three until the first day of spring. 'A good man in a bad way. I'm glad we came this way, Rishka', Kris thought to his horse.

Though not as smart as his Unicorn mentor, the mare could under-stand and communicate with mind pictures. And unlike Emsaph, she rarely talked back, which was kind of like a bonus, which Kris had men-tioned more than once to the Unicorn. A picture appeared in his head of Rishka and Kris blinking from house to house. Kris understood it to mean the question. "Are we going to take this man home now?" He patted her shoulder trying to convey the meaning of patience to his four-legged friend.

Kris turned to right the damaged sleigh. 'I had better not let Hans see me fix his sleigh,' Kris thought to himself.

So he flipped the snow-filled vehicle and willed a sudden wind to whip the dry snow crystals into an impromptu storm between him and the man he'd rescued. Quickly, he touched the Rune Stone at his belt and concentrated on the broken sleigh. The twisted metal ski grew a bright blue and straightened and melded to the frame that had held it to the sled. Kris looked over the rest of the beaten old sleigh. 'Oh, why not,' he thought.

The entire sleigh glowed with a soft light blue and boards that had dry-rotted and were in need of replacing, became as good as new. The metal parts became pliable and reshaped into sturdier versions of themselves.

Kris then set the sleigh down and mentally commanded the packages into the back of the sleigh as the wind died down, letting Hans see the end result of the small miracle.

"Well, I think your horse must have gone on home so," Kris said to Hans, "if you don't mind, I'll hitch up mine."

The man just nodded, swayed a little and had another sip from the flask of brandy that Kris had given him.

Rishka stomped her hoof at the suggestion of being hitched up; she hated the metal bit in her mouth and wasn't going to let Kris use reins on her without putting up a fight. He'd always ridden her bare back, using mind pictures to direct her, and that wasn't going to change without a whole lot of trouble from her.

Kris read his horse's mind. Her life at the farm was playing over again in her head. She'd kick him if he bridled her and he wasn't about to try.

He calmed her private thoughts by putting an image in her mind of her trotting on ahead of the sleigh while it followed behind her, without being hitched to her. She snorted and made a slight whinny in agreement. The tense muscles in her neck relaxed.

Kris turned his attention to Hans. The dazed young man hadn't moved except to take another couple of swallows of the strong honey wine.

'The way he is going, he'd finish the brandy soon and all for the better,' Kris thought to himself.

Hans was loaded into the front seat of the one horse sleigh with the large white mare in front. Kris pretended to pick up the imaginary reins as he put the image of a fully bridled horse in Hans' mind and flicked the lead saying, "Ho, there."

The horse slowly started to trot through the bottom of the ravine. Hans tried to make suggestions but found that he'd drank too much of the long liquor that Kris had given him to make much sense. So he sat back and let the other man drive the horse. It was his horse after all. They entered what Hans remembered was a steep drop off at the end of the ravine as it let out into the valley just where the high road twisted and turned on tight switchbacks that were dangerous enough to use in the summertime.

Kris mentally forced the snow in front of Rishka to harden until they got to the drop off. Rishka stopped at the edge but Kris urged her onward, placing the false image of a gentle slope before her eyes. Rishka blinked and cautiously put a hoof out into what she had thought only a moment before, was thin air. The footing seemed solid enough to her. She took a less cautious second step. Then, proceeded on down the path to the floor of the small valley.

Kris was busy trying to hold the false image of reins on his horse that weren't there in Hans' mind and the illusion of ground under his horse as she walked on a ramp that he'd created with the help of the Rune Stone at his belt. As the full moon crested the ridge behind them, Kris could make out his passenger's destination. At the far end of the valley near the frozen river was a small house that was easy to spot with smoke coming out of the chimney.

Kris managed to get Rishka, the sleigh and Hans down to the valley floor without much trouble. Hans had opened his eyes a few times but whatever the young man had seen, could easily be explained by the strong drink from the flask. Even though Kris had mastered the Rune Stones ability to cloud a man's thoughts and rewrite his short-term memory, he had already been in the Hans' mind enough for one night so Kris would let brandy and reasoning fill in any strange things that Hans had seen.

Soon, they had joined with the mountain road as it met with the low road in the valley. Rishka felt she had slipped a little as they got to the main road. The ground was cold again and had patches of ice that she could see clearly on the moonlit road. The dry snow was being blown around idly by a slight breeze that was coming up frozen river. 'No doubt this was tributary to the powerful Rhine,' thought Kris. And he was right.

Hans and his father had made their living, trading up and down the mighty river that started high in the mountains of Switzerland and wound through Germany and Gelderland out to the North Sea near Rotterdam. But, it was an unusually cold winter and the river had frozen over early that year, so Hans had had to go over the mountains to get more food for his family when the roads were at their most treacherous.

As they neared the house, Hans was coming out to his haze. He shifted in his seat to point out his home and tell Kris that this was his stop. Kris let him mumble excitedly as the full moon continued to rise behind them. Rishka was guided to the small shed that was behind the home. The sleigh came to a silent stop in the crisp, freshly fallen snow.

Hans got out of his side of the sled without checking to make sure his feet were under him and made an impromptu snow angel and he tried to stand.

With a sack of beans under one arm and helping Hans with the other; Kris made for the front door. A sliver of bright light met them as they rounded the corner, then the front door was thrown open wide as the entire family ran to see what was wrong with their kin. Kris was pelted with questions…

"Is he okay?"

"Where did you find him?"

"Is he hurt?"

Kris didn't try to interrupt. The family's anxious energy needed to be vented. Hans' wife was the first to see that more than anything, her husband was drunk. She looked to Kris for an explanation as he unburdened himself of his load, setting the beans on the kitchen table and Hans in an obliging chair. Anna, Hans' wife, stood in front of Kris blocking his path to the exit with her arms crossed and an unpleasant look on her face.

A grandfather was closing the door and Hans' two small children were huddled next to their mother, clinging to her skirt.

Kris related a fairly accurate account of how he found Hans and had given him a flask of brandy to warm his blood. Anna looked at her husband who wasn't known to drink with kinder eyes and finally noticed the bruises on the side of his face and raw skin on the back of Hans' hands, that he had gotten trying to break his fall in the icy ravine.

"My poor husband," her mood softened as she gingerly helped her husband remove his shirt. That drew gasps from his whole family. There were dark purple bruises from the small trees that hadn't broken Hans' fall and the sleigh that had rolled over Hans during his accident. The children rushed passed Kris to their father. The old man hadn't moved but stretched his neck to see his son's battered body.

"Since no one has said it yet," the father said, with more emotion than he was comfortable with, "Thank you. We were expecting him at around sundown," he went on, "I've had a hard time keeping Anna from going out to look for him. Then, when our horse came home without the sleigh, she was inconsolable." The father finished nodding his head towards his daughter in-law.

"You're very welcome...sir," Kris said lamely. He knew the father's name was Jarvis, he had waited to read any of the family's thoughts until he was halfway through his tale, when the fears of the wife and children had calmed down enough for their minds to be read.

"Forgive my rudeness," the man started. "I'm Jarvis, Hans' father. That's Anna," The old man pointed the wife who was examining her husband's hurts, "and those are my two joys in life," he said, pointing to the children who darted behind their mother's skirt. "Ava and Karl," the old man smiled at their shyness.

"I'm probably the first red-haired person they've ever seen," Kris said, to give the children an excuse to be so shy. He turned to face the Ava and Karl directly and watched them fully disappear in the folds of Anna's skirt. "I should finish unloading the sleigh," Kris started to head for the door. "Those oats and salt would be gone in the morning if there are any deer around tonight." He said over his shoulder.

Jarvis grabbed his thick woolen overcoat and followed after him. Soon, all the winter supplies were brought in and Kris pushed the sleigh into the small shed that doubled as a stall for Hans' own mare. He stopped to check on the family's horse. It had avoided a spill into the ravine, along with Hans, only because of a couple of gnarled oaks at the edge of the road. The horse had fallen hard against the stout oaks and managed to keep its hooves under it enough to amble home. Yet the horse had four bruised ribs and a pulled neck muscle. A quick Rune Stone-aided rub down later, the horse slept under a new horse blanket that Kris magicked from his stable in Siberia. His mind turned to the supplies that Hans was trying to bring to his family. Even with rationing it wouldn't be enough to last until the ice broke on the river, allowing Hans to take his boat out for more food. It would be another dangerous trip over the mountains. Kris thought about increasing the family's supplies as he folded space around Rishka to send her back to her heated stall at the great house. He mind-spoke to her, that he would join her and brush her down as soon as he had checked on Hans one last time.

But, when he entered the front door Jarvis met him with some strong alcohol of his own making. The white-haired father insisted that Kris share in the family meal, since he had brought the day to a happy ending.

Kris first checked on Hans, who was sleeping peacefully near the fire. He was full of strong honey wine and a couple of homemade remedies of herbs and alcohol. Kris put his hand under his cloak as though scratching his back and put his other hand on the sleeping man. Using the excuse of checking Hans' freshly bound wounds; Kris quickly healed them, so that Hans would be as good as new in the morning.

'Rishka will be angry if she doesn't get her grooming,' Kris thought to himself as he accepted the family's hospitality.

He turned back to Jarvis who thrust a pewter flagon full of home brew into his hand.

"Come sit," Jarvis pointed into the kitchen area to the table.

Anna had set out what was to be the family's celebration dinner, of the much needed supplies, that would see them through the harshest part of the winter.

The meal was hardly a feast, the goose was a little on the small side; the pie was more crust than berries and the cheese was hardened. But, it was the very best that the family could offer to Kris. After they had taken their seats, Jarvis raised his glass and toasted his son's rescuer.

"Sir, I know not where you hail from or what takes you from your family this day, but tonight here I christen you a member of our family. Tonight you are a Kringle!" Jarvis said, with emotion that he usually he kept to himself. The old patriarch of the family clinked his pewter mug against Kris' to seal the edict.

Kris looked to Anna, who had given him a stern glare when he had brought in Hans, to see that she was smiling and made it a point to touch her glass against his, to let him know that she had also welcomed him to the Kringle's feast. On the other side of the table, the two children held out their own goblets as far as they could to reach Kris' mug. He stood up and extended his own and made sure to softly tap each of the children's goblets in turn, then he sat back down.

Jarvis raised his pewter mug one more time.
"To your health and long life, Kris Kringle," Anna and the children echoed Jarvis' sentiment. This touched Kris in a way that he could hardly explain. The generosity of the Kringles to welcome him in and share what

243

little they had was remarkable. The year had been a poor one for the family; it had rained when they had tried to harvest their crops causing most of their grain to spoil and Hans' trading on the mighty Rhine River hadn't brought in as much as the family had hoped. Yet, the Kringle's were happy with what they had and truly cherished the love they shared.

The meal was finished far too fast for Kris' liking. He would make sure to do something about that.

Filling the Kringle home, was the kind of abiding love that Kris had remembered from his own childhood. The plates were cleared, a portion of the feast was saved for Hans and Jarvis poured the last of his homebrew into Kris mug.

"Well now, tell us a tale of your travels," Jarvis prodded Kris.

"Yes, do tell us," the children chimed in. They had warmed to Kris' presence during the meal and now thought of him as an uncle come to call from far away.

'It must be my red-hair,' Kris thought to himself.

"Very well," Kris thought for a moment. "Here is a tale of my dealings with the Grand Turk, Sultan of the sea of fire. Where sand burns your feet and trees are but a dream to the people there."

This drew oohs and ahs from Karl and Ava who were under a thick blanket in the small loft that was over the kitchen that served as their bedroom. The story was when Kris had to trick the Grand Turk into letting him see into the royal treasury to search for the Evil Loki Stone. Kris fed images of the distance land, where the air was full of spices into the minds of his audience as he wove the tale around plot twists and unforeseen events to the delight of the Kringles.

After the story, the children drifted off to sleep, filled with dreams of far away lands, leaving Jarvis and Anna to talk to Kris. The conversation turned to little Karl. It was easy to see that he was a dwarf and would never grow any bigger than he was now. Anna worried for her son. She had heard stories of the mistreatment of dwarves of other lands. They were sold, by their own families to traveling circuses, performing for the amusement of strangers. Kris hadn't heard of the traveling circuses, between looking for the Loki Stone, helping people in need and having been gone for decades to meet Frey, ruler of the Realm of the Light Elves, he had been too preoccupied to hear about the plight of the 'little people.'

Anna just didn't know how her darling son was going to fare in the harsh world. Jarvis commented on how smart his grandson was, and would go far regardless of how tall he grew. Kris listened quietly and went into Karl's mind, What Jarvis had said was true and not just an overly generous grandfather touting how wonderful his grandchildren were.

Little Karl was very intelligent; Kris felt he had to think about Karl's future and the future of these unwanted children.

Anna turned in first, going up stairs after kissing her sleeping husband on the head.

Jarvis yawned a couple of times before finally saying he was in need of some rest. After putting more wood on the fire, he took a couple of blankets from a chest near the fireplace and settled into a low seat across from his son. Leaving a blanket on the larger padded bench that Kris could use for his own bed.

Kris made sure that the whole family was asleep before he blinked back to the greathouse in Siberia. He had a lot of work to do before morning and first on his list was to take care of his horse, Rishka, who had gotten tired of waiting for him to come back and went into her stall and gone to sleep. Kris quickly filled up a feed bag with her favorite food. Apples and oats with a little sweet grass and woke her up so that she could eat while he groomed her. Mary came down to see why her brother had come in so late. Kris explained the night's events to his sister and told her a detailed account of what was happening to the dwarf children all over Europe.

Mary was beside herself with anger. Though she had mainly stayed away from the great cities of Europe, she hadn't been a total recluse. She had spent a lot of her time with the Tungus tribe and was well loved by all the children in the village. The thought of unwanted children being sold into slavery was just too much for her to take.

"Some...thing must be... done," her voice stammered with the emotion that was overwhelming her. "At once, tonight!" her face flushed with color. "You're better with the Rune Stones than either Olaf or me, bring him here now and contact that Unicorn." She stomped outside to get some air, as Kris touched the stone at his belt and thought of his wayward brother.

Olaf was summoned, though he wasn't happy about leaving the Chinese junk as it sailed the South China Sea to come home to an irate sister.

Kris explained how upset Mary was and how she had demanded that something be done. The two brothers sat in the stables brainstorming, when Emsaph finally answered Kris from just the other side of the portal, mind speaking,

"You rang? It's a good thing that I was near this end of the universe."

Sometimes Kris couldn't tell when his mentor was kidding. Emsaph appeared at the door before Mary came back. The situation was explained in full to the Unicorn, when Kris had finished Emsaph said,

"Elves seem to have a greater respect for life... great and small, than humans do at present. Present company excluded of course." He finished, nodding to Kris and Olaf.

"And that needs to change," Mary interrupted the Unicorn before he could go into a lecture about the evils of the Realms he watched over.

Augustus Krup was busy counting the night's meager earnings and mumbling to himself about how the cold weather kept townsfolk from coming out to see his troupe of little people. The shutters on his wheeled caravan, that served as his office and home, banged back and forth against the sides of the wooden structure. The sign on the side of the wagon, once richly painted, advertising 'Krups collection of gnomes' was now in a sad state of disrepair.

'Maybe, we should winter in Southern Italy.' The balding German thought to himself. 'Yes, they might like my midgets. It would be easier to convince the Romans that I had captured and tamed a strange race of little people.' He thought, as a smile crept across his craggy face as the prospect of profit entered his mind.

Indeed people might, though Augustus was getting older, with thinning hair, he was well muscled and had a look of danger in his eyes. This more than anything else kept people away from viewing the dwarves he had bought and trained to do tricks. The midgets he'd collected from Northern France and the Netherlands numbered only thirteen, but with only a few threats and an occasional beating they learned to do tricks very fast. Juggling and acrobatics were all he required of the little people, skills that the midgets learned, were enough to wow the yokels. Most townsfolk would pay just to see the novelty of something different and that was fine with Augustus.

The shutters banged harder as the wind whipped around the camp.

"Damnation," Augustus muttered as he reached for his cloak. "I'll never get a night's rest with those things making such a racket."

He was starting to hate winters. The cold would seem to stay in his bones from Nicholmas to the May Day festival. As Augustus opened the door to his small-wheeled caravan he was hit full in the face with an icy blast of the north wind. He decided to definitely head south in the morning.

The 'circus master,' as Augustus thought of himself, was met by a rather odd party at the bottom of the stairs. They were easy to make out in the full moon light. A strawberry blonde-haired woman in an emerald green cloak, flanked by two men that were probably her brothers, one full blonde; the other a redhead.

"No shows tonight," Augustus said, throwing up his hand to the trio.

He started to turn away from the group to refasten the caravan's shutters when he noticed a single white horn leveled at his belly. The horn was attached to what appeared to be a small black horse. Augustus stopped in his tracks.

"Is this yours?" thoughts of 'Augustus' Exotic Creatures' was cut short by a voice that rang in his head.

"Listen to the Lady, she is the only one kind enough here to let you live." Emsaph knew what kind of man the 'circus master' was, the kind that would only listen to the sound of money or a threat.

Augustus looked back to the beautiful young woman who hadn't moved and her two brothers, to size them up as possible murderers. The blonde one was much like Augustus was in his prime, muscular arms showed from under his cobalt blue cloak. The other brother was a little smaller but looked just as strong as his sibling.

'Why do redheads always wear red,' Augustus mused, as he noticed the bright red cloak the Kris was wearing. Casually, he looked over his shoulder to see if the Unicorn was still at his back. Now the moon had been covered by a cloud, all Augustus could see were dark shapes and patches of snow that dotted his campground.

"What kind of trickery is this?" Augustus roared, as he turned his full attention back on the three. No one had moved... the man in the red cloak still had his hand out of sight, which could be resting on the hilt of a sword. Still no one moved as Augustus yelled at them again, as he did the dwarves he owned.

"I'll beat you to a bloody...pulp." His voice lost its edge when he noticed that they didn't seemed threatened.

"Are you finished?" the woman spoke for the first time. Her voice had a musical quality to it, not demanding like Augustus' first wife had had.

"Well, um... yah." He came back rather lamely.

"We wish to see your so-called 'gnomes.'" She was referring to the dwarves that Augustus had forced to wear red and green pointed hats, in an effort to make them look like the small forest creatures of legend.

Something in the tone of her voice made Augustus feel that there could be a great deal of money for him if he let these strangers have a private showing of his midgets. Twice he had given exclusive viewing to some nobles who had ended up buying a dwarf for their own household. Maybe as companions or to entertain the nobles, Augustus didn't care; he was well paid for the little men that the nobles wanted. These three hadn't struck him as being nobles; they didn't have jeweled broaches to secure their cloaks. Then, a thought entered his mind, 'nobles that didn't want to be robbed, wouldn't wear expense gems out on a lonely road in the middle of nowhere at night.'

That reasoning made sense to him. Augustus glanced back at the trio as he got a lantern to light out of his caravan. Their clothes were odd. The men were dressed simply but with well-tailored shirts and boots. The woman's outfit was hard to make out because she had kept her cloak drawn tight around her, but at her throat a lacey white material could be seen, lace always meant money to Augustus. Only the very rich could afford such luxuries.

After Kris had erased the presence of the Unicorn from Augustus' memory, he put the thought that he and his brother and sister might be nobles, into the circus master's head. Then Kris mentally told his siblings to relax. Now that Augustus thought there was money in it for him he would be easier to deal with. Emsaph, trotted along after them, invisible to the circus master. The Unicorn volunteered to run the slaver through, but Mary vetoed that action with a withering glance.

As they waited for the man to find a light, Olaf muttered, "We could just take the little people without all this pretending."

"I want to know what's in this man's heart," Mary said, plainly. "What would make a man enslave and mistreat another person." While she had dealt with her own childhood pain of just that act, she still didn't understand those kind of people. Kris offered to read Augustus' mind to his sister but she retorted that the mind and the heart both rarely spoke in males. That silenced the rest of the party quickly.

Augustus lit the lantern and led the three humans that he could see and the one Unicorn that he couldn't, to a smaller, more weathered caravan that housed his little people. As the party rounded the coach, Augustus pounded on the outside to awaken the his midgets and to give them time to get on their lederhosen and felt caps. He knew that even under a threat of being beaten, it would still take them a little time to get ready, so he tried to stall.

"Lady and noblemen," improvising was never Augustus' strong suit. "From far away lands I've collected these forest creatures..." 'damn, not a good time to become tongue-tied,' he thought to himself. "Err, for your viewing pleasure." It didn't rhyme, but it would do. More importantly he had said, Lady and noblemen, loud enough so that his troupe would know that they were to be their best or they would get very badly beaten. Augustus bowed as best he could, 'I'm was getting too old for this,' ran across his mind. He straightened himself with a slight groan and opened the door to show off his little gnomes.

In the doorway were eight little men, smiling like they were happy to be stared at and trying not to notice the cold. They fumbled down the stairway that was much too large for their gait. Augustus thought that having the dwarves struggle on a simple stairway was subtle way to introduce his dwarves to the public. The five smallest came down to the ground while the three tallest gnomes stayed upon the steps.

Mary knelt to view one of the smallest of the little people. He was a man of forty and looked like he had seen better days. Augustus brought his light closer to her so that she could get a better look. The circus master saw that her cloak that she had kept so closely drawn, had fallen open to reveal a richly jeweled outfit of exotic design. The word money, money, money was all that Augustus could hear in is mind.

"Are there no females," one of the bothers asked the circus master. But Olaf was too entranced to answer, let alone notice which brother had asked.

As if in answer to that question, five little women appeared at the top of the stairs of the small caravan. The men had gotten ready faster than the women and had tried to entertain the visitors until the women could get dressed. The little ladies had the same fake smile as the little men, so happy to be seen by such exalted people. The dwarf men on the stairs helped the little women come down as gracefully as they could. Finally, all the little people gathered in a semi-circle around the 'nobles.' In unison, the men bowed and the women curtsied to their guests.

"Would you like to see them do some tricks?" Augustus offered. Maybe that would please the nobles.

"No, no I don't think we'll be wanting that." Olaf said, disgustedly. He turned to his sister and said lowly, "Let's end this."

It was loud enough for the circus master and his troupe to hear. They started to worry. Had Augustus camped near a town that would consider the little people witches? None of the circus folk moved.

"Do not be troubled my little friends," Mary's melodious voice filled the silence.

She turned to Kris. "They are well fed but have been tormented by this...man," she said. speaking of the little people but pointing to Augustus. Before the circus master could speak in his defense, the lantern he was carrying went out. He groped in the darkness back to his own wagon to rekindle its flame.

Augustus didn't know what was going on but whatever it was, he was going to put a stop to it. As the flame grew in the latern the burly man returned to the small caravan to find everybody had vanished. Nobles, gnomes and wagon simply weren't there. Even the small ponies he'd used for the gnome's caravan were gone. Augustus thrashed about in the under-brush looking for some sign of his midgets or the people who had come to see them. The big man raged and cursed for over an hour before he gave up looking for his dwarves.

'There went my livelihood," Augustus said to no one, as he slowly mounted the steps of his caravan. He had a repeating dream every night for a week after that. More like a vision, of a small fishing village in the South of France where he could keep the peace for the village and maybe find some barmaid to love.

Back at the great house, deep in the forest of Siberia, it took a long time to convince the little people that they were free of Augustus or of any other master. What would keep another stronger, bigger man from enslaving them all over again, one of them asked. It was a good point, well made, by the oldest of the little people, the same man who had ap-proached Mary back at the circus camp. His name was Luc, and while he wasn't formally educated, he did have a lot of firsthand knowledge about the way the world worked.

More little people were freed from the traveling circuses that winter. The great house that had seemed so cavernous only a season ago was be-coming a bustling small town. The dwarves were amazed by the kindness of these "big people" and some were worried that there would be a price to be paid for all their good fortune. But their hosts had gone out of their way to be accommodating. One morning, not long after their arrival, Luc found that the main staircase in the front of the house had been somehow magically changed. One side had steps for big people but the new half of the stairs had been changed, made smaller. They were just the right size for little people. Also Luc noticed that his room had shrank a bit. It did seem silly notion at first, but the window sill that had been too high for him when Mary had offered him the room, was now perfectly placed for his smaller stature.

Luc had become the unofficial leader of the dwarves, though he didn't know why really. The new arrivals found out through the grapevine that he was the one to talk to about their new situation. The little Frenchman didn't mind much, he just wasn't used to having any authority.

What will become of us?

How do we please our hosts?

Why have we been freed?

Those were the usual questions that Luc got from the newcomers. He hadn't seen any sign that the tall red-haired man or the strawberry blonde-haired woman, were in anyway being sly or evil. The tall blonde man was a little more gruff than his siblings but he wasn't mean. Food appeared at mealtime and everybody had their own room, it was more than he had ever dreamed of having in his life. There was even a hot bath and sauna over the stables. When the man called Kris wasn't off bringing more little people to the great house, he was making sure everybody was comfortable and somehow teaching the Spanish dwarves to speak German and French. Within a few days, all of the little people could communicate with each other.

Kris was thankful that most of the liberation of the little people had gone smoothly. Luckily, he had had Emsaph with him, in case things got out of hand.

The last rescue had gone particularly badly. Near Paris, a practitioner of black magic called, Desireé, was going to use the dwarves she had bought as human sacrifices. Kris had heard of black magic, but had thought that it was more about mind altering incense and debauchery than about invoking a dark power.

Well he was wrong; the raven-haired beauty wasn't about to give up her 'little people' so easily. She saw through his attempt to manipulate her mind and hit him square in the chest with hex bolt, that shot out of her fingers like lightning. Kris fell back, his arms wrapped around his aching chest. He knocked over some of her magic books and a scrying crystal off of the small table in her cramped, little room, as he slammed against the floor, hard. Books continued pelting him as he rolled back and forth, knocking more of them off the table. Then, Emsaph shimmered into the fray. The small Unicorn's eyes burned a bright blue as he stood between the witch and his friend. Desireé thought that this was the spirit that she was trying to invoke.

"My lord," she started slowly, 'nothing was written in her occult texts about a black Unicorn,' she thought to herself. Desireé tried to phrase her request in the ancient manner, "You come to me... in your chosen form, to smite my enemy?" The books weren't clear whether this was to be a question or a statement, so Desiree tried to make it sound like it could be either.

"Hush my child," Emsaph didn't know which dark lord this woman was worshiping and frankly it didn't matter. They all pretty much had the same shtick.

"Open your mind to me, reveal your heart's desire." As he mind spoke to her, Emsaph thought of some appropriately foreboding music to play behind his words. The witch's eyes widened as she heard the right words in reply to her summons. This was just like it was suppose to be, she'd done the spell correctly. And the eerie music she heard, sent chills up her spine.

'He must be very powerful,' Desireé thought to herself, 'I hope I have enough of the halflings to sate his blood lust.'

'Humans, so predictable,' the Unicorn thought to himself, as he played his part. Her jumbled thoughts came to him in a torrent of passion, both good and bad.

A rich Count, had shunned Desireé and left her alone and pregnant with his child. In her despondency, she sought revenge. After the baby was stillborn she turned to the quickest way that she could, to get revenge that she had known of...black magic. To smite that rich bastard who wouldn't marry her because she was without title and too poor. Pierre had used her, he'd promised Desireé a ring and comfortable home just to get her into his bed. Then, when she became pregnant, Pierre refused to see her. After her repeated attempts to talk to him, Pierre left Paris to his estates in the south.

But that was not all, he went to the south of France to seek a wife. The south of France, where rich men went to find rich women so that they could keep their blood lines blue. God above, she hated that Pierre. All of this and more she poured out of her soul to the black horse-shaped imp with the single horn.

Emsaph pitied her, but couldn't allow her to harm Kris or any of the 'little people' that she had locked in her root cellar. With her defenses down, Emsaph quickly entranced her mind and removed the more painful of her memories that had caused her to take such drastic actions. He deftly removed the treacherous lover and the death of her firstborn from the tormented woman's mind. Then, he filled in the blank spots that he had created in Desireés memory, with a pilgrimage to the Notre Dames of

France. A spiritual trip to inspire the woman's soul. Emsaph continued to fill her emptiness with joy and hope and a need to help others.

Then the Unicorn turned to his pupil who was still clutching his chest. Kris would be fine; Emsaph had seen the energy building up in the woman's hand before she struck, giving the Unicorn time to shield his student from most of the deadly blow. He grabbed Kris' cloak with his teeth and pulled.

"Hey, watch those teeth of yours," Kris mumbled, as best he could with his jaw clenched. "I don't need you to bite me to remind me to keep my guard up."

"Bite, smite it's a mood thing for us dark lords." Emsaph quipped. "Now, go down to the root cellar and tell the little people, that for all intents and purposes that the wicked witch is gone." He whinnied as he turned back to watch Desireé who was still in a trance, as she was feeding the fire with her book of spells and incantations she had written.

When Kris showed up at the great house with the five captive girls that were going to be sacrificed, Luc was waiting to talk to him about the questions that had been nagging him. Questions that all the little folk had wanted to ask but they didn't want to offend their rescuer. But seeing Kris having to steady himself by leaning on the small Unicorn, just to keep his balance, had caught Luc off guard. The little man was taken aback by the pain on Kris' face and decided to wait until later to question his host. The little French man shepherded the girls into the kitchen to get a hot meal into them and left Kris with the Unicorn in the stables.

"That's the last of them," Emsaph mindspoke off-handedly to Kris.

"Uh," was the man's reply as he sat down hard on a low bench.

"So have you thought about what you're going to do with all these persons of smaller stature?" The Unicorn queried.

Kris replied, "Right now, I'm just trying to think of why you let me get practically disemboweled by that witch."

"Serves you right for not being more careful," Emsaph lectured. "Didn't you learn anything at that monastery in Tibet? I'm sure that I told Lobsang to teach you about the dark powers that are afoot in this world."

Kris nodded his head as an answer and tried to change the subject.

"I don't suppose the Light Elves would be willing to take any refugees?" He hoped that his teacher might say yes.

It's not that the little people were a burden, far from it, they hauled water and chopped wood without any complaining, unlike Kris' brother Olaf. But everything had happened so fast. Mary had wanted these people to be freed. Now that they were, the question of how could they have a chance for a life of their own choosing, came up.

"I'll ask the Elves for you, I need to get back there before the frost giants try to start another war anyhow." the Unicorn mindspoke. "You, educate the 'little people,' either in their dreams or hold classes. Knowledge is power, and that has never been more true, than for these people." Emsaph finished by giving Kris a mental image of Mary playing schoolmarm while Kris walked up and down the rows of chairs to make sure that the students were not falling asleep.

Weeks passed and Kris did instruct the 'little people' in their dreams, of languages and geography, of math and science. The dwarves came to see what they could accomplish with their lives. Not juggling for some Noble's amusement, or being gawked a by a bunch of slack-jawed yokels, but having a place in the world, respected and well paid for their knowledge.

This amazed the 'little people,' who had been told their whole lives that, they would never amount to anything.

Luc had seen much of the small miracles, but though he knew more than he ever thought possible, he still had a question to ask of his host. One day, he managed to find Kris working on a small rowboat in the workshop that was between the kitchen and the stables.

"Why do you not magic the wood to do your bidding." Luc asked a simple question of Kris, to break the ice for his much bigger question. The little man remembered the stories that Kris had told them all one night, the building of the great house and the trees bending to the will of the mind. Kris had told them most of the tales of his life. Of his own boyhood village, Haven, and of its destruction by the slavers. Of the blackspire mountain that he called the 'witch's teeth.' As Kris told the stories he'd gently place images of his travels into his audience's minds to help them picture his fantastic tales.

"I've worked on this boat for many years," Kris said, as he put down a chisel he was using to ornately carve the bow. "It's just busy work for my hands so my mind can think. But you didn't find me to ask about that did you?"

"No, no not really." Luc said while looking away. "It's just that you've helped us when others used us. You've taken us into your home and taught us. I guess what I've been trying to ask is... "What is to become of us? Luc's face flushed red. "I mean with all that we can now do and know, are you to send us back out in the world to make our way? Won't we just get beaten, bought and sold just like before? Only instead of just doing tricks, we will also be doing the accounting?"

Luc was troubled, he hadn't wanted to be the leader of the refugees.

The job was foisted upon him. He certainly didn't want to anger his host, rescuer of them all. The little man looked up to see Kris smiling widely.

"Well, I've been pondering those very questions myself. That's what's been running through my mind, these last few weeks." He said, with appreciation for his new friend. Kris went on to explain that there was a place that the 'little people' could go to and not be exploited, in the Realm of the Light Elves. Luc was stunned not only that the old legends that he had heard were true, but that his rescuers had been trying to find a place for them. As the conversation ended, Kris realized he should have told the 'little folk' about his hope that Frey and the other Elves, would welcome them into the Elfin realm. But Kris hadn't wanted to spread a false hope. The decision from the High Counsel of the Elves could take months.

A meeting was called for that night of everyone to come to the front hall, but instead of a story by Kris or his sister, the 'little people' would hear the plan that Kris and the Unicorn had come up with for their future. After hearing about the Elvin Realm, the group wanted to know all about the Elves and what their world was like. Kris and Mary supplied mind pictures and sounds from their own memories of the place to the refugees. Near the end of the meeting Kris heard his mentor's mind calling out to him from just on the other side of the portal.

"Put on your good shirt and pants, young one, I bring the 'Sisters of the Crossing' with me." The sound of a snort was the end of the message. Kris could tell from the tone of the message that it was good news was coming for the 'little people'.

"Well, it seems we are going to have a little more company tonight." Kris told the entire crowd.

Mary made her way through the group and headed upstairs to change out of her dirty work apron. Olaf went out to the stables to ready a stall for Emsaph. He filled the trough with oats and sweet grass and placed a few apples on the rail for his four-legged friend.

Kris stayed in the large front hall and calmed his guests. He sent images of the three elfin sisters with their names to the group as well as their official title.

"What crossing?" One of the dwarves asked about the strange title that the Norns had.

"Good question, Fiona," Kris recognized the curious teenager's voice immediately. "There are only a few who can move between the Realms safely. The Unicorn," Kris reminded everyone of Emsaph, "I think you all have met. Tonight you will meet, Elphaba, Titania and Nula," mental pictures of each one of the Norns appeared as their names were spoken, "They will ferry you across the great distances of the void to your new home."

A nervous excitement seemed to take hold of the group, which quickly built in anticipation of the Elves that were coming from far across the vastness of space just to see the 'little people.'

A few minutes after Olaf and Mary had returned to the front hall, Kris got a mental call from his mentor.

"Would you be so kind as to come get us at the portal?"

'Wow, Emsaph was being far more cordial than usual,' Kris thought, 'He only uses that tone when he's on official business'. Kris touched the stone at his belt, willing himself to the local portal that led to other Realms of Asgard.

The sisters were there, in all their usual finery. Beautiful wine colored gowns with threading and gems sewn into the bodices, the color of fine honey. They looked much as they did when Kris had seen then all those years ago. Perhaps a little older, but only a little.

"If you would be so kind as to take the ladies to the house," Emsaph mind spoke in formal tones. "I'll join you shortly." The Unicorn then trotted off slowly through the forest in the general direction of the great house.

"Oh, don't mind him," Elphaba, the blonde-haired sister, said offhandedly. "He's been in the void so much lately he probably just wants to feel the ground beneath his hooves." She smiled sympathetically after her mentor.

Kris watched the Unicorn disappear behind a stand of trees and then turned back to his remaining guests. The sisters gathered close and clasped each other's hands as Kris thought of an empty room that was just off the large entrance hall of the great house. He had purposely kept it empty of furniture for just that use. The Rune Stone was touched and the four moved in an instant in the 'in-between.' Mary and Olaf were waiting outside the door to welcome the 'Sisters of the Crossing.' After some small talk, the sisters met the 'little people' who were waiting for them in the front hall.

"We would like to offer you a place among our people," Titania started.

"There is much we can teach each other," Elphaba chimed in after her sister.

"And time moves very differently there, so even the oldest among you could easily live another two hundred years." Nula finished.

Questions of what the place was like and what occupations the 'little people' would have in the Realm of the Light Elves. Would they be servants to these taller beings? Would they have places of their own? Did the

Elves want all of the 'little people' to come or just a few?

The sisters thought it best to hear the group voice their concerns before replying. One of the sisters mentally asked Kris to find Emsaph, so that the Unicorn could be there to project the answers of the sisters with pictures. The 'little people' could then see the houses that they could have for their very own and the libraries and workshops that badly needed their help.

Kris headed straight for the stables to find his friend. With all the traveling that the Unicorn had done lately there was a good chance that he hadn't had a decent meal. Kris' reasoning paid off quickly as he found his friend, face deep in the feed bag that Olaf had set up for him.

"You're wanted in the front hall, whenever you stop eating that is." Kris said, as he grabbed a stiff brush from a shelf and started to groom the Unicorn.

"You really think I'm going to move while you're brushing me?" Emsaph countered.

Kris laughed and thought to his friend, "I'll stop when you do, deal?"

"Keep brushing," Emsaph thought back.

In due time, the Unicorn showed up in the front hall and provided the pictures of the Realm of the Light Elves. The 'little people' were beside themselves with joy. If the place was half as good as they were shown, then it would be a paradise. The next day all the 'little people' were ready to depart. What few earthly possessions they had, the 'little folk' could easily carry to their new home.

Mary and Olaf waved goodbye to their new friends. Kris, the sisters, Emsaph and the 'little people' headed up the hill to the portal. Mary was especially going to miss the little ones. They had become part of the family, as far as she was concerned. Olaf was really going to miss all the extra help that Luc and the others done, in cleaning out the stables and feeding the ever growing household.

As Kris topped the hill, bringing up the rear, he mentally asked his mentor how were they going to be able to move over three hundred people at once. The Unicorn relayed his question to the sisters, Nula mind spoke to Kris with a hint of mirth in her 'voice.'

"It's not the number of souls that cause problems for us." Then an image of the sisters and the Unicorn entered Kris' mind, along with a rather angry dragon that they had had to calm and then transport across the void.

"Now, that was a difficult trip." The other two sisters mind spoke as one.

The Unicorn was waiting at the spring, standing slightly about the ground, by a few inches, with the sisters standing behind him. Kris went over to join his mentor as the three sisters had the group crowd in together as much as possible. The 'little people' watched with amazement as a fog formed at their feet and quickly wove itself in and around the group. No one could see the dense forest or the person next to him or her. In a trice, they were gone.

It was a few weeks until Kris returned to his siblings at the great house. That was the time it took here on Earth to travel the incredible distance to the Realm of the Light Elves drop off the 'little people' and return. Kris told Mary that the 'little folk' had been welcomed with a huge feast.

Over the years, the 'little folk' would come back to visit the great house, usually in a group of twenty or thirty. They told tales of being made honorary Elves.

Which is what they have become known in the stories as Santa's elves. And that's why the stories of elves had always confused people, because there are more than one kind you see. Olaf explained as he took another sip of his tea.

Anyway, some of the little elves had gone on to learn to work silver the elfish way. A little 'elf' brought Mary a set of silver-crafted sleigh bells that chimed in a way to enchant all who heard the sounds they made.

These Mary used when she would go out among the people of Russia in her reindeer driven sleigh, when she played the role of the Elf Maiden, Kolyada. Some of the 'little people' eventually came back to stay. They had missed their connection with the Earth.

Many of these 'little people' stayed in Russia. Most went in the service of noblemen in the court of the Czar, offering their skills to the nobles, for good treatment and high wages. The visiting diplomats assumed that the dwarves where there to entertain as they had been in the west. But actually, the 'little people' performed an invaluable service to the court of the Czar. When the ruler left the room for a break in diplomatic talks for instance, his court left with him, leaving the 'little people' standing at attention. This almost always happened when a trade agreement or a treaty had reached a sticking point. Then the French or German dignitaries talked openly in their native tongues, in front of the dwarves, blissfully unaware that they were giving away important information about upcoming treaties and their own nation's economies, to spies that were standing right in front of them.

After several minutes, the Czar would return to the meeting room complaining of a headache or telling the diplomats that he had pressing business and would adjourn the meeting until the next day. The dignitaries, not wanting to offend their host, would accept a postponement and that would give plenty of time for the Czar to consult with his 'little' spies.

The diplomats never could understand how the Czar could drive such a hard bargain, it was as though he had read their thoughts, someone suggested.

These 'little people' were well thought of by the royal court and were attired in uniforms of generals, made from the finest cloth.

In fact, Peter the Great, the Russian Czar, celebrated the marriage of his niece, Princess Anne, by staging a wedding two days later between his own favorite 'little person' Valakoff, and a female dwarf, Anna, who was in the service of a princess. Peter had invitations to the affair delivered by dwarfs who were all given a new set of clothes for the occasion, and the guests included over seventy dwarfs, most of them from the Czar's household, and all had once stayed at the great house in Siberia. I think that was around 1710 if I recall correctly.

I sat there in the booth thinking of how easily my storyteller had fully explained the common misconception of why the legends and fairytales of Europe had always confused tall and little elves.

"That's about it for this week," Olaf stopped himself when he saw the puzzled look on my face. "Now before you ask, Kris also didn't forget to help little Karl Kringle. After a few visits from 'uncle Kris,' the boy could speak and write in a dozen languages. Kris knew that if he taught Karl a useful skill, people wouldn't care about his size. The Kringles soon became known up and down the River Rhine for having a son that could help in trade negotiations. The traders were amazed with all the languages that he could speak. Karl was a much needed addition to the traders on the Rhine. People came from as far away as Scotland to trade for German steel in those days. And most of the people of Gelderland couldn't speak the Scottish brogue. So they overlooked Karl's height, or lack there of, and praised his ability to translate between the different trading groups that came to the city of Hague to sell their goods. In time, people came to trust Karl's fairness as well and he became a judge over trading disputes, living a very happy life."

"So how many more chapters are there to this story?" I asked.

"A couple, I suppose." Olaf replied, then he took a sip of tea. "Actually, I was wondering what you're doing the weekend of December 5th?" He asked. "It's a couple of weeks away."

"Well, are you about done telling the tale?" I wanted to know. I'd had seven chapters of a book but what good would it do anyone, if the ending weren't finished. I could fake it, I guess, but people would be able to tell the difference.

"This might have to come to a close, which should be fine, the parts that need to be told, will be." Olaf said thoughtfully. "In the next couple of weeks you can make a list of your questions, it will be a long car ride."

"Car ride?" I was intrigued 'Would I get to see the Norns.' The thought raced though my head. "Where do you need to go? And can't you just blink yourself there?"

"Over to the ocean or very near to it," Olaf brought his thumb and index fingers close together, between us, at eye level. "And if I did 'just blink myself there' I couldn't finish the story." He bristled at the suggestion of my questioning him. "I'm not sure who's to meet me there so... it'll be a surprise for the both of us either way."

'Now this development was intriguing,' I thought. "Okay, I can rent a car for the weekend." It would be an interesting journey, one way or the other; a small part of me still wanted proof. I really hoped that it was true, that there were portals to other worlds, Elves and maybe I could get to meet Santa Claus.

It wasn't until I'd made the reservation the next Monday that I actually realized I was excited by the prospect of having all my doubts wiped away.

'Be careful what you wish for...' I thought to myself as I fielded calls for 'Ask Aunt Sally' column that was due at the end of the day.

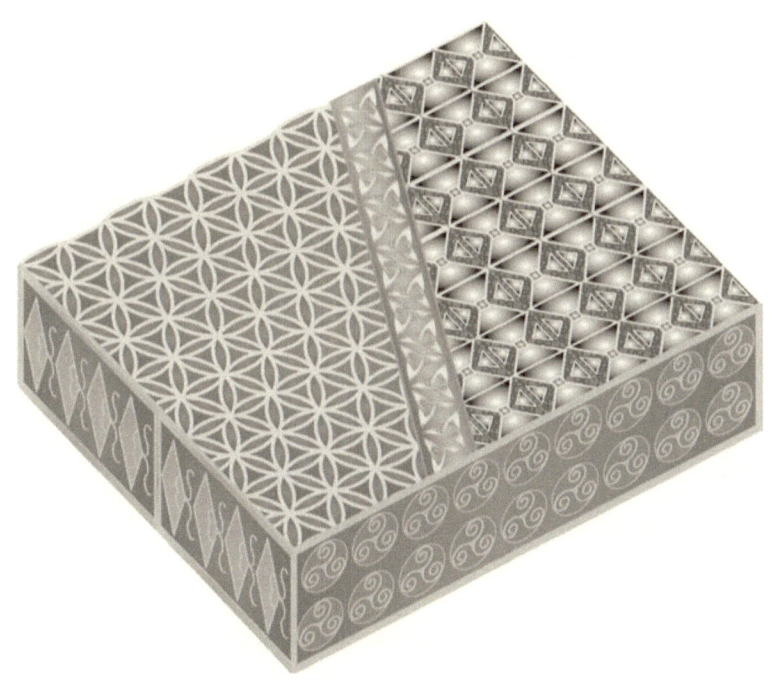

The Oriental Puzzle Box

Chapter 8

Kris plays the role of another Saint

The next Saturday, I'd gotten my mocha and was about to sit in my favorite corner booth when I saw four young women sitting there. 'So this is what a 'glamour' looks like,' I thought to myself. Maybe Olaf was telling me the truth. I was just about to slide in when one of the girls said,

"Hey, we're sitting here! Find your own booth."

I tried to find and excuse, "Ah sorry," I mumbled. "I didn't see you there."

I moved off and looked for another spot. The only seat that wasn't filled was near the front. 'At least, I'll know when Olaf shows up,' I thought.

After a while, Olaf appeared in the doorway of the café. He placed his order and got the backgammon board out of little cupboard that the games were stored in and headed over to the table where the girls had been sitting. He smiled at me and went back up to the counter to get his tea and some sugar packets. I got up from my place and followed him to the booth in the back of the café.

"So, how did you like the glamour I put on the table?" The old story-teller asked.

"I honestly didn't think you were serious about that." I felt like a kid seeing his first magic trick.

I had a whole new perspective on my storytelling friend. Everything he had told me up 'til now was just tall tales. But this display of magick, or whatever it was called, put his story in a new light. Then I thought back.

'Did I see the girls get up from the table and leave?' I hadn't looked in their direction after one of the girls had chastised me. I'd been sitting near the front of the café, looking out one of the bay windows, too embarrassed to look back to see if the girls were still there. My logic kicked in... was this really magick or were there four girls sitting in the booth and Olaf was just using the situation to his advantage?

"Still a skeptic, I like that." Olaf chuckled. Then, he changed the subject. "This week, I thought it would be good to tell you about what happened in the 17th century." Olaf said thoughtfully.

"I couldn't help noticing that you kind of skipped ahead a few centuries. Is there a reason for that?" I asked. It seemed that he'd been leaving a lot out.

"I'm telling the story as it winds through time. I could sit here and tell you about the black plagues and the pestilence that were visited upon the world or about the crusades and the rise of the Roman Catholic Church. But Mary and Kris were busy with the Elves, off world for a lot of that time. I stood in for Kris as Father Frost for a couple of hundred years. It was kind of fun, actually. Also, I kept track of the rise of the wealthy and powerful for Kris while he was away." He explained. "The Unicorn was sure that the Loki Stone would turn up in one of the royal treasuries sooner or later." Olaf smiled slightly. He left that thought and rolled his dice.

The year was 1760; the colonies of America were still under Mother England's rule. The trading in the East India Company was in full swing and France was still suffering from its latest war. The conflict was with England over a colonial struggle that remained unresolved. It was called the Seven Years War.

France, crippled by corruption and mismanagement by the ruling class, was to lose most of its overseas possessions to the British. Diplomats, on both sides of the English Channel, were still busy ironing out a lasting peace accord. In this interplay, Kris had placed himself at the service of Louis XV, the King of France. At the time, Kris was calling himself the 'Comte St. Germain.' It was a title of low noble birth, as though he was the illegitimate son of a minor duke somewhere in Eastern Europe. The title Kris had chosen, had given him access to all the royal courts in Western Europe without too much fuss over who his father and mother were.

As it was the height of rudeness to ask such questions of a nobleman. If you had the right manners and money, nobody would question your nobility in France at that time.

Kris had used the name and title for over one hundred years and the people of Europe began to tell tales of the man who never got any older.

Kris had decided to use the mystique to his advantage. Over the years, he'd watched the people he'd helped, poor young women that he'd given dowries to, so that could marry into wealthier families and improve their lot in life. The children that he'd looked after, making sure that they always had food in their belly and a roof over their heads. People that had lost hope in their lives and that he'd gifted with a bag of coins for a better tomorrow. All of this and more he had done and still it wasn't enough to make the world a better place.

'Little acts of kindness will make a difference over time,' his mentor had told him. But it was hard to see any large changes in humanity after hundreds of years of trying to help people. Finally, after talking the situation over with his brother and sister, Kris came up with a plan. It would take generations to change the minds of the rich and power to get them to unwittingly help but it was worth the effort.

Kris had finally tracked down the Loki Stone in France in 1675 when King Louis XIV 's court jeweler had resized the stone to about half it's original dimensions. The jeweler cut away the flawed bits of the outer surface, which were still beautiful if somewhat less clear. The pieces were then recut again and sold to nobles of the king's court.

The jewel, which became known as the French Blue, was then set in the Royal collection.

At that time Kris, playing the part of the lowly born noble man, had managed to become the talk of Paris. With his knowledge of many languages, the mysterious alchemy lab that he set up wherever he lodged and especially because of all the gems he wore. Louis the XIV became an admirer of the strange eastern european nobleman.

Kris played the role of St. Germain, entertaining the King with many stories of his adventures and for his ability to fix flaws in gemstones. Unfortunately, he didn't get into the King's good graces soon enough to 'fix' the Loki Stone but he did secretly buy or trade the Nobles of the court for their own bits of Loki's evil gem.

The King came to Kris one day with a diamond that was a gift from the Emperor of Austria that was worth five thousand francs, but if it hadn't had a flaw it, it would be worth double that amount. St. Germain took on the challenge of fixing the flawed gem, returning it to the King after working his Alchemy 'magick' on the jewel. The King was overjoyed when he had his royal jeweler appraise the diamond's value at around ten thousand francs. These skills and his knowledge of almost every known language fascinated Louis XIV. Soon, the St. Germain was doing secret errands for the King outside of diplomatic circles. These errands soon made Kris despised by many nobles of the French royal court, because he had earned the King's ear, and many of those same nobles also coveted St. Germain's fabled casket of gems.

It was more of a elongated chest than a casket, that Kris had picked up in India on one of his many trips. He used the ornate box to store all the diamonds, pearls and other gems he'd collected on his travels as he'd searched for the Loki Stone. Emsaph had told him that all those jewels might come in handy one day, but at the tender age of eighty, Kris never would have imagined playing the part of a noble man. Let alone needing all those gem stones to impress people.

Having watched how the politics that the Nobility played at the royal courts all over Europe and Asia, Kris was amazed that they all were pretty much the same. The lower of the noble born would do just about anything to raise their status, while the upper Nobles saw this as a challenge to their position in the court. If the ruler was wise, which was rarely the case, he would use the nobles infighting to further his own agenda. If the ruler was unwise, then he was either a puppet of the power-hungry or soon replaced. In France, Kris found a wise ruler at an important crossroads of history. And if Kris' plan worked out, then not only would he have the last remaining pieces of the Loki Stone, he would also be able to change the course of history for the better.

Kris put to use all the grace and charm of the noble born, that he'd had learned over the centuries. As the Comte St. Germain, he had acquired almost all the pieces of the evil gem. All but one that is, that remained in the collection of the King of France.

Three people waited for the mysterious Comte St. Germain, in the richly furnished salon of Madame de Pompadour, in the apartments she occupied at the palace of Versailles.

Voltaire, a friend of St. Germain's and one of the foremost writers and philosophers of the age was in attendance. As was the Count Maupeou, the President of the French Parliament and Madame de Pompadour. The Madame was explaining the reason for summoning Maupeou.

"I've opened this letter... at the time and date that was written on the front," Pompadour held up the note for the two gentlemen to see the finely scripted letters. "As I was instructed by, St. Germain and in it was written this note," The Madame gave no indication that she would let

Count Maupeou see what was written. "It says to summon you here at this exact time, to collect a diplomatic pouch and take it directly to the King." She said, tapping the letter lightly, then Madame slipped it in with the rest of her special letters that was tied together in with a large pink satin ribbon. Most women of the court kept love letters and poems written to them in such a fashion. Madame de Pompadour kept every scrap of paper that could be of use to her. "I suppose that the courier will be here, shortly." She then placed the packet of letters into her purse and took a long time to fasten it closed.

The Count knew better than to ask to see the letter.

"I really must protest, my lady," the Count said, in an agitated voice. "The government doesn't run itself." He was upset about the mysterious Comte St. Germain character. But while he was there, the Count thought he might as well get information about the low born interloper as well as counsel Madame de Pompadour on befriending St. Germain.

The Madame was once the mistress of the King and still was in his royal good graces. Her station in life had changed from royal mistress to arranging parties and social functions for the royal house. This gave her enormous power over the nobles. They could not attend one of her parties for the King without an invitation from her, so everyone tried their very best to stay on her good side.

"Don't be so cross Maupeou, Madame de Pompadour said, forming her mouth into a pout, "You'll wilt my flowers." She finished coyly.

The Count did his best to keep his blood from boiling.

"It's just that I don't like this man," Maupeou said good-naturedly. "So little is known about him. I've had spies on him in London, here and in Vienna. And I can't say I approve of his being so friendly with the other royal courts." Maupeou tried to seed his dislike of St. Germain on the other two. "He's part of secret societies with strange rituals that I wouldn't dare repeat in the presence of a lady." He smiled deferringly to Madame de Pompadour. "Now he's the diplomatic courier for the lasting peace between England and France? We don't know where his loyalties lie." The Count raised his voice on the last sentence to drive home his point.

But Madame de Pompadour and Voltaire were used to the ploys of politicians and didn't seem to convert to his way of thinking.

"Calm yourself, Maupeou," Madame de Pompadour reassured the red-faced Count. "Have some of these delicious Italian chocolates." She raised her hand fan and tossed her wrist towards the small silver dessert tray that lay on a sideboard. A servant rushed over to bring the delicacies to the obese nobleman, so that he wouldn't have to stand.

"Come, come, now your sweet tooth is almost as legendary as you patriotism." Madame de Pompadour cooed to the troublesome politician.

The Count placed five of the expensive chocolates on his beefy left hand before letting the servant take the silver serving tray out of his grasp.

The Lady Pompadour took out her fan, pretending to fiddle with it idly, and forced herself not to mention that her guest should at least have taken a small dessert plate to pile on the chocolate treasures, so as to not stain the rich silk that covered his arm chair.

"What so you think of him, Voltaire?" Maupeou asked of St. Germain, while gorging on the rich chocolates. "You are always ready to speak your mind."

Indeed, Voltaire had been exiled from France for that very reason. At the moment, he was in the good graces of the royal court, partly due to the former Mistress of the King, Madame de Pompadour.

"Well, if you must know..." Voltaire began thoughtfully, "I think that you don't like a conspiracy unless you're in on it, Maupeou."

Madame de Pompadour giggled behind her fan and blushed with practiced ease of a courtesan, while the Count's face deepened to a darker shade of red.

"Oh, conspiracy indeed," Madame de Pompadour chimed in, "Such intrigues should be left to women, for we are more subtle than men and delicacy is our forte." She stated in a matter-of-fact tone.

"No, no... beauty is your forte, Madame." The Count said, to stop her before she went on about those libertarian ideals of hers.

She smiled, more to conceal her amusement at his clumsy attempt at flattering her, than at the compliment itself.

Maupeou pointed to Voltaire with his chocolate covered finger.

"The man knows everything and never dies, you said that, Voltaire." The Count quoted the writer / philosopher. The Count wasn't sure he could turn these two against Germain. They didn't seem to react to his rhetoric but maybe he could still get some useful information out of them. 'They think I'm an oaf but we shall see who is more cunning here,' the Count thought to himself.

"I've heard rumors of a woman in Vienna..." the Voltaire started.

"Aha! So maybe he is aligned with Austria." Maupeou jumped at the tidbit of information like a fish about to be hooked.

"Obviously, any man as refined and rich as Germain would certainly attract young ladies to his arm wherever he goes." Madame de Pompadour said longingly.

"Blast, where is he!" steamed the Count.

"If he'd managed to catch the tide and sailed from England then rode three horses to death he still wouldn't be here by now," reasoned Voltaire.

"And what's the use of being noble born if you can't be fashionably late," the Madame quipped. "More chocolate, my dear René." Madame de Pompadour rarely used the Count's first name, so that and her practiced look of concern for his comfort had him stuffing the expensive chocolates that Germain himself had brought to her earlier in the week.

Kris, in the guise of the Comte St. Germain, had watched the whole conversation unfold in the salon from his vantagepoint of the in-between.

It was true that he'd had a hand in Europe's secret societies, mainly the Rosicrucians, Freemasons and Society of Asiatic Brothers, but there were others. Where bored rich men took oaths of loyalty to each other and thought that they, the noble born, were being taught the secrets of the Ancients. For Kris' part, he'd turn a brick of lead into gold or cause one of the new members to float in the air. Simple uses for the Rune Stones but he got their attention and then after a few meetings, he would bring forth the doctrine of the 'Philosopher Kings.'

It was a manuscript he'd made up about the distant past. Where the rich gave to the poor and improved the people's lot in life and most of all... educated the children. For all that, the ancient nobles were given great supernatural powers by the 'Ascended Masters' and were worshipped by the people. It was all nonsense of course, if the general populous knew what a royal courts spent every month just on parties alone, there would be a revolutions all over Europe the next day.

Kris knew that in all the wars he'd witnessed, the rich sent the poor to die for petty reasons that really wouldn't matter if the king's honor wasn't at stake. 'National Pride' the nobles had called it, 'but if there was a society of educated people' Kris reasoned, 'then the common folk would have a much better chance at stopping the madness before the nobles let it get out of hand.' It had never been tried before and there was no guarantee that it would work, but it was the best hope that humanity had for any lasting peace.

So the Philosopher manuscript had been written in Old Latin and Greek with the mystic symbol of the Phoenix and the not so mythical Unicorn with some old astrological symbols thrown in for good measure.

Emsaph had been looking over Kris' shoulder when he was creating it at the greathouse in the forests of Tunguska.

"It needs to look older. The Unicorn said. "Rip it a little, then soak it in tea." He suggested. When they were finished antiquating the 'sacred doctrine,' it was good enough to fool several ancient book buyers in the capitals of Europe.

"Have them chant and burn incense, lots of incense," The Unicorn whinnied and showed Kris a mind picture of some very out of place men trying to feel the ethers for signs of the ancient 'Philosopher Kings.'

"Also, you should really think about doing the rituals it in some crypt, that will make the nobles want to believe in the 'old ways.'
The Unicorn went on and on about the importance of location, location, location. "Of course eventually, they will want to build a clubhouse or temple, for all the secret meetings." Emsaph whinnied on about the silliness of humans.

And Kris, as Comte St. Germain, played up the strangeness of it all to the hilt. He'd talk of 'Masters of the East' and the 'Golden Dawn' of man that would come again. The great design that Kris had in mind was to redistribute some of the wealth that the nobles kept hoarding. Getting them to pay for the schooling and healthcare for the children in their countries. And to do it in a way that didn't involve bloodshed.

Maybe a 'revolutionary idea' would suffice, instead of another bloody revolution. Having the rich fall all over each other to learn the secrets of the Ancients' power, and in so doing, having the Nobles giving away their enormous wealth, well, that was just icing on the cake. Only people like Count Maupeou would try and stand in the way of liberty for all. Change, for the Nobility of the French Parliament, which didn't increase their wealth, was looked at with abhorrence.

Kris was standing next to Madame de Pompadour with the papers that would start the process of a treaty between England and France. The nobles of Europe could play at these games of life and death with the lives of their subjects; it didn't really bother them. It sickened Kris, but in the course of playing his role he'd managed to acquire most of the pieces of the Loki Stone that King Louis XIVs' jeweler had re-cut. The small, extra pieces still carried the evil beauty of the original gem that had started the final war between the frost giants and the gods of Asgard.

The scraps of the 'French Blue' were sought out by many of the nobles of France, and the Comte St. Germaine had to part with many of his stones from his casket of gems to trade for the re-cut pieces of the evil jewel.

'These nobles are quick enough to scheme and plot without any help.' Kris mused, as he deposited the pieces of the Loki stone in the chalice back at the great house in Siberia. 'Would that the next king be as trust-worthy as his father, Louis the XIV and I'll have gotten the last piece in a decade.'

Louis the XV however, was very unlike his father. Where the father was outgoing, charismatic and as good as his word, the new King was weak-willed, self-absorbed and shifted his loyalty whenever his mood changed.

Louis XV loved for the Comte to entertain him and Madame de Pompadour though for hours on end. When the day at court was done, the King would stay up until the dawn listening to the stories of the infamous St. Germain.

Sometimes, the King would have St. Germain play the violin for hours and never heard the same piece twice. Kris amused the King to get close to the crown jewels that had the possible last piece of the Loki Stone, the famous 'French Blue.' He'd managed to get to touch the crown but the gem that looked so much like the Loki Stone had been a fake. Either the King was too afraid of losing the stone and had kept it hidden, or his father had a copy made of the real one then sold it to help pay off some of the debt for one of the many wars that France had started.

Kris saw that the Count Maupeou had almost eaten all of the chocolates that Kris as the Comte St. Germain had brought for the Madame and Voltaire, he made a mental note to bring some more the next time he came to visit her. 'Well, I've heard enough what the Count thinks of me, I guess I should make an entrance.' He thought.

Kris fell into the role that he'd used for well over one hundred years and mentally pictured a rarely used hallway in the palace of Versailles. He shifted in the in-between to the spot he'd thought of, in less than a second and looked both ways before stepping out of the in-between, no sense appearing before a servant out of thin air. There were enough strange stories floating around about him already.

A quiet knock came upon the door of the salon, then a servant entered and cleared his throat to announce to the trio that were waiting.

"The Comte St. Germain." The servant then pulled the door fully open to show the visitor into the salon.

The mysterious man had always impressed Madame Pompadour. 'A man who intrigues beats a man of wealth.' She'd always said. But standing there in the doorway was a man who had both of these qualities. He was more than he seemed. Sure, St. Germain had prescribed recipes for the removal of facial wrinkles and for dyeing hair, he had shared those freely with the women of the court. He was an alchemist after all, but there was something in his manner. It was something that the Madame couldn't quite put into words.

She'd seen his famous 'casket of jewels' and hadn't thought they were real at first. All the nobles tried to be more important and rich than they really were. It was just assumed that St. Germain's gems were all fake. It wasn't until Madam du Hausset told her that one day when St. Germain was showing the queen some jewels in her presence, the Madam commented on the beauty of a cross of white and green stones. St. Germain nonchalantly made her a present of the small treasure. Madam du Hausset refused, but the queen, thinking the stones were false, signed to her that she might accept. Madam du Hausset subsequently had the stones valued, and they turned out to be genuine and extremely valuable.

And that very year, Countess Von Georgy heard that a Comte Saint Germain had arrived for a soiree at the home of Madame de Pompadour. The elderly countess was curious because she had known a Comte Saint Germain while in Venice in 1710. Upon meeting the Comte again, she was astonished to see that he hadn't appeared to age, and asked him if it was his father she knew in Venice.

"No, Madame," he replied, "but I, myself was living in Venice at the end of the last and the beginning of this century; I had the honor to pay you court then."

"Forgive me, but that it impossible!" the perplexed Countess, said. "The Comte de Saint Germain I knew in those days was at least forty-five years old. And you, at the outside, are that age at present?"

"Madame, I am very old," Kris had said, with a knowing smile.

"But then you must be nearly 100 years old," said the astonished countess.

"That is not impossible," the Comte told her matter-of-factly, then continued to convince the Countess that he was indeed the same man she knew with the details of their previous meetings and of life in Venice 50 years earlier.

If all that was said were mere bragging, then Madame Pompadour could dismiss it a courtly gossip. A way of drawing the ladies to him, some had said, but though St. Germain was always seen at the parties of the rich and famous, his handsome face and charm were more than enough to woo the daughters of the nobility. The Comte was much more than he seemed and liked to flaunt that fact in the face of any of the nobles who didn't acknowledge him as such.

"Here's our man of mystery," de Pompadour cooed and waved her fan at him. 'Would that you be half of what is told about you.' She thought to herself about Saint Germain. Did she see him turn his head slightly? Had he read her thoughts? Maybe, since she was no longer the mistress of the King, she should focus more of her attentions on St. Germain, she mused.

There, standing in the doorway was a man of middle height, lithe but strongly built, and dressed with superb simplicity. Except for the jewels that he wore that is. Saint Germain had gem encrusted buckles on his shoes, rather large white sapphires as cufflinks and a very large black pearl on a gold stickpin that he used to secure his cravat at his neck.

"I hope you've not been waiting too long?" Kris asked, upon making his entrance.

His two friends smiled as Count Maupeou once again bristled in his chair.

"The King will find the terms of the peace accord harsh but fair, I think." St. Germain stated, as he handed an oriental puzzle box to the Count. The bureaucrat handled it as though it was full of poisonous snakes.

"What price is this peace?" He put to Kris, who was still standing over him. "What makes you the one to state terms for France?" The Count's hatred for this interloper was boiling over.

"In matters of state, it is better to be a lucky negotiator than a capable one." St. Germain replied dryly. Kris was never one to rise to an insult, and humor was much more effective foil than mincing words with a politician.

"It is more difficult to keep peace than to make it." Madame de Pompadour added.

"The English are quite capable to continue the war, though they seem to want an end to the hostilities." Kris finished.

Voltaire chimed in to cut off the Maupeou, before the Count could start a battle of wits that he couldn't win.

"Peace is the greatest good that a king can give his people," The philosopher stated to quell any more protests.

The Count finished wiping the chocolate from his fingers and stood up.

"If France is challenged again, then she shall rise to the occasion." It was though the Count was back in Parliament spewing rhetoric. "I bid you good day, gentlemen." He then turned to Madame "I must take my leave of your company, if your will permit me?" Count Maupeou bowed; as best he was able, to the mistress of the house.

"With all my heart." She smiled at the double meaning of the phrase, she was sure he would take her words only as a compliment. The conceited always did.

With the strange Far Eastern puzzle box that held the beginnings of a lasting treaty, the Count exited the salon.

"To succeed in the world, it is not enough to be stupid; you must also be well-mannered." Voltaire said of the Count as soon as the doors to the salon had closed.

"Peace is good for everyone. Isn't that right, St. Germain? It's just common sense." The Madame fluttered her fan lightly in front of her face.

"Common sense is not so common, my lady," the Comte said to his host, with a slight smile.

"Still if the treaty is to be made... France will lose some of its colonies." He finished in a matter of fact tone.

"Maupeou and the rest of the nobles wouldn't agree with you on that, my dear Comte." The Madame countered.

"It is dangerous to be right in matters on which the established authorities are wrong." Voltaire argued for caution on the part of his friend. St. Germain had made a lot of enemies in the court. Nobles didn't like anyone closer to the King than they were.

Saint Germain quipped to the philosopher; "My good friend, Voltaire, would the world have all of your wit and half your cynicism."

All three of the party laughed at that. Though de Pompadour was most determined to winkle out some of the truth about Germain's origins in the next few days. It must be something juicy, about where he grew up or maybe about his education. 'Oh, even better,' she thought to herself, where he had learned to play the violin as well as any musician in France.

De Pompadour lazily fanned herself.

"Would that I was born a man." She said with a sigh.

"Then the world would be a much drearier." Voltaire had a way with words.

"And who would run France?" Germain added.

She truly blushed at that compliment. So few knew how many plots against the crown she'd foiled by dropping a hint in the right ear. It took a lot of work to be overheard by the right gossiping servant or spy without seeming obvious.

While the current King Louis didn't learn from his father's words, she studied the advice from the former King's personal diaries that she'd read as the current King slept. Poor Louis, he never could hold his cognac. The old King's last words in the diary she'd used as her rule of thumb.

'Let the ambitions of one bridle the other.' She'd kept the Counts, Barons and Marquis' so busy backstabbing each other, that they didn't have time to gang up on the King.

"Intelligence has no gender." It was immodest of her to say it, but the servants were gone and she felt that she could let her guard down. "But thank you for your kind words." She was very touched by this handsome stranger that was the only man of the court that hadn't tried to make a pass at her. She added, "You have to have virtues yourself in order to see them in others." This was a compliment to her male guests.

They talked on well into the night on topics that ranged from Count Maupeou's tax reforms to the latest fashion trends when Madame put a question to St. Germain.

"What one change would you, Germain, make to perfect the world?" The Madame had found that such seemingly innocent questions while seeming fanciful, tended to reveal a lot of the hidden character of a person.

St. Germain paused for a moment and with carefully chosen words said, "I would add to mankind a greater sense of compassion for his fellow man, and woman of course."

This caught the Madame short on a response; she would have to think his words over, so she turned to Voltaire. "And you my dear philosopher, what would you add to this world to make it perfect."

"Madame please," the old writer replied. "You have read my books and you well know that this is the best of all possible worlds." All three of the party laughed at this. It was true that he'd written most of his books using that premise, but the pages were full of sarcasm about the state of the world and the inequalities that all but the rich and powerful had to endure.

From there, Madame de Pompadour tried to steer the conversation into the background of her mysterious friend, St. Germain. She started by asking him about where he learned alchemy, but somehow the topic went onto Nicholas Flamel, the famous 14th century French Alchemist and the fabulous Philosopher Stone that he was said to possess.

"How does he do that," she mused to herself, when de Pompadour remembered the next day that she hadn't winkled-out any information from St. Germain.

As the Count Maupeou walked down the corridor away from Madame de Pompadour's suites, he stewed over having to play the part of delivery boy for St. Germain. The Count hated that St. Germain always spoke with an entire lack of ceremony to the most highly placed personages and seemed fully conscious of his own superiority. The Comte St. Germain didn't hold any office in the government of France and there he was ordering the President of Parliament around, giving him a package to deliver.

The Count hated being put in that position. The papers of the treaty were in one of those damned Chinese puzzle boxes that Germain always used when carrying important papers. Only he and the King knew how to open them so that none could spy on the secrets that St. Germain carried.

Lord knows, Maupeou had tried to get the box open by pressing the tiles that decorated the box in different patterns, looking for a tell tale sign of a locking device or a strange kind of keyhole. But even though Maupeou examined it every time St. Germain had summoned him to deliver one to the King. The Count could never get it open.

Years later, in 1774, during the reign of Louis XVI, St. Germain returned to France to visit Marie Antoinette. Kris found that he wasn't welcome at the royal court, many of his enemies had grown in their power over the throne during his absence, so he turned to the Comtesse d'Adhemar, a long time friend, to arrange a private meeting with the queen. Since he'd left for England to deliver the final revision of the treaty to end the Seven Years War, he had not reappeared in France for over fifteen years, but the memory of him had become a legend. And King Louis XVs' friendship with him was well known. So the new queen felt comfortable enough to meet with the mysterious Comte. She had heard all the stories about his vast knowledge, his ability to speak almost any language and his famous 'casket of gems.'

The old Comtesse d'Adhemar assured the young queen that all the strange stories that she had heard about St. Germain were indeed true and he had never seemed to age.

"My family had known him for over one hundred and eleven years and he has ever looked the same." The old Comtesse assured the young queen.

The two noble born ladies waited for St. Germain in the Cometesse's apartments in Paris. Finally, a knock came at the door of small sitting room off of the central courtyard garden.

Marie-Antoinette, never one to stand on ceremony, immediately asked Saint Germain if he was going to settle in Paris again.

"A century will pass," was his reply, "before I come here again." Kris liked to keep the sense of mystery about being the 'man who never dies,' maybe that would add a little weight to his words and Marie-Antoinette would get him the audience he needed to help the young King before it was too late.

In the presence of the queen, he spoke in a grave voice and foretold events that would take place in the coming years.

"The queen, in her wisdom, will weigh that which I am about to tell her in confidence. There is a movement that desires power, which it will obtain only by the complete fall of the clergy. In order to bring about this result, these conspirators will try to gain control of the monarchy. The Encyclopedists, who are seeking a chief among the members of the royal family, have cast their eyes to one of the Dukes, I'm sure of it. The noble will become the instrument of men who will sacrifice the Duke when he has ceased to be useful to the party. The power hungry Duke will then go to the guillotine, instead of, to the throne of France. The laws of the land will be overturned. The wicked will seize power with bloodstained hands. They will do away with the Catholic religion, the nobility, and the magistracy."

"So... only royalty will be left," the queen interrupted impatiently. She didn't know where this story was going. Was this some sort of sick joke?

"Not even royalty. There will be a bloodthirsty republic, whose scepter will be the executioner's blade." Kris wasn't one to be melodramatic, but he was sure that the Loki Stone had infected the royal court of France. All that he had done to try to change in the nobility of Europe was disintegrating back into a mass of greedy chaos. The secret societies he'd help to start had turned against him. Casting aside the doctrine of the Philosopher Kings in favor of occult practices that would bring them only a little esoteric power, but it was enough for their small-minded self-aggrandizement. The wars would continue, the poor would remain downtrodden and he'd had to let go of the grand idea of an educated society. All that was left to him was to find the last piece of the evil jewel.

His terrible predictions filled Marie Antoinette with foreboding and agitation.

This wasn't the St. Germain that she'd heard about. Where was the courtly flattery and amazing stories that he was to tell to entertain her?

Then, St. Germain asked to see the King, in order to make even more serious revelations, and strangely, St. Germain asked to see the king without his Prime Minister, the Count Maurepas, being told of it. Kris had tried to reason with the Count when he had first returned to France, but it turned out to be a waste of time.

'This Count Maurepas is no different than the Count Maupeou that I had to deal with years ago. Greedy and suspicious of anyone that might threaten his power. Are they all sent to a school to look and act the same way?' Kris had thought to himself.

"He is my enemy," St. Germain said, "and I count him among those who will contribute to the ruin of the kingdom, not from malice but from greed and stupidity." Kris was trying not to scare the young queen; she was only nineteen after all. But from the direction that the court was taking he was sure the Loki Stone was bringing out the worst in the Nobility of France. Why else would they act so stupidly? The Nobility were having extravagant parties while their subjects starved in the streets. Maybe the Loki Stone was lost in the water supply at the court. That would explain most of the greedy and hateful behavior of the 'Nobles' he'd encountered when he had tried to present himself to the King to ask for a private audience.

"The King does not possess sufficient authority to have an interview with anybody without the presence of his minister." The young queen said.

Maurepas pretty much ruled the country. The young King didn't have the experience, so he bowed to the will of the Count. For her part, Marie Antoinette kept to her apartments with her retinue that she had brought with her from Austria.

"My queen, I'm sorry to have to ask you for this favor," St. Germain bowed to her to show her the respect that she wasn't getting at court. "But truly, the future of France is at stake." He finished.

The young queen was impressed by his courtly manners, in spite of his dire warnings. She extended her hand as a sign of her consent; she would do as he asked. St. Germain took her hand and smiled slightly, she hadn't been touched by the Loki Stone. She was merely an innocent in the dangerous times that were about to unfold.

She went back to her apartments in the palace, her mind in turmoil over all that St. Germain had told her. It seemed like he had stopped himself at one point to find the least offensive words for her royal ears. There was nothing in his manner that suggested that he was trying to trick her. And besides, St. Germain had always been a friend to the King of France. Indeed, he was highly respected in the royal court of Austria. Marie remembered all the stories of the famous Alchemist that had visited the Austrian court often over the last century. She had secretly thought that it must have been a father and then a son and perhaps a grandson who had kept up the appearance of an ageless noble. But, the elderly the Comtesse d'Adhemar had swore to her that indeed this was the same man she had known her whole life.

'Very well,' she thought to herself as she entered her salon. 'For all he has done for my family, I will do him this small kindness.' But the meeting would never take place.

As soon as she had asked for the private interview for St. Germain, the King informed Count Maurepas. The Count made the queen relay the interview that St. Germain had had with her and the Comtesse.

Maurepas thought it would be wisest to imprison in the Bastille a man who had so gloomy a vision of France's future. 'St. Germain would spread these rumors of the trouble to come and become the close confidant of the King to take my place as Prime Minister', Count Maurepas thought to himself. "I'll see to this treacherous rogue myself, your majesty." He said to the King. "We should have a royal guard with you at all times."

The Count continued. "Strange stories are told about this St. Germain. He may know of some secret passages into the palace that we do not." The Count finished giving a hint of danger to frighten the young King.

"Make any arrangements you feel are necessary, for the protection of me and my queen." The young King said, in a shaky voice.

"Of course... my King," the Count bowed himself out of the Louis' private room and left to triple the guard at the palace and to secret the King out of Paris to one of the many country estates that the Count owned. 'Better to wield my power in the King's name.' Maurepas thought to himself.

With the King out of the palace, the Prime Minister could make laws without having to clear any of the decisions with the young King.

The next day, the Count went to see if he could find out any more information about St. Germain. The Count paid a visit, seemingly out of courtesy, to the Comtesse d'Adhemar, the woman who had arranged the meeting of the young queen and St. Germain. Maurepas visited her in order to acquaint her with his decision to capture St. Germain and to see if she was in on what seemed like a conspiracy to replace him. She had received him in her salon that looked out over her beloved flower gardens.

"Count, I don't usually receive company this late in the day." The Comtesse knew that her visitor was the real ruler of France but the social graces always came first.

"I am indeed sorry to trouble you this late in the day Madame," how he hated the social graces, "But this St. Germain fellow has been meddling in the affairs of France for too long, and I mean to put a stop to it." The audacity of St. Germain, to try and usurp his power, it made Maurepas' blood boil.

"My dear Count," she was surprised by the venom in his voice. "I've never known him to be anything but open and honest." She protested as politely as possible. "There is nothing artful or malicious in the man. I'm sure if you sat down with him he would explain himself to your satisfaction." There, that seemed reasonable enough to the Comtesse, though the Count would hear none of it.

"I know the scoundrel better than you do," he said. "He will be exposed. Our police officials have a very keen scent. Only one thing surprises me. The years have not spared me, whereas the queen declares that the Comte de St Germain looks like a man of forty."

No sooner had he finished his words than both the Count and the Comtesse were startled by the sound of a door being shut. The Comtesse uttered a small cry. All the blood that was ready to boil in Maurepas' veins went cold in an instant. The Count's face whitened at the sight of his nemesis. He tried to get up to challenge the interloper, with all his might he tried to stand, but found he couldn't move. St. Germain stood before them, dressed, as he had always been known. Elegant simplicity of gray velvet with diamond encrusted buckles on his shoes, enormous white sapphires for cufflinks and a rather large black pearl that held his cravat.

"The King has called on you to give him good counsel," the Comte said; "and in refusing to allow me to see him, you think only of maintaining your authority. You're destroying the monarchy, for I have only a limited time to give to France, and when that time has passed, I shall be seen again only after three generations. I shall not be to blame when anarchy with all its horrors devastates France. You will not live to see these calamities, but the fact that you paved the way for them will be enough to blacken the memory of you for all time." Kris had no respect for this bureaucrat who was more interested in keeping control over the young king than helping France.

Having uttered this in one breath, he walked to the door, shut it behind him and disappeared.

The Count found he could move and leapt up to follow the interloper. He reached the door only a moment after St. Germain had shut it but the long hallway that led to the front door was empty.

The Comtesse was beside herself. She had never known St. Germain to be anything but polite. Could what he'd told them be true? She heard Count Maurepas take his leave and saw him depart, but she was too flustered to try and plead the Comte's reasons to her guest.

'All the better' the Count thought to himself. He walked as fast as a gentleman could, without looking gauche, out to his waiting carriage.

"To the Police station!" he called up to the driver. As soon as he closed the door the horses were in motion. He would rally the police to search the city, as rich as St. Germain was, it should be easy to find the rogue in the nicer hotels in Paris. The Count was so busy with his scheming that he didn't notice that the carriage was headed out to the countryside.

As he departed his good friend's parlor, Kris knew that all that he had seen in using the blank Rune Stone, the one that showed probable futures, was going to pass for France. The revolution was all but ready to start and the shining bright future that he had worked so hard to insure for the children, was being snuffed out like a candle.

Kris was tired. Tired of trying to get the nobility of Europe to be better than they were. As soon as he closed the door on the parlor of his dear friend the Comtesse d'Adhemar, he touched the Rune Stone on his belt, using his thought, he moved into the in-between to just outside of the apartments were the Count's carriage was waiting.

"Driver, your master would have you go to his suite and pick up a parcel that is waiting for him." Kris commanded. The driver looked down at the nobleman who was countermanding the direct order that the Count had given him, to stay there and be ready to leave, at a moment's notice.

The driver was confused as if the world was kind of out of kilter; he clamped his hands down on the rails to steady himself.

When his mind cleared he remembered the package that his master needed him to get. 'I'd better run,' he thought to himself, 'it's only a few blocks away.' Kris watched the driver head off on his errand; he soon disappeared from view in the twilight.

'Now for the Count,' Kris thought. He positioned himself like the driver, placed a likeness of the coachman over himself and waited for the evil politician.

Maurepas didn't keep him waiting long and the order was given to drive to the Police station and not to spare the horses, but Kris wanted to question the toady little man before he let him go. The Count's thoughts were full of hatred that was unnatural even for one of the nobility. With all the time, they had to fill with petty emotions, few had more pure hatred in their soul than Maurepas.

'He must know where the Loki stone is or maybe, since he's now the high counselor to the throne, he will have it in his own secret safe.' It was the only logical explanation for the Count's total disregard for all that was good and right in the world, Kris thought.

The Count was asleep by the time the carriage had traveled more than a few blocks, with a little help, from Kris that is. He let the horses slow to a trot. Most people would see a slow moving carriage in the moonlight at night and assume it was a couple enjoying a romantic evening. This idea was further reinforced when just outside of town, the horse-drawn carriage turned onto the road that ran along side the river Seine. Kris pulled the horses to a stop between the river and a stand of trees.

With so much at stake he had to be cautious. Emsaph was going to be back in Tunguska to collect him in a few hours and take him to the Elves.

Everything that Kris had seen in the royal court convinced him that the Loki Stone, though smaller, was just as potent as ever. Sure, he could have just reached out and touched the Count back at the Comtesses' home. But if Maurepas had the Loki Stone on him he could be very dangerous, so Kris had to get the Count alone first.

Kris dismounted the coach and opened the door to the cab. Maurepas was slumped over like he'd drunk too much wine.

Kris reached out and barely touched the Count's hand. He hated touching the bits of the Loki Stone that he'd found, so he thought that it would be the same with touching someone under its influence. The Count just snoozed away, while Kris read he thoughts. Yes, Maurepas had touched the stone but it had been long ago. Even after all this time, he was still under its effects.

Maurepas was far more hateful and greedy than even a noble could normally be. In the Count's mind, Kris also saw the actions of the other nobles that the young King trusted. Even if he could take the last of the stone with him tonight, the damage to France was done. The economic reforms and policy of more liberty for all wouldn't save anyone from the revolution that was coming.

"Better that I hadn't talked to the queen." Kris said to himself as he thought of the bloodshed that was coming. 'So much for my revolutionary idea' plan, he thought despairingly. His mind turned back to a memory, long ago to the little village of his youth, of the raid and all the unnecessary death that had followed. He left the Count by the river to awake sometime the next morning.

Kris was due back in Tunguska shortly. Emsaph was to take him to meet Frey, ruler of the peoples and lands of the Elves. It wasn't an appointment that could wait.

The Parisians that saw the impeccably dressed man walking beside the river, saw a sad and lonely expression on the handsome face and strong broad shoulders that were slumped over like they had the weight of the world on them.

The next morning, the Count awoke with a start. How had he gotten out here? Where was his driver? He got out of the cab and climbed clumsily up to the driver's seat. By the time he'd gotten to the head inspector of the police, the trail of the infamous Comte St. Germain had gone cold.

All efforts to find St. Germain proved fruitless. The keen scent of Maurepas' police officials was not keen enough. They never discovered what had happened to the Comte de St. Germain.

As the years passed when Kris was away, the Freemasons and other secret societies had changed their agendas, becoming far less philanthropic and much more dubious. Kris saw much of what he had worked for, be corrupted by the wealthy and powerful. At that point, he turned to Emsaph who had always given him good counsel and an objective opinion.

"You take too much on yourself, young one," the Unicorn chided him gently. "Humans will continue to make war until they have lost their taste for it. People will always mistreat others that are different... until everyone, and I mean everyone, realizes that you are all pretty much the same." Emsaph finished and then let his young student absorb his words.

"I just feel... at least some of the people I tried to help... should have gotten what I was trying to teach them." Kris was still struggling with the stupidity of humanity.

"Always bet on vice," the Unicorn whinnied referring the 'noble born.'

"You do good by giving the very young those little gifts," Emsaph showed Kris mind pictures of the children that Kris had brought gifts.

Some went on to become more giving to others. Some held onto that memory of the time in their lives when Santa Claus or Father Frost had thought enough of them, to care about their wants and needs, and that single memory was what got them through the rough times of their lives. "You might want to think of your life as like being a gardener. The kindnesses you've done are like seeds. Some take root and grow into beautiful and fruitful things. Some seeds fall on barren ground." Emsaph waxed on philosophically.

Kris felt the wisdom of his teacher's words and the heaviness of his heart began to lift. Soon he felt better and continued to help people as best he could. Perhaps his grand plan to help could have worked but he had misjudged the greed that still ruled the hearts of men.

February 1784, Kris arrived in Austria, as the Comte St. Germain, who had long since fallen out of favor in the French royal court. This was mainly due to the nobles that controlled Louis the XVI, that had gotten used to their positions of power. It didn't take being able to look into the future to see the bloody revolution that was to sweep over France. But the nobles just ignored the problems of the poor and kept the royal house totally isolated from the cries of their subjects. Kris felt that he'd done all he could do to help to turn the tide of revolution for the young King. Once Louis XV had told him. "After me, the flood." He was referring to the almost bankrupt treasury he was to leave the next King of France.

'Perhaps I can help the next leader of France when he comes to power,' Kris thought to himself. 'Better I find the last piece or pieces of the Loki Stone' The evil that was happening in the world was more in the hearts of men then coming from a stone, no matter how evil it was. There was no sense adding to the woes of the world with the evil, the gem still held. Kris turned his mind to the good that he could do to help the people of other countries.

Luckily, Kris hadn't lost all his friends in the royal courts of Europe. So, he decided to stay for a while in Vienna to help the Queen of the Holy Roman Empire, if she would accept his service.

The Empress, Maria Theresa, had the forethought to introduce the reforms of the Austrian economy, the introduction of civil service and not just giving government jobs to a noble with a title, but to someone who was actually qualified to do the work. And she was credited with a most forward thinking idea, of public education that she introduced. All of these reforms were being implemented while her enemies beset her.

To the East, lay the Prussian Empire with the ever-greedy Fredrick II looking to increase his lands at Austria's expense. And though an uneasy peace had been made with government of France, the Empress knew that without a royal marriage between Austria and France, war would be declared by the French King. Louis would be under pressure from his own greedy nobles who would try to lay claim to the prosperous western part of her empire. The Empress had more than her hands full and welcomed the help of Comte Saint Germain, as long as he stayed in the background of the court. The Empress couldn't afford the idle gossip that she was Saint Germain's pawn and was doing his bidding, rather than just offering advice on the future of France and the motives of its nobles.

Kris felt that he could do some good for this Empress of the Holy Roman Empire of Austria. That had brought him to Vienna, well that and his sister Mary, who had also moved there and had just purchased a store where violins and sheet music were sold.

Mary had left the Netherlands after an extended stay there, where she had lived in the vicinity of the descendants of the small village of Haven, where she and her brothers had been born over five centuries ago.

The origin of where the people of Southern provinces of the Netherlands had come from had been lost in the mists of time. Stories so strange that after a while they are just best thought of as forgotten.

Mary had become accustom to city life over the years, then she contacted Kris, or as he had called himself for over a century, 'The Comte St. Germain.'

They agreed that the capital of Austria would be a much needed diversion. Mary followed her brother's example and brought elegant, yet simple clothes and adorned herself with some of the less gaudy of the gems in Kris' collection. Mary suspected that her brother liked being a mysterious nobleman from Eastern Europe.

As for her part, she had always loved music, from the time that she first heard her mother sing her to sleep. And Vienna was said to be the the place to hear the most talented musicians in the world. Mary looked forward to meeting the composers, but she didn't want to play the part of being the sister of Comte St. Germain. Too many questions would arise and she was more interested in the music than with consorting with nobles.

When Emsaph had taken her to see the Elves, Mary had spent most of her time in the gardens, where songbirds had filled the air with symphonies that seemed to change every day. The head gardener explained to her that the little spotted birds called starlings could mimic and remember almost any tune they heard. So Mary tested that bit of information. She would sing or whistle a small tune and listened with amazement as the starlings repeated it back to her. Then, they would sing it again, changing a few of the notes then adding a few more making it sound similar, but more lively and richer in tone.

One of Frey's daughters, Titania, the red-haired Norn and Sister of the Crossing, had made a present of a several of starlings for Mary, when she returned to the greathouse in Siberia.

The starlings quickly became a flock and settled in and around the house, stables and nearby forest. Mary rarely left the Siberian forest for the next several centuries, preferring her animal friends and the Tungus tribe to the growing cities of Europe with their cathedrals and castles. Only when she was out playing the part of Belfana, the Italian good-witch who left presents for the good children on the holiday called Twelfth Night. Or in early December in Russia where Mary was both the grandmotherly Babouschka and the elfin maiden known as the Lady Kolyada to the children of Russia, did she venture away from her home.

As grandmotherly Babouschka, much like Lady Belfana, who gave presents to children, she would appear as an old woman carrying a large sack full of treats and toys. But instead of riding a witch's broom, Babouschka traveled in a sleigh, drawn by a single reindeer as she did when Mary played the part of the elfin maiden, the Lady Kolyada. Mary loved bringing joy to children, to give them at least one happy memory of childhood.

Like Kris did when he played at being Santa Claus or her brother, Olaf, who took care of the Northern Europe, gift giving while in the guise of 'Father Frost.'

Vienna was becoming the music capital of Europe and composers were creating new masterpieces every month. Kris had mentioned this to Mary when he had come home to get away from all that courtly intrigue and scheming he'd done in order to get the remaining smaller pieces of the Loki Stone. Kris always liked to return to the great house in Tunguska. Mary would listen to his tales and laugh at all the secrecy and pretense that "the Nobles" had to go through to get through a day. It seemed like far too much work to her. But the thought of listening to symphonies and operas in the great concert halls was too much a draw for her not to visit Vienna.

Kris hadn't seen her that excited since she was a small child. So he offered to show her all the sights of the city of music, as it was know then.

Mary was overjoyed. She decided to leave her beloved home to see this city for herself. Kris offered to introduce her to society by way of the Netherlands. So that she could acclimate to the bustle of city life. Mary agreed, but wanted to see if she could manage on her own once they traveled to Vienna. There she had purchased a music store giving the previous owner his asking price without trying to haggle him down. She'd done that with Kris' urging, after all money was easy enough to produce, but Kris knew that word would spread about a mysterious woman of means that had purchased the small but expensive shop as though she were buying a flower at the market. That was publicity that money couldn't buy.

That notoriety would bring the composers to her store; seeking to meet the rich woman they hoped would be their patroness.

Mary was amazed how fast the word had spread about her. Soon, she was asked to parties and balls, hosted by the nobles of the Austrian court.

There, she was introduced to the Comte St. Germain. She greeted him as though for the first time, not as her brother. Many bets were lost on that meeting. Some of the nobles were sure that somehow the mysterious Comte must be related to the equally enigmatic 'Lady Petranova,' as Mary had taken to calling herself. It was a Russian title that simply meant the daughter of Petr. This would drive the Austrian nobles mad, trying to figure out her true origins. Mary would just giggle when they tried to press her for more information. How could a Russian 'Lady' have red-hair and deep emerald green eyes?

'She must be hiding something,' they all thought, well all but Kris, he watched from across the room when she was introduced to the famed composer Wolfgang Mozart. The young Austrian was being very animated in his gestures, as Mozart was known to do, when he talked about his concertos. Kris stayed at the party until it ended, despite all the invitations to other more private parties that would last until the morning. He wanted to keep an eye on his sister. Mary could be as naive as she was sweet and Kris wasn't about to let anyone take advantage of his baby sister.

Yes, he knew that she could pop back to the great house in Tunguska on a moment's notice, but that didn't stop him from looking out for her.

The next day at the music store, Mozart came to see the shop that was so much on everyone's tongue. It was somewhat small, but was well stocked with all the latest equipment for repairing and making instruments. Violins hung from the rafters and harpsichords and piano-fortes lined two of the shop's walls. He was amazed at the price of the sheet music, such finely inked parchment would cost double in his hometown of Salzburg. 'How did this Lady plan on staying in business with prices so low?' He wondered, as he pretended to browse the the store.

The Lady Petranova came down the staircase that Mozart hadn't ever remembered being there. He had been in the store before. It was so close to the Burg Theater and on the way back to his hotel that he used while in Vienna. But, the previous owner had the shop full of clutter so there might have been an elephant in there for all Mozart would have known.

With the new owner, the shop was clean and tidy, with only a hint of the linseed oil that was used to treat the delicate wood of the violins.

Mary had almost fainted the night she had met the great Mozart. The week before meeting him she had gone to the Burg Theater to hear one of his older works. 'Magnificent,' she had thought. Never had she imagined that musical notes could be arranged in such a sonorous manner. Mary had been so moved, she remained seated long after the concerto was over, finally one of the ushers came to ask if she was ill. Mary opened her hand fan and fluttered it in front of her face.

"Just a case of the vapors," She said, in a flushed voice. She knew then that she desperately wanted to meet Mozart and talk with him about the way he composed the melodies and rhythms of his music. Mary thought it odd to go to all the trouble that her brother had, with dressing up like a noble and being mysterious. But it had worked. The doors of the most wealthy of Austria had been thrown open for her and the composer that she would have had a hard time getting an audience with, was seeking her out in the little shop she had bought.

"Why, Wolfgang Amadeus Mozart, what brings you to my little shop?"

Mary said, as though she was surprised to see him.

"Well, I've heard about your fine instruments and we didn't have a chance to finish our conversation." He replied lamely.

She led him up the stairs and through a set of French doors out to a rather large high-walled garden that couldn't be seen from the street below. The statuary in the garden amazed Mozart; it must have been made in ancient Greece. The whole garden had an otherworldly feel about it. The Lady Petranova left him briefly, so he had a chance to look around. The strangeness was nothing he could put a finger on. It wasn't the well-groomed trees or shrubs, not even the large fountain that ran down the back wall. How could the garden be on the second floor with all the weight of the flora and the soil over an empty storeroom? It must be that the garden had been here for well over one hundred years and the shop had been built so that it could easily access this oasis of beauty in the middle of the city. 'Yes, that was a reasonable answer,' Mozart thought to himself.

The Lady returned as he finished his thought and they sat and talked for a very long while about musical theory and inspiration, but he was the one giving all the information. When the afternoon tea service had been removed by one of her servants, Mozart felt that this mysterious Lady Petranova knew all about him and was either going to commission a musical piece from him or bid him good day. Truly, she had only given a vague idea that she was from the East and dabbled in music, nothing more. The Lady's dress was simple, but elegant and the jewels that she wore certainly had the glitter of real gems, and her manner was reserved but lively enough when she talked about music.

Mary had thanked the servant that took away the remains of the high tea and turned her attention back to her guest. He had such an insightful mind maybe he could use one of her little pets. She whistled a high shrill then a lower note, which quieted the starlings in the trees. That whistle meant the little birds that Mary was about to feed them like she did back in Tunguska.

"Would you like to see some magick?" she asked her guest. He nodded quickly as a reply.

She held out her hand and one of the birds came to sit on one of her fingers.

"Please hum or whistle a little of the masterpiece that you are now working on, please." Mary asked, and smiled to her guest.

Mozart thought better than to question a Lady in a situation as strange as this. So he thought for a second and found a difficult passage that he had yet to work out in his mind. It was a piece that had alternating sharps and flats in a robust melody, but it didn't come together the way he had thought it would. He whistled the eight bars with practiced ease, then nodded to the lady.

The bird in her hand whistled his tune back to him then changed the melody and whistled it back again making the changes that would make it a masterpiece. Mozart could hardly believe his ears. He asked for a piece of paper of write down the changes to his music, they were the same notes only arranged in a way that made them more lively, more playful. It was the exact combination of tempo and tone that he had been trying to produce. Mozart had to write it down before the bird started to sing another masterpiece. One of her servants brought him one of the finely scripted pieces of sheet music, an inkwell of fine Indian ink and a sharpened quill. The starling sat on the end of Lady Petranova's finger and waited for another piece of music to make its own.

"Would you like to take this bird with you, my dear Mozart?" The Lady Petranova asked.

"Are you a muse?" Mozart asked the mysterious female seriously.

"You do know how to flatter a woman," she said wistfully. "No, only a person who loves beautiful music, and I dare say some of your best work lies ahead of you." She leaned forward in her chair. "Take good care of the starling and she will take care of you."

Mary then understood why her brother loved playing the role of 'Comte St. Germain' so much.

After Mozart left the shop with a bird cage in one hand and an armload of sheet music that Lady Petranova had given him, Mary turned to her brother who was under a 'glamour' of being one of her servants. The look of an old man in an ornate burgundy coat and breeches fell away to reveal, the velvet clothes and gems of the Comte St. Germain.

"Kris, thank you so much for helping me with Mozart," she grabbed his hand and led him up the stairs to the garden. They sat among the statuary that Kris would send back to the hidden caves were he had found most of the great works of the ancient world. All the trees and earth used to make this old garden, that was really about a week old, would be returned as soon as Mary had completed her business there in Vienna.

"Oh what a good use for the Rune Stones." Mary had a mischievous smile on her face, "who else needs a muse...? I wonder." Her eyes twinkled as she laughed.

Kris smiled; he hadn't heard her laugh like that since she was a child.

"Goodness me," he feigned shock, "wait 'til I tell Emsaph that I've created a monster!" They both laughed at that.

"Well, are you ready for next weekend?" Olaf asked, as I rolled double sixes and won the game.

"Is it close by right, not in Sweden I mean, are we going to blink there?" I still thought that Olaf was being vague on the destination.

"I thought I told you last week that it would be a day trip, if we got an early start," he smiled a far away smile. "I'll make the arrangements on my end, and you drive, Jack." He finished.

It sounded good. Finally getting some conformation on this story would make me know it was true and not just a good bedtime story for some child.

"Since apparently you've lost count Jack, you've won our little backgammon tournament by two games." He said flatly.

I had lost track of the games a couple of weeks ago. I was far more interested in the story.
"Well... okay then, do I get a prize? Are you going to show me one of the Rune Stones or maybe I get to meet the Norns?" I was hoping.

"Well, as long as it's something easy." Olaf smirked. "You want me to summon the 'Sisters of the Crossing' for you to gawk at?" He gave me a good hearty laugh as an answer.

My hopes on seeing the elfin sisters had been dashed, but I still wanted to see what the old storyteller had to show me.

"All, right then, I'll see you next week, Where did you want to meet?" I asked. I didn't want to go hunting all over the market. "How about next to the brass pig?" I thought that was an easy landmark to find.

"In here is fine." My storyteller countered.

Olaf started to collect the game pieces and I took the hint and started to pack up my tapes and recorder.

As I lost sight of Olaf in the bustling crowds of the upper part of the market, I thought that I should reread the story to see if I could think of any questions for the storyteller for our journey.

'Why are you so excited, Jack?' I had to ask myself as I was walking home.

The Hoh Rainforest

Chapter 9
The spirit of Christmas

The day was supposed to be rainy, but in true Seattle fashion, the weather defied the forecasters and I was met with a bright blue cloudless sky.

'Jack, you've got the wrong job,' I thought to myself. Honestly, the weather forecasters up here in the Northwest must use a dartboard that has all the spots marked rainy except one, to predict the next day's forecast.

In their defense, the weather term, 'sun breaks,' which means that the sun might peek through the cloud cover at some point during the day, was invented up here as well.

'So, we'll have a nice trip,' I thought to myself. It's not like I didn't want it to be a nice day, but when you keep hearing that tomorrow will be bad, you kind of mentally prepare for it. Then when it turns out nice, I guess people get angry for not taking the day off or planning to enjoy a picnic lunch.

Really, as much as it rains in the Northwest, almost constantly in fact, when the sun comes out, it is one of the most amazing places to be, that I've ever seen. All the hills are packed with lush green vegetation and the water in the lakes and the Puget Sound are a brilliant deep blue. Since most of the skyscrapers in the city have green glass, it does remind me of the emerald city of Oz, which is Seattle's nickname.

Early that morning, I went down to rent a car. Being from back East and a true city dweller, I know how to drive a car, I just don't own a car. I rented a huge SUV.

I would blend in with all the other Seattle drivers for our outing. It had a bigger interior than my first apartment, but I thought that Olaf would be thrilled, it may be his first car ride, for all I knew.

Parking near the market was a new experience for me though. It's hard enough to find a space if you're in a Cooper Mini, in the 'boat' I rented, it might have been easier to just take a cab from the coffee shop where we were to meet. After much wrangling and yelling at people in the New York manner, I got one of the choice spots, right behind the produce stalls on the brick road that runs in front of the market. Since I'd told Olaf that I didn't know how long it'd take to get the transportation and make any arrangements, I wasn't too pressed for time.

I walked passed the chainsaw-carved Bigfoot statue, up the creaky old staircase with the 30-foot long giant squid made from bronze, hanging down from the ceiling and into the main level of the Market.

The old brass pig stood there amidst the tourists who crowded around the fish throwers at the Pike Place Fish Co. to watch the guys throw twenty pound Coho salmon back and forth. It was a gimmick that was started by a couple of college kids when they got bored one day and is a Seattle 'gotta go and see' attraction. All that morning, I was noticing things that I'd normally taken for granted. If Olaf was really going to show me 'the elves' then I knew my view of the world would drastically be changed forever. So on my way to meet him, I tried to see things as if I were looking at them for the first time.

I turned to go towards the coffee shop and someone grabbed my arm. I don't mind helping the people, but I don't like being grabbed by anyone. As I spun around to give this person a piece of my mind, I saw that it was Olaf.

"Let's go," he said, foisting a large duffel bag at me. I threw the thing over my shoulder and almost threw out my back.

"What so you got in this thing, a horse," I asked seriously.

He didn't say anything, he just headed back the way I'd come, towards the SUV. I caught up to him in due time, the duffel bag had slowed me down a bit in the crowded market. After we reached the bottom of the stairs, I took the lead and wove my way through the people and out to the car. Olaf looked at the behemoth I had rented and then back at me.

"We aren't bringing anybody back you know." He said with a smile.

I put his luggage in the back with the small backpack that I packed some apples, crackers and a couple of water bottles along with my extra tapes and notebooks.

I felt like a kid going to see a rich uncle. After rereading the story from the beginning, I only had a few questions, I also realized that nothing that Olaf had done, had proved to me that there was any truth to his story.

The more I'd thought about the girls in the booth last week, the more I thought that it wasn't a 'glamour,' as he called it. A spell to keep other people from getting our booth, week after week. I had been so embarrassed for almost sitting on one of the teenage girls that I had consciously kept my eyes looking out at the Puget Sound until Olaf had arrived. So, I may not have noticed the girls leaving the café. With that being said, I still couldn't account for feeling so excited about the trip.

"If you can get this vehicle out of this tiny parking space," Olaf was looking down from his seat, on the car parked next to ours, "Head for the ferry terminal in Edmonds. It's a little north of here." He finished. Olaf then turned his attention to the scenery.

I managed to get out on the road without too much trouble, then turned down one of the steep streets towards the water. Everybody thinks that San Francisco has the steepest streets on the West Coast. Well, they might have more of them, but James Street in Seattle will scare anyone who drives a stick shift. After that street, it was easy to follow the signs to get to the boat that would take us across the water.

We got to the terminal just as they were loading the huge car ferry for the trip across the Puget Sound to towns on the peninsula. The price is very reasonable compared to the time and money that a person would spend traveling one hour south to Olympia then another hour north to Port Townsend to get around the huge inlet of the Puget Sound.

After the cars and trucks were loaded, Olaf wanted to get out and go up to the observation deck to see the city as the boat pulled away from the dock.

The deck was fairly empty. After the summer crowds, there weren't many tourists in the Northwest. The weather usually wasn't so mild and the people who regularly traveled this route, usually stay in their cars and read.

Olaf went over to the railing and watched the sunlit glass towers of the emerald city as they got smaller in the distance.

"One should never take beauty for granted, just because he sees it so often." Olaf remarked.

He continued watching the city until the boat went around one of the islands and into a strait that blocked his view. That meant we would soon be landing, so we headed back to the SUV.

"Well, I hope you've got your questions ready," the storyteller said, as we disembarked the ferry and headed up the ramp into Port Townsend. "I still have one more story to tell you though." Olaf turned his head and watched the small town go by the window.

Traffic thinned out quickly, since most of the people on the ferry either lived in the small town or were just visiting for the day. Soon the road to the coast was open before us. With only a couple of small towns to go through, that would be the only traffic we would encounter. It would be a pleasant trip.

"So, now that we're on the peninsula can you tell me where we're going exactly? I'd need to be able to know where we'd stop to get gas and lunch." I explained to my passenger.

"The Hoh Rainforest, it's very close to the coast." Olaf didn't offer any more information.

"Hoh as in ho, ho, ho?" I asked, now this was bordering on the absurd.

All the proof of the story about Santa Claus, Kris Kringle, Saint Nicholas was in a place that was named Hoh? "Come on, I find it hard to believe where this is going." I said with a laugh.

"I didn't name the place," The old storyteller replied testily. "It was named after the Hoh Indian tribe. It was their land, now it's part of Olympic National Park." Olaf looked out his window as I drove on for a mile or so then said, "Let me see your list of questions."

It was between the seats on my yellow pad. I dug it out and handed it over to him.

"Let's see here..." he started to go down the list.

"The diamond that you called the 'French Blue,' is that the same thing as the Hope Diamond? Now that's a well thought out question." Olaf said approvingly, and looked over at me. "Yes it is, it was also in the possession of Queen Isabella II of Spain around 1830 then it was lost again. A lot of things happened after that, some of which I'm going to tell you about today, that stopped the search for the Loki Stone, which is now called the Hope Diamond. It now rests in Washington D.C. in the Smithsonian museum of natural history on the second floor." Olaf stated matter-of-factly.

"You mean, that all this time it's been in a museum and Kris didn't just pop in and switch it with a copy?" I almost lost control of the SUV, I knew that after he'd told me about the French crown jewels I could finally look up some information on the web. The Hope Diamond was said to be cursed, its origins lost in the distant past. Just about everybody who had come into contact with the stone had died in some bizarre or violent fashion. The only one known to be spared, was the last person to own it. Harry Winston, by name, he acquired it in an estate sale in 1948 and donated it to the Smithsonian ten years later.

Olaf just stared at me for a long while. Then, he finally spoke.

"One doesn't just 'pop' into the Smithsonian." He had decided to use his 'lecture' voice. "And if you need proof that the museum really holds the last piece of the Loki Stone," He started to count the fingers on his left hand. "One, Since nineteen eighty-seven, Washington D.C. has more murders per capita than any other city in the nation. "Two," he continued to count off the reasons, "It is arguably the most politically powerful city in the world. Three, the stone has the same properties as the Loki Stone when exposed to intense light. And four, how else can you explain the actions of some of those 'right-minded' politicians? Highly educated men and women acting like pigs at a trough. Feeding on power and indulging in every carnal urge. That's the influence of the Loki Stone. I'm just thankful that the 'Hope Diamond' isn't any bigger. Think how much worse it could be." Olaf shuddered slightly at the thought of it and sat back. He seemed satisfied with his explanation. "As for the why that it was left at the Smithsonian, well part of the reason is in the story I'm about to tell you. And as for the rest, I would be willing to bet a very large sum that if the stone were moved to say... Seattle, then within a few decades it would be the murder capital of the world." That was all that was going to be said about that subject until he'd finished his story.

Olaf scanned over a couple more of my questions, when one seemed to set him off again.

"With all the power the Rune Stones possessed did Kris ever use them in a violent way? The storyteller read from my list. "What kind of a question is that?" Olaf seemed very put out.

"I guess..." I started. "Well if it were me, I'd have killed the Viking

317

slavers, put some of those despots into deep space and set up some kind of reward for the finder of the Loki Stone. Kind of an 'all the riches in life are yours if you bring me the evil rock,' sort of thing." I hadn't really framed the question as succinct as I could have. I had thought that I'd be reading my questions to Olaf instead of having him look over some hastily written notes.

"Kris had seen enough butchery and barbarity in his childhood to know that killing one evil king only makes room for another," Olaf chided me. "If you're looking for nastiness surrounding Christmas..." the story-teller thought for a second. "Oliver Cromwell outlawed Christmas back in 1652 and people celebrated it anyway, in spite of fines and floggings for being merry around Christmas. As soon as Charles II came to the throne in 1659, he reinstated it. Now that's the way to win the people's praise." Olaf said smiling. "Did you know that in this country, it was Boston... about 1659 I think, people were fined 5 shillings for exhibiting Christmas spirit?" Olaf laughed. "And that's not all, in New York around 1830, some bureaucrat thought that it would be a good idea to outlaw Christmas all together. That pretty much guaranteed a riot from the public." Olaf scoffed at the 'powers that were' and their attempt at controlling people. "Enough of that, what else do you have." Olaf scanned through the list of questions. "Where did 'Rudolph the Red-nosed Reindeer' come from?" I could see out of the corner of my eye that he was rolling his eyes at me. "I've told you about the reindeer that the Tungus tribe gave us every year. Mary was the only one of us to even use one of them when she was out giving gifts to the children of Russia under the guise of the Lady Kolyada, an Elf maiden who traveled by sleigh. That was pulled by only one rein-deer, thank you very much." Now he was getting testy again. "Rudolph was a children's promotion for a department store in the fifties that has taken on a life of its own. As for the other eight reindeer, they were the invention of Clement Clark Moore, who was Episcopalian minister of all things." Olaf laughed again. "None of us had anything to do with that poem." He said, speaking of the famous 'A visit from St. Nick.'

Olaf read off another question. "What exactly was Kris' message? Why did he try to help all those children?" Olaf read the two questions that I'd meant to rewrite into one. "Boy, haven't you been listening to the story I've been telling you?" Olaf threw up his hands.

"Yes, I have!" I countered. "I just wanted the condensed version so that if a person asked me I could say..." I tossed my hand to one side as if I was saying 'fill in the blank.'

"You see," Olaf was now looking at me and using his hands to emphasize his point. "It's not the toy... it's the happy memory of being loved... special and well thought of...there is a deep potential for good in people, that is left behind in childhood, when life shows its ugly side...

He stopped for a moment to collect his thoughts. "People reinvent Christmas over and over and I don't care if they do... as long as they keep the meaning true. The importance of the family...tradition... ties that bind us, the love we share and those precious memories are all we take with us throughout our lives. Where's the harm in that?" He sat back and didn't say anything for a few miles.

"That's what people need to hear." I said quietly. "Thanks." I finished.

He scanned the rest of the list. "Okay, well here's one that I was going to tell you about on our way to the coast." He was getting back into his storyteller's voice.

"Tell me more about the Christmas spirit. Good question," Olaf said.

"It was around the turn of the last century.... Give or take a decade or two...."

In Russia, while the Czar still held a little sway over his vast empire, in the mysterious Tunguska region, a vast uncharted wilderness, there sat a lone figure in an unusually carved boat. It floated in a small lake near a greathouse, made entirely out of intertwined trees. Kris Kringle leaned back onto the ornately carved keel to recast his line and once it was in place, his mind turned to other things.

He had been quite pleased with the way his family had been using the Rune Stones to help humanity. It was more than the gifts and dowries that had made people's lives a little better. His brother and sister used what power that remained in the Rune Stones to help further the arts.

Four of Odin's power stones had already disintegrated into dust from use. Moving in the in-between and duplicating bags of gold, food and toys for the people that his family had helped. Now only five remained, one for each of Anika's children, one in the hearth of the greathouse and one that was left in the Black Hat Sect monastery high in the Himalayas, down in the catacombs with the machines of the very ancient times.

Kris' thoughts wandered, finally settling on his brother. Olaf had made it a point to find lost children and help sailors under the guise of Saint Nicholas. This had surprised Kris, since his brother had been a wandering hermit for several hundred years after they had moved to the greathouse. And the 'little people' that Kris had saved from being sold or killed by their parents had become almost indispensable to the elves that had adopted them. Many had become the finest silversmiths and craftsmen in the Realm of the Light Elves. Others had become some of the best diplomats that the elves had ever had. They seemed to have a keen mind for details of some of the more archaic points of the law, that the Elves and Frost Giants had agreed on so very long ago.

Several times, the 'little people' as they liked to be called, had kept the peace between the light-elves and some of the more hostile of Asgards Realms.

The 'little elves' could quickly find a reference in an ancient agreement that the frost giants had abided by, but had chosen to forget. Many such laws were found by the small scholars, thereby stopping the Elves' most troubling foes from escalating a disagreement into an all out war. Kris was very proud of the 'little people' that his sister had insisted on saving.

His thoughts drifted a little more, as did the small fishing boat that he'd made for lazy days on the lake in Tunguska. With a fishing pole over the side that the fish had long since ate the bait off of, Kris laid back, fully putting his weight against the highly ornate bow of the boat, that served as a back rest. The latest red cloak that the Tungus tribe had made for their 'shaman of the forest' he wadded up, to use as a pillow. Kris didn't need it for its warmth. The single Rune stone at his belt was more than capable of doing the job. Kris just wanted to while away a day or two, thinking of what else he could give children that would outlast even the golden memories of childhood. Most of the countries of Europe were actually treating their children much better in the last hundred years and parents had taken up the practice of buying or making gifts for their kids for Christmas, lightening Kris' gift giving load.

Olaf, his brother, had made up for the lost time of being a hermit over the centuries, by moving to England. Staying there in a place called Oxford for a couple of decades. Kris was quite surprised that his once illiterate brother was actually an editor of a newspaper in New York, New York in the United States and had bragged about helping an author named, Charles Dickens, with one of his books. Olaf had sent a copy to Kris. The book lay on the seat next to him. He had meant to read it today but his mind was buzzing with thoughts.

Mary, Kris' younger sister, had continued to play the part of a muse and patron to artists all over Europe and had gone to visit their brother Olaf in America.

"You must come and visit Kris, as soon as may be." She insisted. But duty called and things had still needed to be done. Emsaph had stopped by at the greathouse on his mission to check on the progress of the healing of the 'tear between the worlds,' that he and Kris had done, back at the Witch's Teeth all those centuries ago.

"Stay close to the portal, young one," Emsaph had told Kris. "Now that the tear is healed Frey will probably think that it is safe to destroy the pieces of the Loki Stone that you've collected." He mindspoke with an audible snort.

With that being said, Kris' mentor turned and galloped for the spring that held the doorway open to the Realm of the Light Elves.

'Light Elves,' Kris mused, as the boat had drifted closer to the center of the lake. He'd asked about that term once before when he was to visit the home of the 'Sisters of the Crossing.' All Emsaph would tell him was to wait and see it for himself. Thinking back, Kris didn't remember seeing anything 'light' about the three sisters that took him to Asgard. Sure, they had pointy ears and almond-shaped eyes but apart from that, they could've been mistaken for human.

Finally, Emsaph had arranged for Kris to meet the ruler of the elves.

Frey wanted to see this human who would had been the fulcrum of fixing a tear in the universe and was to vanquish the evil that the god Loki had wrought. Kris was about three hundred years old at the time, but Frey was infinitely older and thought of all humans as children, cursed with such a short life span.

Emsaph made the crossing from the great house portal in Russia alone with Kris. Titania, and Elphaba had been called away on some diplomatic crisis, so the raven-haired sister, Nula was standing in the moonlit courtyard with her father, Frey, waiting to greet the brave young human.

As the mist fell away from Kris and the Unicorn, the Kris was amazed by what he saw. Beings of brilliant light reached out to welcome him to their realm. Immediately, the taller one started to chastise Emsaph.

"You were suppose to raise your charge's vibration slightly," the larger light-being raised his hand towards Kris, who was now getting a throbbing headache. "Before you bring him here," Frey finished.

"He wanted to know..." Emsaph started, "what 'Light Elves' meant." The Unicorn didn't feel the need to apologize.

Kris' pain eased, as the beings became less and less luminous.

"You couldn't have just shown him one of those mind pictures of yours," Nula waved her finger at the Unicorn. "Evil, evil beast. Are you trying to frighten him?" She was long from being finished with her four-legged mentor.

The meeting had gone very well once Kris got used to heavier gravity of their world. Frey had turned out to be a very kind elf. The office he held was High Chamberlain, Lord of the Elves of Light, but much of it was formality since the fall of Asgard.

The war called Ragnarok, that had ended on that plain in the realm of the Norse gods, had laid most of the combatant forces to waste. Only the Light Elves, so called because they existed in a slightly higher vibration, had been spared the ravages of the war. The Elven realm was almost as far from Asgard as that of Midgard, the world where the humans dwelled.

Frey knew that the tear that had pierced all of the Realms would be an opening for the strong to prey upon the weak. Once the Frost Giants had recovered in sufficient numbers, places like Earth would be overrun.

To insure that didn't happen again, the elves enlisted the help of the most powerful creature that they could find.

The Elves had dared to open a portal to a Realm only known as the 'Void.' An infinite black-nothingness, that had probably spawned the multiverse itself. All of their collective will had been poured into the blackness in the form of a wish. The wish was for a guardian to help watch the tear while the elves tried to figure out a way to heal the damage that Odin had done, by using one of the Rune Stones to kill all of his enemies at once.

The Elves were more than a little shocked by the blue-eyed, black-coated Unicorn that trotted out of the nothingness and into the chamber where the elves worked their High Magicks.

"Your plea to the unknowable Void has been answered." The Unicorn mindspoke as he bowed his head slightly to the twelve elves that stood in a semi-circle around the portal.

The oldest and wisest among the elves looked down on the small horned horse.

"We will try again tomorrow," he addressed his fellow mages, "and figure out where we went wrong." The elder started to turn away from the guardian that they had summoned.

"A-hem," Emsaph mindspoke a clearing of a throat.

"Oh yes, find the animal a stable until we get this sorted out." The senior elf idly waved his hand at one of his attendants.

The Unicorn lifted his left front hoof a little and mindspoke again, "A-hem." He then stomped his hoof into the stone floor. Twelve cracks ran to the feet of the twelve elves in the semi-circle as thunder filled the room. Emsaph let the noise die down before he spoke again.

"Now... that was with my weak hoof." Blue fire seemed to burn in the unicorn's eyes. "I would hate to start our relationship off on the wrong foot, as it were." Emsaph snorted. "Oh Counsel of Mages, wizards most high, do not be so unwise as to judge your guardian by his form." Emsaph raised his front right hoof slightly.

The elder elf took the meaning quite clearly and quickly raised his hands. "We are sorry for the misunderstanding... guardian. Tell us what it is that you require of us." The old elf finished lamely.

'Better to get any misconceptions out of the way early,' the Unicorn thought to himself.

With their 'guardian' patrolling the space in the tear between the Realms of Asgard, the elves started to assess the work that lay ahead of them.

While surveying the damage on Midgard, the elves came across a tribe of humans that had a natural ability to work with the Magicks of the human world. These people agreed to help the elves and in return had their abilities enhanced to be more Earth-wise. The human tribe became known as the Druids. With these people working with the elves, Frey felt that they could somehow heal the breech at the black mountain.

All was going according to plan, when one of these Druids had come across the Loki Stone. The elves had thought it destroyed or lost in the void between the Realms, falling into the blackness of space to be lost forever.

The evil gem was a much debated item in the eleven forum, they couldn't bring it to them, it might infect the entire realm, some thought.

It must be destroyed in the realm it was in, nothing else could be done, others argued. Again after lengthy debate a plan was made to make a crucible of the same kind of mineral that held Loki's evil. It would be infused with protective magicks that would counteract the evil and hold the stone until it could be destroyed. Of course, all of this fell apart when Emsaph reported back that the Merlyn, the leader of the Druids, had failed to pick up the evil stone, due to a sudden war.

More debate raged on in the counsel of the elves, as the years sped by on Earth. The Druid they had picked, Anika, had had children of her own by the time they agreed to close the tear first and worry about the evil stone until later. Concerns over the Frost Giants getting through the opening clinched the council's votes and Emsaph was sent back to Earth to get the Druid woman to help in the healing.

That stopped Kris' reminiscing about the past. He knew the end of that story.

Still, he had loved the Realm of the Light Elves almost as much as his sister Mary. When she had been there, she had stayed in the palace gardens almost the entire time. Listening to and singing with the starlings.

Even now, Kris could hear the some of the birds that Mary had brought back, singing in the woods around the greathouse. He slowly rowed the boat to shore as the sun was setting. Maybe, he would go over to see the new official shaman, Mattu, and see how she was settling into her duties.

The Tungus tribe generally didn't ask Kris for much, usually they wanted to know the best places to hunt or if it was going to be a bad winter, the rest of their spiritual needs were filled by a person that was born in the tribe. Kris still had a place in the hearts of the Tungus. He had been their benefactor for hundreds of years. In bad winters, he'd made sure that they all had plenty to eat and he'd bring medicine back from his travels, which Kris freely gave to them. It was just that he was gone for long periods of time so they kept a holy man, or more often, a holy woman in residence.

A week of lazy fishing passed before Kris felt the presence of his mentor in the back of his mind.

"Holiday's over kid, wake up and meet me in the stables," Emsaph's mindspeech grew louder with every word. Kris knew that the Unicorn was almost at the portal near the greathouse.

They met in the stables that were lit with the luminescent glow that came from the living wood of the greathouse. Kris found his four-legged friend waiting on him when he got there, face deep in a large portion of wild oats and timothy hay that the Unicorn loved to eat. Kris had stopped in the kitchen and had also grabbed a bite of food. They both ate in silence, neither of them speaking or using telepathy.

After Kris had finished his apple, he got a good stiff horse brush and gave the Unicorn a thorough grooming. Emsaph ooh-ed and ah-ed at the attention that he was getting, mind speaking,

"You don't know how many times I have to beg the elves for a good brushing. They tell me that if they started, I'd never let them stop." He snorted.

"I can see why they might say that," Kris goaded his friend, as the horned horse leaned into the brush. "So what's the plan?"

"Keep brushing...." Emsaph's mindspeech seemed slurred to Kris.

The Unicorn finished his bag of feed before he stepped away from the grooming.

Images started to fill Kris' mind. It would be easier to explain to Kris, Frey's plan with visual aids. The 'young student' watched the scenes play into his mind as he put away the brush.

"So we have to go back to the Witch's Teeth?" Kris hadn't gone back to the black mountain since he'd first benn entrusted the Rune Stones. The memories that a visit might bring up had subconsciously kept him from returning.

"Not to worry young one." His mentor assured Kris. "It'll be a short trip. Get your belt."

Kris went up the scrollworked back staircase with a little trepidation in his mind. Emsaph had visited the black mountain on his way back to the greathouse. 'On one of his errands for Frey no doubt,' Kris thought to himself, as he strapped the leather belt with the Rune stone around his waist. 'When the Unicorn came here, he told me to stay close by, so what's he not telling me?' Kris wanted to know.

He came down the stairs with several questions on his mind, to find the stable empty. Kris called out to his mentor with mindspeech. The Unicorn answered, "Come into the kitchen."

'Maybe he wants some apples for dessert, what a chow hound!' Kris thought.

"I heard that!" Emsaph's mindspeech sounded loudly between Kris' ears.

The Unicorn was standing next to the crucible looking intently at the gleaming pieces of the Loki Stone.

"I thought we were leaving, oh Spanner-of-Worlds." Kris used one of his friends' many titles.

"Funny." Was the only reply, but the mindspeech inflection wasn't one of humor it was one of concern.

"You mean funny, ha-ha?" Kris asked.

"No more like funny uh-oh." Emsaph countered and images of the problem came into Kris' mind along with an explanation. "You see the crucible," the Unicorn's student nodded his head. "Now look at it with second sight." Kris relaxed his vision and let his breath deepen. The crucible no longer looked like a solid object sitting on top of the small table that held the Rune Stone of the hearth. In second sight, the crucible that held the pieces of the Loki Stone vibrated like a wineglass in an opera singer's hand, ready to break at any moment.

"You see what Frey and I have been worried about." The Unicorn said flatly. "It's a good thing you hadn't found the last piece. That might have been too much evil for the crucible to hold."

Images came of the building of the crucible, of its hurried construction. While Loki had tens of thousands of years to amass and focus malice into his own gem. The elves had only a few weeks to form a container that would shield the outside world from the effects of all that concentrated hatred. It hadn't been designed to hold the pieces for so long and with the renewed problems that the elves were having with the Frost Giants, the matter was left for Emsaph to fix.

"We need to get this thing out of here." Kris said. "Is that why we're going back to the Witch's Teeth? To bury this."

"Aaaah...no," Emsaph said, "There's another way to take care of this.

The elves want it destroyed here on Earth and soon." The Unicorn turned and ambled out to the stables without another word.

"And why do I think I'm not going to like this?" Kris called after him.

The man was starting to question the wisdom of the elves. He was over nine hundred years old after all. 'They may be older than me, but I shouldn't be treated like a child.' Kris thought loud enough and left his mind-path open so that Emsaph could hear his thoughts clearly.

"Alright, since your feeling up to a challenge," the Unicorn went into 'teacher mode,' "take us both to the exact spot where we first met, by the small pool on the upper slope of the crater of the black mountain." Emsaph finished with an audible snort.

Kris knew this was another of those tests his teacher liked to spring on him. The Unicorn stood across from him in the stables, waiting.

"Think back, back to that one moment when I shimmered into your life," Emsaph whinnied.

"Oh joy." Kris shot back. He steadied his breathing and touched the Rune Stone on his belt. His mind cleared of all thoughts, of the crucible, the wind and rain outside the stable and the secrets that his teacher loved to keep from him. All of that drifted away, only the destination mattered. Far off on the other side of the continent, Kris let his mind race up the coast of the far away land, at the speed of thought.

He came to a place that felt right but the landscape had all changed. The once flat plain that he had had to cross with a broken leg, was now eroded away. The black mountain had also changed dramatically.

The first time Kris had seen it, he'd been a boy. The bottom and top of the mountain had been as black as coal with a small band of snow near the middle and the spires of the mountaintop had reached towards the sky, twisted and foreboding.

After so many centuries, the mountain was being washed away bit by bit. Tide and storm were erasing the spot were the last battle of the Norse gods had ended.

Kris looked over the snow-covered mountain then shifted his focus into the crater. Instead of it being snow-filled, there was still a protective bubble. Much smaller now, no longer melting the snow off, but it would be enough space for them to move around.

"Get ready...nag." Kris locked onto the space and willed himself and his teacher through the in-between.

The two appeared just at the spot where they had first met. Kris stood before the small pool on the upper rise of the crater and his teacher standing slightly above a little pool of water that had been used as the portal for their trip to Asgard.

"Very good job of control, young one," Emsaph liked to preserve the student / teacher role when it suited him. "Now how about putting me on the ground."

Kris shifted his position and looked down the slope at the larger pool where the Rune Stones had healed him.

"Don't even think of dropping me in that water," his teacher mind-spoke good-naturedly.

Kris moved his teacher slightly to the left, to the black ground and released his hold on the Unicorn. This freed his attention to the landscape that he hadn't seen since he had been a boy. The ground was the same, though it didn't have the warmth that it had in the past. The sky couldn't be seen for the snow that covered mountain but the strange half light still shown everywhere, allowing him to make out some of the melted armor in the far wall. Emsaph headed down the slope towards the larger pool.

The Unicorn drank a little of the water, while Kris continued to survey the crater in second sight. Nothing was there that wasn't visible in normal sight. Then Kris looked down the slope to where his teacher stood drinking from the healing pool. A bright shine came from the water. So that was the source of the half-light, Kris thought to himself.

"Are we learning yet?" Emsaph goaded his student.

"You know," Kris reasoned, "If you want my help, you're going to have to start offering information... and a little more freely, at that."

"Well now what are you wanting to know?" The Unicorn mindspoke back.

"I've run your errands, followed your advice and put up with your all-knowing-ness. And I've done so without protest. But I haven't been a child for many a year now and even though you are infinitely older, or so you say. If I'm to be a part of these schemes of yours, I want to at least have some questions answered." Kris didn't like to be cross, it could be seen as immaturity, which in this case, would totally undermine his argument.

"Get in the pool," Emsaph said calmly. "That will answer a couple of questions and bring up a whole lot more."

Kris was expecting some logical reason from his teacher as to why he'd been kept in the dark and why it was going to continue. Maybe he'd even get an argument from his teacher. The last thing, he thought would happen was to be given an answer so easily.

"Okay," he said. Kris got down into the pool and felt a tingling on his skin just as he had when as a boy. Though this time he wasn't injured.

"Look into the deepest part of the water with your second sight." Emsaph moved his head and pointed with his horn to the other end of the pool. Since Kris had already calmed his mind, the sight came on quickly, without much effort. A large object glowed with power, about two feet long and a foot and a half wide at the other end. He went to reach for it, wading into the deep end of the water.

It was a hammer... and not just any hammer, Kris knew in an instant. This was the same weapon that he'd seen in the vision of Odin and his son, Thor. It was from their last battle... he was holding Thor's hammer.

"That's right, young one." Emsaph started revealing images as he explained. "The Runes Stones, the Loki stone and Thor's hammer, made of a blue-gray metal, were the only things to survive the blast from the Rune Stone that Odin had crushed in his mighty hand."

Kris lifted it out of the water to get a better look at it. The wooden handle was still intact, rapped in leather that had a sling at the end of the grip.

"That handle is made of a branch of the 'world tree,' Yggdrasil, the tree that spans all the Realms of Asgard. A picture of the great gnarled tree in the Realm of the Light Elves flashed into Kris' mind along with the same type of tree that the 'Sisters of the Crossing' had taught him at, in Asgard.

'Where was the tree in this world?' Kris wondered. Then, another image was shown to Kris of the black mountain, but before the last battle of the Norse gods. It was a beautiful hill with a grove of trees. In the middle of the stand of trees was the 'world tree' that had been destroyed along with the rest of the landscape, all the way out to the sea. The blast had violently pulled bedrock from out of the Earth, making an unnatural mountain out of a small hillock and leveling the forest for almost a mile out to the sea.

"So, if the tree that was rooted in all the realms of Asgard had been destroyed here, why was it possible that all of the portals to the home of the Norse gods were still open, you ask?" Emsaph mindspoke the question before Kris had a chance to ask it. "Because of the handle of Thor's hammer that you hold now. It kept the way open, and it helped more than it hurt, so the elves allowed it to stay here. You weren't given this knowledge because you had already been given the Rune Stones. They held enough power to let you take over the world and rule with an iron fist for thousands of years, if you had wanted." Kris saw in his mind the elves debating over the Rune Stones, if Kris was the wrong kind of person to trust with so much power, he wouldn't need the influence of the Loki Stone to be corrupted. "So, now you see the dilemma we faced." Emsaph continued. "Then, after the 'tear between the worlds' had been patched, Frey wanted to see how you would make your way in the world. In case you're wondering, you exceeded everyone's expectations. You and your siblings took great care, to not try and rule your world. Now with the tear here at the black mountain, or as you call it, the Witch's Teeth, is healed and nine tenths of the Loki stone safely in the crucible, Frey and I came up with a plan that should destroy most of that evil in one fell swoop. But in so doing, pathways between Earth and Asgard should be forever closed. To destroy the pieces of the Loki stone we, meaning you, will use Thor's hammer with the last bit of the 'world tree' thereby uprooting, in a sense, the Earth from the other Realms of Asgard. The good thing is that you won't have to worry about dealing with Frost Giants anymore." Emsaph snorted.

Kris saw the image of the crucible being hit by the hammer and all the pieces of the Loki Stone that he'd gathered being vaporized.

"I'm going to guess that both you and Frey have no clue just how this idea of yours is going to play out," Kris said.

Emsaph let his young ward have time to think about what was being asked of him. After a while of sitting at the edge of the pool, thinking about all that had he'd been told. "And are there any special powers in this weapon of the God of Thunder that I should know about? Just so that I don't accidentally kill us both." Kris was trying to be nonchalant about what he had in his right hand. He could feel the hammer vibrate slightly and he sensed its power where it touched his skin.

"Well, you mean besides being one of the most formidable weapons known to man or god. Forged out of the mystical metal, uruk or urus, I forget.... It sounds something like that. It's an alloy, forged in the fires of the trolls by Odin himself, being magically enchanted at every step of the forging. It was built to be an indestructible throwing weapon, and enchanted by Odin to summon storms and lightning. The hammer can also open portals to other realms. Another good reason to see it destroyed." The Unicorn finished with the description.

"I've seen the wars that are coming." Emsaph told Kris. "They come like waves onto the shore. Not just on your world, but on many of the worlds that I watch over. Can you imagine, one of the armies on this world with a weapon as powerful as this." The Unicorn shook his head violently.

"You know of what I speak, you've seen the near future here on this continent. War bloody and long with only a short reprieve until it happens again." Kris nodded at the statement his teacher had made. The Rune Stone at his belt allowed him to see a little into the future, even though it was shadowy. But with the training at the Black Hat monastery,

Kris had greatly increased his accuracy. His old teacher, Lobsang, had said that it was as if ....'Through a lens darkly, the future reveals itself.'

With the mental exercises he'd learned and the power of the Rune Stone, Kris saw the phantom of 'Nation Pride' again rising, turning sensible, educated people into fanatics, for the honor of their country.

"An arbitrary line on a map," Emsaph said, reading Kris' thoughts. "That makes next door neighbors into sworn enemies. It would be laughable if it weren't so tragic." The Unicorn walked away from the pool and started up the gentle slope to the portal. Kris got out of the water and gingerly held the hammer at arm's length.

"Do you have anymore questions?" Emsaph asked offhandedly, as Kris caught up to him at the doorway between worlds.

"I did want to know more about you..." Kris started. "But, now that I think about it..."

"Exactly," The Unicorn whinnied, "be careful what you ask for... Tell you what, if... and I do mean if, we can pull this off without getting scattered into... atoms. I'll tell you anything you want to know and... hey, we could take a week off and go talk to the Sphinx. She'd love to hear about this." Emsaph snorted, while an image of the three of them having high tea under the roasting noon day sun of Egypt, played across Kris' mind. "She always did like to chat." The Unicorn finished with a whinny.

For the next week, Emsaph was off closing the portals to the other Realms of Asgard, so that all of the force of the blast would be only here on Earth. That would keep the power concentrated here and with no gateways open, it would probably keep the massive amount of energy from tearing a new hole back through the Realms of Asgard. At least, that was the theory. That left a week for Kris, back at the greathouse to make preparations for the evacuation. The reindeer and other animals were given the gentle urging by Kris to leave the area, to migrate to better feeding grounds. He felt that the weapons of Asgard had killed enough things in their time, so even if Kris was only saving some herd animals and a few squirrels, so much the better.

Next, Kris went to tell the tribe that the land would no longer be fertile and would soon turn into a marshy bog. Infested with flies and disease. Mattu, the tribe's shaman, didn't want to be the one to second this information to her people. But after seeing the images that Kris had put in her mind of what was to come, she strongly advised the leader of the tribe to move the village. Then she promptly started packing her few belongings and made a big show of leaving the village and headed South. This more than anything she'd said, convinced the people of the tribe to start evacuating as fast as they could. With that done, the only thing left to do was to tell the Almas of the plan and ask them to leave the area.

Only a few families of Almas were left in the region to tell. Most had moved to North America. They still preferred to stay away from the things of man, so even though they still lived in a slightly higher vibration of Earth, they chose remote regions in the mountains and along the rough seacoast of the Pacific Northwest.

At first, the Almas had seen Kris as a possible threat. Normally, humans tended to use whatever power they had to make slaves of others or kill that which they didn't understand. For over nine hundred years, Kris, his brother and sister hadn't tried to harm any of the Almas. On several occasions, Kris had offered aid when some younglings had gotten lost in a riptide of the in-between and couldn't be found.

On one occasion, Kris and Olaf had found the young Almas quickly, on an island off the coast of Greece. The children had lost their 'mental footing' and been pulled away from home at a fantastic speed. Scared and not knowing how to get home, they materialized on the Isle of Kronos and not seeing anything resembling the forests of Siberia, they hid in a cave near the shore. After the children's safe return, the Almas warmed slightly to the family of humans that lived in their midst.

That tiny bit of trust that Kris had earned from the Almas was to then be tested. Kris told them that this land was to be destroyed and that he didn't know what would happen as a result to their world, that overlapped with the humankind.

Better to go, than to be near such raw power that would be unleashed, they decided. After things had calmed down, maybe they would move back to Siberia.

So, by the time Emsaph got back to the greathouse, a large area that would be needed for the destruction of the evil gem stone had been cleared.

"Let's give it another day." The Unicorn suggested. "You can brush me while we wait. What do you say...."

"I'd say you'd make up any excuse to get some grooming," Kris laughed at his old teacher.

Actually, as Emsaph was being groomed, he let some of his mind go searching for any animal or human was still in the blast zone. He agreed with Kris. Keep the death toll down to zero if possible and only two if they made a mistake. He couldn't find a single heartbeat in forty miles.

"I think we're good to go," he mindspoke to his groomer. "I still have to send a message to Frey that we're ready and close the last portal." He put an image of the little spring up the hill from the greathouse into Kris' mind.

Finally, Emsaph said that he needed to run the last errand of a message to the elves. It was the first time in his immortal life he'd asked someone to stop brushing him. The Unicorn looked into his young friend's mind. He saw a sadness there, was this to be the end of them? His student was thinking over and over. How could they escape the power of the blast?

Odin hadn't survived the breaking of a Rune Stone. How could they survive the destruction of; a Rune Stone, the Thunder God's hammer and the pieces of the Loki Stone?

"Odin didn't have an immortal guardian who also happens to be very wise at his side." Emsaph mind spoke to Kris.

"You forgot infinitely powerful and all-knowing. Or should I say a know-it-all." Kris' mood changed.

"Well I would have, but modesty forbids." The Unicorn sparred back.

He trotted off to finish his last task before the sunset. Kris refilled Emsaph's stall with timothy hay and some oats that his friend always liked.

'With so many unknowns to face we might as well eat a good meal,' Kris thought to himself. He went back into the kitchen to fix himself an evening meal and stopped at the hearth table to look at the sparkling pieces of the Loki Stone. A little evil treasure trove that had started so many events. 'Like a small pebbles that start an avalanche,' Kris thought.

Emsaph hadn't come back by the time he'd finished his own dinner so Kris went back out to the stables and made a bed of straw and used a sack of oats for a pillow and tried to get some rest. There were many beds upstairs, but he didn't want to be alone on that night. 'Life passes by fast, no matter if it's ninety or nine hundred years,' Kris thought, as he tried to settle his mind.

He had already talked to Olaf and Mary by mind speech, amplified by his Rune Stone. They thought the plan was more than a little hare-brained. But, if it meant an end to some of the evil that could harm the world, and if nobody was going to get hurt, and that was a big if, to be sure, then it might be for the best.

Kris let his mind wondered back to his time in Asgard. Where he and his new Unicorn friend had explored and where Emsaph had erased some of the pain that would have eaten at the young boy's soul and left him a bitter and hateful person. Kris caught himself. 'If I go thinking about the 'what might have been' I'll never get any sleep.' And he would need all his wits about him in the morning. After tossing and turning for more than an hour he felt the presence of his old friend in his troubled mind. Without realizing it, he drifted off to sleep A dark, warm... dreamless sleep.

Kris awoke with a start, Emsaph standing over him. It was before sunrise, not even a false dawn was on the horizon, Kris noticed as he looked out the east-facing window. He stretched and splashed water from the trough on his face to fully wake up.

"Well, are you up to this," the Unicorn asked. "If not we could wait one more day."

"You just want more brushing, don't you?" Kris teased his old friend.

The Unicorn snorted and turned and headed out of the stables, having already eaten his breakfast that Kris had set up for him the night before.

Kris secured the red cloak that the Tungus tribe had bestowed on their honorary shaman and protector, and followed his teacher.

They both turned when they reached the edge of the clearing in the front of the greathouse. Teacher and student knew their separate roles in the destruction of the Loki Stone. Emsaph connected with the earth-power that slept in the deep under the forest. He was to form it into a shield to protect the planet from the power that was about to be unleashed. The idea was to have the shockwave of the blast be deflected away from the ground so that the energy could be spread out into the atmosphere or better yet out into space.

Kris' job was two-fold. The first part was certainly the most fun. He touched the Rune Stone on his belt and commanded Thor's mighty hammer to come to him. As the weapon of the Norse god came flying out one of the upper story windows of the house, Emsaph remarked, "You could have just went up and got it, you know?"

The hammer flew over to them at lightning speed and stopped an inch from Kris' hand.

"Now, where's the fun in that?" he said taking the hammer in his right hand. Emsaph snorted as a reply and went back to gently prod the great amount of dormant energy that begin to overlap and bond together. The earth-power that had built up here over the millennia was moving to the Unicorn's will a little faster, the power stirred in the depths. Emsaph wove the strands over and back on themselves adding bulk to what he'd hoped would be enough power to minimize the damage to that isolated part of the world.

Emsaph watched as Kris stepped forward into the clearing and began to swing the Thunder God's hammer over his head. As the weapon gained speed it started to glow a faint blue. The smell of ozone filled the air and tiny bolts of lightning started to crackle around the gray-blue metal at the end of the weapon. Kris let it go. It flew off at an angle, heading skyward.

"Now, for the not so fun part." Kris said, returning to his teacher's side.

Emsaph was glad that he hadn't mentioned the hammer before to Kris. The smile on his pupil's face looked a little too similar to that of the hammer's previous owner. 'Maybe Thor had infused some of his own being into the hammer,' Emsaph thought. Fortunately, that was no longer an issue, with the hammer in orbit around the Earth and about to be used to destroy the crucible and everything in it.

When Kris returned to his side, Emsaph said, "Okay, make a wish." This kind of took his student off guard. 'Make a wish?' what was that suppose to mean?

Pictures began to enter Kris' mind. Again, he saw the destruction of the Loki Stone as it should happen. The great release of energy and shockwave that would sweep the forest clean for twenty miles in all directions. Trees, two feet thick, would be knocked over like matchsticks. It was the same images he'd shown to Mattu, the Tungus tribal shaman. But, this time the vision continued on, he saw the wave encircle the globe becoming invisible to the naked eye but still pushing the upper atmosphere like waves hitting the beach.

Kris turned to his mentor, "I wish we could do this another way." He said, not that he would complain, he had lived a lot longer and done much more than almost anyone alive.

"They have eyes but they do not see, they have ears but they do not hear." Emsaph started. "With all the good works that you've been doing in your spare time, all the saving of small children and dowries that you've thrown in windows of poor maidens so that they could marry a good husband that they loved…" The Unicorn was really into his teaching mode right then. Kris knew better than to interrupt him when Emsaph got like that. "Inspiring people to listen to the angels of their better natures and share a little of the bounty of their own lives with the less fortunate. Kris, you've actually made it fashionable for people to be good to one another and you didn't use threats or punishments to do it. With all that being said," Emsaph was starting to get to his point. Or at least, Kris hoped his teacher was, the sun was rising. He didn't want to be standing there all day. "Don't you realize that thought is just a type of energy?" The Unicorn queried.

Kris remembered something his teacher had told him from when he was back in Asgard. The Unicorn had put most of the lessons into his mind while he slept. Something about purpose or intent, that was what Emsaph was going on about.

"Are you even listening to me?" The Unicorn turned to face Kris directly, his horn very close to Kris' face.

"Yes, yes you just reminded me of lesson that you'd given me back in Asgard. One of the dream lessons." Kris replied quickly. He went on, "Intent is the first step in any action, to know yourself is to... to," 'Boy, that was a really long time ago,' he thought to himself. "To know yourself is to know the right action." He finished rather proud that he still could recall something from a dream that happened so long ago.

"Great," His teacher said quite pleased with Kris, "now what does that axiom mean in relation to what we are about to do?" He tried to stump his student.

"That we, or I should say I, need to intend an outcome that may not be related to the energy that we are about to unleash upon an unsuspecting world?" It sounded good to Kris but would it satisfy his mentor.

"Exactly right, that's why I said, make a wish." The Unicorn replied happily.

'So the thought will be magnified by the blast,' Kris made sure he had it worked out before he thought about how to frame his intent for humanity. He thought back to a tale that his friend, the Sphinx, had told him about a ruler who once asked a jinni for the 'wisdom of the ages.' The King was cursed with undying life for all time. Kris wanted to be extra cautious, knowing how any intent could go very wrong, just like a wish can, if not framed in the right manner.

Peace on Earth and good will to mankind, sounded a little vague. Do unto others... no that could be turned very wrong. Finally, he hit on it. 'Yes that would do nicely,' he thought to himself. Kris turned to his teacher. "Okay, let's do this." He said.

They both turned to face the greathouse. Inside the kitchen, the hearthstone table that the crucible rested on, started to bend to the will of the Unicorn. The crucible with the pieces of the Loki Stone safely inside, began to sink into the table as the wood became soft and pliable. Within a minute, the crucible had sank down to touch the hearth stone where it came to rest as the wood covered over the top rim of the crucible and enclosed the pieces of the Loki Stone. Then the wood returned to it's normal state after having melted like hot wax.

"Your turn," Emsaph mindspoke to Kris. "I'm going to work on our exit." The Unicorn touched his horn to the Rune Stone on Kris' belt to draw more energy; to use; to transport them away as fast as possible from the destruction that was about to take place.

Kris took over from where his mentor had left off. His job would be to lift the enclosed crucible as high as possible into the sky to keep the impact away from the ground. And bring Thor's hammer, that was now circling the Earth in a high orbit, into the floating hunk of wood that held one of the Rune Stones, the crucible that the elves had supplied and the pieces of the Loki Stone.

All that and to bring in the hammer with such force that it would break everything in the wooden block into atoms. Thereby, incinerating the evil gems and releasing the power of the hearth stone with the intent that the waves of power that would encircle the globe would ease the hatred that poisoned one against another on Earth. Giving the world an opportunity to turn the tide of war before it washed over humanity once again. At least that was the theory, as Emsaph kept reminding him.

Kris used his thought to pull the table free of its base, it came away as if it were made out of soft clay. The wood block floated upwards slowly and came out the front door of the greathouse. Kris then concentrated on making the wooden container lift in to the sky. It shot straight up and soon wasn't visible to his eyes. Kris could still feel it though, it was right over the greathouse about a mile up in the air, gently floating in the target area that his mentor had worked out ahead of time.

"Is our exit ready?" Kris turned to look at his long time friend.

"Oh, it's ready... but the timing is going to have to be perfect." Emsaph stepped closer to his student. "Grab hold of my mane," he mindspoke. "It may be a rough landing... what with the incalculable energy that will be released, right on top of us as we leave." He whinnied. "Just so you know.

"If you're trying to comfort me, stop." Kris said with a smile. It was understood that this may be their last minute alive. The blast could be too quick and too much for the Unicorn or that the force could still kill them in the in-between on their way to safety.

Emsaph followed along with Kris' thoughts by lightly reading his pupil's mind.

"Don't be starting that, 'It's a good day to die' stuff," the Unicorn snorted indignantly. A comfortable silence fell over the two as they looked at each other in the morning sun. Finally, Emsaph stomped his front hoof into the soft ground. "I guess I'll miss this place," He turned his head slightly towards the house.

"Now, don't go making me get all misty-eyed." Kris retorted. With his free hand raised, he searched the heavens for the hammer of the mighty thunder god. It was still speeding around the Earth, north of the equator, in a tight, fast orbit.

"Okay, here goes." Kris' hand unconsciously tightened on the Unicorn's mane. With his mind, he reached out to stir the power in the hammer. Electricity sparked around the blue-gray metal, bringing to life the full power of the weapon. Lightning crackled from the mystic metal hammer and it started to glow as it moved faster and faster around the upper hemisphere of the globe. Its orbit becoming lower and the hammer grew even brighter as it came in contact with the thicker atmosphere of the planet.

"NOW!" It was a shout that rang in Kris' head. He didn't know if he or his companion had said the agreed upon word. But as the hammer streaked across the sky, headed for the wooden capsule, Kris concentrated all his will into the impact far above his head.

The day would become known as June 30, 1908. At approximately 7:30 A.M., people viewing the sky over Russia watched a huge fireball streaking towards the Tungus region, followed by tremendous booms and a fiery cloud that could be seen for over two hundred miles.

Forty miles away from the blast center in the town of Vanavara, people were thrown into the air by a shock wave. Windows shattered and ceilings collapsed, and a series of thunderclaps could be heard for five hundred miles. But not a single person was seriously injured.

Hours later, the whole region around the Tunguska was showered with a "black rain," lake water had mixed with dirt that was sucked into the vortex of the explosion and was thrown all over the region.

Other parts of the world reported odd atmospheric phenomena for several days after the event. Colorful sunsets and unusual sunrises captivated the people of Russia, Scandinavia, and Western Europe. There were huge streaks of light that lit up the night skies in the Northern Hemisphere. In London, people reported that the nights remained so bright, a person could easily read a newspaper or book without need of a candle.

The light faded slowly over the course of a month. But because the area of the blast was so remote, the first expedition was put off until 13 years later.

When the expedition finally reached the Tunguska region, they found the forest laid flat for almost twenty miles around a central point but no sign of what had caused the massive explosion.

"Well, I guess that I ended the story at about the right time. The entrance is just up ahead. Up here on the left," Olaf said. Was he impatient?

"Now just hold on one minute," I started. "What happened to Kris? Did he make it out okay?" I wasn't going to let him get off that easily. 'You can't end a story like that,' I thought.

"Yes, yes Kris and Emsaph made it to the temple of the Black Hat Sect. Perhaps a little more singed than they would have liked. But the intent that Kris held onto, even while the fireball was about to envelop him, worked." Olaf said.

I just glanced over to him with a puzzled look on my face.

"Whenever the Rune Stones were used, the action was always more than physical." My storyteller was now looking at me, trying not to roll his eyes. "The force of the blast carried the 'Spirit of Christmas' all around the world. An ever-present... ocean of goodwill for your fellow man." He looked at me, narrowing his eyes a little. "It's easy for anyone to feel, though it's far stronger during the month of December. If people would just stop running around buying things for a few minutes they could feel it. A warm sensation of peace that starts in your heart, relaxes your throat and clears the mind. It's a shame that humanity doesn't embrace it like they used to," he lamented. "Back in thirties, even with the Great Depression in full swing, people felt the Spirit of Christmas. Maybe even more so, because they didn't have so many gadgets and toys to distract them." He rubbed his chin thoughtfully for a second or two.

"Now as for the rest of your questions, a lot can be figured out if you reread the story." Olaf knew I had reread the story he was just seeing if I'd rise to take the bait.

"Yeah, but what about the last piece of the Loki Stone?" I asked. "Why leave it behind?" I wanted to know.

"Well, back in 1908, Kris didn't know where the last piece was and the crucible was barely containing the other pieces as it was. As for why, he hasn't done something about it lately," Olaf pondered. "Kris went to the Realm of the Light Elves, there he has only been gone a few years. While back here on Earth it's been...say almost a hundred years or so." He was counting decades on his fingers. "Yes it's been about that now."

He nodded. "As for Mary, she finished up her business shortly before the Second World War and then Emsaph returned to take her to the realm of the Light Elves as well. I wanted to stick around because things were just starting to get interesting at the beginning of the twentieth century." He finished with a smile and a twinkle in his eye. I assumed that was a family trait.

A small brown wooden sign indicated that the Hoh rainforest was the next turn on the left.

"Well, here we are, Jack." Olaf had a lightness in his voice, that I didn't know that he could have, like an excited child opening his first present on Christmas morning.

"So are we going to meet someone or are you going to show me one of the Rune Stones. Is one of them buried out here?" I looked down the two-lane road for something. "When I heard there'd be a rainforest I expected to see some kind of different trees, geckos, I didn't know... something." I rattled on.

"Don't be petulant," Olaf started. "If you roll down the window you can smell the moisture in the air, the decay of fallen trees and of fresh growth of the forest." Olaf was waxing on poetically. "As for the rest, well, you'll just have to wait." He said tersely.

We followed the river road as it wove its way deeper into the park. Around the next bend in the road, some of the trees had club moss hanging from the higher branches. After another bend and I noticed that the trees that lined the roadside, weren't all pine, like they had been on the trip over. Also, they seemed closer together. I could no longer see Mount Olympus through the breaks in the trees.

We passed a couple of little stores that sold bottled water and snacks to the tourists in the summer months. They were locked up tight for the off-season. A few more twists in the road and we stopped at the ranger station at the park entrance.

"I think you've got the park to yourselves today." The ranger told us, looking at us suspiciously. "Are you on vacation?" she wanted to know.

"I'm visiting my son," Olaf chimed into the conversation, "I've always wanted to see a rainforest. I don't think these old bones could make it to Borneo." His voice cracked and sounded weak. "Is there a level trail that can show me a little of your park?" Olaf was playing his part to the hilt.

'Okay, now he was laying it on a little too thick.' I thought to myself.

"Yes sir, it's just off the main parking area." The park ranger reassured 'my old man.'

We drove away from the booth at the entrance with maps and information pamphlets and headed on up the road a few more miles to the parking lot where most of the hiking trails started.

"Park over there by that work shed." Olaf pointed to the far end of the empty lot. I made out a small building that looked like it might house tools and supplies for the park rangers. It was painted green to match the dense foliage that ringed the parking lot.

I stopped the car in front of the spot that Olaf wanted, and turned to my guide. "Okay, so now what?"

"Now we hike," Olaf said with a smile.

I didn't mind the trip over and I liked the story. But I wasn't sure that I wanted to go adventuring in a remote rainforest in the off season. 'Hey, call me crazy,' I thought as I looked out the window, storm clouds were gathering over the empty parking lot. Okay, so there was one car that I'd missed, still I didn't see any park ranger vehicles. Did they do anything besides sit in that booth and listen to the radio at this time of year? I wondered. 'She could be the only ranger in the whole park at this time of year,' I thought to myself. I noticed my paranoia was starting to pick up steam.

"Come on, lazy bones," I heard the lightness back in the storyteller's voice, now that he'd finished his performance he was back to his spritely self. Olaf practically hopped out of the SUV. I got out and went to the back where I had put my little backpack and his duffel bag.

The air was heavy with the smell of earth and decaying plants, kind of like a greenhouse. I had grabbed the travel guide of the peninsula that was in the glove box, and was thumbing through it to find out any information about our location.

Hoh Rainforest: one of only three temperate-zone rainforests in the world (the others are in New Zealand and southern Chile). 'Okay,' I thought to myself, 'I'll ask Olaf about that.' I read more of the information.

Massive 'nurse' logs of fallen trees serve as starting ground for new seedlings, nourishing them with nutrients as they decay. Moss drips from overhanging branches, and licorice ferns sprout from trees without ever reaching the ground. Everything grows two to three times faster than on dry land; here in the rainforest, Sitka spruce grow to heights over 300 feet and as wide as 23 feet. Roosevelt elk are easy to spot and seem tame enough to let you take pictures of them from the trails, but please don't approach wild animals. The pamphlet cautioned.

'I wish I had brought my camera a long.' I thought, putting the field guide and information that the ranger had given us in my backpack.

"You can always come back later." Olaf said, reading the look on my face. He turned and started to walk over to one of the trailheads.

"Now, before you ask the most obvious question." Olaf was talking back to me over his shoulder. "Yes, there is something special about this place. It's a rainforest that shouldn't exist in this latitude." Olaf lifted his index finger higher than his shoulder and pointed to the club moss that draped every branch of the nearest tree.

"Haven't you noticed that things that are out of place are a sign that there is something special about a location, something that needs careful thought and more investigating?" Olaf went on with his lecture as we passed probably the loneliest phone booth in the world. Its wooden roof was covered with dark green moss.

"Take Stonehedge or Easter Island for example. All those strange alignments and how did the people move those massive stones?" Olaf turned to look at me and almost knocked me down with his duffel bag that he was shouldering.

"There are portals near all of the sacred places." He said flatly. "The Giza Plateau, Chaco Canyon, Angkor Wat and Machu Picchu, all have gateways to other realms." Olaf stopped affirming each sacred site by wagging his finger and opened his palm and lifted his arm in a sweeping gesture. "This 'out of place' rainforest is the closest portal to where I'm going from the Seattle area. There are a couple of portals that are closer, but they lead to off to remote realms, where it's hard to get back to Earth." He turned his attention back to the trailhead.

As we passed the plastic covered map board that showed the three trails for day hikers, I scanned it to see the general path we'd be taking.

"Don't bother looking at those trails," Olaf said flatly. "The portal isn't going to be found on a map."

I hadn't thought that he was taking me to a doorway to another dimension. I hadn't really thought too much about the strange areas on Earth. Like most people I thought that it would be cool to go see one or two of them before I died, but they were just some of the ancient mysteries that even the best scientists couldn't fully explain. I had a job and a life and those places didn't seem real to me. I guess I thought of the ancient sites like I thought of the Milky Way. I know it's out there but you can't see it from the city. So, it gets lost in the jumble of modern life. A wonder that's remote but always there loses its appeal in a way. I'm sure some psychologist will write about 'modern man's selective memory, friend or foe?' some day.

The path wound around one of the giant fallen logs that had some young saplings growing out of the decaying tree trunks. I turned to get a better view of where we just traveled and look back to see the parking lot, but it had disappeared behind the ferns and thick bunches of low hanging club moss that seemed to hang off every tree branch. We tramped on over the pebbles of the path that was reinforced for the regular tourists then after crossing a couple of rough log bridges, I started to feel the spongy ground under my feet.

A little farther on, I noticed the forest closing in around us. Ferns covered the edges of the path, the smell was fragrant with the scents of flowers that I still can't name. Off in the distance, I could hear the sound of the Hoh River as it cascaded down the rocks of a small falls, on its way to the Pacific Ocean. I could only get glimpses of the sky through the dense tree canopy of hemlocks and Sitka firs.

That stopped me in my tracks, here it was the first weekend in December and I was starting to become lost in a rainforest with some guy that for an inexplicable reason, I trusted. Well, trusted up until this point. I tried to get my bearings. I looked around for some kind of landmark. The few breaks in the trees only showed me the misty fog that was rolling down from the mountains that ringed this small valley. Everywhere I looked were trees thickly covered in club moss that hung almost to the forest floor. The ground was covered in dense foliage of ferns and rotting logs. I noticed that the air was actually becoming kind of muggy. It reminded me of that old poem by Henry Wadsworth Longfellow,

This is the forest primeval. The murmuring pines and hemlocks,

Bearded in moss and in garments green...

I was struck with a sense of wonder that pushed my paranoia out of my head.

Olaf had also stopped at the top of the next rise. "Get out your rain gear, if you brought any." He ordered.

I looked up into the tree canopy to see if I could spot the clouds. I couldn't see any blue or white of the sky. I could only see the dark brown-grays of the wet branches, greens of the leaves and moss in a strange yellow half-light of the deep forest. I looked up the incline of the path at Olaf. The lighting gave him the look of a youthful face and straw-yellow hair.

"I won't sport with your intelligence on how you know that." I said, taking off my backpack. I found my rain poncho just before the first fat raindrops found their way through the thick foliage of the upper canopy. The ambient light darkened slightly, 'probably because of the clouds rolling in off the Pacific,' I thought.

I caught up to my guide as the rain increased.

"Hey, didn't you bring a raincoat in that duffel bag you brought?" I asked.

"I like to feel the weather," Olaf laughed at some thought that he kept to himself. "When it rains, I want it to pelt my face and when it snows, I want to taste the snowflakes on my tongue." He turned back to the trail that was becoming more and more overgrown with ferns and moss.

'Well, this isn't what I'd hoped for,' I thought. 'I guess we're just going to hike around in this swampy forest while he shows me the wonders of nature.' I let my mind wander, the scenery had all blended in my head into a big 'save the rainforest' montage. Moss, huge trees and a marshy undergrowth. "Hey, throw in some loincloth-covered natives and you could make a documentary out here." I said, but Olaf wasn't listening to me.

The trail continued to rise around fallen, rotting logs that were taller than me and the occasional mound that could have been a massive boulder that plants had grown over. I looked at my watch. It would be dark long before we got back to the rental car.

"We're here," Olaf said abruptly. The statement kind of startled me.

I looked around to take in the scene. The rainforest didn't look that much different. Water still dripped from the canopy. The storm had passed over and the ambient light had brightened slightly but still had an odd yellow tinge to it. Olaf still looked as though he had straw-colored hair.

"Look more carefully... investigate." Olaf said, referring to his speech about the sacred places that he gave me earlier, when we started this hike.

I listened to the sounds of the forest. I could still make out the gurgling of the river off in the distance and there was a continuing dripping of the rain from the leaves and moss overhead. I scanned the area to see thick tree trunks half covered in moss and ferns and a few fallen tree trunks that were covering the ground. I then looked back to Olaf and shrugged my shoulders.

The scowl on his face told me that I'd better keep searching for something. Halfway up one of the mammoth Sitka spruce trees I spotted a black bird. By the size of it, it must have been a very large raven. It was watching me, watch it. The oily black feathers seemed to shimmer in different hues. The raven cawed twice and seemed to lose interest in me. I continued to scan the rest of the scene for anything else. Finally, I turned back to Olaf.

"Well, there's a big raven in that tree over there." I said, pointing in it's general direction.

"Very good, grasshopper," Olaf said humorously. "Now, what can you tell me about the lore of ravens in the Pacific Northwest?" He stepped over the run-off of a little spring or stream and sat on a mossy boulder in the small open space a few yards away.

I started to pull off my backpack to look up any information that the travel guide to the Olympic National Park might have on the subject.

"You're not going to find any of the old legends of the raven in that bag of yours." Olaf said with humor in his voice. "So I'll tell you," he started. "To Pacific Northwest Coast tribes, Raven represents the shaman's powers, symbolizes change in consciousness and is the mark of a shape shifter. Raven medicine gives you the courage to try new things and not to be afraid of the unknown. And oddly enough, the Raven is the keeper of the portals in this area of the country." Olaf finished. He sat there and let me process the information.

I looked over to where I'd last seen the big black bird. It had left its perch. I scanned around for it in the waning light of the afternoon. When I looked back to Olaf, the bird was sitting above him in the remnants of one of a giant spruce.

The Raven's perch was on top of the spire of wood that had remained rooted to the forest floor as the rest of the giant Sitka had long since fallen and decayed, giving itself to nurture new life.

"And here is where I leave you..." Olaf said. I watched as he got up from his seat and crossed the little spring of water that had suddenly dammed up to make a large puddle. I watched as a mist started to form over the ever-growing puddle.

"Now, wait just one minute," I still had questions and more were popping in my head as the mist swirled and started to form into a small square shape.

"How am I suppose to find my way back to the car? It'll be dark soon. I can't follow a black bird in the dark." I was trying to slow this ending down.

"That's already been arranged." Olaf said smiling. The Raven cawed again, as the square of mist grew into a rectangle and continued to grow.

"Why do you have to leave now and so quickly?" I asked hurriedly.

"Some friends of mine have found my mother's sea chest." Olaf said. "Apparently, the Selke... remember them, beings from prehistory that can change from seals into men. Well, they had collected it back from the sea, hundreds of years ago and stored it in a cave on one of their islands." He finished with a smile. That statement caught me off guard. "You've got enough of Kris' story to write your book, if you will." The storyteller bowed to me slightly. The rectangle had grown to the height of a man and now resembled a doorway with the mist becoming brighter.

"I will," I promised, looking at him more closely as he stood next to the shimmering steamy opening, Olaf's hair didn't just look blonde, it was blonde. I'd just assumed from the first time I'd laid eyes on him that he must be old. Then, after I'd started to believe his tale, it'd just seemed natural that he'd have white hair. He was about thousand years old after all.

"You... you glamoured me." I laughed. The man standing a few yards away could have been my age.

"You noticed," he laughed with me. I watched as the mist seemed to freeze into place. Something moved behind the light, something dark, something small but it was growing, taking shape. The bright light of the misty doorway fell away from the middle of the doorway and was quickly replaced by darkness. Soon the charcoal colored spot in the middle of the portal grew out to the edge of once bright mist. Blacker than the Raven that stood watch over us. The bird cawed twice and a voice came from the inky blackness.

"I'm coming, I'm coming... you flying rat."

I'd never heard the voice but I knew the sarcasm.

"Emsaph," I called out to the portal. Then, my eloquence left me. What does one say to an immortal, semi-mythical, smarmy know-it-all?

"Calm down, junior," the voice from the dark doorway, "I didn't come for an interview. I just came for Olaf." I thought I heard a snort at the end of that sentence.

"We're not done here, you know..." I searched my mind for one of the questions that I hadn't asked. "What about you, Olaf. Were you ever married?"

"Don't start with the public have a right to know crap," a voice rang in my head.

"Apparently, the 'public sure are nosey." Olaf said with a laugh. As he stepped toward the portal. I found that I could move, so I walked towards the doorway after him. The Raven cawed loudly as my storyteller hovered slightly above the puddle and then faded into the black space before him. I was almost there when I caught the sight of a pair of azure blue eyes looking at me from the darkness.

"Yes, now for you..." The voice I heard in my head had a mischievous sound to it. I saw the rectangle grow bigger. It seemed to move towards me. I wished that I was back at the car or home in the city or just about anywhere else on Earth at that moment...the moment that the blackness fell over me.

"Confronting the unknown can show you a lot about yourself, young one." I could hear the words in my mind as I drifted in the inky space, not feeling gravity or ground beneath my feet. "So many questions," Emsaph's 'voice' seemed to say, from far away. I felt as if my thoughts were all in a book with some unseen hand, quickly flipping through its pages. Images and explanations filled in the empty spaces in my head. "The unopened sea chest is in safe hands, on an island off the coast of Ireland. Why didn't he just fly to Ireland already when he found out about it two weeks ago? Good question. If you were standing on the West Coast of the Emerald Isle looking out over the sea, you would never be able to see the Isle of the Selke. In fact, you can't get there from any portal left in Europe. That being the case, I had to politely asked Raven, the guardian of the portals in this region, if I could pick up one of my charges on his turf. You know Ravens can be as chatty as a Sphinx once you get them started." Emsaph was sounding like a teacher, explaining something simple to a first time student.

The images started to blur in my head as I felt that the interview was coming to an end.

"Oh yeah, I have one more thing to tell you, young one, an objective piece of wisdom from a world-spanning, immortal, noble and humble servant of the Light Elves. As soon as a human loses their 'sense of wonder' their spirit goes to sleep. It's just something you might want to keep in mind." I heard another snort and a feeling of warm permeated my body.

One thought was still on my mind. 'How am I going to find the car?'

Then a clear and cheerful voice rang loudly in my head. "Work shed!"

I wouldn't say, "poof I was there," it was more like a thud actually. I lay on the ground, in the waning twilight in the bushes next to the park ranger's dark-green work shed for a few minutes to feel my body get used to the sensation of gravity again.

On the trip back, I waved to the ranger at the entrance quickly as I passed by. Thankfully she didn't stop me, I would have had a hard time explaining that I'd left my 'father' back in the rainforest. The miles rolled by on the empty road, as I was lost in thought. 'Maybe Olaf's mother was in that sea chest,' I thought to myself. Anika might have made it to the safety of the chest in the raging maelstrom, then if the lid had closed behind her; then she would have not aged a day. No wonder Olaf had been so antsy.

I made it onto the last car ferry of the evening and went back to the city. Driving down the festively lit streets seemed somehow less real than the strange experience I'd had in the rainforest. The glass and steel towers gleamed and glittered in the reflected Christmas lights, but to me, they seemed two-dimensional. I drove around a little, looking at this shining example of man's taming of the wilderness.

'Did that Unicorn change me somehow,' I pondered, as I came to a stoplight near my apartment. I parked the car under a street light that had a huge blinking Santa Claus ornament hanging from it. I chuckled at the electric image of Kris Kringle, 'what silliness,' I thought. Then I saw a family crossing the street, from all the packages they were carrying, it was obvious that they had been out late, trying to get the family Christmas shopping done. The three-year old girl in the group pointed up at the Christmas light over my head and asked,

"Santa?"

Her mother looked up in the air to where her little daughter was pointing and replied, "Yes Katie, that's Santa," then she smiled as the little girl laughed.

When they passed by me, I was getting my stuff out of the back of the SUV. My eyes were drawn to look at the face of the little girl in halo of the street lamplight. I saw the look of wonder on the toddler's face. Who was I to scoff at what others want to believe? The thought rang in my head. 'Jack, your brain is full and you'd better call it a day.' I mused.

But part of me tried to concentrate on the feeling of other-worldliness of the events that had happened to me. I didn't want to lose that sensation.

All the next day, as I got back into the routine of doing laundry and paying bills, I felt the feelings of my unique experience start to slip away from me. Like each mundane task that reminded me of my comfort zone, pushed my visit to the Hoh Rainforest further away from me.

Monday came and so did work. The weekend faded into an odd dream as I got a break to do a real story about some misappropriation of city funds. That took up the balance of the week and I managed to scoop the television news on the entire story that was going in the Sunday paper.

Front page of the local news, B section, but hey, it wasn't my usual 'Ask Aunt Sally' column, so I was very happy.

Christmas week came and I hadn't thought of writing down the last story that Olaf had told me on the trip over to the rainforest, for two weeks. I would have off a couple of days and made a resolution to have the chapter written by New Year's day. When I thought back to the trip, a lot of what happened had pushed me out of my comfort zone of how I thought life really was. Like most people, I was of the opinion that: if you're lucky, you get threescore and ten years, Newtonian physics runs the Universe and mankind's destiny slowly marches forward. But what I'd been told through Olaf's story and the trip had shattered those illusions.

I sat in the lunchroom at work, looking out the window over the Puget Sound, lost in these thoughts. Christmas lights twinkled on the far shore over on Bainbridge Island. All of the festive decorations of the downtown malls, giant plastic candy canes, wreaths and a Santa on practically every corner, seemed trite and missing the point. Then I recalled what Olaf had said, "People reinvent Christmas over and over and I really don't care if they do... as long as they keep the meaning true."

'I hope that we don't lose the meaning,' I thought to myself. I was still lost in thought when a friend came in to look for me.

"Hey, the boss wants your column for the deadline. Tick, tock, tick, tock." He said.

I finished the column quickly and clocked out for the week. I felt like I at least owed the storyteller something for all that he'd shown me. Enough to finish his tale at least. I could post it on the Internet if I couldn't find a publisher. Though I kind of thought of Kris or Mary walking through a bookstore, probably somewhere in Europe and seeing their brother's story in print, it might give them a smile.

After the first of the year, I went back to my routine of hitting the coffee shop down in the market on Saturdays, hardly ever getting my favorite booth and kind of missing the next story about days long gone and having some of the mysteries of history being explained. I'd gotten my booth early one Saturday in February as the bitter cold of late winter had kept most of the early shoppers home. Bulldog edition of the Sunday paper in hand, I settled in my booth, putting my mocha near the large paned windows that showed a cold and blustery day blowing in from the Olympic Mountains and over the Puget Sound. Making the water choppy and hard to look at, it reflected the 'perpetual gray' of the clouds that had hung over the city since I'd come back from my trip to the peninsula.

I had just sorted out all of the coupons and ads and got the paper arranged with the sections that I care about in front of me and the other stuff off to one side when I was interrupted by a man who wanted to sit at my table.

"Mind if I sit here..." He said.

"Sure," I replied, without looking up, I was hoping that he wasn't one of those people who mistake tolerance for hospitality.

The Déjà vu alarm rang in my head. I looked up over the top of my paper at the man sitting across from me. Well it wasn't Olaf. At least it didn't appear to be Olaf. The man was thinner in build and had black hair with only a touch of gray at the temples. 'Okay,' this should be an interesting Saturday,' I thought to myself.

"I'm Jack," I said holding out my hand. Something about the man radiated a kindness that made me want to respond likewise.

"Pleased to meet you, Jack," His voice was deep and had a slightly European accent to it.

"I'm Nicholas... Nicholas Flamel," the man said with a straight face. "A mutual friend of ours, named Olaf, said that you liked to hear stories."

I wish to thank all who immersed themselves into another place and time, if only for a little while. And hope you happen this way again in my first book of short stories.
::: The Happy lil' Photon ~ Nap time tales for your Inner child :::
or in the series of five illustrated children's books :::
Plink
Plink in Space
Plink Beyond Yonder
Plink Jupiter Jump Point 4
Plink Mars Mystery
also published through Third Sun Media
at Lulu.com

Until then, have a wonderful life...

www.ingramcontent.com/pod-product-compliance
Lightning Source LLC
Chambersburg PA
CBHW031100030726
47496CB00002BA/313